monsoonbooks

SHAMAN OF BALI

New Zealander John Greet lived in Southeast Asia from 1985 to 1997, during which time he was sentenced to 37 years in prison on a drug charge, but was pardoned and freed after five years. While behind bars, Greet was charged with assaulting a prison guard and spent two years in solitary confinement in leg irons. Following his release from prison, Greet studied for and was awarded a degree in creative writing. *Shaman of Bali* is Greet's first novel and is followed by the sequel, *Blood Money*.

SHAMAN OF BALI

JOHN GREET

monsoon

monsoonbooks

First published in 2016
by Monsoon Books Ltd
www.monsoonbooks.co.uk

No.1 Duke of Windsor Suite, Burrough Court,
Burrough on the Hill, LE14 2QS, UK.

First edition.

ISBN (paperback): 978-981-4625-39-5
ISBN (ebook): 978-981-4625-40-1

Cover design by Cover Kitchen.
Cover photograph©Jack Picone / Alamy Stock Photo.

Cataloguing in Publication Data: a catalogue record for this book
is available from the National Library, Singapore.

Printed in USA

Dedicated to
Mary-Anne Thomson and James George

Life is not always a matter of holding good cards, but sometimes, playing a poor hand well.

Jack London

PART ONE

1

The *Sea Rover* sat at her berth, a fifty-five footer, cutter-rigged with self-furling mainsail, her sleek black hull highlighting the teak decks and wooden bowsprit. Her fresh varnish shone in the midday sun. Her mooring lines creaked against the dock as she rose and dipped on the wake of a passing boat. It was a Singapore delivery; a crewman had just pulled out, and I'd jumped at the opportunity. I'd been living at the Y.M.C.A. and searching the town for a job in hospitality, but the news of my bankruptcy tended to precede me. I'd been met with sympathetic refusals from former colleagues. 'Over qualified,' they said. The same people who'd felt privileged to get a booking at my restaurant only months earlier now rejected me politely over a complimentary glass of wine. Although this job meant I had to sail with Duncan, it did pay well.

His footsteps were heavy on the pier as he came towards me. His grey eyes caught mine but gave no indication they knew me. 'Immigration clearance at 17:00. *Sea Rover* departing on the hour,' he mumbled, as he boarded the yacht with surprising agility for his age.

I climbed aboard and went to the lockers to stow my belongings. My sea bag carried my wet-weather gear, my sextant and compass, and a change of clothes for the flight home.

At three thirty, I called Grace. She would be walking home from school.

'Hi, sweetheart.'

'Dad, why didn't you call? I've been worried.'

'I'm sorry. I'm not comfortable talking to you when your mum and David are around.'

'I know, it sucks. And those guys who trashed your apartment, well, they had their car parked outside her house yesterday. They're really creepy. Just kind of staring.'

My skin burned. I knew Tula would never stop. The numbing powerlessness of not being able to do anything to stop him cut deep.

'You there? Dad?'

'Yeah, Grace, that sailing job came through. I'm leaving for Singapore in a couple of hours, and when I get back I'll make a payment to them.'

A silence followed. I could see her in her school uniform, pushing back her blond curls with her mobile, her blue-green eyes staring at the sky.

'How long will you be gone?'

'Three weeks, maybe four, depending on the weather.' I checked my watch as I tied off a slack docking line. When she didn't answer, I added, 'Grace, I need to get these guys off our backs.'

'I know, but it's so unfair,' her voice rose in anger. 'You didn't hurt anybody, you didn't break the law, and the liquidators took everything from you. They took our life away, as if everything we'd worked for meant nothing.'

I understood her. She'd lived most of her life in the Milano's kitchen; it had been her sanctuary, and she'd been ordering chefs around since she could walk. Over the phone, I heard the sound of a passing car, the chatter of schoolgirls.

'Gracie, I'm going to make it right. I'm going to find a way to pay them all.'

'Does Mum know you are leaving?'

'I'm meeting her now.'

'Good luck with that.' She paused for a moment. 'And try to be nice to each other.'

David stood leaning against a lamp post, smoking a cigarette. He turned away as I walked past him. Elisabeth sat alone on the beachfront terrace. She moved her wine glass and ran her fingers through her hair as she saw me approach. I hadn't seen her for a long time. The years had enhanced her beauty. Her skin was flawless, and the way her sandy brown hair curved towards her shoulders reminded me of Grace.

'Adam, those men have their black car parked right opposite my house. Sunglasses, tattooed arms, those thugs watch everything we do,' she said, diving right in. 'What do they call themselves?' Elisabeth was never one for small talk.

'Kingsnakes. They're Tula's boys,' I said. He had gambled on winning my restaurant, but the liquidators had beaten him to it, and the Matua of the Kingsnakes didn't like to lose. Elisabeth knew Tula from our years of managing Milano's. She turned away and looked at the beach. The sky was grey and swollen, awash with inky shadows. A handful of kids played at the water's edge. An echo of Grace's words came to me: 'Be nice to each other.'

When Elisabeth returned her gaze to me, her eyes sparkled with anger. She steadied her hand on her wine glass. 'How could you do that? How could you borrow money against my share of the restaurant, and from a fucking criminal gang? Without asking me?' Elisabeth's voice was sharp and loud. The terrace fell silent. The waiter cast a concerned glance at us. David flicked his cigarette and moved towards us. Elisabeth held up her palm. He stopped.

'And you are sailing away, just like that.' She snapped her fingers, her voice now a low growl.

'There's nothing I can do. They are not breaking the law. I didn't ask for that money. Tula's boys just showed up with it, so I took it. You know how desperate I was. I thought it could help save the restaurant.' The words came out of my mouth in a nervous tumble.

'You should have sold Milano's years ago. I should have forced you to sell the place, but I didn't, because of Grace.' Elisabeth was trying to keep her anger in check. I didn't answer. I knew that talking to my ex-wife when she was worked up like this was pointless. I got up and left.

*   *   *

At dusk, the *Sea Rover* slipped around North Head with Duncan at the helm. A cool breeze stung my cheeks. I fastened my sea jacket and sat on the transom, watching the lights of Mission Bay flicker on. Between all the orange and red, I saw the glimmer of blue from the neon sign that shone above Milano's. I looked further uphill, searching for my old apartment, and caught a glimpse of the giant pohutukawa tree that marked my driveway. I drifted back in time and saw Grace again when she was five years old, playing in a treehouse I'd built in the lower branches; I heard echoes of her laughter and remembered the delight on her face. Then my stomach hollowed as I recalled the last desperate moments Grace and I had spent in the apartment only a few weeks ago.

A hammer blow shattered the door, until it burst from its hinges and hung sideways. They pushed into the apartment through shards of wood and glass. One held a crow bar, the other a sledge hammer. Looking at their viper tattoos, I knew they were Tula's boys. They moved fast. One twisted my arm, forcing me into a chair. He held me down with his foot on my chest. His thick-soled boot pressed the air from my lungs while the sledge hammer dangled effortlessly in his grip.

'Where's the cash, Milano?'

'I don't have any.'

'Come on, man,' said the guy with the crow bar. 'Tula's

not gonna go for that one, you know that. All you restaurant guys have a stash.' They ripped off the bench top and pulled out cupboards. Plasterboard walls crumbled to the ground. The crowbar screeched as it was slid under anything it could wrench open. The hammer pounded like a dull drumbeat. A fine cloud of dust hung over the room.

Grace stood in the doorway, holding two burgers, their wrappers printed with red brand names, her hair haloed by sunlight, her school uniform the same colour as the sky. The burgers fell from her hand as she walked towards me, her cheeks red, her eyes pinpricks. I took her hand and felt her trembling.

The larger guy eased on the hammer. He looked at us, and his lips opened like a cod's and curled into a hard smile. The light caught his gold filling as he crossed the room. He nudged his mate and tossed his head towards the door. They shattered the remains of the door as they left.

*   *   *

The days rolled on in an endless flow of ocean and sky. We made good time. A week later, we had reached our waypoint south of New Caledonia and charted a passage into Micronesian waters. Duncan slept little and spent most of his time at the helm. I'd known him all my life: he was never talkative, was always a little strange, but his seamanship was excellent. As a teenager I'd spent eight hundred hours under his captaincy. It was Duncan who had signed off my skipper's ticket. Over the years, we ran into him often at the marina. Grace was particularly fond of him and managed to coax sea stories out of him while my father and I worked on our boat, a classic wooden sloop, now in the hands of the liquidators. I'd sat helpless and watched as they'd methodically assessed every item I owned, ticked it off on a clipboard and marched it out to a truck. The leather couches, the oil paintings, Papa Milano's antique coffee machine, all sucked into the void of bankruptcy that was once my restaurant.

My mind refused to give me any reprieve. I would try to read, but after a couple of pages my concentration would drift, and I would find myself rehashing the same old scenarios and wondering what I could have done different, or calculating how much I was being paid for this voyage and how many more yacht deliveries I'd have to make to pay back what I owed. It would take seven or eight years. Grace would be twenty-five by then.

When we sailed between Darwin and Timor, I radioed the Australian Coastguard and notified them of our position. They put us on pirate alert as we were now entering dangerous waters. Later that day, I removed the ship's shotgun from its case, oiled and serviced it, and checked the date of the cartridges. I left the weapon breached on a shelf above the starboard bunk. The sea was calm with a steady fifteen-knot breeze. We passed local fishing craft and transport dhows, and I kept watch from a forward hatch as any of them could turn out to be pirates. Duncan seemed kind of absent and unconcerned but was doing a fine job helming the boat.

The following morning, I was preparing breakfast in the galley when a squall hit us.

We were in the Torres Straits on a tight reach. The boat lurched, and the coffee pot went flying. I cleaned up the mess then scrambled up the companionway. We were being driven towards the rocky coastline, with our gunnels submerged and the sea streaming over our rails. Our hull showed the colour of its anti-foul. A leaden sea tossed up foaming whitecaps. I braced myself as a sudden gust pushed the life rail under, submerging half the boat in swirling foam.

'Duncan!' I hollered, but the wind turned my voice to a whisper. I pulled myself closer, climbing up on the helm, and bellowed in his ear. 'We're carrying too much canvas!'

He looked surprised, as if seeing me for the first time, then he reeled back, brushing water from his face. We were close to the shore, too close. I could see rocky outcrops. Then a sudden shift in the wind changed our course. We were now belting along parallel to the shoreline, with our bow pointing a few degrees seaward, with exactly the right amount of sail. I winched in the mainsheet. Duncan still gripped the helm. His face showed no sign of appreciation for our good luck. He wore the same blank look, the same strange expression.

I went below. We had taken on water, and the hatch was open in Duncan's forward berth. Sea water had filled the bilge and flooded the cabin floors. I pulled the hatch shut and turned on the bilge pump. The forward quarters were soaked, the squabs wet, the locker doors flung open, clattering and banging noisily. Duncan's gear was strewn about. Soaked clothes and papers were scattered everywhere. As I gathered up his things, I found a box of medication. Small white bottles had spilled out of it and lay bobbing about on the last of the bilge water. They had come open, and tablets of various sizes and colour were dissolving quickly. I gathered up a handful of bottles. What kind of condition did Duncan have that required so much medication? Did this explain his lack of sleep and appetite, the blankness in his face, the strange glint in his eyes? The tablets were unsalvageable.

He pushed into the cabin. His eyes flared, and he grabbed frantically at the remaining pill bottles. They were empty. He fell to the cabin floor on his hands and knees, scraping at the wet mixture of powder and water; it sifted through his fingers like wet sand. His mouth twisted. He fixed his eyes on me. 'Do you know what this means?' he said. I tried to speak but he cut me off. He grabbed my shirt and pulled me towards him, but I broke his grip, held him at bay and manoeuvred my way out of the cabin. He followed me into the salon, where he slumped down on a squab with his head in his hands. I kept a good distance from him.

'For fuck's sake man, what's going on? Why didn't you tell me? When do you need to take your pills next? I mean ... your next dose?'

He looked at me with an incomprehensible expression and shook his head. Then the boat lurched, the jib flapped, and the sheets cracked and whipped. We were about to breach. I got to the cockpit, winched in the jib sheets and eased the mainsail. The squall had passed and sat like a distant black smudge to starboard. The sun broke through the clouds and bounced off the boat's decks. A halyard was tangled, and one of the poles had come loose. It took me some time to fix this and get the boat back on course.

When I came back to the salon, Duncan was out to the world. He was curled up in a foetal position, taking short rasping inhales, then holding his breath before exhaling loudly. I tried to wake him but couldn't. His eyes were jammed shut, his face twisted into a grimace. I tried to straighten his legs to ease his breathing, but he wasn't having it. He pulled them back up into a curl then wrapped his arms around his knees and went on with his rattled breathing. I took a survival blanket from the first-aid locker and wrapped it around him.

Back in the cockpit, I thought about radioing for help but then changed my mind. I decided to wait and see how Duncan was when he came to. The wind had dropped to a steady ten knots on the beam. I rolled out the genoa and shook a reef out of the main. We were making good speed towards our next waypoint, the southern tip of the island of Bali.

It was early evening. The *Sea Rover* rose and fell on the ocean's roll, our stern wake bubbling and snapping to the occasional slap of a jib sheet. A seabird followed us, then glided away. The ocean changed hues from blue to grey as dusk fell. I ate a can of tuna with crackers, changed my T-shirt and checked on Duncan. I couldn't tell if his breathing had become worse, or if I could just hear him more clearly since we were on calmer waters. I made a flask of strong coffee and took a few cushions up to the cockpit. We were averaging around six knots in light air, and the wind remained steady as we sailed through the night. By morning, I was exhausted. I'd managed to stay awake all night. Duncan still lay on the squab, breathing hard. The *Sea Rover* held her course. We were fifty miles closer to our waypoint. I put my head down on a cushion.

It was broad daylight when the noise awoke me. Duncan was moving around down below. I checked our position on the navigation station. It was dead. Then I saw that all our navigational gear and electronics was out: the depth sounder, the forward sonar, the radar and auto pilots, the lot. I looked below just in time to see Duncan ripping out our ship's radio. The V.H.F. already dangled by its wires, and so did our short-band radio.

'Duncan, stop!' I hollered as I went below.

'Where are they? Where have you put them?' He waved the ship's radio at me like it were a weapon.

The damage he had wrought was horrendous. In his frantic search for his medication he'd opened the housing case for the ship's electronics and destroyed the wiring. Loose wires hung out of their casing and dangled like colourful threads. While I took stock of the damage, Duncan had moved on to the first-aid cabinet. I caught him just as he was about to swallow a handful of morphine tablets.

'Give them to me,' he screamed as I grabbed the tablets. His eyes glittered with madness.

'Your pills are gone, man. Gone! These are not them.' I threw the bottle out of a hatch. 'And look at this mess. What are we going to do now?' I wrapped my arms around him and forced him back to the bunk. He fought against me but I had him in a vice-like grip. 'Duncan, look at me,' I pleaded. 'I want you to stay here while I try to fix some of this damage. Look at what you've done … Look at this shit! We're fucked, man. Don't move from this bunk. Do you understand me?' From his vacant gaze, I knew that he had no idea what he'd done. I felt his body go limp as he slumped onto the squab. 'Give me my pills,' he murmured, falling unconscious.

I spent the rest of the day trying to get our electronics to work. We were hove to and going nowhere. The boat lolled and bobbed, making even the smallest movement difficult. Every combination of wiring I tried was failing to work: the brown wire with the green, then the red with the black, but nothing, not even a spark. The same with the ship's short-wave radio.

Whatever I tried didn't work. I gave up. Duncan came to a couple of times; he looked at me with a crazed glint in his eyes and then returned to his slumber. I couldn't believe what was happening. I cursed my bad luck. By the end of the day, I'd had enough. I decided to get the boat moving. I could use my sextant and compass, and we had paper charts and a wristwatch on board. I could take a reading and plot a course for the ship while we still had sun. I wasn't sure how we'd manage without a wind vane or self-steering gear, but I didn't want to risk falling asleep, especially with Duncan acting so erratic. I pencilled in some waypoints on the chart and then set sail. I was beyond exhaustion, frazzled and running on coffee-fuelled energy as I tried to helm the boat to a compass course. I kept an eye on Duncan too. The last thing I wanted was for him to wake up and wreak more havoc.

By grabbing myself whatever snatches of sleep and food I could, I managed to sail the *Sea Rover* through the night and into the next day. I took a sextant reading as soon as the sun allowed it and discovered that we'd made good time. According to my calculations we were about twenty-four hours away from Bali, where I intended to land. We would have to sail into Benoa Harbour without notifying customs or immigration, and we couldn't start the boat's engines as we had no ignition. Duncan slept on.

The next day and night were a test of my physical and mental endurance. I spent all my waking hours helming the boat to a compass heading and manning the sails after sudden wind shifts, while snatching food whenever I could. Duncan kept waking up and wandering about in a delirious state. He refused food but

I managed to make him drink some water. He sat with me in the cockpit for an hour or two, and after several attempts at conversation I realised how out of it he was. He muttered and rambled on incomprehensibly, then returned below and lay on his bunk, his eyes wide open and staring at the bulkhead. The next time I checked on him, he was asleep.

When we reached the Strait of Lombok, a gale set in, right on the nose. It howled through the seaway that separated the islands of Bali and Lombok. Try as I might I couldn't point the *Sea Rover* towards our destination, Benoa Harbour, which lay only an hour away. I was weak with exhaustion as I tacked the boat up into the wind. I could see land. Southern Bali lay to port, and the small island of Nusa Penida, which sheltered Benoa Harbour, lay ahead. After countless tacks, I took a bearing against a land point and knew we were losing ground. We were drifting backwards faster than we were moving forward. Duncan was awake and agitated, and I was worried that I wouldn't be able to control him in these conditions. We would have to go about. I managed to bring in the sails while we were still pointing upwind, leaving only a scrap of head sail for steerage, and swung the helm. I had no way to gauge our boat speed but we were sailing fast downwind. I couldn't leave the helm for a second. Duncan's head would appear in the companionway and stare out to sea, then disappear. I'd locked the first-aid cabinet and couldn't think of what further damage he might do.

A short time later we sailed out of the Strait of Lombok, around the southern tip of Bali, and into the calm waters of the Bali Sea. I raised the mainsail, stabilised the boat then sat slumped over the helm. I didn't know how much more of this I could take. I was close to breaking point. On our starboard side I saw the giant wave breaks of Uluwatu, and the surrounding high barren cliffs and outcrops of land. In the distance, beyond the airport runway, lay the white sands of Kuta Beach. I looked at the chart and saw that our best chance to make landfall without a motor would be the ferry port of Gilimanuk, further north. With luck and wind, we might make it by nightfall. My body ached, and my focus was beginning to drift. I plotted a course that I hoped would be our last. An offshore breeze pushed us along at a good clip.

'Get off!' Duncan's voice suddenly pulled me awake. I ran my hand over my face to make sure I wasn't in the grip of a wild dream. Duncan stood in the cockpit stark naked, not a metre from me, pointing the ship's shotgun at my face.

'Leave this boat now!' he bellowed. These were the first coherent words he'd spoken in days. I saw that both barrels were loaded and he'd released the safety catch. I cursed myself for not remembering to put the gun away.

'Duncan, please ...' But my words fell on deaf ears. He was now releasing the boat's tender from its davits with one hand, while pointing the shotgun at me with the other. I knew that I had to tread with extreme caution. In his delirious state, he would shoot me.

'Get in,' he commanded as he tied off a line to the dinghy, which ducked and dived in the *Sea Rover*'s wake.

'Duncan, this is crazy! You can't sail this boat alone. You haven't eaten in days, for Christ's sake, man. Wake up! You really want to put me in that ...' Duncan's answer was to move the shotgun closer to my head. I had no choice. I had to go. My sea bag was in the cockpit with me. I stuffed my wallet and passport into my shorts pockets then clambered onto the transom, almost falling into the dinghy. Duncan released the line and cast me adrift. I watched helplessly from the dinghy as the *Sea Rover* sailed away, her stern rising and dipping on the swell. Duncan stood naked on the transom, the shotgun still trained on me.

I took up the oars and began rowing. The currents were with me, and the dinghy drifted at a good speed towards the island. In the distance, the summit of Mt. Agung rose above a ring of clouds. An hour later, I could hear the traffic on the beach road, and the sound of pounding surf. I thought the best way would be to ditch the dinghy and body surf into the shore. But then the boat started to pull towards the airport runway, which jutted out to sea at the end of the beach. I heaved on the oars but couldn't shift her; my strength had finally given up. I was caught in the grip of a powerful current, and there was nothing to do but to go with it. By taking up one oar and jamming a rowlock into the stern brace, I was able to guide the dinghy a little. I could see the beachfront hotels. They were only a few hundred metres away. As the runway approached, the wave-line curved inwards, forming a funnel that I was being sucked into. The rollers became so large that when I descended into their troughs, I saw only mountains of moving water on either side, and as I was propelled to the top, in quick glimpses, I saw the shoreline and the calm waters of a lagoon. The tide was high. Perhaps I still had a chance. I threw out the oars as the dinghy was sucked into a giant wave. The boat would be my shield. I would brace myself against the coral heads that I could see shining like knives beneath clear waters. The current propelled the boat to the top of the wave, and the dinghy fell forward, beyond the breaking crest. I looked down and saw the enormity of the wave, an almost perpendicular wall of water with a half-moon curve, which swept over black jagged coral heads at a tremendous speed. As I tumbled down the wave, I fell backwards. The dinghy raised its bow and then surfed with me hanging out of the stern. Spray flew out on either side as I sped down the face, clinging to the tiny boat like it were a lifeline, both hands glued to the seat. The shuddering impact when she hit the rocks should have torn her apart but she only capsized. I was trapped underwater, tossing and rolling. My lungs heaved, and sharp coral scraped against my back and legs. I was moving fast, and I was about to let go of the boat when she hit a rock and broke. I rose to the surface, clutching the seat as my lungs sucked in air. The next wall of foam hit me and took me with it. I held the seat under my chin, managing to keep my head out of water. More coral sliced against my legs, and a pain shot through my shoulder. I couldn't use my left arm.

When the foam released me, I stood on soft sand. With my right arm I reached down and touched my wounds; they were bad, and my shorts were gone, and my arm felt broken, and blood from the coral cuts coloured the water around me. Then a bolt of pain set in, and I was sure it was over. I was going to drown. My legs refused to support me, and I was exhausted and nauseous. Another wave knocked me over. I came up sputtering, spitting seawater. I saw an outrigger canoe manned by four men paddling towards me. Wrapped in a blanket of darkness, my vision became a tunnel through which I kept the outrigger in view. I tried to fight the suffocating blankness but my body gave out, and my legs gave away, and I slipped underwater.

The last thing I heard was the stroke of paddles, drawing nearer.

I came to for an instant, and I saw that I'd been laid out on a restaurant table. Worried faces peered down at me, their eyes searching, their hands rubbing my shoulder. A cold cloth was pressed to my forehead. I felt a sharp pain stab at my shoulder. Then the faces changed, and as I slipped back into unconsciousness, I smelled garlic and heard the hiss of a frying pan. I was back in the Milano's kitchen, and I could see it all again.

Grace is at a table. She is rolling pizza dough, her blue school uniform stained white with flour. I am standing at the stove. I have more orders on the rack than I can cope with.

Elisabeth walks in. 'Look at your uniform, Grace. How am I going to get that flour off? Adam!' I keep my eyes on the stove. 'Adam would you look at me?' I don't move. 'I am sick and tired of talking to your back.' I hear her anger, then Grace's voice.

'Mum, please … Not now,' Grace pleads. 'He's got to get through those orders. Antonio is sick, and he's on his own.'

'She spends too much time here, Adam. It's not healthy for a girl her age. She should be at home, doing homework, or playing

with other kids.'

'I've done my homework.'

'Don't interrupt me when I'm talking to your father!'

'Adam!' Elisabeth shouts. The skillet flares orange then blue. Her words drown in the hiss of the flames.

'Mum, I'm ready. Let's go.' I turn and see Grace pulling her through the door. Elisabeth's eyes are violent points of blue, her lips tight.

I hear the screech of tyres as she races out of the carpark.

2.

Consciousness returned to me slowly. One minute I was floating, and in the next I was pulled back by a violent pain in my shoulder. The buzzing in my head cleared, and I became aware of the tangy smell of papaya. Footsteps and voices sounded near. I opened my eyes and saw I was lying on a bed. I was in a hotel room. Palm leaves and twine were wrapped around my chest and legs to hold pieces of papaya against my skin. A Balinese man wearing a white sarong entered the room. He was bare-chested and with a lean muscular frame, his oiled black hair tied in a ponytail. He had an air of authority and was clearly in charge. A man and a woman stood behind him.

'Anak,' said the man, standing by the bed and placing a hand on his chest. 'Thankfully you are now awake and we can reset your shoulder; it's dislocated. You've been unconscious for some time.'

I made an attempt to speak but couldn't. Anak held a glass filled with a liquid the colour of blood. He raised it to the light and chanted something. Then he fished a small stone out of the glass, folding it into a cloth and tucking it into the sash of his sarong. The woman raised my head while Anak put the glass to my mouth. I sipped the red water. He mounted the bed and motioned for me to remain silent, then took my arm and pulled, putting all his weight on my body. I heard an audible scrape, the sound of bone against bone, followed by a click. I knew he had reset my shoulder, which should have caused excruciating pain, yet I felt only movement, no pain. Instead, I was overcome by a deep peacefulness, a feeling of detachment, as if all of this was happening around me and not to me. Anak rubbed his hand over my shoulder, then stood with his arms folded. The woman stood beside him, occasionally catching my eye and smiling. She had a sturdy squat frame and warm eyes, a small nose and a full mouth, and thick glossy hair tied into a bun.

'By tomorrow we can remove the papaya,' said Anak. 'But your coral cuts will not infect because you are under the protection of the bloodstone.'

'Where am I?' I asked.

'You are at my hotel, the Sandika. Ketut here, and his wife, Wayan, run it. You are in good hands. We saw you come over the reef in that strange boat and we were quite sure you'd drowned. We paddled out to retrieve your body but you popped up in front of us, very alive. You were clutching a piece of wood and raving, waving it about.' He paused and his dark brown eyes met mine. A smile flickered on his lips, and his voice changed to a mocking tone. 'We nearly left, thinking you were a sea demon. But then you passed out, so we knew you were only human. Now rest. Your shoulder will be stiff for some time,' Anak continued. 'I'll come back when you're ready to tell me how and why you washed up on our shores.'

'Did you find my shorts?' I asked.

'No, but you no worry. Ketut will give you some shorts,' said Wayan.

*   *   *

As my head cleared, I began to notice my surroundings. I was in an upstairs room with batik wall hangings, rattan furniture and a large plate-glass window with a view that reached as far as the reef. The room had no ceiling. I was looking up at the underside of a grass roof with its intricate thatched patterns and tight stitching woven around carved wooden battens that held dried grass in place. Through the window I saw the trimmed eves

29

of the grass roof, which were at least a metre thick. Further out, as I raised my head, I could see an unruly garden of palms and vines. At the end of a sandy pathway stood a giant banyan tree, and underneath it was a coffee shop. Across the calm waters of the lagoon, glassy waves peeled away. Surfers dived in and out of the pipeline, weaving and riding them with ease. I'd survived that reef. I thought of Grace, and I quietly thanked Anak for rescuing me. I looked down at my legs and remembered the bad coral cuts I'd seen before I lost consciousness; I pushed the papaya aside and saw only faint lines of scar tissue where they should have been. Wayan returned with food. She fussed about, cleaning the room, and when I'd finished eating, she removed some papaya from one leg and took a long look.

'More time,' she said. 'I put some new papaya now, then one more day, and you can leave the bed.' I asked her about the blood-coloured water, but as soon as I mentioned it she put a hand over my mouth. Her eyes darted from side to side and she whispered, 'Shhh, no speak. *Leyak* maybe hear you, many *bata* and *kula* around here.' When she saw my uncomprehending look, she cupped her hand around my ear and hissed, 'Devils listening'.

That evening I propped my head on a pillow and watched the sunset. It began in turquoise, streaked with magenta, then the sun became a glowing orange orb as it balanced on the horizon. How Grace would love to see this. She was fascinated by sunsets. I remembered her asking me as soon as she could speak, about where the colours come from. I listened to the hum of the surf. A dog barked and silenced the crickets. I had to find a way to call her. I wondered how she was making out living with her Mum. Were Tula's boys still hassling them? Regardless of what had happened between us, Elisabeth didn't deserve to get harassed for my debts.

I remembered the night he had visited my restaurant. Although in his seventies, Tula was still a powerful-looking man. He had eaten alone while two of his boys stood outside. He was dressed in black, his long silver hair done in a plait, and with a large spiral of jade hanging from his black collar, denoting him as a Matua, a Tongan tribal leader. He was more than that. In his youth he'd founded a gang called the Kingsnakes. They'd started out as a biker gang, but with Tula's business acumen, not only did they take control of the drug and prostitution trade, but also established a legitimate security business, a chain of strip clubs and more. Tula had a taste for Italian food and was a regular customer at Milano's. I recalled the fear he'd inspired in me as a child, but my father had said, 'Our customers' business has nothing to do with us. As long as they behave and pay for our food, we will treat them with courtesy and respect.'

That night, with my father's words in mind, I dismissed the waiter and took his food to him myself.

'How are you doing, Adam?' he asked.

'I'm okay.'

'No, I mean the restaurant. You going to be able to hold out in these hard times?'

'If I had a couple of hundred grand, yes,' I said flippantly as I laid down a plate of seafood pasta before him. Tula then spoke of my father with fondness, enquired after my family, and I left him to dine alone.

The following night one of his boys had shown up in my kitchen. We went into my office, and he opened a case containing two hundred thousand in cash, plus a contract: it stated that if I was unable to repay the money, Tula would take ownership of the restaurant. I didn't hesitate. It sounded too good to be true. Of course I could pay him back. This economic downturn had to bottom out. Hadn't it always? Tula had come to my rescue even though the banks had given up on me. This money would see me through the tough times. I could finally pay my staff and suppliers. I didn't stop to think that Elisabeth still owned a forty-five percent share of the business and that I should ask for her consent. I signed the contract on behalf of the both of us and began paying our creditors. However, Tula's money was too little too late. Only three weeks later, and without warning, the tax department put me into receivership. Tula lost his money. I lost everything.

*　*　*

In the morning, a cool breeze rustled the curtains. Wayan bustled in with a smile. She untied the bindings on my legs and wiped away the fruit. I rolled onto my side as she inspected my back and grunted with satisfaction.

'You get up now, shower and put clothes. Here,' she said, pointing to a faded brown batik shirt and a pair of shorts she had put on the bed. 'Ketut give you. I come back soon.'

I found my balance, and moved to the bathroom. I washed away the papaya and looked into the mirror. I was in good shape, considering that I had dislocated my shoulder. I realised that with each movement the stiffness eased. Wayan returned. She took me by the arm and led me down a flight of stairs and along a sandy pathway to the coffee shop. The Sandika Hotel was smaller than I'd imagined, with six rooms upstairs and six more downstairs. The grass roof sat on top of the building like a giant oblong mushroom, and the wild and colourful vegetation that surrounded it created an Alice-in-Wonderland effect. It seemed as if the building had sprouted rather than been built. Wayan told me it was one of the last hotels to have such a roof.

'They called it lady-grass. Before, every building in Bali had them. Now they too expensive to build. We lucky we have ours.' Bougainvillea, hibiscus, frangipani and mango trees lined the pathway. A tropical wilderness of a garden lay to our right, and on our left was an overflowing swimming pool, which threw dancing patterns of light onto the leaves of the giant banyan tree. At the base of the tree's trunk, in a cavity framed by aerial roots, stood a small temple. An offering tray of fruit and incense was placed before it.

'For Anak's father,' said Wayan. She made coffee while I sat with Ketut. A plate of tropical fruit lay on the table: mangosteen, rambutan, plantain and red mango, pineapple and jackfruit.

'Eat, eat,' said Ketut, pushing the platter towards me. 'We have plenty fruit from our garden, and soon I will go to sea. We have fish for lunch.'

The coffee shop was decorated with batik-covered cushions and comfortable rattan chairs. Chess sets sat on tables, ornaments and painted carvings hung from the walls, and a faded, gold-framed, black-and-white photograph of a dignified Balinese man dressed in white turban and robes hung over the bar. An incense holder and a lit candle were placed beneath it. From the man's resemblance to Anak, I guessed it was his father. The blinds facing the beach were rolled up. In the shallows of the lagoon, fishermen stood waist deep in the water, casting circular hand nets, which blossomed out before them then sank. Slivers of silver caught the sunlight as they retrieved the nets. The reef hummed in the distance. I could see clusters of black rock, visible one minute, submerged by rolling foam the next.

'This Kuta Reef. World famous for surfing,' said Ketut, pointing to the wave-break two hundred metres beyond the lagoon. 'But you come in here with your boat,' he pointed. 'Airport left. They call it big waves, and only big surfer do that one.'

We could see the airport runway. It jutted out to sea, and while we ate, a Boeing 707 landed. It arrived from the left, appeared suspended in the air briefly and then made its noiseless dash down the runway. Wayan refilled my cup and replenished the fruit platter. I thanked them for their kindness, the food and the clothes.

'Is there anything I can do?' I asked.

'Yes, can you tell us your name?'

'I'm sorry. My name is Adam. Adam Milano.'

Wayan smiled. 'Welcome to Bali, Mr. Adam.'

*　　*　　*

I took my coffee and walked to the sea wall. Beyond the reef, a thin blue line separated sea from sky. Seagulls cawed above. I took a deep breath, and a flood of questions washed through me like a wave. What had become of Duncan? What was I going to tell Grace? Where was I going to go from here? And with no money, passport or means of identifying myself? I briefly considered calling a couple of friends for help, but then imagined what I would say to them: 'I have been left washed up and broke in Bali.' No, I couldn't do that. I thought of calling the New Zealand Embassy, then realised that I'd entered Indonesia illegally and would be arrested. I looked out to the spot in the lagoon where I'd stood days earlier, so sure I was going to drown. I had survived. I closed my eyes and thought of Duncan, hoping beyond reason that somehow he'd survived too.

I heard the roar of motorbikes. A couple of surfers pulled into the carpark, their surfboards and bags strapped to their bikes. Ketut and Wayan rushed out to meet them and pulled them into the coffee shop. After a while, a blond guy came over to speak to me.

'Hey, man, you the guy eh? They tell me what happen. Big surf, man, you crazy in a little boat? I'm Geno. There, my brother Paolo.' He pointed to the darker of the two with his thumb.

'We from Brazil,' he said, pumping my hand. He asked me to join them and share a bottle of arrack. Wayan brought us shot glasses and iced water. I welcomed the distraction offered by the soothing liquor, the company and the conversation. The brothers told me they came here to surf and had lived at the Sandika off and on for the best part of a decade.

'Wayan and Ketut, they like family to us, man,' said Geno, after knocking back a couple more shots. 'Anak, he's a good man too, but watch out for that one. He got big magic.'

'Magic?'

'Yeah, man, he a shaman. White magic, spirits, healing with hands, he can see what you gonna do before you do it, all that shit man. We have those guys in Brazil too. Scary stuff, watch out for that. They can fuck you up big time. We Catholic.' His hand reached up to a gold crucifix around his neck. 'But I tell you something,' he continued, 'he's the best cock fighter on the island. The hotel here stay mostly empty. Sometime he make money with cockfighting, sometime he lose big time.'

We drank and ate fish and fruit. Our talk lulled as Geno took out a guitar and sang in Portuguese to samba and bossa-nova rhythms, and after each song the arrack was passed around.

They didn't look like brothers. Geno was blond, and Paolo dark. Geno had green, calculating eyes that looked out from an untidy shock of sun-streaked hair. He was edgy and wired, except when he sang. Paolo had a gentle demeanour.

The sunset that evening was softer, with streaks of pastel blues and turquoise that stretched across the length of the horizon. The sun, blotted out by a single grey cloud, was outlined by an aura of gold.

Anak arrived and called me over to his table. He inspected my legs and approved.

Then he sat with folded arms and looked at me with an expression that was austere yet warm.

'You were lucky the moon was full when you arrived. The bloodstone's power is strongest at that time.' I wanted to ask about the bloodstone but Geno's earlier warnings had made me wary.

It was hard to put an age on Anak. His hair showed no sign of grey, his eyes held a youthful sparkle and his smooth skin was the same tone as the earth. Later, Wayan told me he was fifty-two. Anak was a direct descendant of the royal family of Bali.

'We Balinese are the only island nation to regard the sea with a sense of dread,' he told me, unfolding his arms. 'We believe that demons and evil spirits dwell beneath the waters, and we are constantly trying to appease them by leaving offerings at the shoreline. So, you, my friend, to have survived these waters and to be tossed up by the sea, and to arrive on our shores in such a spectacular manner, we should really treat you as a god.' There was a hint of mockery in his tone when he added, 'You are blessed.' As he poured tea I told him what had happened aboard the *Sea Rover*.

'Ah, there you have it. You see, your captain was possessed by sea demons, and you did right to leave. You took the best course of action under the circumstances, because unless you have a remedy for a man possessed, they can cause you great harm.'

'Anak, my passport and credit card were in the shorts I lost,' I said, feeling a little uncomfortable with the talk of sea demons. 'I have no money to pay you for the room and food. And no means to get any just yet, because I can't identify myself.'

Fruit bats swooped and squealed. A cluster of moths swarmed, hissing and crackling against a bare light bulb. Wayan's pans clattered on a gas hob.

'So you were a restaurant man?'

'Yeah.'

'You could stay here, work with Ketut and Wayan. They need help, particularly with our coffee shop, and I'm sure that you will find your way. Your destiny has brought you good fortune so far, and I'm sure it will continue to do so.'

'Good fortune?'

'Of course, it has brought you to the Island of the Gods,' he said as he rose to leave.

It was late. The coffee shop was empty. Fruit bats swooped out of their perches in the banyan tree. Rat monkeys chattered and squealed, and the croaking of tree frogs rose above the hum of the surf. I climbed the stairway to my room and from the rear balcony, by the moon's light, I saw the manicured gardens and pristine lawns of a luxury hotel that lay directly behind us. Only a stone's throw from where I stood, a handful of tourists bathed in a backlit swimming pool while sipping cocktails from a floating bar. Further on, through the glass windows of the main building, guests in evening wear were being served by uniformed waiters under a sign that read 'The Bali Haj Hotel'. I glanced back at the overgrown wilderness of the Sandika's gardens. The coffee shop was now closed for lack of guests. Fireflies flickered in dark recesses, and honeysuckle vines dangled from palm trees. Then, as if it had something to tell me, a rat monkey jumped onto the balcony, stared at me with its beady red eyes, and scampered off.

3

In the morning, a grey sky shrouded the sun. The air was still and sticky. The coconut palms drooped. The fruit bats were out early, swooping and fluttering. The chattering of rat monkeys couldn't be heard, and the tree frogs had stopped their croaking. I recognised the signs of an approaching storm. Anak arrived and ordered Ketut to the airport to get a weather report. He soon returned with the news that all flights in and out of Ngurah Rai Airport were cancelled due to a cyclone that was forecast to hit the southern tip of the island soon. Within minutes, several Balinese men arrived. Geno, Paolo and I offered to help.

Soon the cyclone hit us. Palm fronds rustled furiously as the winds rose beyond gale force. The reef, no longer visible through a darkened sky, and the sea, now a mess of foaming white caps, surged forward. The wind became an incessant howl. Waves exploded at the sea wall, surging onto land.

We hunkered down in the cinder block office with its sturdy tiled roof. The coconut palms were bent almost horizontal, their fronds trashing about, reaching out like furious hands. Spumes of sea spray drenched the seaward window. With an ear-splitting crack, the coffee shop disintegrated. Pieces of thatch and furniture flew past us, smashing against the office walls and hurtling into the garden and beyond. Coconut palms split, shrieking above the howl, toppling across the garden like Chinese sticks.

Then came a break in the storm. We looked around us at the devastation. All that remained of the coffee shop was the tiled floor and Wayan's cast-iron stove. The garden, with its vegetation ripped away, had been reduced to half its size, and we could see through to the Bali Haj grounds and its tiled roof, swimming pool and white deck chairs. Then a sudden gust of wind hit us with such force that we stumbled back into the office. Another onslaught. From the rear window we saw the lady-grass-roof's front bindings break. It lifted up, like a gigantic mouth opening. The whole structure rose up like the sail of a mythical craft, held only by its rear bindings; it was balanced vertically on the hotel. As the gust eased, it began to reset itself, in fits and starts like an arm-wrestling match. When it was almost in place, another powerful gust hit it. The roof rose up again, screeching and groaning, then its rear bindings broke. The roof fell. It turned three-sixty and landed with a ground-shaking thud on the lawn of the Bali Haj Hotel.

The storm left as quickly as it had arrived. I guessed it was only the perimeter that had hit us. The centre of the cyclone must have passed further seaward. We wandered towards the decapitated building, silenced by the havoc the storm had wrought. Tears streamed down Wayan's face. She held out her hands towards the scant remains of her kitchen. I heard the sound of a person wailing and then the baying of a dog. Behind the Sandika, occupying almost the width of Bali Haj's lawn, lay the lady-grass roof, the right way up, like a giant tomb. The Sandika had taken the brunt of the storm while the Bali Haj had sustained little damage; there was debris scattered across the hotel's property, and its poolside furniture had been blown into the pool, but its buildings were intact.

A man strode out from behind the roof. He was tall and wore a white, flowing, full-length kaftan and a black skull cap that identified him as Muslim. His skin was a polished brown, and he sported a pencil-thin moustache as manicured as the hotel's gardens. Greying hair at his temples suggested he was older than Anak.

'Mahmood Bas,' whispered Ketut. 'He own the Bali Haj Hotel.'

He came closer, stopping ten metres before us. His teeth flashed, his jaw muscles and throat working, and his coal black eyes zeroed in on Anak. Mahmood Bas's words came in short staggered bursts.

'Get this monstrosity off my property. You have until ... in the name of Allah I will show compassion ... until tomorrow night. If this thing is not gone by tomorrow's sunset, I will torch it. I'll burn it to the ground. I give you my word.' Mahmood Bas then strode away.

*　*　*

The brothers and I moved into a downstairs room.

'My board, man. My best fucking surfboard's gone,' said Geno as we were sorting out our beds. 'I gonna look for it tomorrow, and if that Bas asshole try to stop me, I gonna ...'

'Geno, there's a board by the Bali Haj pool. Green stripe down the middle.' I suddenly remembered seeing the thing.

'That's it, man!' he said, rushing out the door.

'Take care, brother,' Paolo called after him. 'Don't let Bas stick a flaming torch up your sorry ass.' Geno slipped over the border and into the Bali Haj. Paolo and I sat listening to the night noises. The rat monkeys had lost their home and were jostling for perches in the banyan tree, their chatter upsetting the fruit bats. One swooped close to where we sat, its wings beating a muffled rhythm. 'Geno, he okay. It's just sometimes ... It's like his life catches up with him and it's stronger than him, know what I mean?'

'Sort of.'

'Yeah, I know, you have to know him to understand, but he lost a lot, you know ... I gonna tell you about it one day.'

*　*　*

In the morning, the Sandika's grounds teemed with local people; workers were refitting the thatched walls and roof to the coffee shop, and men sawed at the fallen coconut trees. I saw Anak on the beach. The seashore was covered in debris, with coral sand banked high against the sea wall. Men were shovelling it away. I looked back at the hotel and saw that the beams of a temporary roof were being laid and sheets of corrugated iron nailed in place.

'Anak, the roof?' I asked.

'Impossible, we can't dismantle it in the timeframe Bas allows. He knew that before he opened his mouth.' We looked back at the half-finished corrugated iron roof.

'We'll cover the iron with palm fronds and hang batik cloth for the ceiling. At least the hotel won't be ruined in the rains.' By late afternoon the roof was on. A truckload of new coffee shop furniture arrived, and the last palm fronds were attached to the roof. Wayan's stove had worked all day, feeding the workers.

As sunset approached, the joking and laughter stopped. Workers laid down their tools. We filed up to the rear balcony of the Sandika. Below, the grounds of the Bali Haj were deserted. Minutes passed. So complete was the lady-grass roof, it looked as if it had been purposely built on the ground it now occupied. People shuffled about anxiously. I heard Paolo whisper, 'He only bluffing, man.'

Then Mahmood Bas appeared from behind the roof. He walked with long strides, holding a flaming fire torch in one hand. He stopped before the roof and looked up at Anak. 'I warned you!' he shouted, waving his blazing torch.

Bas lit each corner of the roof. The fire reddened his face as he went about his task methodically. Yellow flames licked up the sides of the roof, turning orange, and then red. Within minutes the whole structure was alight. Enormous flames flared skyward, throwing up hot embers, and the air filled with tiny black fibres. The heat was intense. Soon, wads of burning lady-grass fell inwards, exposing the timber frame. The fire burned out rapidly, leaving behind a smouldering mass of grass and timber. A funnel of black smoke rose and twisted into the night. The stench of burning grass was overpowering. Bas came back into view. He tossed his torch into the embers, threw a chilling look at Anak and left.

* * *

At breakfast, we heard that the airport was open, and only the teardrop peninsular of southern Bali had been affected by the cyclone. Anak pulled into the carpark with a copy of the morning's *Herald Tribune*. He opened the paper to page three and placed it on the table before me. There were photographs of the damage the cyclone had caused to the islands south of Bali, and mention of serious damage to Timor and Darwin, but what caused my throat to tighten were the few sentences at the end of the article: 'The search was called off last night for the two New Zealand sailors. They are believed to have drowned in the waters. The wreckage of their sailing vessel, the *Sea Rover*, was discovered on a reef off the coast of southern Java. The names of the sailors will be released once their next of kin have been notified.'

I turned cold. Duncan must have been sailing in circles after he'd ordered me off the boat. He must have been caught by the full force of the cyclone. And what about Grace? They would be receiving a telephone call in New Zealand soon, if they hadn't already. Elisabeth would be telling her that I was presumed drowned, dead. Perhaps I could reach her first. I checked the time: New Zealand was four hours behind Bali. Grace would be on her way home from school.

Wayan took me to the phone in the office. I dialled Grace's cellphone but heard hollow rings. There was no answer. I hung up and ran her number through my mind again: yes, I was sure it was right. I dialled, but again there was no answer. I paced the pathway. Ten minutes later, I tried again. The phone clicked on, and I heard Grace's soft sobbing. She blew her nose then answered with a tentative, 'Hello'.

'Grace, it's me,' I said in the calmest tone I could muster. I knew she was about to scream. Then she composed herself, spoke in a muffled voice. 'What's going on? Are you safe? Oh my god, Dad! I, like, thought you were dead ... And there's a room full of people at Mum's place, and they think you're dead.' She blew her nose.

'I was never on the ship during the storm. I landed in Bali a week ago, and that's where I'm calling from. Grace, are you there?'

'Yes, I just need a minute.' She blew her nose again. 'You know, I never believed it. I just knew you'd make it, that you couldn't be dead ...' She jabbered into the phone. 'But I just didn't feel it. I was crying my eyes out here in the ... Wait a minute, Dad. What are you doing in Bali?' I told her what had happened. I could feel her spirits rise. I heard her voice pique with curiosity, then flag again as she thought of her old friend. 'And Duncan?'

'Yeah, I know.'

'So what do we tell Mum? And those people inside? You know, they're the same people who trashed you before you left, but now that they think you're dead, they're, like, saying you were such a good guy ...' Her voice trailed off.

'Gracie, I called to let you know that I'm alive and okay, and if you can hold off telling anyone where I am. I need to figure out what I'm going to do first.'

'Wait, Dad! That's it, I got it! We don't tell her, we don't tell anyone! It's as simple as that,' her voice rose with excitement. 'We just don't say anything. Think about it ... You're dead, so Tula will back off. Your creditors will have to chuck out your debts. You stay there until you figure out what to do. I mean, if you do hand yourself in, what will you be coming back to?'

'Let me think about that ... I'm not sure. But for the meantime just hold off, will you?'

'Yeah, I will, and thank god you're okay. I've been missing you big time.'

'Miss you too, Gracie. I have to go now. I'm on a borrowed phone.'

Walking on the hard sand at the waterline, foam swirling around my feet, I looked out across the sea. Duncan's leathery old face seemed to rise out of the swell and hover before me. I didn't hold it against him for forcing me to abandon ship. In a roundabout way, he had saved my life. I slowly came to terms with the fact that Duncan had drowned. I consoled myself with the notion that he'd gone down with his ship and perhaps avoided the indignity of spending the remainder of his life in a mental hospital. A rogue wave slapped at my legs. The sand shifted beneath my feet. I moved to solid ground, picked up a stone and hurled it into the sea.

* * *

The Sandika's gardens grew back at an astonishing speed. And soon the honeysuckle, bougainvillea vines and giant palm fronds obscured the view of the Bali Haj Hotel. The monkeys returned, and the fruit bats hung like dead leaves from the banyan tree. I worked with Wayan in the coffee shop's kitchen. I would keep my head down and work. I would stay around the Sandika and not venture out. The last thing I needed was a New Zealander on holiday, or perhaps a customer from Milano's, recognising me. I didn't call Grace after that, but had come around to her idea of staying in Bali for a short time. Not to avoid paying my debts, as she had suggested, but to take a moment for myself. My run of bad luck had been extraordinary, and with all that had happened over the past few months, I was severely stressed, becoming insomniac, and my nerves were stretched. Under the warm tropical sun, surrounded by laughter, friendship and good food, I was beginning to feel better.

The coffee shop had a meal menu so old and faded it was barely readable. The place served traditional Indonesian fare, and I thought we could try something new for a change. I tweaked the presentations of the dishes and taught Wayan how to glaze and garnish a grilled fish European style. We worked on tropical salads and introduced a fruit smoothie with a dash of arrack to the drinks list. The cocktail menu needed attention, but as we didn't have the full range of spirits, we worked with what we had, giving each new cocktail an exotic name, such as Arrack Attack, Mango Paradise and Tropical Tease.

Wayan asked that I accompany her on her morning temple rounds. She told me the Balinese day didn't officially begin until the gods were offered food and water. The tray she carried had small baskets of rice, fruit and incense. As we strolled through the garden, she would pick up honeysuckle and mango blossoms along the way. The Sandika had temples with carvings of fierce-faced gods in each corner of the property. We placed fruit and lit incense before them, then Wayan knelt and prayed. From the temple on the far right of the property, I could see Bali Haj's grounds again, and wondered about Mahmood Bas and Anak, their intense rivalry.

That evening I asked Ketut about what had happened between the two men. He told me that the land the Bali Haj was built on had once belonged to Anak's father. There was an issue over how Bas had acquired it, and this was the main cause of their animosity. The Bali Haj was one of the finest hotels in Bali. It was a five-star luxury hotel with fifty rooms, but it had one major problem: no beach access. The Sandika Hotel, with its twelve rooms and rustic flavour and overgrown gardens, lay directly between the white sands of Kuta Beach and Mahmood Bas's dream of creating the perfect beach resort. He had offered to buy the Sandika, but Anak had refused. Bas had tried acquiring beach access through the Sandika's gardens, but the negotiations had turned sour, and insults had flown like knives. The two men's hatred of each other had developed a deeper intensity.

* * *

Wayan called for me from the office. 'From New Zealand,' she said with one hand over the mouthpiece. I wasn't going to take the call until, through the muffled mouthpiece, I recognised Grace's voice.

'It's me, Dad. How are you?' she said. 'I can't stop worrying about you, so I found the number you called from before.'

'Gracie, I'm fine. And I don't want you to worry anymore, okay? How's things with you?'

'Well, Mum's a little suspicious, and she, like, keeps asking if there's something she should know about, something I'm not telling her. So I've bought a new mobile. One that has only your number on it, and I keep it turned on all the time. It's on vibration, so you can call me whenever you want, or I can call you. I miss you big time, Dad.'

'Me too.'

'How are you? Are you looking after yourself?' she asked.

'Yes, I am. You know, there's something to be said for being dead.'

Her laughter rang through the receiver. 'Here's my number,' said Grace. 'Call me when you can, or I'll call you.'

'Hey, Adam, man,' said Geno the next day. 'You coming with us today? You too skinny man, look at you. Paolo and me, we gonna show you how to surf.'

'Geno, I'm not sure …'

'Not sure ain't in it. I check with Wayan already. I got a big board for you to start on. Get some sunscreen on those skinny shoulders of yours, put some white shit on your nose and get in the truck. We gonna start with the small wave at Nusa Dua.'

We pulled up under a tree near the sand dunes. I saw the waves. If these were small, I didn't want to see the larger ones.

We paddled out, with Geno reaching over and hooking me back onto my board every time a wave knocked me off. After countless tries, I caught a wave. Sea spray whipped about my face as I hung on with both hands.

'Now stand the fuck up!' hollered Geno, who was surfing beside me.

'Stand up, Adam. Just let your hands go,' came Paolo's easy voice.

I found my balance and surfed. But it was not more than a few seconds before I tumbled into the wash with the ankle strap pulling at my leg. When I surfaced, the brothers were ecstatic.

'You did it, man! You surfed, and on your first day!'

That night I came home exhausted and slept deeply. The next day I asked Geno when we could go again. 'Every day, man. We gonna go every day until you learn this thing.'

In a short time, my body became lean and brown, and my hair grew longer. Gone were the chef's slouch and the worry lines that I thought were permanently etched on my forehead.

* * *

Anak often came to the coffee shop in the evenings. Once, over a game of chess, as we saw Geno and Paolo pulling out on their motorbikes, he told me, 'Watch out for those two. They're up to something … We have an arrangement that they keep their business away from the hotel. If they do that we'll be okay. They're good paying guests.'

I listened without taking my eyes off the board. Anak had trapped me with his king, and I couldn't find a way through.

'That Geno guy, he's famous in Brazil. He showed me some newspaper clippings once. He was a sportsman, a pole vaulter in the Brazilian Olympic team. He's won all kinds of medals and trophies and was one of the best pole vaulters in the world.'

'What's he doing here?'

'He got busted for doping. Steroids, I think they call it. It was just before a big Olympic event. He was expected to win gold for his country, and all his countrymen's eyes were on him. He was disqualified and banned from the sport for two years. Such was his shame that he never returned home. He came to Bali to surf. That was years ago, but I remember it well. Geno swore he was innocent and told me he was set up.'

'What is it they're up to?' I asked, moving my queen two squares to the right.

'Ask Ketut,' he said, as he checkmated me with his knight.

Later, as Ketut and I sat at the sea wall, listening to the surf, I casually wove the question about Geno and Paolo into our conversation. His gentle face clouded with worry. He pulled his chair closer to me and whispered, 'Cocaine. I think maybe cocaine, Adam. Not sure.' Then he added, 'They brothers.'

Anak arrived the next day with a truck laden with coils of barbed wire and metal battens. He ordered the staff to come to the back of the hotel. Over the course of the day, we had constructed a border between the Bali Haj and the Sandika: it was a hideous-looking barrier of barbed wire and battens, like something you might find in a war zone, running up to thirty metres. It lay on our side of the boundary and out of sight of our hotel, yet in full view of the Bali Haj guests. There was nothing Mahmood Bas could do but watch.

4

Late one afternoon, I'd settled into the hammock on my balcony and was lazily admiring the tenacity of a gecko hunting a fly on the wall. With its suction-cupped feet it moved closer and closer to its prey. A hammering on my door; the gecko froze; the fly moved. I almost fell out of the hammock in my rush to open the door. Geno grabbed my shirt front.

'Adam! Something bad happen, man. Come quick!' He pulled me towards his brother's room. As we entered, the look of horror on Paolo's face made my throat tighten. He pointed to the couch. Lying on it was a guy with his head lolled back, his lips blue and bloodless, and thick white saliva dribbling down one side of his mouth, his eyes open but rolled up, his arms and legs splayed lifeless.

'He dead ... Gone, man. I do everything. I give him the kiss, bang his chest, everything, but he dead, man, finito!' Paolo cried.

'Who is he?'

'We know him. Mikey his name, surfer guy from Australia. What we gonna do now, man?'

'Why are you asking me?'

'Because you our friend, man, and we need help.'

On the glass coffee table, there were three white lines of powder, and a banknote rolled up beside a credit card. Two-thirds of the middle line was gone.

'Strong coke, eh?'

'No, man, not coke. That heroin,' said Geno with an odd expression.

I wanted out of there. This had nothing to do with me, and I moved towards the door. But Geno cut me off and held my arm.

'What do you want from me?'

'Help us, man. We got a plan.'

'Geno, I …' His fingers dug into my flesh.

'Just listen, okay? We not gonna get you in any trouble, man, but if we don't get rid of this body we in big shit, man. Big shit. Tell him, Paolo,' said Geno, holding my arm in a vice-like grip.

Paolo moved towards us and released Geno's hand from mine. Then he walked me past the body and out onto the balcony. 'It's simple, man. You gonna be our lookout. We gonna dress him up, pour whisky in him, and then Geno and I gonna shoulder him down to the motorbike, like him really bad drunk. You know between us, like this,' he mimed how they would carry the body. 'We put him on motorbike, three's up Bali style, him in middle. I hold him from back. Geno drive and we go, eh, man?'

'Go where?'

'To Blue Ocean Beach.' Paolo looked at me, his palms spread open.

'Wait a minute, let me get this straight … You're proposing to put this dead body between you and Geno, three's up on a motorbike, and drive through busy traffic and crowded streets of Kuta, to Blue Ocean Beach?'

'Yeah, man.'

'That's mad, that's fucking crazy! Let me go, let me out of here.' I saw that Geno was standing guard at the door.

'Not so mad, Adam. Now you just listen,' said Paolo, his voice soft but insistent. 'You get whisky from coffee shop, then you go downstairs to make sure no one's around. Give us a sign, then we fix him on bike and you borrow Ketut's bike and follow us, so we safe from back like that. Anybody look they gonna think him drunk. And Blue Ocean, man, many people drown there. We wait till dark and drop him by the water. In the morning, when they find him, they think he drunk too much, go swim and drown.' Paolo was waiting for an answer. I turned my eyes away from the body slumped on the couch, and towards Geno, who sat in the doorway, head in hands.

From the balcony, I saw turquoise streaks of the sunset, and heard the call of a beach hustler chasing a tourist. Blue Ocean Beach, a surf spot about two kilometres further down the beach, where the brothers had taken me for surfing lessons, did have a strong rip. The same rip that had caught me in the dinghy. I'd heard that every year a number of tourists drowned there. But to get the body from here to there ... Wouldn't a car be better? No, in gridlocked traffic with a body in a car, it could turn into a trap. Motorbikes could get through traffic where cars couldn't. Besides, we didn't have a car. Motorbikes were definitely our safest option. I could ride vanguard, covering them from the rear, blocking other bikes from cutting in and getting too close. Three's up on a motorbike was a common sight on the streets of Bali. It could be done.

What was I thinking? I didn't need to be part of this! I'd caught myself buying into their crazy plan without realising it.

Paolo stroked my arm and said quietly, 'Do this, Adam, and we owe you big time, okay?' I looked over the balcony and briefly considered jumping from it, and fleeing, but the thorns on the bougainvillea bushes below would tear me to shreds.

'And anyway, it is better for you too, man.'

'How can that be?'

'Well, you know, man. If we don't do this, we leave the hotel, and they find body, and then find you and ...'

He didn't have to say more. I had no passport, and if the police caught me, it would mean the end of Bali, as well as some immigration jail time. And considering that I have already seen the body, I was already implicated in their crime whether I liked it or not. I didn't answer when Geno said, 'You got it, eh? Now go get one bottle of whisky and borrow Ketut's bike.' He pushed open the door.

Wayan was fussing over a table of early diners and didn't notice me slip in and take a bottle of whisky from the bar in the coffee shop. I found Ketut, and he handed me the keys to his motorbike. Back at the room, the brothers had dressed the dead man in a red T-shirt and cleaned him up. He was already wearing board shorts, which he'd need if he'd been swimming. I handed the whisky to Paolo.

'What about the face?' I asked. 'That face gives it away!'

'No worries, man. We put him face down on Geno's shoulder. He drunk.' Paolo opened Mikey's mouth with his fingers and poured in the whisky; it overflowed and ran down the red T-shirt, then for good measure Geno took the whisky bottle and poured some in his hair. Then they hauled Mikey up and draped his arm on their shoulders.

'How we looking, man?' Paolo asked. As long as one couldn't see the blue bloodless colour of the man's dead face, the three of them looked passable. I grabbed a baseball cap that was lying around and put it on Mikey's head, pulling the visor down low over his eyes.

I went out first. The hotel staff and guests were on the beach, their backs turned, holding cocktails and staring at an exploding skyscape. The hotel grounds were empty. I gave the brothers the all-clear sign, and they shouldered Mikey towards the motorbikes in the hotel parking lot. No one noticed anything unusual. I kept some distance between myself and the brothers. As they positioned the body onto the motorbike, I heard Geno say, 'Come on, Mikey, good boy, Mikey,' and as Paolo was about to mount the bike from behind, the body slipped. Paulo's arm shot out and grabbed him from the neck. 'Motherfucker!' He pulled Mikey back up and gave him a hard slap. I started my motorbike. Geno led the way as we left the hotel grounds. We drove towards the centre of Kuta. It was the only way through.

At this time of night Kuta's traffic was brought to a standstill. In the cool of the evening, everyone came out. Tourists and Balinese went about their evening business, jostling for space on the narrow walkways. Footpath hustlers competed with noodle stands and hot-grills for the choicest spots. The smell of barbecued satay blended with exhaust fumes as we crawled through the teeming traffic. Geno revved the bike, moving forward in short bursts. I kept my front wheel almost glued to their rear one, making sure traffic couldn't pass me from behind. Paolo kept the body upright. Under the cover of darkness, we came out on Beach Road.

An Indonesian cop stepped out of the dark side of the road suddenly. He held a flashlight that looked more a weapon and flagged the brothers down. I wanted to accelerate and get out of there. One cop couldn't run after us after all. For an instant I thought Geno was about to do the same. But, no, he brought the bike to a halt. I drove past, and as soon as I was out of sight, slung my bike onto its stand. I looked back and saw why Geno had stopped. A second cop sat in a police car hidden behind the coconut palms.

Using the palms as cover, I moved closer towards the brothers. I saw the flashlight cop slowly circling their bike. He shone a beam on Geno's face and then on Mikey's body, which lay head-down in the crook of Geno's neck.

'Get off the motorbike.'

'No,' said Geno, looking hard at the cop. He took out his license and passport from a travellers pouch and handed them to him. 'Sir, it was a lot of hassle to get this guy on the bike. Took a long time. He very drunk, he dead drunk, and if we move him, he vomit. Not nice, sir, not nice for you, sir.'

The cop unclipped his gun holster. I took a deep breath. I could smell salt air and feel the sand under my feet. People on the other side of the road began to gather, locals mostly.

'Brazilian?' asked the cop, shining his light on the passport and in the same breath asked, 'You know three on motorbike is not allowed in Bali?'

'Sorry, sir, we have to get this guy home. He sick, really drunk …' Geno's voice was cut off by the slamming of a car door. The second cop stepped out with a torch in one hand and a gun in the other. He walked towards the brothers. He wore leather boots, a tight-fitting military style uniform and a high-peaked cap with a badge, which indicated he was the higher-ranking official of the two. I hardly had time to take in what was happening when he stopped in mid-stride. In the light of his torch I saw why. Paolo held a wad of American dollars in his hand. No words were exchanged after that. I watched from the shadows with an acidic taste in my mouth: Paolo sat on the back of the bike, one arm around the body, the other holding out the money. Both policemen feigned disinterest at first, but then in a casual movement, the higher-ranking cop moved in behind the bike and pocketed the bribe.

The onlookers dispersed. Geno started the motorbike, and the police guided the trio on to the road with hand signals and flashlights. Geno glanced at me as he accelerated past my bike. His green eyes caught mine, and a grin puckered his face. We rode down Double Six Road and onto Blue Ocean Beach. Geno and Paolo drove their motorbike onto the sand towards the water's edge. I parked and kept lookout. Apart from a lantern-lit restaurant further along, the place looked deserted. I saw the white caps of waves, heard the sound of surf pounding. Then the brothers returned, just the two of them on the motorbike. They gave me a nod. I rode back to the Sandika Hotel, following the brothers.

In the solitude of my room, I thought I would feel relief that we were out of danger, but instead I felt cold and empty. It had all happened so fast. My first instinct had been to run. Then I had been caught by an urge to protect myself. Who was Mikey, the Australian surfer who had died tonight? Did he have a family? The image of him lying on the sand on Blue Ocean Beach in his board shorts and red T-shirt came to me again.

Unable to stay still, I paced my room. The monkeys' chattering irritated, and the tree frogs' croaking mocked. A knock came on the door. It was Paolo.

'Just come to say goodbye, man. Geno and I, we going, we

outta here.'

'Yeah, that would be best,' I said. But first I wanted to talk to Geno.

The brothers' luggage lay in the centre of the room, packed and ready to go. The place looked tidy. Geno sat on the couch. The bottle of Johnnie Walker stood where we'd left it on the coffee table. I took a shot glass from the mini bar, filled it to the brim with whisky and knocked it back.

'I thought you had an understanding with Anak. No drugs at the hotel. But heroin? What's up with that? And who was Mikey anyway! How could you fucking do this?' My voice got louder with each word until I realised I was shouting.

'Okay, okay, stop right there, man,' said Geno, putting up his hand. 'First thing, we never bring dope here. Never, man. We always honour our thing with Anak, always. Mikey, that motherfucker, we did not ask him here. He just show up, and he got a big bag of Thai smack. He want to change it with us for coke, because he can't sell smack in Bali, and he sit right here, make three lines. And you know me and Paolo, we don't do that shit, and we was just telling him to fuck off when he roll up a note and … Well, man, you see what happen.' I took another shot of whisky and it went down easier.

'Where's the heroin now?'

'Gone. Paolo, he dump it in the beach somewhere.'

'You guys feel anything about Mikey?'

'Fuck him, man!' said Geno, holding up both palms. 'Look at the trouble he make for us … Hey, don't beat yourself up, Adam. He dead, we here, that's life. What you gonna do?' The third shot of whisky hit the mark, and I felt its numbing effect. I reached for another but Paolo took the bottle.

'Easy, man.'

'And look at it like this: we do that junkie scumbag a big favour.'

'How?'

'Think about his family, man. What they gonna like better, a son who drowned surfing or by heroin overdose?'

I thought about Geno's strange logic. The whole thing brought back memories of Duncan. I couldn't see or understand what the connection between Duncan and Mikey was, but it was there.

'You guys coming back?'

'Yeah, give it a few weeks, man. Let it blow over.'

5

The heron outside my window flapped its wings. From my balcony I looked out at the reef. Glassy waves peeled away in a steady pattern. On the beach, women sat in a circle, weaving frangipani blossoms into garlands. Ketut fished leaves out of the swimming pool with a long bamboo pole. The smell of freshly brewed coffee wafted up from the shop. I heard the distant ring of the office phone, then I saw Wayan waving to me.

'David's being really weird since you've been gone,' Grace sounded rattled. 'You know, he like, keeps trying to talk to me like he's now my father, and he even tried to put his arm around me. He really creeps me out, Dad. What should I do?' she asked, her voice as clear as if she were standing next to me. The hairs on my arms bristled as I thought of my ex-wife's partner. Grace changed the subject before I could answer, 'Oh, and Tula's guys came to see Mum the other day. They said that because she owns half of the restaurant, she's responsible for half the debt.' The words brought me back to reality with a jolt. I was about to speak when she cut in again, 'I'm going flatting with some friends and they're, like, really cool. You'd like them … And I forgot to tell you: I've left school, and you know Pierre who has the French café? I'm working front of house for him.' The news hit me like a slap in the face.

'Whoa, Grace, slow down, one thing at a time, and why didn't you talk to me first before you quit school.'

'Because you would have said no.'

'Damn right, I would've!'

'Sorry, Dad. I should have asked you, but you're not here, remember?'

I pulled up a chair. A couple of young tourists about Grace's age wandered past the office window. They were dressed in their swimming clothes, headed for the pool. Wayan brought in a coffee and placed it before me. My daughter was eighteen, I reminded myself. I was already running a restaurant at that age.

'Okay, Grace, you have my blessing. But in the future, tell me before you make these big decisions.

'I will! Thanks, Dad.'

* * *

In the coffee shop, the same young couple I'd seen before were sitting at a table, playing chess. A couple of surfers passed me on the way to the beach. How I envied their carefree existence. I would have liked Grace to travel overseas, to do something other than hospitality, but I had to remember that she loved everything to do with the restaurant business.

I sat under the banyan tree, sipping fresh coconut juice and watching new customers wander into the coffee shop. Word had spread that our restaurant was a good place to eat, and we had begun to pick up business. Wayan liked my changes. I made garnishes of local herbs and diced fruit. I found a linen glass cloth and taught our staff how to polish cocktail glasses with it; I also taught them to make sure the dining plates went out to customers without fingerprints or smudges. The fruit and vegetables from the morning market were fresh, and the fish always caught on the day. We also made sure the meals weren't overcooked and we didn't use too much garlic or salt. And so, Wayan received regular compliments on her cooking.

As a kid I loved seeing the delight on our customers' faces as my father did his rounds through Milano's dining room. He would move from table to table in his chef's whites, shaking their hands, telling them jokes and inquiring after their food. He was a big man with considerable Latin charm. In the kitchen, I remember being fascinated by the way the hot oil flamed up in his skillet as he cooked, pan in one hand, me on his hip, barking orders to a bevy of kitchen staff. My grandfather was given the task of looking after me. His wife had died while giving birth to my father. He'd raised his son on his own, just as my father was raising me.

I can still see my grandfather, Papa Milano, standing before his antique coffee machine. It was a tangle of polished copper and brass that stood on a plinth at the entrance to the restaurant. 'I bring this from Italy,' he would say in a distant voice as he picked up a cloth to polish the brass.

By the time I could speak, I wanted to know where my mother was and when she was coming back. Every kid I knew had a mother, except for me. I thought all I had to do was to ask my father to bring mine back.

'Papa, where's my mother?' He continued cooking. I tugged at his apron.

'Basta! Enough!' he barked. His tone would've silenced any kid, but I was determined to know. I barely came up to his knees and was about to tug at my father again when an arm reached and scooped me up. It was Papa Milano.

'Tell him, Salvador. He's old enough now.' My grandfather held me close. I could see my father's face grimacing. He ground his teeth, and his cheeks flushed. He wouldn't look at me.

'Catzo, Papa, what you doing to me!' My father cupped his fingers in an exasperated gesture. 'This picilo stronzo, he's too young!'

'Tell him, Salvador!' The kitchen had gone quiet. The chefs, kitchen hands and dishwashers had their ears peeled to hear our conversation.

'Salvador, you talk to your son. You answer his question like a good father, or I gonna tell him myself in front of everyone!' Papa Milano took the skillet from my father and pushed me into his arms. The staff lowered their heads as we walked past the prep

benches. We pushed our way through the swinging doors into his office.

I felt grown up and important sitting in my father's swivel chair. He uncapped a bottle of whisky and slugged it down. 'Come here.' He lifted me up and sat me on his knee. He smelled of whisky and garlic. 'Your mama's name is Rosa, and she ain't never coming back here.'

Tears welled up in my eyes. I couldn't stop them, but I kept my face still. I wasn't going to cry, not in front of my father. He took my face in his hands, and his voice became a murmur.

'She was no good, son, no good.'

'Why?' My voice cracked.

'She worked here for two weeks, and we, well … You know, we got together.'

'Were you married?'

He laughed, which made me smile, and I brushed away my tears with the back of my hand, 'Yes, son, she was married. But she just wasn't married to me.' He laughed again, ruffled my hair then drank some more.

'Where did I come from then?'

'I hardly knew her, you know. Two weeks is not long enough to know someone. She disappeared, and I thought she'd gone back to her husband in Italy, but nine months later she showed up in the kitchen with a bassinette, and you inside it.' He took another slug from the bottle. 'She say, "I can't do this, Salvador. He's your child." Then as quick as she arrived, she left. I try to track her down, but the only thing I know is that she came from Verona, and you know, son, I never even knew her last name.'

His words had a finality to them. I knew I would never find my mother, and I knew that she wasn't coming back. I sobbed against his chest until his apron was wet with my tears. Papa Milano came in then and led me to my bed.

'You know, Adam,' he said as he tucked me in, 'your father never had a mother either, and he turned out alright. Sleep now *child, and tomorrow, everything gonna be okay.'*

My grandfather died when I was six. After that I was looked after by a succession of Italian girls who worked at Milano's. Each usually lasted a year or two. My father never married.

From an early age, I was determined not to go into hospitality. I had watched my father's life becoming consumed by it. I knew the kitchen had stolen his life, and finally killed him. When I turned sixteen I enrolled in a marine school. I hoped to become an offshore skipper.

My father was disturbed. 'What do you think I do this for? Why do you think I work so hard in front of this stove?' he said. But then he had relented and paid my tuition fees.

* * *

When a casually dressed Indonesian ate at our place one night and walked out without paying, I was surprised. 'Eddi Medan,' whispered Wayan. 'Security ... Same like the police ... Him Muslim.'

The man returned the following night and asked me to join him at his table. Wayan's words put me on edge.

'Know anything about this guy?' he asked, pulling out a snapshot of Mikey from his wallet. I shook my head. 'You're looking a bit pale. Anything you need to tell me, Adam?'

'How do you know my name?'

'It's my job to know. Hey, relax, mate. I'm on your side. This guy was a known drug courier, and I've been trying to track him down for some time. Just need to know where he stayed, so I can clean out his room before the local police get to it and take a large bribe from one of my clients.'

'He didn't stay here.'

'You sure about that, mate? He was seen around here.'

'Positive.'

'Okay, I'll strike this one off my list. Hey, I hear you're a chess player?' Eddi then ordered a chess board and two beers over to our table.

Over the course of the game, he told me he was from southern Java and his family had emigrated to Sydney when he was a kid. After finishing high school, he had become a police cadet and joined Sydney's police force. In his mid-twenties he had decided that traditional police work wasn't for him. He took three months' leave and came to Bali, where he found a job that suited him: an affiliation of hotels hired him to work as liaison between them and the famously corrupt Indonesian police. I relaxed a little when he told me that the Sandika was included in this group. Being fluent in both English and Indonesian, he had a network of Indo beach hustlers who were his informants. He could track down a stolen credit card before it was used. He dealt with rental car accidents and guests skipping out of hotels without paying; they would find Eddi waiting for them at the airport.

Eddi was big man with a gangly gait. He had a cop's wryness, which was countered by gentleness, particularly evident in his brown eyes. I wondered why he hadn't asked me where I was from, then guessed that he'd chosen not to. I asked him about the Bali Haj and the story between the two hoteliers. Eddi exhaled as he told me: 'I work for them both, so I can't really say much. A story like theirs is steeped in thousands of years of history; they were born to hate each other.'

Eddi drained his beer as I moved my queen in for the kill. He shrugged and called for two more beers. 'Anak's an interesting guy,' he said. 'One time I'd done in my back, and I went to every doctor I thought could help. Nothing worked, and I was all strung out on painkillers. I was in a bad way. Anak heard of my condition and called me to his house on a night of the full moon. You know I'm a Muslim and I find the Hindu ceremonies too strange, but my back hurt so much that I was prepared to try anything. Anyway, Anak gave me some water the colour of blood. I drank that stuff ... Then I remembered I had an appointment with my acupuncturist.' Eddi leaned across the table and said, 'You know, he couldn't get one of his needles to go in. He kept trying, but the needles just broke. It freaked him out, and he still hasn't gotten over it. But here's the strange thing: I went home, and the next morning, my back pain had vanished. Gone! My back has given me no trouble since. Figure that one out, mate.'

* * *

After a few weeks, Geno and Paolo returned to their room. Once more, the evening sunsets were accompanied by Geno's bossas and sambas. I resumed my surfing lessons and often hung out with the brothers at the Blue Ocean bars. I enjoyed their company but always kept a weather eye out lest they lure me into their business again.

One day, Geno invited me to walk along the beach with him. 'Adam, I got something for you,' he said. When he handed me a large manila envelope, I was uncomfortable. We walked a few more paces in awkward silence.

'Open the fucking thing, man,' he said. In the envelope, folded between two sheets of paper, I found an Australian passport. It was printed under the name of Michael Brown, but it had a photo of me, my correct age, and on the first blank page a one-year residency visa for Indonesia.

'Geno, where did you ... That's not my name, and where did you get the photo?'

'I took the fucking photo when you weren't looking, and its Mikey's passport. At least we got something from that motherfucker for all the trouble he caused us. We had it fixed, and the work visa, man, those rip off Indos at immigration. Anyway, listen up. We square now. You help us and now we help you. Finito, okay?'

'I can't accept this.'

'You can and you fucking will. What else you gonna do if the police stop you, eh?'

I thumbed through the passport. The photograph had been touched up, and it gave me a possum-in-the-headlights stare, but the likeness was good. I didn't want to be Michael Brown, but on the other hand, this passport would give me the freedom to move around Bali. I'd never ventured too far from the Sandika for fear of being stopped. I'd be safer with it than without it.

'Okay,' I said tentatively.

'Of course, man, of course,' said Geno, and we shook hands.

A stray gust of wind blew in, causing a flock of seagulls to lift off and resettle further along the beach.

That night I borrowed Ketut's motorbike and rode towards Kuta. I slowed down as I came into a built-up area. Behind thatched bar fronts with tacky neon signs flashing names like 'Froggies Bar' or 'Peanuts Club', I heard the drunken drawl of late-night revellers. I recognised Australian and Kiwi accents. An empty beach road stretched out before me. A strip with the ocean on one side and hotels set back from the road on the other. I rode the bike, slowing to a crawl as I passed the spot where Geno and Paolo had been pulled over – that night seemed like ages ago. I passed Legian village. On the main road heading out of town, I saw a signpost that said 'Beach', followed by an arrow. I swung into the narrow lane. At the end of the track, sweeping white foam surged and receded on an expanse of flat sand. Coconut palms rustled. Attached to a trunk, swarming with moths, shone a single light bulb. I pulled up under its glow, cut the motor and sat on the bike, enjoying the warm sea air.

I had the urge to swim suddenly. After dropping my clothes above the tide line, I raced into the sea, my feet sinking in the soft sand. I jumped over a few incoming rollers and found a good depth. Beyond the waves, I floated on my back, looking up into the starry skies. Then I became aware of a current. With memories still fresh of the rip that'd pulled me onto the reef, I swam for the shore, body-surfed on a wave and came out some distance away from my clothes. I could just see the light on the coconut palm.

There was movement to my right. People were walking along the beach at the water's edge. I stood waist-deep in the sea. I would stay there until they passed.

Moonlight and phosphorous foam cast a translucent light on three approaching figures. They came out of a sea-spray mist, two jet-black hunched animals and a tall white woman. The animals wore chain collars and leads, and they loped along, almost pulling the woman faster than she wanted to walk. They were close, not twenty metres to my right, and I could see them clearly: two huge orangutans with hairy manes, and a tall elegant woman dressed in white. They passed directly in front of me. I saw the fiery-red eyes and human-like faces of the apes, but the woman held my attention more. A shawl, embellished with white lace, covered her shoulders. Her silver hair curved across a high brow and fell draped to her shoulders, where it became a plait woven with sea shells and other trinkets. The only non-white adornment she wore was a pair of black wrap-around sunglasses. Her face was delicately sculptured, and her body, under wind-touched fabric, moved gracefully.

I walked out of the water keeping well behind as they moved up the beach and towards the light. One ape stopped at my clothes and sniffed. Its eyes flashed my way for an instant, and I froze. Then it diverted its attention to the woman's shoulder bag. She pulled at its chain and the ape heeled. Under the light she rummaged through the bag. I couldn't see what she took out from it, but whatever it was interested the apes, and they pressed towards her, clutching her. The woman in white, haloed by the light of the lamp, was held aloft by two enormous black apes. I watched transfixed as they disappeared through the coconut palms.

6

I awoke to a dusk with no moon. A grey mist hung low over the coffee shop, making the glow of the oil lamps brighter. A swarm of night moths circled and hovered around the electric light, hissing and popping. The tide was out. I padded down from my room to the shop. I saw Wayan pointing to a smattering of dead moths under the light. She ordered a waitress to take a broom and brush them away, but unsatisfied with the way that the waitress did the task, Wayan came out from behind the cash register to show her. She was halfway across the floor when she stopped. I saw her terrified expression. Her face flushed red, and she stood transfixed, then let out a scream. She fell to the floor writhing, making gurgling sounds and clutching her throat, as if she was trying to pry away invisible hands. The terrified waitress knelt beside her. Ketut rushed in. I helped him pick her up. She fought against us, scratching our faces. Her eyes rolled white as she thrashed and twisted. Ketut wrapped his arms around her, lifting her off her feet. Together we carried her out of the coffee shop to a deck chair by the swimming pool.

'Call Anak!' Ketut cried. I rushed to the telephone in the office. Anak sensed the urgency in my voice and hung up immediately. I returned to the coffee shop to assure our guests that help was on the way, then went to stand by Wayan's side. We waited long moments. Ketut strained to keep himself together while his wife's condition worsened. By the time Anak arrived, Wayan was soaked in sweat, and her eyes were wide open, her face flushed.

'It's a spell,' said Anak, touching her forehead. 'It's a strong one, too. Ketut, get me a glass of water, and tell the staff to return to their work. Adam, you take over Wayan's work. Stay in the coffee shop, and don't allow anyone to come near us.'

'How bad is she?'

'Very bad. I must use bloodstone.'

I took up Wayan's place behind the cash register. I slipped a recording of calming gamelan music into the shop's sound system and told our waitresses to offer each guest a cocktail on the house. Through the thatched blinds, I watched Anak hold up a glass of red liquid to the light.

The coffee shop was almost empty when Anak called for Ketut. Together they held Wayan's head up and poured the contents of the glass into her mouth. Still unconscious, she gagged and spluttered. Our staff sat around a table, silent and scared. Then Anak called us over. Wayan lay peacefully on the pool chair. We rolled her onto a stretcher and carried her to her room. I walked back to the coffee shop with Anak.

'She'll be okay,' he said. 'The blood water will stop the spell from becoming worse. But, unfortunately, it will have less power as there is no moon tonight.'

I'd been in Bali long enough to know that spells and magic were very real to the people here. These magical forces and unexplainable energies were as real to them as the air they breathed. Demons and gods were given equal importance. One couldn't exist without the other, I'd been told, and they went to great lengths to appease them both.

I wanted to believe that Wayan had been struck down by a spell, and that the magic of the bloodstone had cured her, but a small voice in the back of my mind kept telling me it was nonsense. I remembered drinking the blood water myself and seeing the cuts on my legs vanish. At the time my feelings had ping-ponged between disbelief and amazement, until I had finally come to the conclusion that my incredible cure was due to the papaya. The next day, Wayan was back at her post. Ketut told me she had no recollection of what had happened the night before.

Several days later, I saw Anak wandering along the shoreline. He was investigating bits of seaweed and turning over rocks and shells with a walking cane. As I approached he looked up, acknowledged me with a nod and went back to his fossicking.

'Anak, please, I would like to see the bloodstone.'

'And so you shall, my friend,' he answered quietly, as if he'd been expecting my question. 'Come to my compound for the full moon ceremony.'

I knew that in his capacity as a shaman, Anak cured afflictions ranging from small ailments to spirit possessions through the laying of hands and chanting of prayers. Wayan had told me how patients queued up outside his compound on nights of the full moon with baskets of offerings in exchange for healing sessions. These sessions, she said, were part of an elaborate Hindu ceremony to invoke the power of the moon. The bloodstone was only used on rare occasions when all other remedies failed.

On the night of the next full moon, Wayan dressed me in a dark blue sarong with a gold embroidered sash, along with the appropriate headgear for a Hindu layman. I climbed onto the back of Ketut's motorbike, and we headed out of the quiet of the hotel grounds into the madness of Balinese traffic. We were met at the entrance to Anak's compound by his wife, Dewi. She adorned us with frangipani garlands and ushered us inside. A large banyan tree grew in the middle of the compound. Lanterns hung from its lower branches, and in the cave-like root cavities of the trunk were placed statues of Hindu deities, honoured with incense and tiny baskets filled with rice and bits of paper currency. About a hundred devotees sat cross-legged before the bamboo dais where Anak was perched. He was dressed in a white sarong, with his hair oiled and tied back. A patient undergoing a healing lay before him, chest bare, sarong rolled up.

A bell rang, and a group of priests struck up a chant,

accompanied by the beating of drums and gamelans. A hundred voices joined in, the sound vibrating through me. The sound of chanting and the heady smell of incense made me feel light-headed. Ketut sat next to me, his palms pressed together, his face enraptured. The chanting ended with the priests sprinkling holy water over the crowd. Each devotee reached out with open palms to receive the blessing.

Soon, the healed and the priests had left. Only Anak, Ketut and I remained.

'Come,' said Anak. He pointed to a seat on the dais. As I sat, he placed the bloodstone in a glass of water. After several minutes a thin blood-like substance oozed out of several points in the stone, turning the water red. Anak removed the stone from the glass and returned it to its cloth.

'Drink some,' he said, handing me the glass. I raised it to my lips and drank a couple of mouthfuls. He then took the glass from my hands. 'Once again you are under the protection of the blood stone.'

I had heard the same words when Anak had set my shoulder. I remembered the reverence in Ketut's voice when he spoke of the bloodstone, and of course the fascination in Eddi's voice as he told his story. 'Protection?' I asked.

'Yes. Nothing can hurt you now. Let me show you.' Anak reached for his kris, a small razor-sharp curved dagger that Balinese men wear tucked in their sashes. He handed it to me. I felt its sharpness with my thumb.

'Hold out your arm.'

'What?'

'You cannot be harmed.'

He took my arm and quickly slashed it three times. I could feel the sharp blade cutting into my skin. I tried to pull away but his grip held me firm. To my surprise, no marks showed on my skin. There was no indication that I had been cut with a sharp knife. Again he slashed my arm, harder this time; once more I felt the blade piercing my skin. Yet no mark showed. Anak told Ketut to hold out his arm then lightly dragged the kris across his skin. A thin line of blood appeared. Ketut had been cut. He smiled at me as he wiped the blood off his arm.

I was experiencing something so far outside the realm of what I knew to be possible, yet it seemed believable. Anak was believable. He had no reason to trick me. But that's what I thought it was: a trick, a hoax, a sleight of hand. I felt the weight of disappointment settle in me. I picked up the kris and felt its blade once more. He must have seen the disbelief on my face.

'One day, you will understand,' he said.

I thanked him for the demonstration as he left.

A gust of air rustled the leaves lying about the deserted compound. An oil lamp flared, illuminating a small golden statue of a god at the base of the tree. We were about to leave when Ketut reached for the remaining blood water. The glass was still two-thirds full. He raised a toast to the moon and drank it. 'No need to waste it,' he said as we climbed onto his motorbike. Although the moon was full, the coconut palms that lined the road made it gloomy. Fireflies flickered in and out of our headlight.

I saw the dog rush out before us, and I felt Ketut swerve to miss it. The motorbike went over. We skidded along the tar seal right into the path of an oncoming truck. I was thrown off into the gravel. I turned my head to see Ketut disappear under the front wheels of the truck. The sound was sickening: a dull crunch, and then the same horrific sound again as the back wheels of the truck ran over Ketut's body a second time. The motorbike lay on its side, front wheel spinning. The headlight was still on, and it pointed at Ketut's inert body lying on the middle of the road.

I picked myself up and staggered towards him. His face looked strangely serene. He opened one eye, and then the other, cocked his head to one side and looked down at his body. Then he stood up.

'Ketut!' I shouted. 'Are you all right?'

He ran his hands over his body, checking. 'Yes, I am.'

We picked up the motorbike. Apart from the bent handlebars and a cracked headlight, it was undamaged. There was no sign of the truck that had run over Ketut. We got back on our bike and drove home.

Back at the hotel, a single bulb lit the deserted coffee shop. Wayan had left a plate of fruit and a thermos of tea for us. An offshore breeze rattled the rattan blinds. Waves thumped against the sea wall. A loose piece of thatch flapped noisily.

'We might have some bad weather,' said Ketut.

'Are you sure you're okay? Do you feel anything? Any bruises or pain?' I wasn't interested in the weather. If I'd thought Anak's performance with the bloodstone was a trick, I knew Ketut being run over by a truck wasn't. 'Ketut, did you not feel anything when the truck ran over your body?'

'What?'

'Ketut, you were run over by a truck. You went under the front wheels, and then the back wheels too.'

'I did?'

'Yes, I saw it.'

'Strange.'

'What do you mean?'

'I know we fall off bike because of dog, but I don't see no truck.'

'Ketut! I saw it!' My voice rose in frustration.

He sipped the tea and then unpeeled a mangosteen. He popped the white flesh of the fruit into his mouth and flicked the peel over the sea wall. The wind grew stronger, causing a tablecloth to flutter to the ground. I could see he was deep in thought. I stared out at the sea. After some time he turned to me and smiled.

'Maybe I explain a little. You see, Wayan and I, we been working at Sandika Hotel for long time and I see many foreigners. One thing, the Westerner, he always need an explanation for everything. How much this? How much that? Where? Why? What? And also the Westerners have only one god. And I know him always angry: Don't do this, don't do that. So, many Westerners cannot believe in him. You see, we Balinese very lucky. We have many gods, happy gods, sad gods, fighting gods, gods for this and that. So many gods. Even me, I can't remember them all.' Then his face darkened, and as he spoke, he lowered his voice. His eyes scanned the surroundings as if he were afraid someone would listen. 'But also we have *leyaks,* devils and demons. They very bad, Adam, watch out for them. You see already what happen to Wayan.'

'Yes, but ...' I was not sure what Ketut's discourse had anything to do with the night's bizarre events.

'Wait,' he said, 'I'm not finished. You see the bloodstone, and you don't believe its powers, but I believe. Do you believe the Americans put man on moon?'

'Yes.'

'I do not. I can't believe that one, because the moon is a god, and how can a man walk on a god? But I try to answer your question now. Anak show you the bloodstone and you no believe, so a god who's watching said, "Ah! I gonna show him." You understand?'

'No.'

'Adam, not everyone see the same thing at same time. Maybe that god, he want to show you the power of blood stone with the truck. But me, I believe already, so he no need to show me. You understand?'

'So what you're saying is the truck didn't exist. It was only an illusion manifested by some god?'

'Ah! There you go again. You see the Western mind is so hard, Adam, like a rock.' Ketut slapped his forehead in frustration. Then he leaned over and rubbed my arm as he spoke, 'Of course, the truck exist. You exist, I exist, and even the thinking in your head exists. Adam, please don't worry yourself anymore. You see the truck. I did not. That's it.'

At that moment, a gust of wind blew through the coffee

shop and pushed the blinds aside. Moonlight illuminated Ketut's face as the wind rose stronger. The chorus of crickets and frogs became silent, and the fruit bats grew still. I thanked Ketut for his explanation and headed up to my room. I lay awake listening to the rain pound on the roof.

* * *

Grace rang the following morning. 'Hi Dad, are you sitting down?'

'I am now.' Her tone made me anxious.

'Hey, are you okay?' she asked. 'You don't tell me much about what's going on with you in Bali.'

'Gracie, what is it?

'Well … I'm with someone.'

'What do you mean?'

'I have a boyfriend,' she blurted out the words so fast, I nearly missed them.

'Whew, you had me worried there. I thought it was something serious.'

'It is serious,' she said quietly, and with a slightly indignant tone.

'Okay, who is he?' I stood and looked out the office window to the coffee shop. Wayan was serving a couple of surfers. Sunlight filtered through the banyan tree, casting shimmering patterns of light on the ground. Grace had a boyfriend; should I be concerned, worried? I had to admit it kind of bothered me. I still saw her as my little girl.

'His name is Steven,' she said carefully. 'He's two years older than me, and he's studying Accounting at Auckland Uni. He's not really good looking but he's, like, kinda cute in his own way. He's kind and caring. Dad, he really loves me.'

'Do you love him?'

'I think so,' she paused. Wayan came in and bustled about the office looking for a receipt book. Grace continued, 'I can talk

73

to him, and he listens. Since my dad's not around, I haven't had anyone else to talk to.'

'That's not the reason you're with him, surely?'

'No.'

'Have you two … you know?'

'Know what?'

'Made love, had sex?'

'Dad … I'm eighteen.'

'Okay, okay.' I suddenly felt foolish. 'Well, Grace, what can I say … I wish you both the best and don't get pregnant.'

'Hah, listen to you! Mum had me when she was seventeen, didn't she? Now tell me about what's going on with you? Are you looking after yourself? How are you feeling?'

After our conversation, I took a seat by the pool and watched the wind ruffle the water's surface. A leaf blew in from the banyan tree, and I scooped it out, the water cool against my hands. Not only was I in a relationship at Grace's age, we owned and managed Auckland's finest Italian restaurant. I'd met Elisabeth when we were both sixteen. I was studying then for my offshore yacht masters ticket during the day and working at Milano's at night. She worked as a waitress at the restaurant.

I can see her now in her tight blue jeans, her hair piled up on the top of her head and held together with a Japanese comb, her teasing green eyes, her easy laugh as she served a table. I loved everything about her. I remember her voice, low and husky, as she pulled me aside in the kitchen and said, 'Hey, I know this really cool club downtown where they don't ask for IDs … Wanna come?' That night Elisabeth took me to her room, and under her sheets, with her hand clamped over my mouth so her parents couldn't hear, I lost my virginity to her.

Soon, we were spending every moment we could together. Our hormones seemed to run our lives. We couldn't get enough of each other. If her shift finished before mine, we were gone, running out of the restaurant even as my father stood in the doorway, chef's knife in hand, shouting obscenities after us in Italian.

When Elisabeth got pregnant, our families disapproved and counselled us not to go ahead with it: we were too young, they'd said, but for us there was never any doubt about it. We were keeping the baby. Grace was born premature, and both mother and daughter had to spend many weeks resting and recuperating at the hospital.

I found a two-room apartment not far from Milano's and asked my father if he could sign the rental agreement as we were both under age, and if he could help us with the rent too. He didn't speak a word as he signed the document and handed me a cheque. He sat in his swivel chair, rested his hands on his generous girth and looked at me with a sorrowful face.

Elisabeth and Grace came home soon. The baby was tiny and fragile, with her delicate face and Buddha belly. We were good parents for a couple so young.

For one year we lived in a bubble of domestic bliss. It was hard trying to make ends meet, and to juggle work, study and family, but looking back, it was still one of the happiest years of my life. At the end of my shift, my father would sometimes haul me over to the stove and slip a roll of money into my top pocket. When I tried to thank him, he'd raise a palm and say, 'Basta, it's for bambina.'

A year later, at the age of forty-eight, my father had a heart attack. One minute he was preparing a slab of scotch fillet, and the next, he was dead. His huge body lay on the kitchen floor, eyes open, covered in the calamari rings that had toppled from the table and landed on him as he fell. A desperate kitchen staff tried to revive him while I watched, paralysed with shock. Moments later the ambulance staff pronounced him dead. I didn't go with the body. I picked up the filleting knife and continued preparing the scotch fillet my father had left unfinished, barely able to see if I was cutting the steak or my own flesh. The staff looked at me in confusion.

7

Not long after the full moon ceremony, Anak arrived at the hotel. He came riding in his chariot: the extraordinary vehicle had the lower half of a silver Mercedes Benz, and he sat high in the back seat, with his cocks in wicker cages placed on either side of him. Anak had won the car in a cock fight. However, he'd decided the vehicle was too hot and unsuitable for transporting his cockerels to the fights, so he ordered for the upper half of it to be cut off. This job went to a local handyman named Bung, whose only qualification for the job was that he owned some antique welding equipment. Bung had made a dog's breakfast of it, leaving an ugly jagged edge of burnt black metal around the car. To correct this, Anak commissioned a temple carver to create a railing out of coconut logs. The artist took his commission to heart and carved images of Hindu gods wrestling with serpent-bodied dragons and of fierce-faced *barong* and *rangda* rising out of the wood, while a multitude of lesser gods adorned the rear. A deep groove had been cut on the underside of the carved logs so they sat neatly over the botched metal. The carvings ran down both sides of the car and a further piece was added to traverse the rear. Once bolted and fitted, they created a wooden boundary, like a set of horizontal totem poles, framing the red-leather upholstered interior of what was left of the Mercedes Benz.

The carvers must have been caught in a creative flow because they forgot about the doors. And since it would be considered sacrilege to cut through an image of a deity in order to accommodate a car door, Anak simply got into the vehicle as if mounting a horse. The final adornment on the car was the placement of a large, carved Garuda head with moonstone eyes in place of the Mercedes Benz emblem on the bonnet. The end result was curiously pleasing: the vehicle was an interesting blend of modern Teutonic automotive design and ancient Balinese artistry. The shine of the silver-bodied Mercedes complemented the speckled grain of the coconut wood carvings, and breathed life into the eyes of the ancient Hindu bird-like deity. When travelling, Anak sat cross-legged on the back seat's leather cushion, his arms folded, and his black hair cascading out from under his straw hat. His driver and cock-handler was a high-born man called Gusti. It was in this manner that Anak travelled to every major cockfight on the island of Bali.

I had been expecting him that morning when his chariot pulled up under the banyan tree. Wayan had told me that he was coming. She'd groomed the coffee shop in preparation of his arrival. The palm-weave matting and bamboo had been brushed and the tiled floor polished. On the tables were placed coconut bowls with floating frangipani petals.

While Gusti and Ketut fussed over the cockerels and placed their wicker cages in the shade, Anak got out of his chariot and strode into the coffee shop, smiling. Slightly anxious I rose to meet him. The last time I'd seen him was on the night of the episode with the blood stone, and the incident with Ketut and the truck.

'How are you, Adam?' he asked, and in the same breath, 'I want you to meet someone.' Anak clapped his hands and called, 'Gusti, bring Ali.'

A moment later, Gusti placed a magnificent cockerel on the table before us. The bird shone with good health: his plumage was a deep red, shimmering with golden highlights and hackles of iridescent blue. With his neck poised and tail extended, the bird cocked an eye towards me. Anak held Ali in both hands and bounced him up and down, while gently ruffling its feathers.

I'd observed Balinese men paying more attention to their fighting cocks than to their wives. They were petted, lovingly fondled and spoken to in soothing tones. *Ba mantap!* I'd heard women shout to groups of men squatting idly in the courtyard, each with a rooster between his legs – it meant 'cock crazy' in the island's dialect.

'Ali here has never lost a fight,' Anak told me proudly as he handed the bird to Gusti. 'Adam, I want you to do me a service. That is why I am here, to ask this of you.'

He called Wayan to him and whispered something into her ear, and the coffee shop was immediately cleared. Staff shuffled away quietly, heads bowed down. Anak waited with folded arms, and when he was satisfied we wouldn't be overheard, he leaned forward and said, 'There is a major cock-fighting tournament the day after tomorrow. I want you to come and bet on Ali, place large bets, a million rupiah each. But you should come as a tourist. Bring Geno and Paolo with you. You can all bet.'

'Where's the tournament?' I asked. I was aware that cockfighting was illegal in Indonesia, and I didn't want to get involved in something that might land me in a police station.

'Don't worry, far away from here: Singaraja, north of the island. No police. There are very rich competitors coming in from Java. But there is one in particular … I want to take his money.'

'Who?'

'Mahmood Bas.' Anak spat his name out like a curse. 'Bas has a flock of the best fighting cocks money can buy, and he hires the top Javanese handlers. But Ali can beat them all. The bird has a god-given spirit,' Anak said. He caught my gaze and held it. 'Will you do this?'

Of course there would be some risk involved in this, but on the other hand, it would be a way to repay Anak for all that he had done for me. And if we were rounded up by the police, I would have my forged passport to show them and a pocketful of cash to give them, should a bribe be necessary.

'I will,' I said.

That night I spoke to Geno and Paolo. They were into the plan as well.

'Hey, man, if we can take down that motherfucker Mahmood Bas we in, we coming,' said Geno.

* * *

The next morning Anak dropped off a package of three million rupiah. The tournament fights would be held at a yet-to-be disclosed location the next day. We were told to bet a million each on Ali, when Anak's cock was pitted against one of Mahmood Bas's birds. Anak would send someone to inform us when that would be, well before the fight. Gusti filled me in on the finer points of the rules of cockfighting. As game-cock owners, Anak and his opponent held the central bet, and therefore were not permitted to side bet. The side betting was run by money lenders and independent bush bankers with large amounts of cash. In Bali, fortunes were made or lost on a single, one-minute cockfight. The big money was in the side bet. That's where we came in. Gusti told us there were always a couple of tourists at the fights, and they generally bet big, and of course Mahmood Bas didn't know us. Although we were neighbours, I'd never met the man.

The drive to Singaraja took us through Ubud, a mountain village renowned for Balinese fine arts. Artists displayed their canvases on easels outside studios that were set against a backdrop of tropical foliage. Braced against the brisk mountain air, we continued our ascent of Mt. Agung, moving up a winding narrow road, past terraced rice paddies carved precariously into mountainous ridges, and to the crater. Geno pulled the Jeep to a stop on the ridge, the most elevated road on the island. On one side, we saw a panoramic vista of the southern slopes of Bali, and on the other, a mist-shrouded crater lake, and further on, the summit of Mt. Agung. Through breaks in the mist, we saw on the eastern shores of the lake a burial ground reserved for high-born Balinese.

After lunch at a roadside stall, we began our descent. The

hour-long drive twisted and turned through the densest rainforests on the island, towards Singaraja, the old Dutch colonial capital on the northern shores of Bali. We checked into the second floor of a Dutch pension, a place with overhead fans, creaky wooden floors and planters' chairs set on a balcony that overlooked the town centre.

Singaraja was cockfight crazy. All the cockfighting aficionados had descended on the town and were gearing up for the tournament. There were wicker baskets of birds on the backs of motorbikes, tucked under arms, and there were groups of men squatting on pavements, comparing their birds, cooing to them, blowing on their beaks and setting them in mock combat against each other, only to retrieve them quickly before any damage was done.

Although cockfighting and gambling were illegal in Indonesia, owning fighting birds wasn't. The game birds didn't have to be concealed. For this reason, the organisers of the tournament wouldn't reveal the location of an up-coming fight until the last minute. They often set up a decoy fight in another location just to confuse the police. Word of the real location would then spread quickly before the fight, and the town would quietly empty, leaving the police looking at deserted footpaths covered in bird shit and feathers.

We heard a soft tapping on our door, and a small boy stood there. I recognised him as one of Anak's. His face beamed with pride as he handed me a folded piece of paper and ran off. It was a map, leading us to the location of the fight. With Geno navigating, we set off in the Jeep. Earlier, we'd divided the money – a million rupiah per man. The tournament, according to our map, would be held behind the temple ruins about three kilometres outside the city. We turned down a rutted dirt road overgrown with vines and creepers, and came out at a clearing under some scrub trees. The number of dusty motorbikes and parked vehicles indicated the grand size of the tournament. I saw Anak's chariot parked by the temple wall. The entrance to the cockpit was through crumbling brown terracotta pillars covered in lichen moss and honeysuckle vines. Once inside, it took us a moment to adjust to the frenzied atmosphere. A fight was underway; a dense crowd of noisy, gesticulating men circled the arena, calling for side bets. Their shouts drowned the raucous laughter and the calls of food sellers hawking their wares. Wicker cages encircled the periphery of the cockpit and all outlying grounds of the temple ruins, while cock handlers displayed their birds. Tournament officials, in black and white turbans, paired off competing birds.

The crowd cleared when the fight ended, and I finally got a glimpse of the cockpit. The bird that'd lost, a speckled black-and-white cockerel, lay dead in the centre of the pit, soaked in its own blood. The owner bent over and retrieved his valuable metal spurs by hacking off the bird's feet with a machete. Then he picked up his cock by its stumps, blood dripping from its beak, and hurled it into a growing pile of carcasses. Gusti had told me that cockfights were often held in or near temples. The spilling of blood onto the ground became part of a religious rite. This way, the losing cocks contribute to the appeasement of small animal-like demons and spirits, the *bata* and *kula* that lurk in the undergrowth around temples.

I looked around for Anak and spotted his group under the shade of some scrub trees. They'd built a colourful shelter out of sarongs to keep the sun off their birds.

A cockfight generally lasted only three minutes, so up to twenty-five fights were scheduled for the day. Another fight began, and Geno and Paolo were getting their feet wet, waving their money at the bookies and making their own small bets. Mahmood Bas's group, dressed in white kaftans and skull caps, were sitting close to where I stood. I recognised the hotelier under a white umbrella surrounded by cages. His cocks looked magnificent and his handlers were many. I hoped Anak knew what he was doing. I moved away quietly, having decided to appear only when the big-money fights were on. I bought an iced mango juice and marvelled at the ingenuity of the seller who'd transported ice, mangoes and glasses on a bicycle to the tournament. In the shade of the ruins, I sipped my drink, wondering how such a large event was kept secret from the police. An hour later, the same boy who had brought us the note earlier walked past and caught my eye.

Anak's and Bas's cocks were on. I manoeuvred my way through the dense crowd to the edge of the cockpit. Geno stood opposite me; Paolo further around. Anak was positioned at the edge of the cockpit, his arms folded, watching the razor sharp steel spurs being tied to Ali's legs. Gusti squatted on his haunches holding the bird. At the other end of the cockpit, Bas's men were doing the same. The referee inspected the tying of the spurs on both cocks – a part of the preliminaries. Gusti and Bas's handler moved to the centre and squatted, holding their birds. They both plucked hackle feathers and flicked at the birds' beaks to rouse their fighting spirit.

On the strike of a gong, the birds were released, and the fight began. Bas's cock, a powerful-looking bird, dark buff, with a silvery blue mane, circled Ali, its head extended and hackles flared, head cocked to one side. The betting, permitted until the first engagement, was furious. It took only seconds to place my million-rupiah bet with a bookie. The transaction passed without notice amongst the jostling throng.

The crowd fell silent with a sudden awed hush. The buff bird rushed towards Ali, crashing with such force that it fell backwards. Ali reeled back. The buff bird regained its footing quickly. The birds were in the air again, striking at each other. Spurs flashed. Wings beat in a whirl of motion. The birds dropped to the ground and crouched, heads extended towards each other. Hackles flared in a standoff. The crowd inhaled as one. Then the buff bird dashed in, trying to knock Ali off its feet. The red bird feinted expertly sideways, and the buff bird tore past, missing its target. As the charging bird whirled about, Ali was on top of him in a flurry of legs and spurs, pinning the buff to the ground with its beak. A dark blood stain appeared below the buff bird. Ali had drawn blood. The silvery buff bird, pierced through the breast by Ali's spur, lay motionless. The fight had lasted less than thirty seconds. Ali had won. Pandemonium broke as the bookies collected and paid out. The winners called for their money while the losers retreated. As I picked up my winnings, a parcel of two million rupiah, I noticed Anak looking directly at Mahmood Bas across the pit. As their eyes met, I felt once again the chilling force of their hatred.

Cockfighting rules dictated that the owner of the losing bird had the right to one rematch against the same winning bird. If that bird wins twice, the third fight is the winner's choice. This almost never happens. Because of wounds and exhaustion, most birds don't survive three fights in a row. But when it does, the central bet is tripled. If a bird wins three times in a row, the amount the challenger has to pay is huge, often running into tens of millions. If the bird loses the third fight, the owner forfeits only the original central bet.

Bas's team selected a pure white cock for the next fight. The bird was almost invisible against the white kaftans of the handlers who squatted centre pit. Gusti took his time pampering Ali, repairing ruffled feathers and blowing on its head. The spurs were tied and inspected, and the fight was on. Bas's team were going pound for pound. The white bird was huge. Without hesitation, it charged at Ali. The white bird rose up and planted its spur firmly into Ali's breast. I noticed that both Geno and Paolo had placed their bets. We had two million rupiah riding on this fight.

Ali lay beneath the white cock, pinned to the ground by its beak. The crowd's rumbling quickly faded into silence. Both birds were at a deadly standstill. Slowly Ali managed to get one foot out from underneath its body and used this as a lever to push itself up. Ali stood, pulling along the white bird, even as its beak was still firmly attached to Ali's neck. Again, I saw a flurry of spurs from the white bird hit Ali in the breast, but these blows had no effect. Anak's bird shrugged them off and, finally, the white bird could no longer hold its grip and let go. Wings extended and head craned forward, it turned and ran, with Ali in pursuit, straight into the hands of its handler.

Cockfighting rules also stated that if a bird retreated twice, the fight is forfeited. Once again, the two birds were pitted against each other. The white bird charged but stopped in front of Ali, who stood wings flared and hackles raised. Once more the white bird turned and retreated, with Ali in pursuit. The fight was over. Ali won by default. The crowd's spontaneous burst of applause stopped as Mahmood Bas came to the centre of the pit, holding the white bird under his arm, looking directly at Anak. His face contorted with rage. Bas held the cock out in front of him and wrung its neck with such force that the white bird's head separated from its body with an audible snap. Thin lines of blood shot out from the severed neck and sprayed over Bas's white kaftan. He stood gripping the head in one hand and the bird's bloodied, thrashing body in the other. He threw them on the ground in front of Anak and shouted 'Tiga! Tiga!' (Three! Three!). The crowd started to chant 'Tiga! Tiga!' but Anak seemed oblivious to it. He kept his eyes fixed on Bas, as if he expected the man in the bloody kaftan to lunge forward, drawn kris in hand. He shook his head slowly from side to side, motioned to Gusti to gather up Ali, and then, turning his back on his adversary, walked away.

I felt relieved it was over. We had achieved what we'd set out to do. Both Geno and Paolo collected a million apiece, and between us we'd won three million rupiah for Anak. Furthermore, he had humiliated and antagonised Mahmood Bas in front of a large audience. And now, it was time to leave.

We were almost at the temple gate, when I looked back and noticed that the atmosphere had changed. There were no cocks fighting in the pit anymore. Some of Bas's men were arguing with the referees while another group of his men, including Bas himself, were walking towards Anak's saronged enclosure. I saw no sign of Anak or his crew, and guessed they must be inside. I sensed something was wrong. Leaving Geno and Paolo, I dashed along under the cover of the temple wall and arrived at Anak's enclosure. Bas was about thirty metres away. I pushed through a sarong at the rear and entered.

It took only seconds to understand what I was seeing. Gusti held Ali under his arm and, with his free hand, pried the bird's beak open. Anak sat next to him on a mat, with the bloodstone placed in a glass of blood water, just as I'd seen it on the night of the full moon at his compound. Anak had a plastic syringe in one hand and was drawing the blood water into it. On seeing me, Gusti put a finger to his mouth. I now knew why the silver bird's spurs did not cut. Ali was under the protection of the bloodstone. Anak was forcing the blood water down Ali's throat with the syringe.

'Anak! Bas is outside.'

He tossed the syringe aside immediately, and retrieved the stone from the glass, pocketing it. Then, flashing a strange look at me, opened the enclosure to find Bas standing before him. A heated debate erupted. Bas, keeping his eyes fixed on Anak, reached into the pocket of his vest and pulled out a note. He handed it to his man, and in a halting voice, the man read aloud: Mahmood Bas would gift the Bali Haj to Anak if the fighting bird Ali were to win the third fight. Should Ali lose, however, Bas would be given beach access through the Sandika grounds for his Bali Haj guests and a signed contract to that effect for eternity.

When I grasped the enormity of this wager, I swallowed hard. Bas was going to stake his entire hotel on one cock fight. Gusti's face paled. Anak instantly agreed. 'Give me a minute to prepare.'

'No, you must come now. My men cannot hold the fights off any longer. The crowd is impatient. You must come this instant or it is no deal. Where is your bird?'

There was a brief pause.

'Gusti!' Anak called. 'Bring Ali.'

Gusti crawled out with the bird.

Before I left through the back entrance, I pocketed the plastic syringe and emptied the remaining blood water onto the earth, an offering to the local *bata* and *kula*. I made my way back along the temple wall towards Geno and Paolo. I couldn't help grinning at the audacity of what Anak had done, but I was feeling anxious over the fight about to take place. Did Anak's cock have enough of the blood water in it to survive? I realised that if Anak had refused the third fight he would have aroused suspicion. Perhaps Bas suspected foul play already? Had he also seen those spurs fail to penetrate Ali? Had he wagered such a large bet because he knew he would win? It came to me in that instant; I knew what I had to do.

I came out at the temple entrance and found the brothers. I was thankful to Gusti for explaining the finer details of the game. Cockfighting rules stated that the referee must call out the amount of the central bet. After conferring with both contestants, the referee announced, 'In a third fight against Anak's bird, Mahmood Bas bets the Bali Haj Hotel against the granting of right of access through the Sandika Hotel grounds.'

A shocked silence descended on the crowd. Geno looked at me in disbelief. Men stared with mouths open as Bas and his crew moved about making preparations.

'Never has such a bet been placed on a single fight,' an awestruck punter told me. Anak stood at the side of the cockpit, while Gusti squatted in front of him doing a most extraordinary thing: he was stuffing a split red chilli up Ali's anus. I recognised it as a bird's-eye chilli, the hottest chilli in Indonesia. This was not against the rules but a common practice, I had heard. The burning chilli would drive the bird wild with aggression.

On the other side of the cockpit, Bas's crew were preparing for the fight as well. The handlers' solemn expressions indicated that their entire livelihoods rode on this single fight. Referees paced nervously around the cockpit, making sure the correct amount of arena space was available. The crowd had fused into a single body, packed tightly around the ring, brought together by a collective awareness of what they were about to witness: a fight that would surely be talked about in the villages for years to come.

Bas had chosen a speckled black-and-white bird. The spurs were tied to the referee's satisfaction. The cocks were massaged, fluffed, pulled and prodded. Ali was agitated. The chilli was clearly working. Finally, the two birds faced each other in the centre of the cockpit. Gusti held Ali, and Bas himself held the speckled bird. Both men squatted. The cock's beaks were inches apart. The birds' hackles flared. Their owners waited for the sound of the gong. The referee allowed for the betting to start. It was clear that every man with a rupiah in his pocket was going to wager.

I pulled in Geno and Paolo close so we would not be overheard. 'We are going to place three bets. Two million a man – all on Bas's bird, the speckled cock,' I said evenly. Geno looked at me as if I had lost my mind. He mumbled something in Portuguese to Paolo, who opened his mouth as if he were about to say something then closed it. Chaos surrounded us. Men yelled at bookies, waving money, making unfathomable signals with fingers and hands to the deafening sounds of, '*Merah, Bintik*! (Speckled! Red! Red! Red!)

We had to place our bets quickly. 'I can't do that, man, you fucking crazy?' Geno cried.

'Trust me!' I grabbed him and yelled in his ear,

He looked at me for a brief moment then relented, nodding at Paolo. We each grabbed our wads of rupiah and headed separately into the fray calling, '*Bintik*! *Bintik*!' (The speckled bird!)

With our bets placed, we pushed our way to the sidelines. Both birds had been teased into a fighting fury. The handlers retreated five paces. At the sound of the gong, they released their charges. The birds went at each other in a flurry of feathers and flying spurs. My eyes could hardly follow the feverish action. The birds met in mid-air with their spurs beating together, seeking a lethal strike, but failing as they dropped back to the ground. Regaining their feet, they flew at each other, battling savagely with beak and wing. Dropping to the ground, both birds seemed unharmed, but stood panting with beaks opened, necks stretched menacingly, circling each other as they sought an opening. Then the speckled bird charged, knocking Ali off balance, drawing a gasp from the crowd. A louder cry arose as Ali, on his back, managed to sink a spur into the speckled bird's wing, holding the bird long enough to plant his other spur into its body. Blood haemorrhaged from the breast of Bas's bird. As the birds lay immobile on the ground, Ali could not be declared the winner, so the referee called for a separation. Gusti and Bas rushed in to retrieve their birds. My heart thumped. I had just bet all of Anak's winnings on his opponent's bird, who was about to lose. Geno glared at me, squeezing his fingers together in the Latin sign for 'asshole'. Bas's team worked frantically on their wounded, but still-standing, cock. They tried every trick to revive it. Some kind of paste was pressed into the wound. One handler blew into its beak, forcing air into its lungs, while another massaged its legs; a third plucked at its hackles.

On the other side of the cockpit, Ali appeared undamaged and ready to fight. The birds were released once more at the sound of the gong. The speckled bird faltered in its step, attempting to rally its fading strength. Ali sensed the weakened state of its foe and moved in, head extended, circling with wings spread, preparing to charge. Any last glimmer of hope for us vanished as we waited for the death strike. Again the speckled bird stumbled and almost fell as Ali careened in for the kill.

But then, as if drawing strength from some unknown source, Bas's speckled cock burst into the air with wings beating, as if pounding at drums, and as it came down, it sank a spur into Ali's heart. The big red bird died instantly, blood oozing from his beak.

Seconds passed before the crowd realised what had happened. Ali was dead. Then, as one, they erupted screaming, red-faced and wild, shouting, '*Bintik! Bintik!*'

The speckled bird stood, wandered a few wobbly paces towards its handler and collapsed on the floor of the pit, blood seeping from its wound. It died in the hands of Mahmood Bas as the referee declared it the winner.

Bas's team burst into a frenzy of back-slapping jubilation. They lifted their boss onto their shoulders and, while still holding the dead-speckled cock, paraded man and bird in a victory lap around the pit.

Anak conceded formally to the referee then tossed a grim nod to Bas. Geno, Paolo and I collected our winnings. Over three bets we'd collected a total of twelve million rupiah – about twenty thousand US dollars. We stuffed the money into a shoulder bag and moved away as quickly and quietly as possible. We slipped out through the crowd to the Jeep. Another series of cockfights was about to begin as we drove back down the rutted dirt track and out onto the main road. As soon as we were safely away, Geno and Paolo roared with laughter and slapped me on the back.

We spent a rough night in a pension somewhere between Singaraja and Kuta. On the following morning, we pulled up under our banyan tree in the hotel courtyard. Never had the Sandika felt so welcoming. An offshore breeze carried a soothing coolness, and the familiar scent of freshly lit temple incense greeted us. The morning sun reflected off our swimming pool and shone patterns of light on the palm fronds. The flame trees and bougainvillea blossoms were a palette of brilliant colour. Wayan and Ketut rushed out with a pitcher of iced tea. News of the cock fight had already reached them through the bush telegraph. It was the talk of the town, they told us.

I slipped away and, after a brief explanation, Ketut and I deposited the cockfight winnings in the hotel safe. Geno and Paolo were leaving the next day on a surfing trip to Java and returned to their room to prepare.

Anak's chariot soon swung into the courtyard with Gusti at the wheel. 'Adam!' he called, 'Come with me.'

We walked down the pathway and came out behind the hotel. Through the barbed-wire fence, we stared at the Bali Haj Hotel. Anak spoke quietly, as if to himself, 'I was thirty seconds away from reclaiming that.' Then he turned to me with a disturbed look on his face. 'For my father,' he said and stopped suddenly as if he didn't like where his mind was taking him. Once again my curiosity piqued. What had happened between him and Bas? The expression on Anak's face told me that now wasn't a good time to ask so instead I said, 'Anak, I bet your stake and winnings on Mahmood Bas's bird. There's twelve million rupiah sitting in our safe.'

He turned and looked at me with surprise. From one gambler to another, I saw on his face a twinge of grudging respect. He placed a hand on my shoulder, and then he turned and walked to a small shrine housed in the shade of a mango tree. Several deities were represented there on a covered pedestal, with a basket of recently offered fruit, lit incense and frangipani petals. He held the incense sticks between his palms and prayed. Then, placing them again in the holder, he turned to me with a serene expression. 'Thank you, Adam. With that money we are going to build the best lady-grass roof this island has ever seen.'

8

That evening, I went to the Blue Ocean terraces for a farewell drink with Geno and Paolo. A thin moon hung low in the sky amidst a smattering of stars. The sea hummed and rolled. Fire flies shone in the darkness beneath the shade trees that lined the beach, and a soft breeze danced in the oil lamp flames, casting shadows over the group of expats on the terraces. Geno gestured impatiently for the waiter. 'If I have to wait any longer for this motherfucker, I gonna get my drink myself.'

'Hey, man, relax. What's the hurry,' said Paolo.

Geno slid his green-eyed gaze to me and pointed a finger, 'You got some style, man,' he said. 'That was some fucking bet.'

We ordered Long Island iced teas as Geno talked about how cockfighting worked in Rio, 'Very different, man. People kill each other over those fucking birds.'

A young guy came up to our table. A gesture, a look, and without words Geno left with him. Paolo ordered me a drink.

'Thanks for keeping it away from the hotel.'

'Of course,' he said. 'You know, Geno do most of that stuff, and sure, we make a good money, but it's really not my thing. I'm the kind of … the watch-out guy, you know. I keep an eye on my brother, make sure he don't go too far,' Paolo explained. 'Surfing's our main thing. The other thing we do so we can stay here in style.' He flicked the rim of his cocktail glass.

'You guys got family in Brazil?'

'Yeah, we from the *favelo*, you know, what you say in English, the slums. Big family, man. Our mama, she still there. Sometimes I think we should send some of this money to her, but I know her, and she know Geno too much anyway. She wouldn't take it.'

'I heard he was an Olympic pole vaulter?'

'That's true, he was, man. Probably one of the best ever. You know, when we were kids, we hang around the beach. Our thing was collecting bottles and cashing them in. We always took the money home. Sometimes it was the only money our family have. Volleyball was a big thing on the Copacabana. We were very young, you know, just teenagers. Geno and I, we sitting there with our basket of bottles, watching the game. Then Geno ask one of the players if he can join in. This black guy who was the top player said, "You dreaming kid, what can a bottle boy do with a volleyball?" Geno, he stand up and he only come up to the black guy's shoulders, and he say "What can I do with a volleyball, I show you … I take that ball, and I jump over the volley net with it!" The black guy started laughing. "Hey, listen to this kid," he said, and the other players and beach people come around. Geno say, "If I do it, I want to be on the team," and the black guy say, "Kid, you got yourself a deal".' Paolo paused, savouring the memory of his brother's audacity. He took a long drink and leaned back in his chair. The waiter came over, and I ordered two more drinks.

Then, with a faraway look in his eyes, Paolo continued, 'Both teams stood aside. You could see the looks on their faces, a bit of fun between games … Watching the bottle kid make a fool of himself … They sure Geno never make it. That he hit the net and fall in the sand like a donkey. But Geno, he always had *conyos* bigger than his mouth. Anyway, he take the ball and then he take a net pole. He go way back, way, way back. Then he run like fuck, pole out in front, ball under arm, like a mad warrior. Then he plant the net pole in the sand, fly up higher than the net. While he in mid-air, he throw the volleyball above him and as he land on the sand, he roll and catch it. It was an incredible jump, like an acrobat, and everyone burst out clapping. Players came over and gave him money, but the black guy say, "You not on the team, kid. That wasn't a jump, it was a vault". Geno was pissed, and I have to pull him away from the black guy before he got a slap on his head. But after that, every time we go to beach they ask Geno to do his trick. He got better and better. He was doing backflips, juggling ball in mid-air, all kinds of crazy stuff! And of course, I pass the hat after he finish. We make more money off this than bottles.'

He leaned back and stirred his drink with a straw. The last embers of the sunset faded between a darkening sea and sky. Fishing boats lights flickered faintly in the distance.

'Hey, I boring you, no? With my kid story,' said Paolo breaking the silence.

'Not at all.'

'Anyway, I cut it short,' Paolo said. 'One day a Swiss guy saw Geno do his thing. This guy was sports promoter back there. He find some sponsorship money from corporate companies and get Geno into professional sports academy in Switzerland. My brother had only one condition: that I got to go with him too. Man, it was fucking cold up in those mountains, but after a couple of seasons, Geno was winning every pole vault event in Europe. By nineteen he become a world champion.' Paolo's tone became measured. 'Adam, you know what that meant? A bottle boy from the *favelos* becoming a world-champion sportsman. Every time he was in an event, they run it on Brazilian national television. The whole *favelo* stop to watch. That's my brother's story, man. He was a hero. Every street kid look up to him, and think "if he can do that maybe I can too".' Paolo exhaled. I felt his pride mixed with regret.

'And he got accused of doping?'

'Nah, man. Sure he fail the test. Look, I tell you, at that time we didn't even know what steroids were. Nah, Geno was innocent, but his trainer, the guy I told you about, always giving him pills and shots, said they vitamins to stop dehydration, something like that. Just before the Olympics, man.' Paolo snapped his fingers. 'And it was all gone, man, all gone.'

The terraces were nearly empty. We finished our drinks. Geno returned and tossed his head to Paolo, 'We gotta go.'

'Hey, Geno,' I said, 'before you go, I have to ask you something. I saw a woman walking along the beach with a couple of orangutans. Know who she is?'

'All white?'

'Yeah.'

'That one's as crazy as a mother fucker. What you want with her, man?'

'Nothing, just curious.'

'Janna, man, she called Janna. She a drunk, talk to nobody, and she been here longer than me. She a freak show,' Geno made circular movements with his forefingers around his ears. 'Okay, you curious? She over there at Omar's, the end of the strip. Turn right, and she in there at the back. You curious, you go look. Paolo, man, let's go.'

I followed his directions and found Omar's, a bar well off the main strip with few customers. I ordered a drink and turned to find myself looking directly at Janna. She sat at a table near the entrance with her orangutans chained on either side. They squatted on their haunches, their paws before them, remarkably passive. The only movement was their eyes, like smouldering red flames in the light of oil lamps, continually moving and looking for small prey, like insects or moths, then regarding them unworthy of further attention. From their muscular bodies, long black manes and fully developed cheek flaps, I guessed that they were mature male apes. From what I'd seen of orangutans, they always had comical facial expressions, a sort of Homer Simpson quality. Not so Janna's beasts; they had sharp, tapered snouts with smaller mouths, sloping foreheads and deep-set eyes. They were not the normal rusty brown colour. Their coats were as black as a panther's. I put their weight at over a hundred kilos each. As if it had read my thoughts, one ape turned to look at me. Its eyes centred on mine for a second before flicking away.

On the table stood a half-empty bottle of arrack and a bowl of fruit. Janna poured herself a glass. She peeled two rambutans and handed one to each ape. As she raised her forehead, I saw her heavy white make-up, her white necklaces and bracelets and her white-gloved hands. I felt her perplexing allure, her luminous sensuality. She made me think of a rare orchid in need of sustenance. I wanted to talk to her. I wanted to be near her. I couldn't understand why I felt so fascinated with her. Her face had come to me at odd moments since the first time I'd seen her. Her beauty was undeniable, but there was something more. I left the bar with Geno's words on my mind: 'She talk to no one.'

PART TWO

1

Elisabeth and I drove our old Toyota Corolla into the carpark outside the office of my father's lawyer. Grace had fallen asleep in her car seat. We had come directly from the funeral service for the reading of the will. I wound down the window, and the cool air woke Grace. Elisabeth brought her to her breast. She then put her free hand over mine.

'You okay?' she whispered.

'We never talked. I never knew him, not really,' I mumbled. She placed Grace on my lap. I held my daughter raised over my shoulder and rubbed her back. As I held her, and she cooed and smiled, the overpowering love I felt for her momentarily obliterated my grief.

'Hey, Adam,' Elisabeth said, raising a palm to my cheek. 'He wasn't an easy man to know.'

We followed a secretary into the lawyer's office. Simon Taylor had been at the funeral so we dispensed quickly with the condolences. He seated us together on a couch so Elisabeth could continue feeding.

'As I'm sure you are aware,' he began, 'you are the only beneficiary Salvador Milano has, therefore the reading of his will is a simple matter. However, before we proceed, I must tell you that your father has given me a letter, quite recently actually. He asked me to give it to you in the event …' He looked over the rim of his glasses towards me with practiced concern, 'I could read it if you would prefer?'

I agreed. Elisabeth had just passed me Grace, and her head nestled on my neck, her breath warm on my skin. Simon read the words in an emotionless monotone, and as he read I could hear echoes of my father's gravelly tones.

Adam, if you are reading this, then the doctors were right. They'd told me to stop working, drinking, smoking and just about everything else. I ignored their advice: what is a man supposed to do, stop living? I had a business to run. Before you read my will, I want to say a few words. I know how hard it was for you to grow up without a mother. There were so many things that I could change if I could. I saw the sadness in you. But then Elisabeth and bambino came into our lives, and for the first time I see you happy, and that made me a happy man too. I know you don't want to be in that kitchen, but, Adam, I ask you to give it a go. Things might change. You've got what it takes. It is in your blood. I ask you to consider this.

And one more thing, I loved you as best as I could, and I'm proud of you, son.

Your father, Salvador Milano.

Grace began to cry – a cry that turned into a bellowing, blue-faced howl. We walked her up and down the hallway but to no avail. Simon looked on sympathetically while his secretary came in, making funny faces and shaking a rattle, which only made Grace scream even louder. We left the office, went downstairs and walked her around in the carpark until she had cried herself into an exhausted sleep. We then returned to the office for the reading of the will. It was pretty much as I had expected: we inherited the business, but there was more.

'Read that last bit again, Simon. I'm sure I heard it wrong.'

'Six hundred thousand,' he stated flatly. 'Non-taxable and to be held in this trust account and paid out to you in full on your twenty-first birthday, on the precise condition that at that time, you still own and run Milano's restaurant.'

'How is that possible? I thought we were just getting by.'

'Adam, your father was a very frugal man. I'm not at liberty to discuss his affairs until after probate, but I can say this: he started your trust fund over ten years ago and saved every cent of this amount for its intended purpose.'

'What happens if I don't want to do this? If I sell the restaurant, for instance.'

'Of course you are free to do that, but I must inform you that under the terms of the will, if this should happen, the trust fund, the entire six hundred thousand, will be donated to the Salvation Army.' Simon again looked over the top of his glasses. 'You know how fond your father was of the Salvation Army's brass band.'

* * *

As we drove back to the restaurant to get ready for the evening shift, I could feel Elisabeth's eyes on me. 'Well,' she asked, unable to hide her excitement.

'We're selling,' I said quietly as I turned the car onto the waterfront road. An ocean of dazzling blue lay before us. On the breakwater, waves crashed against barnacle-encrusted rocks, and below us, the mud flats of Orakei Bay reached out to meet the oncoming waves. I glanced at Elisabeth. Her eyes were on the road ahead.

The service at Milano's that night was hectic. Condolences from customers flooded in from the floor; the staff worked extra hard. I was now their new boss, and I felt the subtle shift in their attitude. As I stood before the stove, juggling the skillets, flicking herbs and spices, flaming wine with metal pans scraping and hissing, my father's words came to me: *'Proud of you, son … I saw you happy … in your blood.'* Was it true? Could I really do this?

That night, in our tiny room above the grocery store, Elisabeth and I made love. She then moved to the side of the bed and wrapped a sheet around her waist. Her breasts were swollen with milk, her skin glowing in the light of a single bulb.

'We are eighteen years old, Adam,' she said. 'We own a good business, and if we stick it out, we will be rich by the time we're twenty-one. We are *so* lucky. Do you know what this means?' I didn't answer. My father had planned it well; there was no way out. Elisabeth bent down and kissed my forehead.

'I knew you'd understand,' she said as she brought Grace to her breast.

* * *

Elisabeth took over the front of house while I ran the kitchen. We worked seventy-hour weeks and hardly saw each other outside of work. When we arrived home in the early hours, we were too exhausted to make love. Milano's was unrelenting; the more successful we made it, the more it demanded of us. In a short time we had changed the restaurant from a family business to a substantial enterprise with a large roster of employees. We extended the dining room to double the amount of tables. We catered to weddings and functions.

Elisabeth thrived in her role. Her transformation from waitress to maître'd was quick and effective, and she soon evolved into an excellent hostess and a good businesswoman. Milano's received positive reviews in the local press. Our restaurant became noted for its authentic Italian cuisine. We were booked out for months in advance, and we made more money than we could spend.

Three years passed by in a whirl of frantic expansion and activity. In the meantime, Grace was growing into a beautiful young child, wise beyond her years. When the inheritance money came in we bought a house. A Remuera villa with a sea view. Elisabeth began extensive renovations. The interior was gutted and given a modern minimalist make-over, with stainless steel, black-leather couches and stark lines. I thought it made the house cold and unwelcoming, but said nothing to her.

Elisabeth suggested that because our working hours often clashed, we should have separate rooms. I reluctantly agreed. If I could point out a turning point in our relationship, if I could remember when it was that we began to drift apart, it was then.

2.

When Anak asked me to become the manager of the Sandika, I felt uneasy with the proposition. The binding contract with its dire consequences that had been my father's will came back to me. Of course I needed money and the wage Anak offered, which included a percentage of any future profits; it would allow me to send something to Tula. I'd often looked at the Sandika and seen its potential for growth. I walked about the beach, thinking over it, but then swung around, my heels digging into the sand as I headed back to the Sandika. I'd decided to take up the offer.

With the cockfight money in hand, the building of our lady-grass roof began. Of course we had to remove the barbed-wire fence and build a new pathway of coral sand leading up to Bas's hotel.

The first of the Bali Haj guests wandered in cautiously, as if entering a strange new land; they peered through our tropical wilderness to discover hidden shrines and temples, fruit bats hanging in dark recesses and exotic flowers and fruits dangling from vines.

The tourists were quick to discover our coffee shop with its view of Kuta reef. They came for breakfast, returned for lunch and at sunset wandered down the pathway to drink our cocktails. Our traditional Balinese food and flavours appealed to them, and they stayed on. We hired a gamelan orchestra. Musicians played nightly together with *barong* and *kecak* dancers. We attracted more guests from the Bali Haj Hotel and added tables and chairs to cope with their numbers. Wayan hired extra kitchen staff, and I ordered a stock of ingredients for our cocktails.

Anak's loss at the cockfight became the Sandika's gain. I

wondered how Bas felt about that. As the new manager, my mind went into overdrive thinking of the financial possibilities of a joint venture between the two hotels. Then Mahmood's cold black eyes came to my mind, followed by Anak's chilling, hateful gaze.

The Sandika owned an outrigger canoe with an outboard motor. About twenty-feet long, the boat was painted red and blue, and adapted from the traditional Balinese fishing canoes – Adze marks were visible through the paint on the hull, which had been carved out of a solid piece of teak. The outrigger gave it stability and such a shallow draft that the fishermen could go out fishing or diving, and then make it back into the lagoon in front of the hotel by surfing over the reef.

I often watched our boat speed down the glassy face of a large wave, with Jimmy the Fish at its helm. Sometimes we lent our boat to him in return for a portion of his catch. He handled it with the skill and expertise borne of a lifetime spent diving and fishing.

Jimmy the Fish was Balinese, but with ginger hair and the most extraordinary yellow eyes. I did a double take the first time I saw him: his eyes had dazzling specks of gold flecked in a luminous base of yellow, with just a tinge of bright red. Jimmy knew his eyes had an unsettling effect on people, and so he wore shades most of the time. On account of his unusual colouring and his association with the sea, he was excluded from his *banjar* and even his own family. And so, he lived the life of an exile, in a hut behind the sand dunes at the far end of the beach. He'd grown up an outcast, a fishing hermit. Beauty is revered in Bali: hair is oiled black, eyebrows darkened and plucked, skin massaged with coconut cream and kept out of the sun. To the Balinese, the best thing you could be is *alus*, refined. Ginger hair and yellow eyes were not *alus*. Far from it, they were colours associated with the underworld.

As Anak had told me when I first arrived, the Balinese regarded the sea with a sense of dread. They believed demons dwelled beneath the waters to seek chaos and destruction. Hence fishermen are treated with suspicion. And so Jimmy the Fish had two demons to battle: his people's aesthetics and their superstitions.

There were a couple of stories explaining Jimmy's colouring. His mother, a beautiful, young high-born Balinese, had a difficult first pregnancy. So painful was her condition that she drove her husband and family to despair. When she had been eight months pregnant, her pain had become unbearable, and she waded out into the lagoon, hoping the cool sea would give her relief. It didn't. With one huge contraction, the baby was born. The husband heard her agonised screams and rushed into the sea. He saved his unconscious wife from drowning, but the baby boy required no help. The umbilical cord kept him afloat, and he was found drifting belly up in the calm waters, gurgling contentedly.

As was customary, when the baby was twelve days old, the family contacted a spirit medium to determine which ancestor had been reincarnated in the form of the new-born. The medium went into a trance and became distressed. It took him several moments to compose himself in order to reveal the mystery: reincarnation had been interfered with by a sea demon, in the form of a yellow fish known to inhabit babies and devour their entrails. The medium announced that the baby's birth was not premature: the demon had hauled the baby out of his mother's womb while she was in the lagoon. The sudden appearance of the husband had caused it to flee, leaving the reincarnation incomplete and the new-born stained with the demon's colours, giving him the yellow eyes and ginger hair. The medium suggested that the family return to the lagoon with the baby and a *balian*, a high priest who could communicate with demons.

'Let the demon return to the child and retrieve his colours,' said the medium. 'Only then can this child live a normal life.'

But the baby's mother didn't accept the medium's findings and refused to follow his instructions. Forty-two days after the birth, the baby's naming ceremony fell due. But it was boycotted by the *banjar* priest, the medium and the family's community, and thereby was considered invalid. At two hundred and ten days, Balinese children have their *odalan*: in this ritual, the child's head is shaved and he is officially welcomed into the community. This ceremony is of paramount importance in a child's life, but it was denied to the boy on account of the priest's unwillingness to officiate it.

As the child grew, his hair and eye colouring became more pronounced, brighter. Other children pointed and threw stones at him, taunting him with calls of '*anak leyak, anak leyak!*' (demon child!). Parents shielded infants as he walked past. At an early age, the boy came to realise he would never have the things other children were given easily: love, friends and family. He would always be considered a freak, a demon, an ugly and unwanted thing.

The boy found grudging acceptance amongst the fishermen of Kuta Beach. They were also outcasts – the Balinese notion of the sea haunted their existence, like it did the boy's. They took pity on the yellow-eyed child and allowed him to live amidst them.

The boy quickly became an expert diver and fisherman. He developed an uncanny sense of the nature and habits of fish and of the movement of tides. The youngster could effortlessly find the hiding places of the best crayfish and could predict which way a tuna would turn in a chase. The fishermen realised his gift and consulted him for advice. Some said he could read the minds of fish; others said this was because he was part-fish. The boy was a seven-year-old then.

Years later, surfers noticed a fin, a snorkel and a head of ginger hair diving in the most dangerous areas of the Kuta reef. One curious board-rider paddled over to ask the boy his name.

'Idi,' the diver replied. The board rider thought he said, 'Jimmy.' And so the yellow-eyed boy became Jimmy the Fish.

The other account for Jimmy's colouring was much shorter:

a ginger-haired American surfer had boarded with Jimmy's family some eight months before his birth.

* * *

Whatever myth created Jimmy, I wasn't bothered about it. I was particularly fond of him. I was touched by how he endured his solitary existence. His hut stood not far from the Sandika, and he often passed by on his way to the reef and back, carrying a spear gun and gunnysack. After a cursory chat about the weather, we'd sit together on the sea wall in silence. Our relationship didn't require many words. He was a young man, his tanned body honed and sculpted from years of diving. His ginger hair was salt-stained, sun bleached and tied back in a ponytail. He wore a pair of Ray-Ban sunnies with a faded-green lucre back strap. The corner of Jimmy's lip was always turned up and seemed faintly mocking, as if he understood something other people didn't.

'Jimmy, could you take me out over the reef?' I once asked as we took our seat on the sea wall.

'Sure, Adam, no problem. Tomorrow morning I go fishing, I come get you early, okay.' He reached down into his gunnysack and handed me a parrot fish he'd speared that morning. 'For your lunch,' and he gathered up his things and left.

* * *

There was a knock on my door just before sunrise. Jimmy the Fish stood there shuffling impatiently while I pulled on my shorts and T-shirt.

'Big tide this morning, Adam, big tides, many fish, hurry.'

Within minutes we were in the outrigger, motoring across calm lagoon waters, with the outboard pushing us at a steady five knots. In the light of a breaking dawn, the reef looked formidable. The waves were glassy and huge. A couple of early morning board-riders were surfing. I watched them ducking in and out of the pipeline and weaving over white crests. On the shore side, the first rays of sunlight highlighted the peak of Mt. Agung. Before us, spumes of spray peeled back from the tips of breaking waves. Gannet-like birds circled and cawed, diving into the waves to catch the swimming herring.

We rolled over a couple of walls of churning foam, which felt like they'd topple the boat, and then we were breached against a giant wave. Jimmy must have seen the fear in my face because he raised a hand in reassurance. He reached down and pulled the motor's throttle on full, swung the helm so we were now face-to-face with the wave and pointing into it. We rode up the glass wall. The screaming outboard motor pushed us upwards, even though, caught in the wave's momentum, we were moving backwards at a faster rate. The outrigger's bow hovered directly above me. I wedged my legs against the hull and tightened my grip. In seconds, we had reached the crest of the wave; Jimmy made a deft manoeuvre by swinging the helm to port, putting us out of the wave's grip and behind the breaking peak just before it broke. We motored towards the horizon until we lay well beyond the forming waves.

I relaxed my grip on the rails, released my legs from their vice-like clutch and turned to Jimmy with a big smile. He pushed his sunglasses up onto his forehead and said, 'Not so bad, eh?'

The next few hours I spent alone on the boat while Jimmy dived. I waited, listening to the cawing of seabirds and lapping of small waves against the hull. He occasionally surfaced with a trevally or a small tuna or a Spanish mackerel; he speared many fish and filled his gunnysack. The tide soon began to turn. I felt the strength of the rip beneath the boat. Jimmy surfaced once more, threw his spear gun and gunnysack aboard, and then climbed in.

'You no worry yourself. Go back, easy, okay?' said Jimmy as he put on his Ray-Bans. He fired up the boat and headed back over the forming waves. As we came precariously close to the reef break, Jimmy swung the outrigger to face a wave. We rose high. I looked down from a moving mountain of water. The crest of the wave took us with it. As it began to break, peeling white water to starboard, Jimmy swung the steering oar again, bringing the boat vertical to the wave, then he cut the motor. The wave's thrust lifted our stern and held us in its momentum. We gathered speed and surfed. We moved faster, careening lengthways along a sheer wall of water. On the starboard side, a wing of spray shot away from our outrigger like the fin of a giant flying fish, and to port, rolling water climbed to a towering azure wall beside us, so close that I could reach out and touch it. Beneath us, through thin crystal water, black dagger-like coral rocks sped by. The wave's crest, now a ton of white water, loomed above. It broke with a pounding roar. Erupting sea foam almost swallowed the boat. Our bow rose, and the stern lifted, and we raced headlong on the cascading water. The wave's final thrust carried our boat into the calm waters of the lagoon.

I'd done it. I'd finally nailed my fear of the reef. As I shook Jimmy's hand he looked at me strangely, not quite sure what I was doing.

We fished together often after that. Jimmy taught me to dive. But more importantly, he showed me the helming techniques he used to cross the reef. Within a short time I could manage the boat without his help.

3

'Duncan's alive!' Grace's voice jumped out of the phone.

'How so?' I stammered.

'He washed up in the *Sea Rover*'s life raft on the northern tip of Australia, and a group of locals brought him to Port Douglas. Flew into Auckland yesterday. It's in all the newspapers.'

'Grace, sweetheart, this is great news.' A surge of warm relief washed through me, but then I froze as she continued.

'Dad, don't freak out, okay? Because it gets bad. He's saying that you were never on the *Sea Rover* during that storm that wrecked him, says that you left the boat somewhere off the coast of Indonesia – they didn't, like, mention Bali, but the newspaper says that they will try and find you.'

I felt like a hand had reached into my stomach and was squeezing my intestines. I could say nothing. Grace's matter-of-fact voice changed to pleading. 'Dad, can you think about coming home? I'm over this. It's getting really complicated, and I have to tell so many lies. Come home, Dad, please.'

The telephone receiver felt like a lead weight. Sweat dripped from my forehead. I could hear Grace's breathing as she waited for an answer. Of course I wanted to go home to see my daughter and clear my name. But I would first be charged and jailed in Indonesia then deported. Once home, my creditors would be at me like a pack of hungry dogs, not to mention Tula. And what could I do there anyway? How would I repay my debts?

'Dad are you there?' she asked.

'Yeah.'

'Oh, and by the way, Mum is so pissed off. She said that it's just like you. She says that you're probably clinging to some rock somewhere, just like you clung to the restaurant that nearly killed us all. What are you going to do?'

'Grace, I want to stay here. I'm managing the Sandika Hotel, and I know I can make something of it.'

'But that's what you used to say when Milano's was going broke ...'

'I know but this time it's different. I have a chance here. There are some real possibilities, and I want to try. I need to do this.'

'What if they find you?'

'I'll take my chances,'

There was a long silence, followed by a resigned, 'Okay'.

I'd started the phone conversation as a dead man, *presumed drowned*, but had ended it as an illegal immigrant, a fugitive even. The good news was that Duncan had survived and, regardless of my situation, that knowledge brought relief.

I was heading across the carpark when Eddi pulled up beside me. He had a copy of *The New Zealand Herald* rolled up in his hand. He handed it to me. 'Thought you might like to read about yourself.' I waited. 'Look, Adam, as far as I'm concerned you're Michael Brown. As it says in that passport Geno got you.'

'What?'

'He asked me to help him get the work visa. The way I see it, mate, whatever happened back in New Zealand is not my business.'

'Who else knows?'

'Nobody, and we'll keep it that way. If something happens, and if they start looking for you here, it'll come through me, and I'll get to you first.'

As Eddi and I walked on the beach, I told him what had happened. 'Incredible, mate! Stay here, make the Sandika into something. It needs someone like you, and if I were in your shoes, I'd think about growing a beard.'

Two weeks later, with a thick stubble hiding my face, and with my shoulder-length hair and sun-bleached skin, I looked nothing like myself in the newspaper photograph.

* * *

After the rafters and framework were completed, the tedious work on our roof began. Lady-grass was wrapped around the bamboo battens before being stitched in place. Wood carvers chipped away at the teak rafters. Mythological figures and stories appeared along each beam. Another group of workmen built bamboo-scaffolding towers at either end of the hotel block. These were to stabilise and guide the roof when it was ready to be hoisted into position.

I awoke to the laughter and chatter of the workers' women and children. From my balcony, I looked down at the roof, now covered with its first layer of lady-grass. Once again, it looked like a massive oblong mushroom, like our previous roof, and was as large as the hotel. It covered the entire carpark.

The roof builders' insatiable appetites multiplied our need for food supplies, so I contracted Jimmy to use our boat daily and supply the Sandika with his complete catch. Wayan negotiated a price for the fish, and each morning Jimmy laid out his catch behind the coffee-shop kitchen for Wayan's inspection. He brought us mangrove snapper, parrot fish, striped eel, blue bream, rock crayfish, sole and, the tourists' favourite, the prized yellow-fin tuna. Some said Jimmy had an affinity with this species on account of its colour. Envious fisherman said he didn't have to hunt the yellow fin, that they came to him on their own accord and he simply made his choice.

Regardless of rumours, thanks to Jimmy our restaurant served the freshest fish on the beach. Our sole meunière and char-grilled crayfish became a hit with the Japanese tourists coming through from the Bali Haj Hotel.

* * *

I was in the coffee shop with pad and pencil, working on a business plan, when an idea stared me in the face. I'd noticed that the Japanese men coming through from the Bali Haj had an obsession with fishing. Decked out in expensive fishing gear, they came to the coffee shop in the morning as if they were prepared for a major fishing tournament. They wore green waders, jackets with an extravagant number of tiny pockets, each containing a fishing gadget; cloth hats complete with flies and lures attached; and carried two or three expensive fishing rods. They waded out into the lagoon and, to the amazement of the locals, seemed content catching tiny herrings and sprats.

One morning, after watching these fishermen's frantic casting and futile endeavours at the lagoon, I casually suggested to Jimmy that he might want to take them out over the reef to go after bigger fish.

'Big problem, Adam. Japanese no dive. Fish around here no eat lure.'

'Take them out anyway. They can't do any worse than what they're doing here.'

I put Jimmy in charge of our boat, and he took the Japanese fishermen out to the ocean daily. Surfing back over the reef became a talking point. Our boat was booked out every day. The Japanese were glad to pay a good price for their fishing obsession, and the Sandika fishing tours became our first steady money-earner outside of the hotel and coffee shop.

*　*　*

It bothered me that our fishing boats often came home without fish. Sometimes they picked up a few small trevally, only slightly larger than the fish in the lagoon. But surely the point of the tours was to catch decent-sized fish.

'You making good money these days?' I asked. Jimmy had just sat down at my table, and removed his shades. His eyes glowed like incandescent amber in the light of an oil lamp.

'You know it, Adam. You pay me.'

'Yeah, you do a great job.' Jimmy shrugged. 'Is there any way we can catch more fish with the tourists? What's the problem? Do we have to go out into deeper waters or is it the type of bait they're using? The tours are booked out already, but imagine if we had good catches. We could put more boats on. There's some serious money to be made in this business, Jimmy!'

'I know it, Adam. I know it. But Japs, only have short time to fish, too hot in day time, water too warm, fish no eat, look,' Jimmy pointed to the faint glimmer of lights on a moonlit horizon. 'They fishermen, and they catch good fish. But Japs no go night-time. They too scared, Adam. I ask them already.' He slipped his Ray-Bans back on and looked out at the sea. A distinct crescent moon hung in a smattering of stars, and a rising tide sent sweeping white foam splashing on to the sea wall before us.

'Adam,' said Jimmy in a whisper, 'I got an idea.'

Over the next thirty minutes, with animated hand movements, Jimmy the Fish laid out his plan. He would go out with our boat at night and catch a number of good-sized yellow fin tuna, which he would keep alive in a large woven basket strung between the outriggers. He'd drop the enclosed basket, weighted with stones, on the deep side of the reef and return to give me the location using a set of land bearings. The next morning, Ketut and I would take the Japanese out fishing in our boat. Before our departure, Jimmy would slip away over the reef with a scuba diver's oxygen bottle, allowing him to stay submerged and wait for our arrival. As the two boats came past the pre-arranged location with lures out, Jimmy, with a tuna fish in one hand and a steel boat hook in the other, would catch the lure and give the Japanese fisherman the simulation of a tuna strike. He would then attach the fish to the lure, and the fisherman could reel away to his heart's content.

Jimmy poured himself a shot of arrack, swallowed it and looked out to sea. The wind had dropped and the moon shone a silver pathway towards the horizon. We both watched the fishermen's lights.

'Jimmy, my friend, that's a wild plan.'

'Make them Japs very happy. Big fish, big feed, big photo, big money for us,' he said as he smacked his lips in contentment.

4

The Sandika was making money with the fishing tours and the coffee shop, but whatever we earned was getting used to build the roof. Anak had gone over budget. He'd spent all of his cockfight winnings on it and needed more money daily. The lady-grass roof had become his obsession. I knew it had something to do with Mahmood Bas; Anak had something to prove to his opponent. I was acutely aware that our current earnings came from the Bali Haj guests. If Bas closed the pathway, he could cut off our income, and it wouldn't surprise me if he did.

The following day I called over Jimmy the Fish. 'I'd like to give your plan a try.'

'Sure Adam, start tomorrow?'

'Okay.'

'I go tonight, and I catch fish.'

The next morning, I told the six or so Japanese tourists, who were about to board our boat for the day's fishing tour, that we were taking two boats. I'd skipper one myself, and Ketut would take the other. Jimmy and I had decided not to tell Ketut about our plan.

Earlier that morning Jimmy had given me instructions about where we should make our crossing. He also told me that the night's catch looked good and he had four large tuna ready in the basket.

Kuta's dependable offshore wind caused waves to break in an even formation as we powered the outboard motors and shot over the reef between waves. From my position in the bow, I lined up our bearings and gave Ketut hand directions. Trolling rods went out when we found deep water.

Within minutes a fish had struck. One of the rods bent double, and its ratchet screamed as a Japanese fisherman, red-faced with trembling legs, fought for control. I told Ketut to cut the motor and ordered all the other rods to be wound in to avoid tangles. The fisherman's line paid out at a fast rate, with the reel making a high-pitched whistle. The fisherman braced himself for the fight. His nylon line cut through water, giving off a fine spray. A sudden series of sharp tugs almost ripped his rod from his grip. Then it stopped. Movement ceased. The rod bent double again and the ratchet sounded. Beads of sweat erupted on the fisherman's forehead. His rod rose and fell, slowly gaining line. Ten minutes later, a firmly hooked yellow-fin tuna lay beside our hull. We hauled it aboard with a gaff hook and net. It was a large and elegant fish, with yellow fins, large black eyes and a horizontal green-blue striped midriff crossed with shimmering silver lines. Cameras snapped and flashed as the tuna shivered helplessly in the grip of the fisherman. I heard a shout from Ketut's boat and the sound of the motor being cut. They had a strike.

'Good luck!' I called, cupping hands to mouth, knowing well that luck had nothing to do with it. We motored closer to watch the fight. The same scenario played out aboard Ketut's vessel. The opulent colours of another gaffed tuna shone as Ketut's fishermen held up their fish for our inspection. The jubilant atmosphere among the fishermen made me almost forget about Jimmy hiding underwater with hook and fish, waiting for the next lure.

* * *

That evening Wayan and her kitchen staff prepared a tuna feast for us. The fishermen invited our entire contingent of roof builders and the Bali Haj regulars. Under a mango-streaked sunset, with a receding tide leaving swirls of silver on sand, our dinner guests sat at tables on the sea wall. One after the other, plates laden with sashimi tuna, fish marinated in coconut cream and stuffed with crab meat and lime butter, and grilled tuna-steaks with mango-chilli sauce were brought out of Wayan's kitchen, along with platters of steamed saffron rice and tropical fruits. A gamelan player's bell chimes played to laughter and different languages. The feasting and drinking lasted until the early hours of the morning.

I didn't see Jimmy the Fish all evening and wanted to speak to him about the following day's tour. I had an uneasy feeling about his absence. I sent Ketut down to his hut, and he came back with the message, 'He fishing, Adam.'

Anak came to the coffee shop for a game of chess.

'I hear that Bas is seething about the fishing tours. I saw him today: binoculars up on the water tower, watching the boats leave. I looked at today's take and realised we make more money from these boat trips than we do off the hotel. Well done, Adam.' Anak's delight about antagonising Bas showed in his quick movements and sly grins. 'I hear that Bas has bought his own boats and will offer the same deal as us. Only he has inflatable rubber dive boats with powerful outboards. He will use a side ramp by the airport runway to avoid the reef. He has those kinds of connections ... Be careful out there, Adam. Watch out for him.'

*　*　*

The next morning I padded down to the coffee shop. As I came round the corner, I was set upon by a group of Japanese fishermen, all talking at once and bent on going to sea. Word of yesterday's success had spread. Three times the number of people we usually had space for on our boats wanted to go fishing.

Ketut pulled me aside. 'I got it, Adam. I bring three more boats from local boys. We have enough,' he whispered. 'Here, Jimmy leave you this,' he handed me a rolled paper note tied with a single strand of lady-grass.

I walked out to the sea wall and untied the knot. It was a

perfectly drawn miniature sea chart giving exact coordinates and bearings, with a large X to mark the spot where Jimmy would be waiting. I recognised the place. It was a black protruding rock known to surfers as the Beacon, about half a mile offshore beyond a part of the reef called Airport Left. I crushed the paper map into a ball and stuffed it into my pocket. What had I gotten myself into? I hoped Jimmy had plenty of fish in his basket.

We set off with the Japanese tourists. No sooner had our fifth boat crossed the reef when I saw the bow-wake of two black Zodiacs hurtling towards us at about thirty knots. Both boatmen were wearing skull caps. As they came into view, I recognised Mahmood Bas's right-hand man and cock handler. They had a couple of Japanese fishermen in each vessel, rods held high. The black boats remained twenty metres behind us and watched our every move. When our fleet cruised past the Beacon, a fish struck. It was a diamond trevally with trailer fins streaming, caught by Boat No. 2. A blue-striped eel caused havoc by tangling all lines around a couple of boats. Then a brown-spotted shark came thrashing and snapping aboard our boat. How had Jimmy managed that? On it went, with a couple of yellow fin, followed by a dogtooth tuna. A pair of good-sized Spanish mackerel went to Ketut's boat. Jimmy the Fish was doing us proud.

The men aboard the Zodiacs had their lines out and were trawling directly behind us. They pointed and shook their heads in disbelief and frustration as they moved in closer, watching us land fish after fish. To give Jimmy a break, I ordered the fleet to the south end of the Beacon. The Zodiacs wound in their lines empty-handed. Our fishermen boasted by holding their fish up, cameras clicking, hurling guttural Japanese expletives between the two boats. Before they left, the Zodiacs circled us at speed, cutting dangerously in front of our bow, their wake rocking our outriggers and soaking us with sea spray, but it didn't dampen out fishermen's spirits. They responded with the one-fingered salute.

We tied the boats together and hoisted a sun shelter. As I

sucked on a piece of watermelon and looked around at the faces of satisfied fishing customers, I realised that Anak was right. We had to watch out for Bas.

*   *   *

Sunday's call from Grace came as a relief. She'd heard nothing more about the search for Adam Milano. She told me that she and Steven had found a flat and moved in together.

'That's good, sweetheart. I'm glad you're with someone who cares about you. I'm looking forward to meeting him. Is your mum getting used to the idea?'

'She's still pissed off, but now that we don't live at her house I get along better with her. I'm working fulltime now for Pierre at the French Café.'

'Okay, is he paying you well?'

'Yep.'

I'd known Pierre from the day he'd arrived from France. He worked front of house at Milano's, and we became friends. Grace was a good manager but I suspected he was looking after her as a favour to me. I quietly thanked him for taking a load off my mind.

*   *   *

Jimmy the Fish never tired or complained about his heavy workload, and of course I saw to it that he was paid well. On account of the tours, and because the roof was nearly finished, the Sandika's accounts were looking healthy. Once the hotel was back in business, I intended to use that money to instigate my marketing plan, a strategy I'd developed to increase our turnover. Once I'd achieved that, I would ask Anak for a share of the business. I felt positive he'd agree. Once, during a chess game, he'd almost suggested as much.

Late one night, I pulled a chair onto the back balcony and

gazed out over the grounds of the Bali Haj. The underwater lights cast the heart-shaped swimming pool in a turquoise glow. Oil lamps lit a coral sand pathway that led to an outside bar. I heard shouts of '*kanpai*' followed by laughter; the fishermen who had been on our boats that day were celebrating. I looked back at the Sandika's grounds. I understood why Bas had made that mad wager at the cockfights. If the two hotels worked together, they could create one of the most unique and profitable hospitality centres in Bali. With the Sandika's sandy beach and local aesthetics, and its grounds large enough to accommodate not only fishing tours but perhaps car rentals, bus tours, poolside smorgasbord dinners and much more. I thought of the many business possibilities that a joint venture could create, and I resolved to myself that if ever a chance presented itself where I could bring these two hotel owners together, I would take it. Furthermore, I would proffer my services as manager, and I would grow the business and put enough money in both their pockets that they would eventually have to consider me their business partner.

The Zodiacs appeared daily and always went home empty-handed. The following day we found that the same tourist fishermen from Bas's tours had signed on with us. The Bali Haj Hotel were giving us a continuous supply of Japanese tourists. Word of our fishing tours reached Tokyo, and they arrived in even larger groups. Jimmy always managed to supply our tours with a good number of fish. Some days, when the tuna weren't running, he speared parrot fish and sand sharks. Both species were not known to take a lure. Thankfully, our fishermen appeared none the wiser.

*   *   *

Weeks earlier, Satchimoto, a Japanese guest had arrived. Being a keen fisherman, he knew of our tours and booked directly into the Sandika. Satchimoto was a stubby little man with bow legs and bad teeth. He had a contagious laugh. It started with a shaking in his belly, rose up and erupted from his florid round face like a burst of machine-gun fire. In the short time he lived at the hotel, together with the heron's cry, the squealing of rat monkeys, the hiss of waves against the sea wall and the chime of temple bells, Satchimoto's laughter became part of the Sandika's morning sounds. He'd soon made the hotel his home and appeared comfortable. He was respectful of the staff and took a sincere interest in their families and affairs. Wayan believed he must have been Balinese in a previous life. But his most endearing quality was his consistent eruptions of laughter.

Since living in Bali, he'd changed his wardrobe. Gone were the standard Lacoste T-shirts, fishing jackets and cloth hats. Instead he'd bought himself a collection of colourful oversized board shorts, which he wore with the waist band pulled halfway up over his round belly, his hairless bow legs sticking out at odd angles. He'd acquired a deep suntan because he liked to leave his Hawaiian shirts off as much as he could. To the Japanese tourists arriving weekly, Satchimoto was already an authority on the island, a role he relished. He spent his mornings in the Sandika coffee shop, dispensing advice to fresh groups of tourists about where to get the best buys, who were the honest traders and so forth.

One morning, while sipping his coffee, Satchimoto told us about why he had moved to Bali. He had spent most of his working life running a successful travel agency in Tokyo, hence his connection to Bali. Some time ago, he returned home from a work trip to find his apartment empty and his wife of thirty years gone. There was a note on the table that began with, 'I'm leaving because I don't love you anymore …' Satchimoto accepted this. In fact, he told us he was almost relieved since the feeling was mutual, but it was the last part of the note that set him on a course of action. His wife had fallen in love with his best friend and business partner, Hiro. They now lived together in Tokyo and were asking for half of Satchimoto's considerable estate. Satchimoto was the principal shareholder of his travel agency, and years ago he had brought his friend Hiro in as partner with no capital. Legally, the business and its assets belonged to Satchimoto. He owned one-hundred percent of the shares but under Japanese matrimonial law, his wife stood a chance of receiving half of the estate through the courts. After an exchange of lawyers' correspondence, it became clear there would be a court battle that could drag on for years. Satchimoto acted swiftly. No official papers had yet been served contesting his estate, so he sold the business and transferred the bulk of his cash and stocks offshore. Some stocks and bonds went to a Japanese bank based in the Philippines and most of his cash to an Indonesian bank. He gifted his wife a large property, and then within forty-eight hours he had boarded a flight to Bali.

His story, punctuated by short bursts of machine-gun laughter, ended with Satchimoto stating emphatically that he would never return to live in Tokyo. Naturally, I could sympathise with him, although I noticed a hardness in his eyes that didn't match his bursts of laughter. I felt that what he chose to tell us was far less revealing than what he kept to himself.

* * *

Early one morning, Jimmy knocked on my door. He looked beat-up, with coral cuts and gashes on his legs and arms. His wet matted hair dripped salt water, and his troubled eyes darted from side to side. 'Adam, I catch a big one.'

I took Jimmy into my room, sat him down and tended to his cuts. He told me he'd been fishing last night as usual and hooked onto the largest yellow fin tuna he'd ever seen.

'His eyes like this.' Jimmy made a circle with forefingers and thumbs the size of a plate.

'Where's this fish now?'

'In the basket, Adam. I fight him long time,' Jimmy grimaced as I dabbed iodine into a graze on his right arm.

'Why didn't you let him go? Cut the line?'

'No,' he looked offended by my suggestion. After a reflective short pause he said, 'Fish and me fight. I win.'

I poured the last of the iodine into a deep gash in his left leg. 'How did you stop him?'

'Ah. Fish make big mistake. He swim past anchor line from my canoe, Adam. I catch it and tie two line together. And the fish turn away to sea, but now he pull a canoe with me on it. He go long time and next time he stop, he all finished, no more fight. He stop by the basket. I put anchor and swim for basket ... I pass the fish, and I see his big black eye watching me.' Jimmy paused as if he wanted to be sure he remembered exactly what he had seen underwater.

'Fish eye follow me ... He quiet in water, the hook in good, line tight, not moving, but big eye following me.' Jimmy's voice dropped to a disturbed whisper, 'I take basket and swim to him. Then I put him in the basket. I come from behind, and he just fit inside, with tail out. I tie basket to rock with big anchor rope, and come here to you.' Jimmy slumped forward, holding his head. I walked out to the balcony. A heron rose from its nest in a palm tree, squawked and flapped its wings. I heard voices from below and looked over to see three Japanese tourists coming along the path, kitted out in their fishing regalia, heading towards the coffee shop. Back in the room I said, 'I can cancel the tour today, Jimmy.'

He looked up. 'No! We bring them like always, go very slow, very slow, give me plenty time and plenty line, and I hook that fish. Him big, so you make Japanese use big line with the big hook. We bring that fish up.'

'Okay, Jimmy, we'll take the boats out now. You okay?'

'Me okay, Adam. You no worry.'

I told the fishermen gathered in the coffee shop, 'An enormous yellow-fin tuna was sighted off the reef at daybreak and was still in our fishing grounds.' This set off a round of excited murmurs and anxious mumblings. 'And use your heaviest gauge fishing line this morning,' I added.

Satchimoto raced back to his room and returned with a heavy-duty big-game fishing rod complete with harness and reel wound with a thick gauge-braided line. He would be coming on our boat. The boats took to the water. Including Satchimoto, Ketut and I had three fishermen aboard our vessel, fewer than usual. I wanted to keep it simple. We took the lead and powered over the reef. I knew where Jimmy and his fish lay: fifty metres to starboard on a bearing we'd used on an earlier trip. I needed to get it exactly right, then make sure that Satchimoto let his line run so Jimmy had time to hook up the fish.

Satchimoto selected a silver imitation fish lure with a hook the size of my hand. He held it up for my approval. I nodded. Over the side it went, and the braided line paid out. Once Satchimoto had his rod in the harness and his feet well-placed and his body braced on a cross beam, I asked the two remaining fishermen to hold off with their rods and took the helm from Ketut. The strong rip of a receding tide caused eddies and swirls and bursts of churning white caps. A flock of seabirds hovered above.

I heard the roar of the engine before I saw it. A Zodiac came speeding towards us, rising until it was almost airborne, thumping into a trough, spraying foam like wings. Mahmood Bas stood in it, holding the guy-ropes while his man helmed the boat. No fishermen were on board. He circled us then cut the motor a short distance away. As the boat dipped out of sight, Mahmood Bas appeared to stand on water like some biblical character, his white kaftan whipping in the wind. Then the boat reappeared and dispelled the illusion.

Satchimoto's rod bent like a whip. The line paid out, and his ratchet screeched like a high-pitched electric drill. I cut the outboard and scrambled the length of the boat. As I reached Satchimoto, I flicked the ratchet lever off his rod and pushed the tip down. His line ran silent.

'Let it run! Let it run!' I told him, raising my hand.

This was not standard fishing procedure and Satchimoto knew it, but he followed my instructions. I sat by him while his reel ran free. Minutes passed. A seabird keened from above. I glanced at Bas. His wet kaftan stuck to his lean frame, he held his skull cap in hand. His eyes were fixed on the line. Satchimoto's hand went towards his drag control. I laid my hand over his. I visualised Jimmy underwater with the lure caught on his boat hook, swimming towards the basket. Satchimoto desperately wanted to raise the rod and set the hook. With his reel nearly empty, I felt the line slacken. I released my hand. Satchimoto flicked on the drag lever. The fish struck! The power of the strike almost pulled Satchimoto off his perch. The boat shuddered as if it had hit a rock; Jimmy had made the hook up and released the fish.

With bow legs braced, Satchimoto raised his rod, set his ratchet and applied more drag. With the line on his reel dangerously low, he needed to gain it back. He leaned into his harness and using his legs hauled the rod up then lowered it, winding fast, picking up line. He settled into a steady rhythm. Up went the rod while sweat rolled down his face. The ratchet whined when he lowered the tip, then groaned machine-like as he wound it in.

The fish made a sudden burst and ran. The hard-won line quickly lost as it sliced through water. Bare metal showed on the spool of the reel. We were only seconds away from the line snapping and losing the fish. In that instant, the yellow fin tuna jumped. Its huge body rose out of the sea, thirty metres from our boat, streaming diamond water. It thrashed and arched in a majestic display of vertical power. Colours flashed, yellow, blue, silver, the tuna's head twisting in an effort to throw the hook. With an eruption of white water, it landed sideways and disappeared as quickly as it had come.

Silenced by what we'd just seen, by the sheer size of the fish, we looked at each other. One of the fishermen had tried to take a photograph, but he'd missed the shot by a second. As he passed the camera around, on the digital screen we saw the tail of the fish, its body obscured by the splash. The width of the tail confirmed that the fish was indeed enormous. From the Zodiac, Bas stared at the spot where the fish had jumped.

Satchimoto raised his rod. The fish was still on. As he gained line. The rod rose and fell. The muscles on his face and forearms were taunt, his knuckles blue, his breathing heavy, and his fishing jacket soaked in sweat. Another fisherman squirted water into his mouth and mopped his brow with a damp rag. There was no sign of the fish, only the slap of waves against our hull, and the incessant groan of the reel as the Japanese worked the rod. But the fish was close. With nearly all line retrieved, we knew it lay below us. With three gaff hooks and a net kept ready, we craned over the side, peering into water. Just as I turned to hand a gaff hook to Ketut, one of the Japanese fishermen near the rail screamed – a long shrill 'Aaaiii!' I looked into the water, and in that moment Satchimoto gave the final pull on his rod.

With ginger hair streaming behind and ghoulish yellow eyes opened wide, Jimmy the Fish emerged from the water, attached to the line. A macabre grin was spread across his face, an unnatural, hideous expression: his lips stretched from ear to ear; his eyes stared straight ahead, unfocused; blood streamed from his mouth, colouring the water red around his limp body. I couldn't move, think or speak. I couldn't tear my eyes away.

Satchimoto, further back in the boat, unaware of what we'd seen, lowered his rod. With the release of the line, Jimmy slid underwater. His body rolled, and I saw what had happened: Satchimoto's hook was lodged under Jimmy's chin. It had pulled his jaw bone out of its sockets, spreading his jowls, forcing his face into that gruesome grin. I jerked into action. With knife in hand, I reached down and cut the line, releasing Jimmy. Only the top of his head was visible in the blue depths. He was sinking fast, his ginger hair trailing free, waving like tentacles. Then it came to me. Jimmy the Fish was dead.

Ketut dived into the water. He wrapped his arms around Jimmy's body and pushed him to the surface. The boatmen helped bring him towards a boat, then we pulled him aboard together and lay him on a platform.

I knelt beside him and mumbled his name. I put my cheek against his mouth. No breath. I took his limp arm in my hand and felt for a pulse. I pushed a damp wad of hair away from his neck and searched for his jugular, pressing with a forefinger. There was no pulse. I looked up at the Balinese faces and moved my head from side to side. On its jump, the tuna must have thrown the hook. Travelling underwater at a quick speed, it had struck Jimmy under the chin. Clearly he couldn't dislodge it or cut the line and had drowned in Satchimoto's relentless pull.

His body was stretched out on the wooden platform, his head resting peacefully on matted hair. The hook, fixed firmly in place, protruded from his dislocated jaw like a tribal piercing. I tried to remove it but it wouldn't budge. A small trickle of blood dripped from its entry point under his chin.

Then I saw something. My eyes stared at a spot on Jimmy's neck. There was movement! A faint rising of his jugular. I reached down and touched it with my finger. Yes, feeble and intermittent, but definitely a pulse. I pinched his nose and was about to apply mouth-to-mouth resuscitation then realised I should first empty the water from his stomach. I applied rhythmic pressure to his chest. I pressed and pressed but to no avail. Long moments passed, and my head spun with exhaustion, and I had no strength left to push on his chest, and I couldn't hold enough breath to blow into his lungs. Still I kept trying. I stopped for breath and was about to reach down when Ketut held me back.

'Let him go, Adam.'

I stood. Anger rose up from the soles of my feet. 'Damn you, Jimmy!' I cried, looking down at him.

The Zodiacs had moved closer. Bas's gaze was on Jimmy, his

face impassive. I reached down and pulled Jimmy up. With one hand on his hair and the other on the band of his shorts, and with the strength of a madman, I lifted him high. I wanted to throw him back into the sea, to be rid of this whole cursed thing. My muscles gave out. Jimmy's body slipped from my grip and fell hard on the wooden platform below. He landed on his shoulder. A great gush of water issued from his mouth. A pink frothy foam surrounded his head and bubbled onto the platform. Then he inhaled, taking in a gurgling strained breath. More water gushed out, followed by more pink foam.

His gasping breath was the best sound I'd ever heard. Jimmy the Fish was alive. I knelt down beside him. His eyes opened, a blurry pool of flecked yellow and red, and centred on me. He tried to speak. The pain of his jaw found him. He raised his hand to it, tentatively feeling the hook. In a voice so faint that only I could hear, 'Fish win … Him big, Adam.'

'I saw the fish, Jimmy. I saw it … Sshhh, now.'

* * *

We needed to move fast. I wasn't sure that Jimmy could survive the reef crossing. I looked towards the reef and saw an outrigger breaking through a wave. It was Anak with two fishermen ploughing through the choppy sea towards us. They were coming to help us. Jimmy had lapsed into unconsciousness, his pulse growing weaker, his breathing dangerously laboured. Anak was ten to fifteen minutes away. Bas's Zodiac lay ten metres to port.

'Help us!' I hollered to the Muslim. He didn't react. His attention was focused on Anak. Bas reached into his waist band and pulled out a military style handgun. I heard a metallic click as he rammed a loaded magazine into the gun's chamber and released the safety latch. I swung around to warn Anak, only to see him standing there, bracing his legs against the hull, a rifle pulled against his shoulder and trained on Bas.

'Ketut, what's going on?' I asked desperately.

'Maybe Anak watching from long way. Maybe he think Bas kill Jimmy … Don't know. Anak crazy sometime.'

'Send a boat. Stop him. Tell him what happened. It was an accident for Christ sake!'

One of our crew swung an outrigger away from our fleet and pushed out towards Anak. Our terrified Japanese fishermen slid down into the hulls of the outriggers.

'Why doesn't Bas leave? He could be out of rifle range within seconds?' Ketut's look confirmed what I already knew: like at the cockfights, neither man wanted to back down.

Jimmy's breaths were coming in short staggered bursts and his pallor was becoming death-like. Bas's Zodiac drifted closer to our remaining vessels. Did he intend to use our hull as cover? I cupped my hands to my mouth and hollered, 'Mahmood Bas, I ask you in the name of Allah to show compassion. This man is dying.'

Holding his gun pointed at the oncoming boat, Bas waved his pistol as if dismissing my request, and looked down at Jimmy. He rubbed a hand over his face, gave his boatman an order then re-aimed his weapon at Anak. The Zodiac pulled alongside us. I jumped aboard. Ketut quickly unfastened the wooden platform, and we eased it into the rubber boat. I left the stunned and silent Japanese fishermen in the care of our boatmen. Another command from Bas and the engine roared. We bounced over white caps at twenty knots. Bas returned his handgun to the folds of his kaftan and held the guy-lines. Not once did he look down at Jimmy or me. Within minutes we were on a boat ramp beside the airport runway. We lifted the platform to the tarmac. Airport staff and onlookers came rushing, quickly regretting their curiosity. Jimmy lay on the wooden plank, eyes open, like a sacrificial human offering. A black limousine arrived and with the help of one of Bas's men we placed the platform on its back seat. As the car door shut, I turned to thank Bas, but he was already gone.

The driver, wearing a Bali Haj uniform, sped along the edge of the runway. He turned and asked in the coolest manner, as if we were a couple of rich tourists he'd just picked up from the airport, 'Where to, sir?' I knew Eddi Medan's cellphone number and asked the driver to dial it. I knew it would be hopeless going to the public hospital. We could be stuck in a waiting room for hours.

'What's up, Adam?' Eddi's voice crackled through the phone.

'Fishing accident, local kid. He's only just hanging in there. I need a doctor urgent. Eddi, it's touch and go.'

'Bring him to the Sanur Beach Hotel. I'll meet you out front.'

'Got it.'

Twenty minutes later, we pulled into the grounds of the hotel. I knew this was where Eddi had his office, and I also knew he had some kind of arrangement with the management.

'Jesus Christ!' Eddi stammered after taking in the extent of Jimmy's wounds. He rushed us to a doctor's surgery inside the hotel – a white, immaculately clean room with fluorescent lights and ceiling fans. We transferred Jimmy onto the surgery bed.

The doctor entered and inspected him. 'I will take out the hook and reset the jaw, but first he must gain strength. Saline drip with antibiotic, morphine and rest. You will have to leave him here overnight. Who will be paying? I must have money before treatment. These are my rules.'

Eddi pulled out a couple of hundred dollars from his wallet.

The tension drained from Jimmy's face as the morphine took effect. He closed his eyes and drifted into a slumber. Eddi took me to his room, where I showered and borrowed a fresh T-shirt and shorts. Over a beer at the beach bar, I told Eddi about what had happened, leaving out the fact that I knew Jimmy was underwater.

When I got to the stand-off between Anak and Bas, Eddi said, 'Mate, I swear, one day those two will shoot each other. Why don't they get it over with, you know. One of those duels at sunrise, pistols at twenty paces like in the movies.'

The relief that Jimmy was alive countered my regret that the fishing tours had to come to close, and with them most of the Sandika's revenue. I leaned back, my arms and legs aching, my head still reeling.

Back at the Sandika, I took a bottle of arrack from the bar and went my room.

5

I slept well into the morning and awoke to the sound of temple bells and gamelans. Every muscle in my body cried out in stiff protest, and my head thumped. From my balcony, I saw that the ceremony preparations were well underway and then remembered that today the roof was to be hoisted into place. Wayan looked up towards me and waved.

'Adam, if you stay there, they will take the roof from your head,' he said to an outburst of cackles and calls from everybody around him. Then I heard the sound of hammers and looked up to see workmen dismantling the old roof above me. I had time for a quick shower before the corrugated iron was ripped away and sunlight flooded into my room.

I found Ketut in the coffee shop. He told me Anak had bribed workmen from a high-rise building in downtown Kuta to tow over two construction cranes in order to raise the roof. While we spoke, the cranes came rumbling in, and the ceremony began. Balinese women, decked out in their best silks and lace, carried palm baskets laden with saffron rice and offerings. They streamed into the Sandika's grounds. Men in black-and-white chequered sarongs and white turbans gave directions. Wearing a white satin sarong and gold embroidered jacket, the same *pedanda* who had officiated at the blessing ceremony sat on a chair, resting his hands on a gemstone-encrusted walking stick.

Members of a gamelan orchestra arranged their stage, placed instruments and tuned drums. Jimmy the Fish's family arrived. His mother, now in her forties, carried herself with the elegance and poise of the high-born. From the coffee shop, I observed her discreetly. She was a beauty indeed and as Anak and she exchanged greetings, I recognised something in her face, the curl of her lip, the way her hair followed the curve of her neck. I saw the son in the mother, but there was something else. What was it? Then I saw it again. In her quick secretive glances towards Anak, a subtle flirtatiousness, a capacity for something other than the tightly regimented life of a Balinese woman. I understood then why Jimmy had ginger hair.

The ceremony began with the chanting of mantras and prayers. The *pedanda* checked the roof for any *bata* or *kula* that might have been be hiding in there and inspected the structure for violations of the spiritual laws of building. The ceremony was for purification, a rite of completion called *melaspas*, during which the previously dead materials became alive as life was breathed into them by the gods. The hotel's foundations were considered its feet, the pillars its body and the roof its head. We were thereby giving our hotel a new head. After hours of chanting, music and the mandatory sprinkling of holy water, it was time to lift the head onto its body. This event went smoothly. The bamboo towers did a perfect job of holding the roof, while construction cranes lifted it high above us and onto the hotel. Anak and a few workmen placed terracotta tiles along the top ridge and attached two small protective statues of gods on either peak. The Sandika Hotel now had its head. It stood redeemed. It was once again the only hotel on Kuta Beach with a handsome lady-grass roof.

* * *

Anak cancelled the fishing tours. He mumbled something about angry demons and crazed sea gods as he stood admiring our new roof. We pulled our outrigger onto higher ground and put the outboard in storage. I puttered around the place, not knowing what to do with myself. We had no guests, and our restaurant customers had dropped off. Wayan's face was etched with worry lines, and Ketut spent hours pulling dead leaves from our empty swimming pool.

I hadn't heard from Grace in over two weeks. It was unlike her not to call; had something happened to her? All my efforts had come to nothing. Anak told me that he couldn't pay my salary until business picked up. Getting my life back on track seemed to be slipping away from me.

I wanted to get away from the Sandika for the night. At the Blue Ocean terraces, I threw the bike onto its stand and pulled up a seat at Geno and Paolo's table. They were with Satchimoto and were entertaining a group of Japanese from the Bali Haj. I'd noticed earlier that the brothers were tight with the expat fisherman. I ordered a Long Island iced tea for myself, drank it quickly and ordered another one. Cold droplets of water ran down the glass. A smattering of rain had left the air hanging like a wet blanket and the earth smelling musty. I watched Satchimoto and the brothers talking to the fishermen. It sounded like they were trying to sell them something. Geno's eyes were like stoned marbles, and his hands waved about as he talked. Paolo sat back, quietly watching.

A grinning waiter hovered around our tables, knowing that the Japanese would offer him large tips. Satchimoto leaned into my ear and in a drunken slur told me how sorry he was about Jimmy. He asked if I could talk to him the following day, because he had some ideas about how we could restart the fishing tours. As he was talking, I saw Geno take his shoulder bag and disappear into the shadows with a local expat. He then returned and nodded to Paolo. For a moment I envied the simplicity of their business, their easy lifestyle, but I knew it wasn't for me; my cloth wasn't cut that way. I twirled the cocktail umbrella between my fingers and crushed it into my hand. I wished Grace would call, even if it was just to remind me of who I was and what I should be doing. I felt trapped, drifting in limbo, lost in a tropical wilderness, unable to move forward, unable to go back. I paid the waiter and wandered out onto the beach, waited until the salt air had cleared my head then drifted over to Omar's café.

Janna sat at her table, peeling a piece of fruit. The orangutans were tethered on either side of her, calmly waiting for their next morsel. I'd heard that orangutans made great pets when they were young but became aggressive when they reached maturity. Janna's apes were remarkably passive however, as if she had mysterious control over them. She filled her glass with the last of her arrack and drank it in one shot. I saw the silken beauty of her neck, her smooth skin. The strong liquor seemed to have no effect on her as she moved with a dancer's ease, unhooking the ape's chains and talking to them in a soft lilting voice.

She walked through the coconut trees and out onto the beach, with an ape loping along on her either side. I followed her from a distance, stumbling along the moonless beach, her white figure glowing before me in the darkness. I kept well behind. They stopped where I'd first seen them, at the light tied to a palm tree. She fumbled through her bag, and the orangutans became animated, reaching towards her, almost smothering her. I couldn't see what she was giving them. It was the same ritual I'd seen on that first night. I watched fascinated, but then as my head cleared, I felt kind of creepy, hiding out of sight and spying on someone I didn't know. I left, walking back along the beach.

At the terraces, Geno was having trouble getting four drunken Japanese into a taxi. He signalled for me to help. Satchimoto was in a terrible state and when he saw me, he pulled my ear to his mouth. The vapour of his breath was foul as he said, 'I want to talk to you … We talk soon, huh?'

'He been going on about it all night,' said Geno, 'driving us crazy with that shit. Hey, you still boss of the hotel or not? Well, this guy is your fucking guest, so look after him!'

* * *

Morning came, and I hung around the office, waiting for a call from Grace. It had been three weeks now and there was still no call. A heavy tropical downpour pounded on the coffee shop's roof like applause. Steam rose from the earth and hung in wisps in the carpark. Disturbed fruit bats swooped by, gibbering and squealing. I left the empty coffee shop and walked purposefully towards the office. I had decided to take the risk of calling Grace.

My ex-wife answered, 'Hello, this is Grace's phone. Can I take a message?'

I hung up immediately and pulled my hand from the receiver as if it had given me an electric shock. A minute later it rang, long shrill calls that vibrated through me. I stood there, unable to move. The phone was still ringing when Wayan appeared in the doorway and looked at me strangely. I picked up the receiver and put my hand over it then nodded to Wayan.

'This is the overseas number that called my daughter. I want to know who this is?' came Elisabeth's sharp voice, followed by, 'Is that you Adam?'

I placed the receiver onto its cradle as noiselessly as I could and swallowed hard. Elisabeth would know it was me. I looked around. The rain had stopped. Wayan was hanging out the tablecloths. I waited until my chest had stopped thumping and the lump in my throat had settled then headed out to the beach. The receding tide had left a large expanse of flat sand. The beach was deserted. I walked at a steady pace. I suspected that she would call the New Zealand Embassy and give them the Sandika's number. My days in Bali were surely coming to an end.

6

When I returned to the coffee shop, Satchimoto tried to approach me, but then saw my sour expression and moved away. I went to the bar and downed a shot of arrack. A short time later Wayan called for me, 'Telephone, Adam.' I suspected it was the Embassy. Wayan's voice came again, 'Hurry, Adam, it's your daughter.'

'Dad! Why did you ring? You nearly blew it,' said Grace in an agitated whisper.

'Because I was very worried. I thought something had happened to you,' I said.

'Listen, I'm outside the house, can't talk long. I'm staying with Mum because Tula showed up in person and she's scared. He said something about how she's still okay for her age and if she came to see him, she could work off some of your debt … He's disgusting. Oh, and after that David walked out, said he can't handle all this shit.'

'Wow, that's heavy. I knew something was up but I thought it was more like she might call the Embassy …'

'She was going to, but I came downstairs and managed to talk her out of it.'

'Did she know it was me?'

'She's not sure. She asked me if you'd ever called me.'

'What did you tell her?'

'I lied. I'm getting so tired of all this. Tula knows Mum can't pay him anything. I'm sick of him, and Dad, I know I keep on saying this, but you need to come home. I don't know how long I can keep it together over here. We need you here. I need you here.'

'Be strong, Gracie. Hang in there a while longer. It'll work itself out, it has to.'

'I wish we could go back to how we were.'

'That's over, forget about Milano's … It's history!' I felt my voice harden.

'If Tula keeps threatening us, I'm going to do something.'

'Grace, listen to me. I'm your father and I'm telling you: stay away from Tula. He's not some kitchen cook you can boss around. He's a serious gangster. Don't go near him!'

'Here comes Mum … Gotta go.'

'Grace, wait!'

Back at the bar, another shot of arrack helped soothe my nerves. My daughter had no idea who Tula really was or what he was capable of.

Satchimoto came up to me again, but this time I was ready to listen to him, ready to entertain any money-making idea he had so I could make a payment to Tula.

Wayan served us breakfast. The tide was in, and waves lapped at the sea wall. Seagulls dived and cawed, fighting for scraps as the night fishing boats cleaned their catch. Satchimoto waited until we'd finished eating before he began.

He wanted to set up a tour company in Bali and do both diving and fishing. He had contacts with travel agents and with diving and fishing clubs in Japan. I was relieved to hear that he didn't intend to use our boats or to even cross the reef. 'Too dangerous,' he said. But he wanted to use the Sandika as his base. 'This hotel feels like home, and you are like family to me,' he said, buttoning up his Hawaiian shirt and firing off a round of machine-gun laughter. He wanted a building on the Sandika grounds to work from. He would front up a large amount of cash to purchase the necessary inflatables, Land Rovers, dive bottles and air compressors. When he said that he was confident about bringing in at least twelve fishermen every week, I paid more attention. Geno and Paolo would be his dive monitors, and he wanted Jimmy the Fish as his dive manager. 'Will you ask Jimmy? I will talk to Geno and Paolo. And could you talk to Anak about the plan?' Satchimoto pushed a packed envelope across the table, 'Give him this.'

I was in the office, discussing Satchimoto's idea with Anak over the telephone when I saw the expat from Blue Ocean whom Geno had dealt to the night before. He went past the office window and seemed to know the way to the brothers' room. Anak and I were still talking when the Blue-Ocean guy returned, carrying a shoulder bag he didn't have with him when he'd arrived. His eyes were as wide as jack apples. It bothered me that Geno and Paolo had not respected my request to keep their business off the Sandika. We were on the verge of receiving serious financial support for the hotel, and I didn't want the brothers to jeopardise us. As soon as Anak and I were finished, I would talk to them. I wondered if Satchimoto, who was about to employ them, was aware of what they really did.

Anak agreed to the proposal. He would lease Satchimoto the land, and as long as the correct building procedures were observed, we could begin immediately. Anak would send an architect and help him personally with the purchasing of the equipment. When I told Satchimoto, he flashed his bad-toothed grin and pumped my hands. I excused myself and made my way up to Geno and Paolo's room.

The brothers were sprawled on their beds. The door was open. Geno got up when I entered. On the coffee table I saw a razor blade and scraps of white powder.

'What's going on? I saw that guy come and go. I saw his eyes and the shoulder bag.'

'Hey, who the fuck are you? Some kind of fucking policeman. Not your business, man. We set you up with a fucking passport, and we tell that Japanese down there he gotta do his business here, just for you, man, just for the hotel, because we love this fucking place.' Geno was pacing up and down. There was sand in his hair, on his face and on the floor. Surfboards were stacked in the room. I remembered that it was from this very room that we had removed a dead surfer.

'Okay, I hear you, but if the hotel gets busted for having cocaine, it'll all be for nothing.'

He turned towards Paolo, 'Listen to this, motherfucker.'

'He only doing his job,' Paolo shrugged, but his brother didn't seem to pay any attention. Geno put an arm around my shoulder and said in a cloying voice, 'Okay, man, Paolo, he right. Forget about it, no more dealing cocaine from the hotel, okay? No more, okay.'

I left the room, uneasy about whether the brothers would keep their word. From the pathway I looked back at the Bali Haj. Thankfully a few of their guests still came to our coffee shop, just enough to keep us afloat.

* * *

Janna's face came to me at odd times during the day, opaque and shrouded. Sometimes she shone like a heroic character, and other times she looked lost. That evening I returned to Omar's, but she wasn't there. I waited and as it got late, I realised she wasn't coming. I asked Omar. He was concerned about her. 'She always comes, always,' he said while stacking chairs on tables.

I knew where she lived, in a walled compound not far from the palm tree with the light. I rode along the beach, then down the small alleyway that led to her compound. I continued along the narrow pathway, ducking palm fronds, when she appeared. I cut the motor. She stood only a half-metre before me. Her hair was an unruly white tangle and her clothes dishevelled. She wasn't wearing her shades; there were dark shadows beneath her blue eyes.

'Are you okay?'

'My boys have gone …' she said, not making eye contact.

'Can I help?'

She threw me a distrusting look. The path was too narrow for her to pass but she pushed away the plants and vines to force her way past. The path was so narrow that I could not turn around and had to continue forward. I guessed that it would lead me out onto the beach again and I could return to help her find her orangutans. However, the further I went, the denser it became; vines and branches blocked my way. I could hear the surf so I knew the beach was close. With the motorbike's engine revving in short bursts, I struggled forward.

An ape's paw landed on my handlebars suddenly. Two fire-red eyes fixed on me. The ape's body was a vague outline before me. I wanted to call out to Janna but I quickly realised she was too far away to hear me. As my eyes adjusted, I made out the ape. Its large body blocked the way. I kept my eyes glued on it, watching for any sudden movement. The ape released its grip on my handlebars. It wrinkled its nose and emitted a sharp grunt, then flailing its arms and grimacing, it began a series of deep-throated sounds punctuated by bursts of percussive clucking. The ape's throat puffed out, pulsating, growing larger until it was the size of a balloon. Then it raised its head and opened its enormous mouth. A howl burst from the animal. I was gripped with fear and hoped Janna had heard her ape and was on her way back. It was a spine chilling sound. The ape's throat worked like a bagpipe's sack, the howl rising and falling, strangely musical yet terrifying. Then it stopped abruptly. Its red eyes were still on me but now held a strange expression. I gripped the handlebars and put my foot on the kick start. If the beast came at me, I would give the motorbike full throttle and charge. The orangutan raised itself up to its full height, and it was then that I saw its erection: a long dagger-like penis with a flared, red head protruded out of its hairy groin. Its intention was now terrifyingly clear to me.

I was about to hit the bike's kick start when another arm reached over my shoulder. Before I could move, it had latched onto my genitals and was squeezing. I felt the second ape's body pressing against mine from behind. It had mounted the passenger seat and was clutching my balls in a vice-like grip. My leg pushed down on the kick start and the motor roared. I jammed back the throttle. The grip on my balls from behind broke as the bike reared up, charging forwards. The ape in front of me moved aside. My bike hit the trunk of a coconut tree, throwing me over the handlebars, my landing softened by the dense undergrowth.

I was on my feet and stumbling through the bush to the beach. My fear gave me an astonishing speed, and I ran driven by terror, by what might happen if the apes caught me. They were close behind. I could hear their clucking and panting. Then an orangutan's paw swiped at my back. I managed to slip its grasp, but its claws had ripped through the fabric of my shirt and cut my skin. Then, a voice in my head echoed: *Apes can't swim*. It had a clipped British accent. It came again, flashing. I remembered where I had heard the words before: on a documentary I'd seen on orangutans. *Apes can't swim*.

I hit the beach, legs pumping the hard sand. I glanced back. One ape was close, loping fast in great gangly strides, legs akimbo, holding its penis in one paw, while the second ape trailed behind. I ran into the surf. A large wave knocked me off my feet and I went with it, allowing my body to be carried out by the receding water. I stood waist deep in the water, gasping. Planting my feet into the sand, I looked for the apes. They were at the water's edge. As the foam swept up the beach, they scrambled away, and as it cleared, they ambled towards me again.

I waited, ducking under the waves, while the orangutans loped at the water's edges. They could see me, yet their fear of water held them at bay. Waves rolled past me in a steady pattern, pushing the apes back with each sweep.

Janna came across the sand, unsteady on her bare feet. Her hair was wild and windswept. She wore a sheer night dress and held a bottle in one hand. The animals rushed to her, reaching for the bottle. She admonished the apes as she held the bottle high, out of their reach. When she saw me, she broke free of the animals and walked into the water. A wave rocked her, but she found her balance and waded forward. The next wave submerged her. She came up coughing in the waist-deep water, still holding the bottle. I swam to her and caught her just as she was about to go under again. I held her in my arms. Her make-up had washed away, and her hair was swept back. Through her wet sheer dress, I saw the rise of her breasts. So enraptured I was by her beauty, her sensuous curves, her satin skin, that for an instant I was spellbound. I'd forgotten about the apes until her trembling voice brought me back, 'Put me down, please.'

I stood her up and steadied her against the next wave. She pushed the bottle of arrack into my hand. 'Walk to the boys and give it to them,' she said. I reached out once again to steady her but she moved back, bracing herself. 'Do it,' she said.

Holding the bottle, I stared at the apes. They sat quietly on sand above the waterline, watching us. 'If you don't want to stay here all night, do it!' said Janna, as she took my arm, and we waded out of the water. When we reached dry sand, the animals rushed to us. I wanted to return to the safety of the surf, but she had a firm grip on my arm. The apes were now as docile as I'd seen them at Omar's.

'Give them the bottle,' said Janna.

Both orangutans sat on their haunches expectantly. I handed one ape the bottle. It took it gingerly, unscrewed the cap and sucked on the liquor, its paws grasping the bottle. After a moment, Janna wrenched the bottle away, handing it to the second ape. There was a brief scuffle, a little hissing and pawing like two kittens fighting over a bowl of milk. Janna raised her finger and the orangutans settled down.

'Go now,' she said, 'they won't hurt you.'

From the force of her gaze, I knew I should leave. I moved away slowly. The wind had risen. The sea whipped and frenzied. With quickened pace, I turned and walked backwards. The three figures remained above the water's edge, hunched together in a bizarre communion. I watched until I could no longer see them.

7

Geno and Paolo kept their word. If there was any cocaine business going on, it happened well out of sight. And they involved themselves in Satchimoto's diving and fishing business with an enthusiasm that was out of character. I wondered about their motivation; they surely didn't need the money.

'Hey man, I thought you gonna be happy, eh? We working, man, just like you,' Geno was clearly irritated by my question.

Satchimoto named the business 'The Bali Blue Fishing and Diving Company'. He had his Land Rovers and inflatables elaborately signed and glossy brochures printed up. The company office that bordered the carpark had a lady-grass roof. They intended to dive the shipwrecks on the eastern side of the island and fish in the deeper waters of the same area. It turned out that Geno and Paolo were both experienced scuba divers. When the first group of Japanese fishermen arrived, we met them at the airport. Wayan showered them with frangipani blossoms while Ketut and I led them to the Land Rovers. At the Sandika, we put on a smorgasbord seafood dinner with complimentary cocktails, and Geno and Paolo entertained our guests with Brazilian music.

The first days of diving were a success, and in the evening, I was astonished at the capacity of the Japanese to drink cocktails. If this continued, with the room rate added in, we would do nicely. With the Bali Haj guests starting to come through again, my job as hotel manager changed from casual to fulltime. Our accounts were becoming healthy, and if this kept up, I would be sending some money to Tula soon.

When our lady-grass roof had blown off in the storm, the rat monkeys had moved into the banyan tree. Now they'd returned to our roof, and in their much improved habitat, their numbers increased. The incessant chatter of these animals began to bother our Japanese guests. These tiny cheeky-faced, long-tailed monkeys kept our roof free of mice, rats, snakes and lizards, but I had to weigh up those benefits against their cacophony.

The best way to deal with the problem, according to Anak, was to buy a leopard cat and keep it in a cage near the hotel block. The scent of the cat alone would scare away most of the monkeys. We could buy the leopard cat at the Satria pet market in Denpasar.

I found the market and strolled around, admiring exotic collections of caged birds, pangolins, snakes and every breed of monkey, all of them looking forlorn, housed in rows of makeshift cages. The market was crowded. The Balinese loved pets, especially birds. Every compound had a caged bird. I asked about leopard cats and was shown to the rear of the market. As most pets at the market were the staple diet of the animal I wanted, the leopard cats were kept in a far corner to preserve the peace. They were striking-looking animals, about twice the size of a domestic cat, with bright-yellow and black markings that resembled a leopard's, and downturned ears with tufts of hair growing out of them. Their eyes looked evil as they paced their cages, hissing and snarling at anyone who came near. They were perfectly wild, having been recently trapped by hunters on the jungle floor.

'You got monkey problem?' said the vendor.

'I do.'

'Him fix it,' he said, pointing to the largest of the cats. 'Give him one fruit bat every day, him happy.' I wasn't sure I was going to do that. I was fond of our fruit bats. After lengthy haggling, I paid the equivalent of fifty dollars for the largest cat and its metal cage. The vendor heaved the cage onto his shoulder, and I led him to the Land Rover. The cat glared at me with demonic eyes, baring teeth and hissing. Such a magnificent animal should not be caged, I thought. I could imagine it on the forest floor, running free, sleek as silk.

At the Sandika, Ketut and I carried the cage to a quiet spot under a mango tree at the far end of the hotel where a large family of rat monkeys lived. Suddenly there was silence. I'd forgotten what the place sounded like without the monkeys' peeling laughter and chatter. They sat up on the eves of the roof as quiet as temple statues, hugging each other, their wide red eyes staring down as the leopard cat paced back and forth in its cage, snarling and sniffing out its new surroundings.

'Him skinny, him hungry,' said Ketut and returned with a slab of buffalo meat. When he slipped it into the cage, the cat pounced on it and devoured it in one gulp. I sat, watching the cat. Eventually it stopped pacing and rested its head on its paws, its eyes darting between me and the rat monkeys.

That night, without the monkeys' chatter, the crickets and tree frogs could be heard once again, along with the curling and tumbling of waves on the sea wall.

It was a moonless night with no breeze. I pulled my bed onto the balcony, where it was a couple of degrees cooler. I couldn't stop thinking about Grace going to see Tula. My imagination conjured up images so vivid and unhealthy that I had to force them away. I trusted that Grace wouldn't do anything too silly, but Tula was a master manipulator. All I could do was wait for the next phone call.

I thought of the two bodies that had been found by a tramper in the Waitakere Ranges years ago. They belonged to a couple of young girls who had worked in one of Tula's clubs. The newspapers were all over it. The murders were the talk of town. Tula was the prime suspect.

I was ten years old then. During that time, he ate at our

restaurant. A posse of news cameras stood by the front door, so my father let him leave through the back door. I watched from a corner of the kitchen as he moved through with his men. He was laughing and joking with our staff and stopped to sample some pasta. Then he caught sight of me sitting at the prep bench with my homework. He came over and put his hand on my cheek, 'Don't worry, little Milano. They can't touch me.'

The next day, he was arrested on suspicion of murder. A week later, there was no more news of the investigation. I came in from school one day, and my father had a newspaper spread on the prep table. He was reading the article to his staff. I caught only the last sentence: 'Owing to lack of evidence, all charges have been dropped against Tula Mahe.'

* * *

I woke up under the veil of my mosquito net to the usual chirping of crickets and frogs. I could smell temple incense and mango blossoms. Wayan would be doing her rounds. Satchimoto's laughter came from the coffee shop. Then I heard an unfamiliar sound, a giggle from the room next door, followed by a guttural Japanese expletive.

I showered and went down to the shop, ordered a coffee and absorbed myself in the morning's newspaper. Again I heard the giggle. I looked over the top of my newspaper and saw two local bargirls, wearing bright red lipstick, high heels and low-cut Lycra tops. They were boarding a taxi under the banyan tree. An hour later, I received an urgent call to the office. A Japanese fisherman's wallet was missing from his room. His cash and credit cards were gone. By the time we phoned his credit card company in Japan, it was too late. A large amount of money had been withdrawn.

Later that day I asked Satchimoto where the girls came from. He told me that a local taxi driver could supply any number of young girls for a very low fee.

'How much?' I asked. The word 'young' bothered me. I was having wild dreams about what Grace might be up to. I was astounded by the large amount Satchimoto quoted.

'That is what we pay in Tokyo,' he said, justifying the expense. 'These men are away from their wives, and they will visit prostitutes. It is a Japanese tradition.'

I knew there would be more trouble if these girls were allowed to stay at the hotel. That evening, I called in on Geno and Paolo for advice.

Geno roared with laughter, 'I see them already. Dirty girls, Adam, too young, too cheap. That one with the wallet, she back in Java already. Trust me, I know. Forget about it.'

'How can I get rid of them?'

'You can't,' Geno shrugged. 'Look man,' he continued, 'Paolo and I, we know a place in Legian with good girls, clean girls that don't steal. A mamasan called Putu, she runs the place. She has all her girls checked up by a doctor every week. We can go there later and check it out. Bring Satchimoto, maybe make a deal. How much you say the Japanese they pay?'

'I don't think we'd be into making money off prostitution.'

'No man, of course not,' said Geno, his voice conciliatory, 'but we are.'

Around midnight, Satchimoto, the Brazilian brothers and I visited Madam Putu's brothel. Her compound sat tucked away in a coconut grove behind the Legian night markets. Geno informed me that you could always tell a newly arrived girl by the black rings around her lower legs. 'It's a watermark, from years of working in the rice paddies. Wears off after a year or so.' I learned that most prostitutes working in Bali were Javanese girls, generally from the Banyuwangi region in southern Java, usually poor peasants or farm workers forced into the profession. One working girl in Bali could support her entire extended family in Java with her earnings.

Once inside, the brothers were surrounded by a group of

girls. They sprang from couches in a pleading chorus of, 'Pick me, Geno. Pick me, Paolo.'

The girls were beautiful. Their skin tones ranged from café au lait to dark brown, without the gaudy makeup and lipstick that bargirls wore. These girls could easily be mistaken for students from Jakarta or shop workers from the boutiques along Jalan Legian. They were mostly Grace's age, and I was starting to have trouble with what we were about to do. I should have never involved Geno and Paolo.

A palette of warm colours, gold-framed mirrors and lace-covered windows decorated Madam Putu's lounge room. Tube lighting wrapped with amber cellophane cast a soft glow around us, creating a womb-like interior. Posters advertising Indonesian movies and local pop stars hung on the walls, above couches and cushions. The sugary sound of an Indonesian love song eased out of the wall speakers. The girls returned to their lounge positions once they realised Geno and Paolo were here on other business.

We sat on stools before a wooden bar laden with backlit liquor bottles. Madame Putu took a seat beside us. Dressed in a baize sarong with a filigree blouse exposing her tight midriff, she was as beautiful as the girls, perhaps more. As we explained what had gone on at the Sandika, she gave us a knowing look. 'I'll try to find out who that thief was,' she assured, pouring us drinks. As she moved, a blue star sapphire set in her taut belly button caught the light and shone like a firefly. Her neck, wrists and ankles carried a collection of gold chains, rings and bracelets; they were a subtle reminder to clients that this is not a cheap establishment.

On our way to her place, Geno had informed me that as a young girl Madame Putu had married an American and spent a decade in New York. With her divorce settlement, she had returned to Bali and opened this high-class brothel. Her fluent English had the slight twang of a Bronx accent, 'Let me suggest something. We know Japanese men don't like to come to us, so if you give me an idea of how many girls you will need, I'll have them ready. You must provide safe transportation. I'm not going to subject my girls to these Javanese taxi drivers. I'll promise you, there'll be no stealing or disease. You must give me your word that you'll look after my girls.'

I took my drink and walked away. What we were doing was necessary. It was how things worked here, but it bothered me nevertheless. I saw Grace's face in every young girl in the room. My daughter was young and pretty, promiscuous in a naive kind of way. Tula would see that. I was worried about her. I was caught in a helpless situation, unable to protect my daughter from herself.

Back in the room, I heard the brother's satisfied laughter as they negotiated prices for the girls, a flat rate along with a fee for the brothers. With the deal set, Satchimoto shook Madame Putu's hand and she escorted us out.

*   *   *

I lay awake, unable to sleep. I stared at the book I was reading but couldn't concentrate on the words. I rose and walked out to the balcony. The pounding of the surf couldn't compete with the sounds emitting from the hotel. Beds squeaked and groaned, and squeals of laughter silenced the chirping of crickets and croaking of tree frogs. I paced the bare floor of my room, feeling like a pimp. When I finally fell into fitful sleep, I dreamed of Grace.

She wore a skimpy bikini and was pole dancing in a strip club. The seedy dump was deserted. Overflowing ashtrays and empty glasses covered glass-topped tables. Blue and red lights flickered on and off. Tula sat in a chair with the leopard cat at his feet, watching Grace dance. From the doorway I yelled, 'She's only a child … She's …' My mouth moved but no sound came. I reached up and touched my face. It was numb. Tula smiled and spat at the leopard cat, which lunged towards Grace and sunk its teeth into her leg, pulling her towards Tula.

I fell out of the bed onto the hard-tiled floor. I ran to the far end of the balcony and looked down at the leopard cat. It stared up at me, its demonic eyes glowing in the moonlight.

*　*　*

The Bali Blue diving tours became the Sandika's main source of revenue. Every week a new group of divers arrived at the hotel, determined to spend as much money as they could. Not only did Geno and Paolo work as dive monitors during the day, but also spent most evenings showing the divers around Kuta's bars and clubs. Satchimoto and the Brazilian brothers had a good working relationship and spent a lot of time together.

I'd helped Ketut carry a comatose Japanese fisherman to his bed late one night. As I was returning to my room, I stopped on the rear balcony. A full moon illuminated the grounds of the Bali Haj Hotel. I liked the simplicity of it. Bas's hotel had a modern feel but with a hint of tradition, in contrast to Anak's overgrown wilderness. Both hotels had their own unique flavour yet oddly complimented each other. If the two hotels would join forces, we could … I dismissed the thought immediately.

*　*　*

'Just one time more?' asked Satchimoto as he stood in my doorway, his board shorts pulled high. I thought I'd made it clear to him that I wouldn't be coming on anymore midnight excursions to Madame Putu's. But from Satchimoto's pleas, I gathered that he and our Japanese clients were going to the brothel for another reason tonight.

'Why do you want me to come?'

'To make a fair price,' he said matter-of-factly.

'Fair price for what?'

'For snakes,' he said, and shot off a burst of machine-gun laughter. This sounded like something the Brazilian brothers should do – then I remembered that Geno had gone to Japan, on invitation by one of our divers, and Paolo was away in Brazil. Later that evening I followed Satchimoto's Land Rover on my motorbike to Madame Putu's.

'Why haven't you been to see me?' She came towards me with her hands outstretched as I dismounted my motorbike. She wore flat sandals with gold straps, and her fawn-coloured satin pants fitted her as tight as a tattoo, revealing her small perfectly proportioned figure. An emerald had replaced the blue sapphire on her belly button and matched her burgundy top. Putu's strong face with flat cheek-planes and a small, curved sensuous mouth was hard not to like. Her dark eyes held a mischievous sparkle. She smelled of sweet vanilla and sandalwood.

'Come now, everything is ready,' she said as she pulled me by the arm and escorted our group from the minibus to the entranceway and on to a room behind her compound.

A table with a green Formica top stood in the centre of the room. There were plastic buckets placed underneath it. A machete lay on the table. A single overhead fluorescent bulb gave off a stark light, and the room smelled like a butcher's shop. Our nervous fishermen sat on the only furniture, a set of badly matched chairs. Satchimoto, Madame Putu and I remained standing.

'So, we are nine men? Ten, perhaps?' she asked with amusement as she glanced my way.

'Count me out,' I said.

'Okay, I can do it for a hundred dollars per man, no less,' she said, her face giving away nothing. 'And don't try to bargain,' she added, raising a commanding index finger. I had no idea about the price of snakes but I knew a thousand dollars was a large amount of money in Indonesia. 'Two-fifty for the group,' I said, pulling a random number out of the air and keeping my eyes on her.

She looked at the ground and then at me indignantly. 'How can you insult me like this? After all that I've done for you … I look after your clients. I send you my best girls. Vipers are hard to come by. The snake man spends all his time in the forest hunting them.' She turned to leave. 'I'm sorry. You're wasting my time,' she said.

Satchimoto looked askance at me. I'd discovered that the Japanese hated to bargain. It was not part of their culture. They found it demeaning to haggle over money and usually paid the asking price – one of the reasons why they were so well liked in Bali. I knew Madame Putu and her girls made a lot of money from our Japanese clients, and I sometimes wondered if the success of the Bali Blue diving tours had more to do with these girls than the diving. I realised that we couldn't afford losing our divers. They were important to our business. One accident or bad experience, and word gets around.

Madame Putu's eyes were fixed on me. 'Alright, seven hundred,' she said. 'And not a dollar less. These vipers are a good size and as I said the snake man has gone to a lot of trouble to get them here. Please understand this.'

'Three-fifty,' I said. Was I pushing my luck?

'You humiliate me. I have my girls to look after. I am not a rich woman,' said the Madame.

'Four.'

'Five.'

'Deal,' I said, offering her my hand. Madame Putu took it in both of hers. The warmth returned to her face, and she squeezed my arm. I knew she was satisfied with the price. Satchimoto looked pleased too.

'Come,' she said, 'let me take you to Joko.'

Nothing could have prepared me for what I saw. The snake man entered. He stood before us holding a gunnysack that writhed and twisted. Smiling, he placed the sack on the table. At least I took it to be a smile; it was hard to tell for his face was so covered in scar tissue that the only recognisable features were his eyes and teeth. He had no hair apart from an odd dreadlocked tail that hung from behind his bald head. As he moved, he dragged his right leg. Two black holes served as a nose. His puckered mottled skin made tiny craters and valleys on his face. The skin on his head was thin and translucent, stretched over a fleshless skull. Beneath it, I could see the outline of his cranium. His temple veins pulsed blue. I realised he wasn't smiling. He had no lips. I stepped back and looked away, but the fascinated Japanese pulled out their cameras. The snake man turned away and let out a groan.

'He doesn't like photographs. You can film the snakes, but not him,' said Putu as she arranged shot glasses on the table and filled them with rice wine.

Our clients were here to drink snake blood, a well-known aphrodisiac and a time-honoured tradition in Asia. The blood of the viper is rumoured to be more powerful than Viagra and infuses men with vitality, energy and health, and most importantly to the Japanese, gave an enduring erection. The blood was to be drunk instantly, as soon as the snake was killed, or it would have less effect. Prostitutes had been arranged for the men. After they'd drunk their share of blood, Satchimoto would escort them back to the Sandika. With the negotiation done, I was ready to leave. As I walked out of the room, I felt Putu behind me.

'Please stay.' She took my arm.

I stopped. Her grip was firm. Although I wanted to leave, Putu's business was a necessary part of our business at the hotel. I didn't want to offend her.

'Tell me about the snake man,' I said as I sat on a lounge chair.

Putu perched on the arm of the chair, her hand resting on my shoulder, and she unravelled the snake man's past to me. A blue viper, the most poisonous of snakes, crawled into his car one night and wrapped itself around the driver's pedals. This happened before Joko had anything to do with snakes and was just a young coffee farmer. He was bitten as soon as he entered the car. He tried to drive himself to the local hospital, but the snake's venom took effect quickly and he lost consciousness on the way.

The car crashed into a wall and burst into flames. When the fire died down, the local villagers pulled his body from the burning wreckage and placed him in a barrel of iced water then rushed him to the hospital. Thanks to this, he didn't die. His whole body was burned though, and his right leg paralysed by the bite. The doctors told Joko's family that there was no hope. He was very close to death when his family brought in a local *balian* who went into a trance to ask the gods if there was a cure. Snake blood, the gods told him. If Joko drank the blood of vipers, he would survive. This he did. The blood of two vipers per day were fed to him for a long time, and his skin gradually grew scar tissue and he could move around. He never returned to his village. He became friends with the old snake man who'd brought him the vipers. They lived together in the forests of southern Java, where Joko learned how to hunt vipers.

Putu's voice became a murmur as her fingers kneaded the tension spots in my back. I felt my muscles soften. We returned to the room as the first snake was about to be killed. The men had consumed the rice wine, a necessary prequel to drinking viper's blood because it lines the stomach and allows the snake's blood to be digested instantly. Holding the machete in one hand, Joko reached into his gunnysack. The vipers hissed as he pulled one out by the tail. He twirled the snake around in a slow lasso movement then landed it onto the table. The machete came down on the snake's head with a dull thud, severing it. Joko held the bloody end of the writhing snake over a glass of rice wine and milked it. Intermittent spurts of snake blood, like a cut jugular, trickled into the glass, creating a murky blend of white and red liquid. Joko ran his hand up and down the snake's body squeezing out the last drops. With the machete, he then deftly cut the snake open. Searching the intestines with scarred fingers, he found the snake's heart encased in a blue-white membrane. He cut away the casing and freed it, a tiny, perfectly formed heart, still pulsating vigorously. This he flicked into a shot glass. He stirred the blood-wine and handed the glass and the shot to the first fisherman.

'Drink the blood in one mouthful and swallow the heart while it still beats,' Putu told him. I couldn't look. My eyes dropped to the floor, and I saw something move. At first I thought it was a rat. I looked again, and there on the ground lay the snake's severed head rolling and turning. I looked closer, repulsed by this hideous sight. Its reptilian eyes were searching, the black stubby snout snapping open and shut, its silver reedy tongue darting in and out.

'Careful,' said Putu, 'they can still bite like that.' She scooped the snake's head into a plastic bucket.

Joko worked with intense concentration, producing a glass of viper's blood and a beating heart per man. They applauded as each man swallowed, relishing the ritual. Blood-filled glasses were held up for the cameras. I noticed that the men became more animated, their conversation more lively after drinking the blood. Our session came to an end when Satchimoto gulped down the last glass. The other men applauded loudly with many *hontos* and bowing. The fishermen, herded by Satchimoto, then filed out of the room. I stayed. The snake man took the last remaining snake from his bag, killed it, milked it, and offered it to me – complete with a beating heart in a shot glass.

'That is for you,' said Putu. 'It's Joko's way of saying thank you, and he wants to offer you this viper for free.'

'No, I couldn't.'

'You will insult him if you don't.'

'Can you thank him for the offer? It's very generous but really … No.'

Joko held the two glasses closer, his scarred face pleading for me to accept them. I desperately wanted to decline, but the sincere look in his eyes made me reach for the glasses. I held them in my hands, looked straight ahead and tried to pluck up the courage to drink. I knew that if I looked down at that tiny throbbing heart, I wouldn't be able to do it. Putu stood in front of me, her face taunting. I raised the first glass to my lips and gulped down the mixture of blood and wine. It didn't taste too bad, just bland. It was the shot glass and its contents that caused me to gag. I could feel the snake's heart beating all the way down my throat, on its slow journey to my stomach, where it seemed to pulsate endlessly.

The snake man left, and Putu guided me to the lounge. Her girls were with our clients, either in the rooms here or at the Sandika. She mixed a Long Island iced tea for me, replacing the vodka with arrack. As I sipped the drink, my stomach returned to normal. More so, I felt good, really good. I had a pleasant rushing sensation to my head. I looked at Putu as if I were seeing her for the first time. Her skin glowed in the soft light. Her lips were full and inviting, and her eyes held a sensuous allure. She undid her top-knot and let her hair fall. She removed her gold bracelets and necklaces one by one and placed them in her purse. She then took me by the arm. I didn't resist; I no longer wanted to leave.

Her bedroom was covered in lush cushions and velvet covers, with an alluring scent of vanilla and sandalwood. She led me to an adjoining bathroom, built in the traditional Indonesian style. She undressed and ladled water over her honeyed brown skin. The spill of moonlight shining through the open roof turned the water droplets on her body into gleaming pearls; they ran down her waist and bounced off the astonishing curve of her hips. I couldn't move, entranced by Putu's naked body. I glanced at her vanity cabinet. There was a mother-of-pearl necklace spilling out of an intricately carved box. Hadn't I bought a similar necklace for Grace's sixteenth birthday?

Putu had her back to me as she ladled water through her hair. Quietly I slipped out of the room and into the night. I found my motorbike and pushed it down the track before I jumped the kick start.

8

Moths and insects swirled around the oil lamps that lit Omar's café. Janna sat at her table, the orangutans on either side of her watching as she peeled a mango. I didn't want to look at them, didn't want to trigger any memories.

Omar leaned over and said, 'She told me what happened the other night. Close call, man. You okay?'

'Yeah, just a couple of scratches.' I told Omar about the voice that had come to me as I'd run: *Apes can't swim.* He laughed, and Janna looked our way. I noticed that she recognised me.

'They're gay,' said Omar under his breath.

'Who are?'

'Her orangutans, they're homosexual.' He poured two shots of arrack, knocked one back then pushed the other towards me and continued, 'We Indonesians believe that orangutans are ancient humans, and many thousands of years ago they took to the forests to avoid being captured as slaves. 'Orang' means people and 'utan' is the forest. We call them the forest people. The males are often homosexual, one of those weird nature things. Like these guys here ...' Omar indicated with his head towards Janna's animals. 'All I can say is that at least Janna's safe. You get what I mean?' He took a full bottle from the shelf and went to her table.

When he returned he said, 'She wants to speak to you.'

As she'd left her apes unchained, I approached Janna while keeping my eyes on the animals.

'They won't hurt you. They know you now. Can you walk with us?' Her shades hid her eyes. She wore seashells woven into her braids and a pair of white fingerless gloves. Her words smelled of arrack. When we reached the beach, the apes pulled at their chains, and Janna ordered them to heel.

'Have you told them?' she asked tensely.

'Told whom?'

'The police, about my boys chasing you …'

I was puzzled. Why would I go to the police? 'No,' I said.

'Have you told anyone?'

'No.'

'I'm asking you not to tell anyone. They can take my boys away just like that,' Janna snapped her fingers.

'I don't intend to tell anyone. You know, for me, it's … Well, it's a little embarrassing.'

She smiled, and I saw her perfect teeth. She looked out to sea. Fishing boats' lights shone on the horizon; the tide was out and the water unusually flat. I asked her where she was from, and it was sometime before she answered.

'My name is Janna Petro Karackavich. I am from what used to be called Yugoslavia. My family are all dead now, and my country is gone. I have one brother somewhere … Don't know where.' She waved her hand towards the sea, as if her brother might be out there in the darkness. A few minutes passed. We walked at the water's edge, the apes trotting beside us. She began hesitantly, speaking in disjointed words, then as she gathered her thoughts, her words flowed, bubbling forth like water from a hidden spring. I didn't interrupt or ask questions.

Janna's father had been the minister of finance under the Milosevic regime. He had amassed a huge private fortune. With the regime about to fall under the United Nations' attack, the family fled to Switzerland, where her father had transferred his fortune. They took up residence in Vevey on the shores of Lake Geneva. Janna was too young to remember the move. She grew up in a lakeside mansion, lived a privileged childhood, and money was never a consideration to her. However, she was extremely lonely. Her only friends were the gardener and housemaid. Apart from her father's employees, she had little contact with the outside world. As she came of age, she attended private schools but remained an outsider. Students whispered behind her back that she was Karackavich's daughter. Yugoslavia had fallen, and members of the former regime were wanted as war criminals. Janna's father had immunity in Switzerland but was unable to reconcile himself to a life in exile and drank himself to death. Her mother developed alcohol-related dementia and took her own life in a private hospital.

Janna had continued to live in the lakeside mansion with her brother, who drank heavily and was also dabbling in drugs. When a young Indonesian refugee she met in a café in Vevey showed an interest in her, the first man to do so, she fell in love with him.

His name was Tan, and he came from Aceh Province in Northern Sumatra. He was a fiery revolutionary who'd dedicated his life to achieving independence for the province.

In accordance with their father's will, lawyers sold the house in Vevey and gave both siblings a sizeable amount of cash and a large monthly pension for the duration of their lives.

Janna then moved to Aceh with Tan, and he persuaded her to donate a large sum to the Aceh Liberation Front, a rebel group that operated out of the Sumatran jungles. The couple got married and lived on Janna's pension in a rented compound in the capital. Janna was close to the women in Tan's family. She had friends and for the first time in her life felt content. One day, she saw two baby orangutans in a pet market and bought them on a whim.

One night a truck pulled up outside their compound. There was a hammering on the door, and Janna and Tan's mother rushed to open it. On the ground before them lay Tan's bullet-ridden body. A note, written in blood, was pinned to his chest with a knife: it said *Pengkhianat*. Janna knew what it meant: 'Traitor'. The women saw the tail lights of a government military vehicle driving away. Tan's family didn't attend his funeral for fear of repercussions from the government. They told Janna she had to leave Aceh. As she couldn't travel by air with her orangutans, she took a bus to Medan, and then a boat to Surabaya. From there she travelled the short distance to Bali, where she has lived ever since.

The light on the coconut tree came into view. The apes strained at their chains. Janna said goodnight and quickened her pace. From the beach, I watched her for a while, then walked back to Omar's.

That night as I lay awake, Janna's story came to me again, like images from an old film clip. I felt pleased that she had opened up to me. We had made a connection, and I didn't want to lose the momentum. I decided to go and see her again.

*　*　*

Satchimoto's tour group had left the Sandika, and Wayan was attending to a few guests in the coffee shop. From the bar I took a bottle of arrack and slipped it into my shirt front. I also took the Land Rover rather than the motorbike. I was going to meet Janna, and if there were any loose apes around, I wanted to be prepared. But before I could pull out of the carpark, I was called to the phone.

It was Grace. I was relieved at the sound of her voice. 'Dad, how long is this going to go on? Can you please come home?'

'Grace, listen to me. I've been worrying myself sick about you having anything to do with Tula. I've been having nightmares about it. Please tell me what's going on.' Grace didn't answer. 'Talk, girl! Tell me!'

'I made a mistake. I should never have gone to see him.'

'Tell me!'

'Stop yelling, please ...' I forced myself to calm down. She began hesitantly, 'Well, I went to the Kingsnakes' headquarters, you know, that place in Grey Lynn, and asked the hoody at the door if I could see Tula. He laughed and told me to go away. So, later that night, Steven and I went to that club he owns up on K. Road. We hung around in there for a while, and I slipped a note to the barman and asked him to give it to Tula. I wrote, "Salvador Milano's granddaughter would like to speak to you." And, like, an hour later, one of those guys that trashed your apartment came up to us. He pushed Steven away and said that only I could go in. Steven wasn't cool with this, but I told him I'd be okay and to wait for me. Tula was sitting at a desk, writing in a book, and he didn't look up. Both of those guys who were at your apartment were sitting there too.' Grace's voice was now weak and troubled, 'Dad … I can't tell you what happened … It's too embarrassing.'

I was so wound up that I wanted to holler into the phone but the sound of her sniffling stopped me. 'All I wanted to do was tell him that you … that there's no money coming and that he should leave us alone, and I think I blurted that out. Then …'

'You didn't … You know?' I heard myself saying, horrified.

'Didn't what?' she asked.

'You didn't go to work for him, did you?'

'How could you say that! Do you really think … Dad, it's just wrong that you think that,' her voice rose in indignation.

'Grace, don't take that tone with me. Just tell me what happened. What did you do?'

She steadied her voice and continued, 'I suddenly felt this hand grab me from behind, pinning my arms to my back, and then there was an arm around my neck, and another clamped over my mouth. It was all happening so quickly. A guy came over and lifted up my dress, and took off my bra and panties. I tried to fight but they had me good.'

'Grace!' I shouted. My little girl …

'I was stark naked, just my dress around my neck. I couldn't move,' she mumbled. 'It was so humiliating. I wanted to scream but I had to be calm. Tula looked at me … He wasn't looking at me, but just checking out my body, kind of looking up and down.

Then he shook his head and said, "Nah, too skinny", and went back to his books. The big guy let go of me, and I fell to the floor. They didn't move as I put on my clothes again. I wanted to cry but I was too scared. I ran out of the room. They were all laughing. Big ugly laughs, still ringing in my head. Steven and I rushed out of the club, and when we got to a dairy shop doorway, I broke down,' Grace's words trailed off.

I was filled with an anger so fierce that my skin felt like it were on fire. My hatred for Tula threatened to consume me. I saw myself holding a gun to his ... No, ramming it down his throat.

'Dad, are you there?' Grace's voice brought me back.

'You were lucky that you got out of there. It could have turned bad, really bad. Why didn't you listen to me? Did you not hear me?' I said, forcing myself to sound calm.

'Sorry,' came her voice between sobs.

'I'm going to sort this out. But in the meantime, I want you to promise me that you will not go anywhere near Tula. Stay away from him! Do you understand?'

'Yes.'

*   *   *

I walked straight to the brothers' room and rapped on their door.

'I want to borrow some money,' I blurted as I walked into the room. I was burning with rage. 'A lot of money, twenty thousand dollars.' Geno's face showed no emotion as he poured me a shot of arrack. My hand shook as I took the glass. Paolo gave me sympathetic looks from across the room.

'Hey, Adam, what happen? You okay?'

'Can you do it?' I stammered, ignoring Paolo's question.

'We can talk about it, man,' said Geno. 'Twenty grand's a lot of moolah. What you need that much for?' Between shots of arrack, I told the brothers what had happened to my daughter in New Zealand.

'So, you think twenty grand going to fix things?'

'It's enough to buy me some time, until I can sort something out.'

'If we lend you this money, how you gonna pay us back?'

It was a question that I didn't have an answer to. The brothers knew I was broke. Geno paced the room. Paolo stood against the wall with a nail file, absently trimming his nails. A breeze rustled at the curtains.

As I calmed down, I realised the futility of my situation. I was about to leave when Geno spoke. 'Look, let me talk this through with Paolo and … You need this money now, eh?' I nodded. 'Okay, I come see you soon. We talk, eh?'

Back at the coffee shop, I took a slab of meat from the kitchen and fed the leopard cat. My rage had turned to numbness. As I focused on the animal's markings, my dream came back, the one where the cat had lunged at Grace. Mosquitoes bit my legs, and I watched them suck my blood. Soon Geno found me, and we were walking out onto the beach together.

'We gonna do it, man. We gonna give you the twenty big ones, man, though you sure as shit can't pay us back now. But we might need something from you one day … We will ask you to do something for us.'

We stopped on the beach. Geno looked at me, his green eyes holding mine in an intent gaze. The wind was blowing sand against our legs.

'That's a bit vague. What is it you think you might want me to do?'

'How the hell do I know, man? Let's just say, me and Paolo, we investing in you.'

'I …'

'Hey, you want this money or not? No more questions. This a one-time offer.'

'I'll take it.' The words fell out of my mouth.

'Of course, man, of course.' Geno reached into the pocket of his board shorts and, like a magician, produced two neat stacks of hundred-dollar bills. 'Twenty thousand, man. Now go pay that motherfucker gangster of yours.'

9

In the morning, I drove over to Janna's. Her compound was silent. I heard something suddenly crashing through the bushes and waited in the Land Rover while a pig grunted past. I'd parked against the wall; sharp pieces of glass were embedded along the top of it. This was often done in Bali as protection against burglars. I touched the bottle of arrack tucked in my shirt front, got out and knocked. I put my ear to the wooden door and could hear the scuffling and grunting on the other side. I knocked louder. I heard footsteps and sounds of the door being unlocked. Janna was not wearing her shades, and her dull eyes squinted in the light. She looked sick as she tried to figure out who I was. Then her face sharpened and her mouth fell open. 'What do you want?'

She didn't wait for an answer. She cupped her hand over her mouth, whirled around and ran back into the house. I heard a door slam. Then came the agonising sound of retching. The apes sat together on the compound floor, their eyes fixed on me. I pulled out the arrack. One beast slid towards me and, as if it couldn't believe its luck, reached out a hairy paw and tentatively took the bottle from my hand.

Ape droppings, some fresh, some dry, covered the courtyard. I walked as if through a minefield, towards the door. I reached the veranda. It was a typical Dutch–Indonesian house, stucco walls with slatted windows. I opened the door. The front room was a hellhole: it was filled with uneaten, decaying fruit; broken furniture; overflowing ashtrays; mouldy piles of white clothes. I followed the sound of vomiting and came to the kitchen, where piles of empty arrack bottles covered every surface, strewn on tables, benches and the floor, clear bottles, all the same brand. I pushed them aside and found the bathroom.

Janna was slumped against the wall, semi-comatose, too far gone to recognise me. Her face and eyes were puffed and swollen, her hair hanging wet and limp. In one hand she held a bottle of arrack.

She didn't resist as I removed it from her. She didn't move as I picked her up in my arms. Her head rested on my shoulder, her breath faint. She was losing consciousness. At the front door the apes, snarling and hissing, rushed to me. I held out the half-filled bottle I'd taken from Janna. One grabbed it, did an about-turn and sped away, and the other ape chased after it. I moved quickly. Janna was light as a child. I placed her on the front seat, and she lay curled up, head buried, legs tucked in. I locked the Land Rover's doors. I'd latched the compound on my way out.

Where to now? Janna was desperately ill. I'd dealt with some very drunk restaurant customers in my time, but this was different. She was sick. The slightly bluish tinge to her face reminded me of dead Mikey's.

* * *

Anak's wife helped me with Janna as we carried her across the compound. We lay her on the dais. Anak was silent, his arms folded, his eyes on Janna. Dewi cleaned Janna with a bowl of water then wrapped her in fresh sarongs. Janna's eyes were still closed and she lay curled on one side, facing Anak. He put his hand on her forehead and held it there for some time. I was expecting him to say something to the effect of 'She is possessed by a demon'. Instead he said, 'Alcohol poisoning. You caught her just in time ... I suspect that left alone she might have died.'

'What can we do?'

'Nothing. As long as she doesn't drink more alcohol, it will wear off. Leave her with Dewi. I'll call you when she comes to.'

As I drove back, I thought of the apes. I picked up a selection of fruit and a bottle of arrack from a roadside stall and returned to Janna's compound. I put my ear to the door; there was no sound. I opened it slightly, just enough to see inside. Both apes were collapsed, lying spread-eagled in the shade of the veranda. Too much arrack, more than their daily dose, I suspected. I slid the fruit and the bottle through the door and latched it.

Back at the Sandika, I paced the sea wall. The night was hot, with no wind. There was a smattering of late night customers finishing up in the coffee shop. The pungent and pleasant smell of frangipani hung in the air. Crickets chirped at a high pitch. A stray dog followed me as I walked. Its sad eyes looked up at me until I bent down and patted it. I could hear laughter coming from the coffee shop, followed by the ring of Wayan's cash register. I pushed aside my worries about Janna and thought of Grace. I could think of her with relief now that a payment had been made to Tula. Earlier that day, Wayan had given me a message from my daughter. It was one word: 'Done.' Hopefully, Elisabeth wouldn't be getting any more threats from Tula.

*　*　*

The fishing tours continued to be a success. The Japanese fishermen returned with large catches. Paolo was in Brazil, and Geno had just returned from Japan. Paolo often came back from Brazil with gorgeous girls: front-page calendar girls who rarely spoke English, and spent their short stay in Bali sunbathing poolside. Satchimoto travelled back and forth to Tokyo, but the tours continued in his absence.

The hotel was doing well from the Bali Blue tour spin-offs and room rates. But I came to realise that with only twelve rooms, I was never going to be in a position to make me the kind of money I needed to sort out my debts in New Zealand, and also pay back Geno and Paolo. I needed to do something urgently.

Mahmood Bas came to mind. I hadn't seen him for some time. Wayan had told me that the cockfighting season had started, so I suspected that's where Anak and Mahmood would be.

* * *

In the cool of the evening, I walked over freshly cut lawns, past a deserted heart-shaped swimming pool to the main building of the Bali Haj Hotel. I heard the hum of voices and the clatter of cutlery. The hotel's dinner service was in full swing. On a white upholstered deck chair at the far end of the pool lay Mahmood Bas, asleep in his swimming trunks. There were no other guests. A cocktail glass stood on a table beside him, with an ashtray and a half-smoked cheroot. As I came closer, he heard my footsteps and awoke blurry-eyed.

'To what do I owe the pleasure?' he said, smoothing his moustache between thumb and forefinger. His sarcasm put me on guard.

'I came to thank you for helping us rescue Jimmy.'

'The Koran states that as a Muslim I cannot refuse the request of a dying man, if it is a reasonable one of course … A notion that would be beyond Anak's comprehension.'

I saw his black eyes assessing me. An awkward silence followed.

'The Sandika is doing very well off your guests,' I said.

'The Bali Haj also is doing well from the arrangement. I have incorporated beach access into my promotions, and my hotel is full on account of that.'

'You took a huge risk with that cockfight.'

Bas looked away. 'Not so huge, really. I'm not completely naïve. I've been around cockfights all my life. Tell me, what was he doing to that bird? He was up to something. I knew that if we could get his bird in the cockpit before he could continue doing whatever he was doing, we'd win. Come now, you can tell me, what was it? Adrenalin injections, a drug of some kind?' Bas's voice mocked. I remained silent. 'Anyway,' he continued, dismissing the question with a wave of his hand, 'We both won. We are both making money off that wager.'

'Would there be any chance of reconciliation between you and Anak?' My question hung in the air for a few seconds.

'This is a question you should be asking Anak.'

*   *   *

Wayan had probably noticed that some of her best cuts of meat were missing. I was spoiling the leopard cat. It snatched the meat from my hand as I offered it, and ate it in great gulps, then took up its position with its head on paws. Wayan found me and informed me that Anak wanted to see me.

When I reached his compound, Anak pointed to the main house. Dewi was at the door, looking worried. 'I've locked the door because she tries to wander off,' she said. As she opened the door, Janna ran at me, screaming, beating her fists against my chest. I wrapped my arms around her and held her in a bear hug.

'I am a prisoner here. Let me go … Let me out. You have no …' She stopped and rested her head on my chest. She didn't resist. Her body trembled and convulsed. We stood like that for a moment. 'What are you doing? Why did you bring me here?' Eyes wide and confused, she looked up at me. Her convulsing stopped but she still shivered like a trapped bird.

'You were sick. I didn't know what to do.'

'Well, I'm not sick now, and I want to go home! Now!' She started to heave. She rushed to a bucket by her bed and retched. Holding her head, she collapsed on the floor and curled into a foetal position, weeping quietly.

Dewi stood beside me, 'It's been like this all night. I hardly slept. She wants to leave, but she is so weak and so sick.'

Anak was waiting for me on the dais. He had the bloodstone

out, and the water in the glass was dark red. 'If you can bring her to me … I think this will help.'

Back in the room, I gently gathered Janna into my arms and carried her to the dais. She opened her eyes, looked at me then at Anak, and saw the glass of red water before her. She snatched it up and drank it in one gulp. She looked at the empty glass with disgust and let it fall from her hand, then turned to me and beat her fists against my chest. 'Take me home!'

I pulled her to me as her chest heaved and her tears fell. Her struggling weakened, and she slumped against me, her breathing growing steadier, her eyes closing.

'The water is working,' Anak said as held his hand on her forehead, 'Her heart is sound, her spirit is healthy, but her addiction is strong. Take her back to her room. Let the bloodstone do its work, and when she wakes, Dewi will make her eat.'

When I placed her on the bed, she pulled her knees up to her chest and hugged them. She looked at me for a brief second before she let her head fall forward limply. I sat with her for a long time, my hand resting on the side of her head. She mumbled and spoke in several languages. A few times, she sat bolt upright, then fell back asleep. If I tried to remove my hand, she'd pull it back and hold it against her head like it were a pillow. Dewi looked in on us occasionally, and after a while she came and stayed. 'I'll take care of her. Go home, Adam.'

The courtyard was quiet. The last candle flickered before an altar in a recess of the banyan tree. There were a few sticks of unlit incense before the image of a god. I took one, lit it with a candle flame and placed it before the deity while a family of rat monkeys watched me pray.

* * *

The following morning, I returned to Anak's compound. In her room, Janna was sitting up on a rattan chair, staring at the wall.

Her face had some colour, a slight flush in her cheeks. Her hair had been washed, and there was an empty soup bowl beside her. She looked at me with a wan smile as I entered. It was some time before she spoke. 'Are my boys alright?' she whispered.

Damn! I'd completely forgotten about the apes. 'They are fine. I'll feed them shortly.'

'I drank more of that red water. What is it?'

'Anak's a traditional healer. It's something he uses.'

'Like an herb?'

'Something like that.'

'Adam, how sick am I?'

'Very.'

She turned to the wall. I held out my hand, and she took it. She put her arms around my neck. I smelled the lemon scent of her hair. She was almost asleep when we reached the bed. Her body fit perfectly against mine. She raised her head and looked into my eyes. She squeezed her arms tighter around me and said, 'Don't let go.'

I held her while she slept. I wasn't aware of the time but soon I was becoming concerned about the apes. They hadn't had their arrack, and they would be wild and crazed. I hoped they were still in the compound. I left as soon as Dewi came and took responsibility of Janna.

I drove to her compound, picking up two bottles of arrack and a bunch of bananas on the way. They clawed and pounded at the door. I recognised their desperate noises from the night they had escaped. I wasn't going to open the door. I wrapped the bottles in palm fronds and hurled them over the wall. I heard their scuffling, and then it was quiet. I waited for twenty minutes, opened the door a crack and peeked through. Both the apes lay comatose on the veranda. I placed the bananas beside them and left.

10

Anak sat reading. On hearing the sound of my motorbike, he looked up, and he indicated that I should sit with him. He pushed a cup of green tea towards me when I joined him. I took a sip.

'I'm using a combination of the blood water and what you would call hypnosis. In Bali we call it trancing. It will allow her dreams to travel back in time and help me find the cause of her sickness. I let her stay awake only to eat and drink – which she is doing. Then more blood water and sleep. This process will take some time. We must be patient.'

I had faith in Anak's healing methods. I sipped my tea and watched a flock of peacocks wander freely around the compound. Fighting cocks cooed, and Gusti passed us on his way to the coop. It all reminded me of Mahmood Bas. I'd almost forgotten about our conversation from days before.

'Would there be any possibility of a reconciliation between you and Bas?' I tried to sound as casual as possible. It caught Anak unaware, and I saw the distaste on his face.

'Go on …'

I told him how I'd met with Bas earlier, and that I had initiated discussions regarding a possible truce, and that Bas had indicated some willingness.

Anak grunted and sipped his tea. 'You're becoming quite the diplomat.'

'From a business perspective, it makes a lot of sense. Both hotels could benefit.'

'I'm sure that is true,' said Anak, 'but there is a lot more to it. It goes much deeper and a long way back.'

'Bas said something similar.'

'Have you ever wondered why we own the front piece of that block of land while Mahmood has the back?'

'Yes, I have.'

'At one time, my family owned it all … All the land the Bali Haj sits on.' Anak gave me a minute to think about this before continuing. 'In order to understand what happened, we need to go back to 1963. I was ten years old then. Being the oldest son, I was forever by my father's side.' Anak poured us more tea. When he looked up, his dark eyes were distant. 'We were not rich. My father was a cousin to the king, but he married a woman of lower caste. This put him out of favour with the royal family. This was the reason he was given a parcel of land by the ocean. At the time, the land was worthless. Nothing could be grown on it except coconuts. Fortunately, my mother's family gave us this land we are now sitting on, and we were able to grow food and live off it. The beach land brought in an income from the coconut harvest, but it wasn't much. In the early sixties, however, tourists began to arrive, and my father had a vision of building a hotel. In order to finance the building, he mortgaged the bulk of the land to a Chinese money lender – Li Cheun was his name. He only kept the beachfront land we now have.'

'We had just finished building the hotel in 1963 when Mt. Agung erupted. Fifteen-hundred people died in the lava flow, and many more died in the famine that followed. As we lived by the sea, we were unaffected, but my family took in refugees, and we helped where we could. On account of this disaster, many families had to mortgage their land to the Chinese money lenders in order to survive. It was a terrible time, and it took a couple of years for recovery to begin, only for it to get worse again. At the time, many Balinese were P.K.I., Communist Party members. My father wasn't one, but he was a sympathiser. I don't think we were real communists like the Chinese or Russians. It's just that with our traditional *banjar* system in Bali, where everyone worked for the community, communism made sense to us, but we didn't bother with all the rhetoric that went with it.'

'Anyway, at that time the country was in political turmoil. Sukarno, the president at the time, had a Balinese wife so he was sympathetic towards Bali. The island, being Hindu, was always isolated from the rest of the archipelago, economically and politically. But the new military command, under the leadership of General Suharto, wasn't sympathetic at all. On the contrary, he saw Bali as a hotbed of communism and ordered his Javanese troops into the island to quell it. And as they had all over Indonesia, mass killings followed. Anyone who was a member of the P.K.I. was taken from their village and shot. Eighty thousand innocent Balinese died in the massacre, and some say over a million Indonesians were murdered in total throughout the republic. It was one of the bloodiest genocides of this century, but the rest of the world sat back and watched. They were aware of the atrocities but did nothing to help.'

Anak's tone changed as he remembered. He still raised his cup to his lips although there was no tea left in it. He re-crossed his legs, straightened his back and continued.

'Suharto was a military man. His troops worshipped him. He was also a power-hungry political animal. According to Suharto, the Chinese were all communists. This was untrue. Our Chinese had lived in Bali for hundreds of years, and they were no more communist than Suharto himself. The General had his death squads round up all members of the P.K.I. and ordered his men to execute them. I look back at that time as a time of shame. To this day, I am ashamed of my countrymen's actions. I will tell you why ... As most Balinese owed money to the Chinese, their debts would have been cancelled by the death of the money-lenders. And so, many Balinese helped the Javanese troops in this massacre of innocent Chinese. As the Balinese had no guns, they used their curved rice harvesting machetes to carry out these killings ...' Anak stammered. 'And this of course worked in

Suharto's favour. He freed people from their debt. Although he was a mass murderer, he gained in popularity. Yes, my friend, we Balinese have blood on our hands. Underneath our smiles and our ceremonies, behind our peaceful beliefs and continual striving for balance and harmony, we have a history as violent and bloody as any nation has ever known.'

Anak stopped to gather himself.

'The first time I saw Mahmood Bas, I was twelve years old,' Anak recalled. 'It was in 1966. He was a young lieutenant in charge of a squad of soldiers. They arrived at the Sandika. Our Chinese money lender, Li Cheun, was beaten and bound. He couldn't see out of one eye, and his mouth was a bloody hole with most of his teeth broken off. Bas was surrounded by a horde of machine-gun toting soldiers, thugs more like it, common murderers. Anyway, Bas held a few papers in his hand. They were the mortgage agreements for my father's land ... "I know you are a P.K.I. sympathiser and I should have you shot," Bas said to my father. I was twelve years old then, and I stood by my father's side. I couldn't believe a man so young, for Bas couldn't be more than twenty-two, could speak to my father, a member of the Balinese Royal family, so arrogantly and point rifles at him as well!' Anak's indignation rose at the memory. 'Bas said, "I believe you owe this communist a considerable amount of money, for a parcel of three-hundred *arrat* of land." My father didn't answer. Bas continued, "I am prepared to let you and your family live if you sign the mortgage over to me." My father knew he was beaten, that he had no choice. Many of our family members and friends had been shot on account of their connections to the P.K.I. So he agreed. But he had one request: he wanted Li Cheun's life to be spared. My heart pounded. My father was on the verge of being executed, but was still bargaining for another man's life. "Take this worthless piece of buffalo dung and do what you will with him," Bas said and kicked Li Cheun from behind. My father then signed the papers. The land belonged to Mahmood Bas.'

Anak re-crossed his legs and refreshed his cup of tea. 'We took Li Cheun in and tended to his wounds, but there was nothing we could do. His wife and children had been massacred in front of him with machetes, and all of his relations had met the same fate. He died one week later of a broken heart. We cremated him at the Sandika and scattered his ashes out at sea in the hope they might find their way back to his ancestors in China.'

My mind whirled in a confused mosaic of images and history as I tried to comprehend the enormity of the events Anak had survived as a child. I sat alone thinking long after Anak had left the dais and gone into his meditation temple.

*　*　*

It was early evening when a ruckus broke out by the pool. Guests had filed through from the Bali Haj to watch the sunset. On the pathway outside the office, a girl was screaming at Geno, pulling things from her handbag and hurling them at him. I'd seen her arrive with him several days earlier. A striking Brazilian beauty, lithe and tall with a deep tan, and green eyes like Geno's. She had her bags packed and an airport taxi waiting in the carpark.

Without warning, she turned to Geno and raved, 'You think you can pay me off with this cheap fucking jewellery, asshole? Give me my fucking money!'

'You've had your money, bitch. You spent it on all this expensive shit you wearing. Look at you! You look like a fucking Christmas tree. So shut the fuck up!' The violent look in Geno's eyes worried me.

'You, you promise me! You know how much you promise me! I am not leaving until I get my money.'

'Shut the fuck up! You fucking *putana*, you get a holiday, all these fucking clothes … What you doing before eh! Fucking old men from the beach in Rio.'

'Geno,' I cut in, 'the guests are watching. Stop this.'

'Stop this? Yes, I gonna fucking stop this right fucking now.'

He had the girl over his shoulder before I could stop him and was marching towards the swimming pool. He carried her kicking and screaming, and hurled her into the water. She came up for a moment, gasping, her wide-brimmed hat floating beside her. She grabbed a lungful of air and went under again. I saw her stilettoed feet pumping frantically, her dress billowing up to her face, her arms waving.

'That stop you, bitch! Come on, tell me now, bitch, tell me what you want!'

'She can't swim!' I screamed at Geno.

'Fuck her, man. That bitch can drown.' He turned to her and spoke, cupping his hands to his mouth, 'You happy now, bitch? You see what you make me do? You make me shame myself in front of all these people!'

I was in the water. The woman had stopped struggling and was floating listlessly. I'd managed to get her to the pool's edge but I couldn't get her out.

'Geno, help!' I yelled. He reached down and pulled her out by the hair then slapped her face hard. She lay crumpled onto the tiles.

I was out of the pool, thumping her chest with both fists. Water gushed out of her lungs. She slowly sat up, coughing and pointing a finger at Geno, 'You gonna pay for this ...' she spluttered and gasped. 'You fucking dead, you asshole. You come back to Rio and the Marco crew ... You fucking dead.'

Geno shut up. Mention of the Marco crew had stopped him. The woman then turned to me and spoke politely, 'Can you take me to change my clothes? Ask the taxi to wait.'

I settled her in the office while Ketut fished out her Versace hat and gathered her bags. Geno had disappeared. As we helped her into a taxi, she began, 'And you can tell Geno ...' But she stopped abruptly. She then pursed her lips and with a faraway look in her eyes said, 'Tell him nothing.'

11

I took a cleaning crew from the Sandika over to Janna's, along with two bottles of arrack, mops, buckets and a trailer. I asked the crew to wait outside while I checked on the apes: the animals were comatose. We went to work.

The women grumbled at the mess and wrapped scarves around their faces as they cleaned. Ketut and I carried the arrack bottles out to the trailer. We all kept our eyes on the apes, watching for the slightest movement. A few hours later, Janna's compound was clean. It smelled of bleach and disinfectant, and with the wood furniture polished and the shades raised, it looked good.

I had to figure out a solution for the alcoholic apes. Janna couldn't come home sober and have to buy arrack daily for her animals. Anak said her cure would take some time. I had to come up with a solution by the time she had returned.

*　*　*

Late that night, I was returning a drunken Japanese guest to the Bali Haj when I saw Bas. He was standing by a palm tree near the pool, smoking a cheroot. He offered me one, and we leaned against the tree and smoked. It was difficult to imagine that this slightly dishevelled older man, greying at the temples, had been the ruthless young lieutenant of Anak's narrative. A man capable of ordering the execution of women and children, and appropriating land for his own benefit.

After some time, I said half under my breath, 'I spoke with Anak.'

'And?' he asked, keeping his eyes on the ground.

'He told me about how you had acquired the land this hotel is built on. He also told me about the money lender Li Cheun and his family.'

'Anak,' he said, and his body slumped as he flicked the stub of his smoke to the ground. He began pacing. 'Anak and I are destined to be enemies for life. I can assure you that if I could turn back time ...' He paused and set off on another train of thought, his voice hardening, 'Let me tell you about some of the things that have happened between us over the years. You know I am Muslim, and most of my guests back in the day were military men and their families. We didn't have the sophisticated artesian wells then as we do today. In those times we pumped the water up into a holding tank with a petrol pump. One day there was a taste of something rotten in our water, and all my guests came down with diarrhoea. I climbed up to look in our water tank and found the body of a decomposing pig there. Have you any idea what that means to a Muslim, to be drinking and bathing in pig water? I knew this was Anak's work. There are many stories like this, but the worst was when Anak finally agreed to sell me the Sandika Hotel. I couldn't believe it at first, but when I heard that he was struggling financially, it made sense. I knew he'd taken heavy losses at the cockfights. When we met, he was civil. He told me that in view of our history, he would require a substantial cash deposit from me as an act of good faith. I agreed to this and in hindsight I acted too eagerly. I paid him the money. To cut a long story short, Anak cancelled the sale and kept the cash deposit, which was about one-third of the hotel's value at the time. He sent me a note that read, "Consider this part-payment of what you owe my father." There was nothing I could do. My lawyers told me that I hadn't followed protocol so I couldn't retrieve my money. I had to borrow heavily and almost lost the Bali Haj on account of Anak's trickery. I watched while Anak used my money to build that beautiful overflowing swimming pool you are all so proud of.'

'I know how difficult Anak can be, but you stole his father's land. You were part of those massacres, and although I don't agree with what Anak did, I can understand him. And I'm sure over the years, you gave back as good as you got.'

'That I did. These are things you could never understand. You are out of your depth here, Adam.'

'Try me.'

'Okay, so you want to know?' Mahmood began. 'It was 1966. I was young and just rising through the ranks of the military. I was a Suharto loyalist and one of the youngest lieutenants to be given command of a squad of men and assigned to Bali. At the time, we military men trusted Suharto implicitly. He was our hero, and he told us the Indonesian Republic was about to be overtaken by communists. I was a nationalist and an idealist, and I had no reason to doubt him. Thankfully, mine was one of the last squads to be sent here. We were on a clean-up mission, since most of the executions had already taken place. I was given a list, and our brief was to hunt out those remaining communists, the ones who had escaped or gone undetected, and execute them. Yes, I'm guilty.' He held up both his palms. 'Yes, I ordered executions. I believed the survival of the Republic depended on it. But I had nothing to do with the deaths of Li Cheun and his family. He was on my list, but when we arrived at his shop, he was already badly beaten but alive. His family lay dead around him. It was horrific ... They had been butchered by machetes, so I knew it was the local Balinese nationalists who were responsible. Li Cheun handed me a bunch of papers and said, "Don't kill me. I will give you this big piece of land if you will send my family's bodies back to China ... I beg you to shoot me and send my remains with them." It was a bizarre and desperate request. I looked at the papers and saw they were land deeds. I recognised the name of Anak's father and checked my list, realising that he was one of the communist sympathisers I was ordered to execute!' His voice shook as he spoke. His eyes were fixed on me, his hands clenched behind his back,

'We took Li Cheun with us, and I'm sure Anak has told you the rest. But let me state this,' Bas said as he waved a finger. 'I disobeyed orders by not executing Anak's father. I took that risk although I could have been branded a communist sympathiser myself. Anak's father lived, not because I wanted to spare him, but because I had seen enough killing and couldn't stomach anymore.' He slumped back against the wall. Long moments passed before either of us spoke again. There was a chill in the air. The pool's underwater lights cast a turquoise light on Mahmood's face. He lit another cheroot, flicking the struck match onto the ground and crushing it with his foot.

'If you owned the land, why didn't you give it back to Anak's father once everything had settled down?'

Bas considered my question while smoothing his moustache. 'It wasn't that simple. You see, it was only years later that we found out about Suharto's true motives. That the communist kills had been a sham, a fabrication, part of the inhuman military propaganda he had used to gain popularity with the people and to depose Sukarno. He had hood-winked us all. By the time I found this out, I had already built the hotel. In order to develop the property, I borrowed heavily from the generals in power in Jakarta. They lent me the development finance at an extortionate interest rate. I built the Bali Haj Hotel on loans, and I had no means to pay when they fell due. I knew the generals would not hesitate to repossess the hotel. Half of the hotels in Bali had already met this same fate. I had to resort to cockfighting. It had always been a hobby, and something I was very good at. The tourist trade flourished at the same time and finally, only a few years ago, I could pay off my last remaining loan. So, to answer your question, no, I couldn't have given the land back. It was the security against the loans. And remember that what I got from Anak's father was a coconut grove. Not the Bali Haj of today.' He paused for a moment, then said evenly, 'And let me tell you, not a day goes by that I don't regret being part of the Bali massacre.'

Before I could speak, he had walked away, his face as tight as a fist.

* * *

Anak came to the coffee shop the following day. Wayan prepared a table for him by the sea wall with his customary meal, and he ate in the traditional manner with his hand.

'How is Janna?' I asked when he had finished eating.

'She is doing very well. Dewi cares for her. Janna's Indonesian is fluent, and she's speaking a little now. She needs more time. This cure must work the first time or it doesn't work at all.'

'Thank you, Anak. That is good to hear. But there's something else I want to tell you.'

He sat stone faced as I recounted word-for-word the story Mahmood Bas had told me. When I was finished, he made no comment and left. That evening, I got a message from Wayan: 'Anak wants to see you.'

I rode to his compound and took a place on the dais, where Anak sat, holding the same fighting cock I'd seen him with some days earlier. He returned the cockerel to the cover of a basket and came back to the dais. 'I have had time to consider what you told me this morning. I want you to take an offer to Mahmood Bas. It is an offer that will settle our dispute once and for all and bring peace to our lives. I want you to tell him that I am doing this in my late father's name.' Anak took a deep breath, closed his eyes then exhaled.

'I am proposing a cockfight to be held on the boundary between the Sandika and the Bali Haj. One fight only. I will pit my best bird against Bas's, and the winner takes all. If he wins, I will give him the Sandika Hotel. If I win, I will take the Bali Haj. The fight will be a private affair. We will hire two judges, one of his choice and one of mine. Same with the spur-tiers and cock handlers, and I want to keep the fight a secret. We will have our respective lawyers draw up the deeds in advance and be present at the fight.'

As the enormity of the proposal sunk in, I interrupted, 'Anak, please, no! Don't do this. There are other ways. We could lose everything.'

'Do not tell me what to do! Carry my message to the man. Leave now!'

*   *   *

At the Bali Haj, I was ushered in through a carved entranceway by a uniformed doorman. I was told to wait outside Bas's office by the receptionist behind the main desk. Crystal water flowed down a marble statue in the centre of the lobby into a pond below, spraying lotus leaves with glowing drops of water.

Bas strode in, clean and groomed in fresh robes. 'You look worried. Is there something wrong?'

'I am here with a message from Anak,' I said, and he led me into his office.

Careful not to leave anything out, I related the proposal. Bas flew into a rage. 'That is preposterous. How can he suggest that? The Bali Haj is worth ten times the value of the Sandika. It's an outrageous proposal, typical of Anak. How do I know this is not another one of his tricks?'

'Because your lawyers will be there, as well as Anak's. I know it sounds crazy, but I can vouch for Anak's integrity. And you do have the right to refuse the offer.'

He didn't answer, so I continued: 'And in terms of money, yes, the Bali Haj is worth much more, but the Sandika is worth more to Anak because it's the fulfilment of his father's dream. It wouldn't surprise me if he broke down the Bali Haj Hotel and planted coconut trees in its place if he won.'

Beneath his moustache, Bas's lips curved into a smile. 'That he probably would.'

'And it doesn't seem so long ago that you wagered your hotel against beach access for your guests,' I added.

'That was different. I knew I would win.' Bas paced the room, hands clasped behind his back. 'I need time. I want to think this through. I will call you tomorrow with my answer.'

I sent a message to Anak immediately. It was a note that read, 'He'll answer tomorrow.'

*　*　*

Valium was the answer. In Bali it could be bought at a pharmacy without prescription.

I crushed twenty-milligram tablets of Valium and dropped them into two bottles of arrack, then took them to Janna's compound. I pushed the bottles through the door and left. When I returned an hour later, both apes were sprawled unconscious on the veranda.

While our crew had been cleaning the courtyard, we'd found an enormous barred iron cage behind the main building. We talked about putting the apes in there, but no one, including myself, wanted to move them. Janna must have had it built years earlier but never used it. It was overgrown with vines. I cleared away the tropical growth and saw that it had raised wooden sleeping platforms, a woven rope centre piece for the apes to climb and a sheltered area in one corner. The cage was about twenty-metres long and rose to the height of the compound wall. I went to a local hardware store and bought a decent-sized chain and lock for the cage's door.

Back at the compound, I took the first beast by the legs and dragged it towards the cage. As we descended the veranda, its head thumped on each step, but the ape didn't wake up. I realised I'd better cut the dose of Valium in half; twenty milligrams was clearly too much. I dragged the hefty beast all the way to the cage and returned soaked in sweat for the second one. We'd just landed on the ground below the steps when it awoke. Its eyes rolled unfocused as it came to its feet unsteadily. It saw me and tried to rush towards me, but staggered sideways and fell. I wanted to run. I had enough time. Instead, I pulled out a bottle arrack from my shirt front. The ape reached out its paw towards it eagerly. I inched towards the cage, holding the arrack before me. Too weak to stand, the ape followed me crawling, intent on having the bottle. As I reached the cage's door, I tossed the bottle inside and the beast went after it. With the door now chained and locked, I took a deep breath of relief. I watched as the ape undid the bottle's cap clumsily, spilling most of the contents as it drank from it.

* * *

'She's in her room, much better. She's been asking about you,' Dewi said. The door to the room was open. Janna sat inside, holding a mirror. She didn't see me. Sunlight filtered into the room. She was wearing her sarong Indonesian style, tight, with a fold above her breasts. She'd swept her hair to one side, highlighting her forehead. Her hand reached up and touched her nose. With a satisfied look, she tucked a wisp of stray hair behind an ear.

I walked to her and put my hand on her shoulder. She turned, and her hair smothered my face as she put her arms around me. I held her and felt her warmth, the beat of her heart.

* * *

The next morning, I was greeted at the coffee shop by Bas's messenger. 'He is ready,' he said.

I had breakfast as usual and then rather than walk through the pathway I rode my bike around the road to the Bali Haj.

Wayan and Ketut were already looking at me strangely, and I didn't want to worry them further. I found Bas waiting for me, pacing nervously in the lobby. We walked together to his office.

'You must have received my answer,' he said. 'I agree to the terms of the cockfight. But I want the wager to be for my land as far as our swimming pool. That is over one-hundred *arrat* and at least double the value of the Sandika. It is a fair wager, and I'll have my lawyer draw up a land deed accordingly.'

'That piece of land against the whole of the Sandika?'

'That is the bet.'

Anak was waiting when I pulled up at his compound. I stayed seated on my motorbike as I relayed the counter offer. He grunted. 'Go back and tell him I said no. It's all or nothing. My original offer stands, and I want an answer now or the wager is cancelled.' I rode back to the Bali Haj, hoping this would be the end of it. Surely Bas would refuse.

He seethed with rage when I delivered the message.

'The man is impossible. He lives on another planet from the rest of us. This is a game to him. He is doing this to humiliate me. He is using you to embarrass me, knowing I will refuse. It goes on and on. It never ends, and it never will.' Then suddenly Bas swung towards me. I took a step back. His moustache twitched furiously. The veins on his temples pulsed.

'Tell him yes!' he yelled, 'Yes! I will do it. Go now and tell your madman that my answer is yes!'

12

The cockfight was on. The age-old battle of Hindu against Muslim, of the twelve-year-old boy against the nationalist lieutenant, of three-hundred *arrat* of prime real estate, on which stood one of the finest luxury hotels in Bali, against a twelve-room, rundown ramshackle structure that had only just survived a storm, although it had amazing beach frontage. The fight date was set for the following week.

Gusti worked with Bas's men on the arrangements. The cockpit was measured out to the correct size and the dirt surface flattened and watered daily. The boundary of the two hotels ran through the centre of the pit. Tourist access was closed for the week by a makeshift thatch fence erected on either side. It became impossible to keep the fight a secret from Wayan and Ketut, so I asked Anak if I could tell them, and he agreed. It was decided that the fight would take place at sunset. The fight would last for only a few minutes.

There was nothing else for us to do now but wait. I knew my future was intricately linked to the result of this fight, and I hoped, maybe, just maybe, Anak might win.

Bas had a stipulation over which Anak hesitated: both fighting cocks were to be kept under guard for a twenty-four hour period before the fight, by their respective crews of men. This was to make sure that the birds would arrive at the fight in their natural state, as Bas put it. Since both hotels were being wagered in their entirety, the lawyers' work was minimal. They simply had to be present with the land deeds ready to be signed, witnessed and transferred.

However, a complication came up when both camps of lawyers argued that they could not attend the fight as cockfighting was illegal. This baffled me. These corrupt Indonesian lawyers worked so far out of the realms of the law, yet became so particular over such a minor legality. A compromise was reached: they would await the outcome of the fight in the dining room of the Bali Haj Hotel.

I had to mediate again when Anak and Bas couldn't agree on which cockfight judges to employ. Furthermore, we couldn't officially offer them the job for fear of the fight becoming public news. Both Anak and Bas felt too many people already knew. We drove in Anak's chariot to Singaraja, with Bas following us in his black Mercedes. We tracked down the same judges who had presided over the fight when Bas had wagered his hotel against the Sandika's beach access. For an amount of cash, these men were brought back with us to Kuta. One judge rode in Bas's car and the other in Anak's. Neither was told of the wager. It was agreed they would be housed separately and kept under guard by men from both camps to ensure they couldn't be bribed.

In the days leading up to the fight, I would ride to Janna's compound and feed the apes, then spend the rest of the evening with her. We talked, and our rambling conversations about our lives helped calm my nerves. I saw Anak on the night before the fight, and he was calm. When I asked him how he felt, he said, 'It is now out of my hands. It is up to the gods ... I will accept the outcome whatever it is.'

*   *   *

At last, the night arrived. The weather was calm with no wind. The setting sun was hidden by rain clouds. The Sandika crew, Anak, Gusti, Wayan and Ketut arrived at the pit, as did Bas's crew from across the Bali Haj grounds. The judges decided to forgo the traditional gong in case the sound attracted attention. Gusti and

Bas's handlers removed the wicker baskets from their respective birds.

Both birds were equally matched in weight and other than Anak's bird being black with blue iridescent hackles and Bas's bird a speckled red there was no indication that these two fighting cocks, upon which so much was at stake, were anything more than two common roosters. The atmosphere was as sombre as an execution ground.

The judges took their place. Both birds had their spurs tied and inspected. The fighting cocks had been roused to a fury by the plucking of hackles and flicking of beaks. Anak and Bas looked at each other from across the pit, each man standing on his own land. Anak stood with folded arms, dressed in a blue sarong and sash, his kris at his side. Mahmood Bas was wearing his usual white robes, his hands behind his back.

As a judge read out the central bet, he stated that there would be one match and one match only, with no rematch. The three-retreat rule was cancelled, and the fight would continue until one bird lay dead. Anak and Bas nodded, and the judge clapped his hands. The fight began.

The birds flew at each other with intense ferocity. They bounced back and circled, both looking for an opening. Anak's bird was bleeding; Bas's cock had drawn first blood. Wayan gasped. Ketut turned pale and looked away. The birds stood motionless, hackles flared and panting, beaks open.

There came a loud popping sound suddenly, like a small explosion, and Bas's bird was disintegrating in front of us in a bloody mess of feathers and entrails. Another pop, and Anak's bird fell dead, severed in two, a wing and a foot torn from its body, blood seeping into the earth. We all stood totally confused by what I'd just seen.

We didn't notice the uniformed policeman until he had walked into the middle of the pit and raised his pistol. He pointed it squarely at Anak. He wore a peaked cap, tight-fitting uniform and a row of commander's colours above his shirt pocket.

'You are Anak, the owner of Sandika Hotel?' Anak nodded. Suddenly we were surrounded by police. They appeared out of nowhere; clearly this was a planned operation. Some men were in uniform, some plain-clothed, and all were training guns on us. They came from the cover of the garden and from behind the hotel block and quickly circled the pit. There were twenty or thirty of them, all armed, some cradling their guns, others pointing them.

'You are under arrest for the possession of cocaine,' the commander said, as two policemen handcuffed Anak from behind. Then he spoke to our small gathering, 'I could have you all arrested for cockfighting, but that is not why we are here. Return to your homes.' The commander waved his pistol at us in a sign of dismissal. With a barrage of weapons pointed at him, Anak was led away, and the remainder of the police followed, leaving the rest of us standing around the pit in a state of shock.

Bas strode over to us quickly. 'Cocaine possession? I've known Anak to do some crazy things but he's never had anything to do with drugs, has he?'

'He is against drugs.' My eyes were still on the dead roosters.

'I think you should all follow me until we know more. Our lawyers are waiting in my lobby.'

Wayan, Ketut, Gusti and I followed Bas across the grounds of the Bali Haj, along with the handlers and the two confused cockfighting judges. Seated in the lobby, we began discussing the situation with the lawyers. We agreed that Anak's lawyer would go to the Sandika to find out what was going on.

My suspicions were confirmed when he returned an hour later. 'The drug squad has left the Sandika and taken along Anak. So you're free to return. I don't think there is any suspicion with regards to the staff, so I suggest you go back to your jobs. The guests will need settling down because the drug police searched all twelve rooms. It seems a Brazilian man named Geno Roberto was arrested at the airport with ten kilos of cocaine strapped to his waist, and the drug police found a connection to him and the Sandika. In Geno's room, they found another kilo stashed under the tiles in the bathroom. They believe Anak has something to do with it. There is nothing we can do to help until tomorrow. I will go to the holding cells at the Polda police barracks and do what I can. I will keep you informed.' Then Anak's lawyer, a dapper little man with an identical moustache to Mahmood's, picked up his briefcase and left.

The rest of us filed out of the lobby. As I reached the door, Bas caught up with me. 'I'm very sorry,' he said. 'Please keep me informed of what happens.'

We saw a stray dog chewing on the bodies of the dead cockerels as we passed the pit on our way back to the Sandika. Wayan, Ketut and I looked at each other. We knew that our problems had only just begun.

In our absence, Satchimoto had thankfully herded all the guests into the coffee shop and reassured them that there had been a terrible mistake. Such was Satchimoto's indignation and anger at the treatment meted out to his friend Anak by the drug police that several Japanese tourists offered to contribute to Anak's defence fund. Wayan arranged for our staff to have the rooms reinstated while we offered the guests free drinks. Once everyone was settled, we sat together and speculated on what would be the outcome of this mess.

I lay in bed that night, wide awake and cursing Geno. He'd broken our agreement by keeping drugs at the hotel and putting Anak in a life-threatening position. The maximum sentence for drug trafficking in Indonesia was death by firing squad. Ten kilos of cocaine was a serious amount of drugs.

* * *

The following morning, at the restaurant, Wayan handed me a copy of the local English newspaper. There was a photograph of

Geno on the front page. His shock of blond curls almost covered a bad bruise on one cheek. His face was almost unrecognisable due to a fat lip and a black eye. On either side of him stood a uniformed policeman, their hands on Geno's shoulder, their faces grinning with pride. They looked like a couple of big game hunters standing over their trophy. I recognised one of the cops as the commander who had shot the cockerels.

Before Geno, spread out on a table, lay the evidence: three large cellophane packets of a white substance.

I heard the sound of a motorbike and looked up to see Eddi Medan dismounting. 'Trouble in paradise?' he said, as he pulled up a chair and sat beside me.

'Eddi, Anak has nothing to do with this. Is there anything we can do to help?'

'Not much. The drug squad here in Bali are a force of their own. For them, having their photographs in the newspaper seems to be more important than accepting bribes.'

'Anak's innocent!'

'We both know that doesn't really matter. Look, the best I can do is pull in some favours and arrange for you to visit him.'

Later that day Eddi called and gave me an address in Denpasar. He informed me that my name was with the guard at the gate, and for fifty dollars cash I would be permitted to visit Anak.

I rode to Denpasar and found the Polda police barracks. The gate guard checked my packages and took the money, along with an apple. I followed him down a corridor to a line of cells while he took noisy bites of the fruit. Each cell contained a traditional toilet and a bucket of water. Prisoners slept on mats on the floor. The cell walls were covered in graffiti, and the only light was a bare bulb in the corridor.

Anak sat meditating. I waited. Soon he opened his eyes and smiled. 'Not quite the outcome we would have hoped for, was it? Both birds were shot so we'd have to consider it a draw, wouldn't you agree?'

'Anak, what should I do?'

'Nothing. I told you the outcome of the fight was up to the gods, and if that means the firing squad, then I accept it, and I'll face it with dignity.'

I handed Anak the food Wayan had sent for him; there was enough to last him a week. 'Thank you for this,' he said as he selected a rambutan and began to peel it. I couldn't understand his casual attitude. It was as if he had no interest in his predicament.

'We'll need a lawyer, the best we can find.'

'Ah, those scoundrels. I refuse to pay them one single rupiah.' He finished another piece of fruit and said, 'Why don't you go and see Geno? He must be further down the corridor. They've been beating him, but in between the beatings, I've heard him singing. Take him some of this food. He must be hungry.'

'Have they beaten you?' I asked.

'They wouldn't dare. They'd be too scared that I'd put a curse on them or their families. Now go and see Geno.'

I took a few parcels of food and walked further down the corridor. On seeing me, Geno rushed at the bars and snatched the food from my hand. He ripped off the wrappings and stuffed the food into his mouth. He spoke between mouthfuls. 'Man, Adam, man, they keep beating the shit out of me. They want me to confess that Anak was in it.' He was halfway through a banana. 'Hey, man, this my shit, and my shit alone, and I tell those motherfuckers that. Hey, what else can I do? But they beat me, man, all day. I never say Anak involved in my shit because he wasn't. You tell him that, man.'

'But why at the hotel! If you hadn't done that, Anak wouldn't be here!'

'Whoa! Stop right there, man. I had no fucking idea the cocaine was in my room, I swear, man. But I gonna confess anyway ... I know who put it there though, and when I get outta this shit, I gonna kill that motherfucker.' Geno was into his second packet of food.

'Where's Paolo?' I asked.

'He's okay. He in Japan, man. Make sure you talk to Satchimoto and tell him to keep Paolo there.'

'Why, Geno?' I cried. 'We had a deal, and you had a deal with Anak, but look at us now. We're fucked and …'

Geno's hand shot out between the bars and around my neck like a striking snake. 'I fucking told you, man. I know nothing about that shit, so you better listen up and believe me. Because you owe me big time … You owe me twenty grand, and now it's payback time.'

'Hey, I …' His thumb and forefinger pressed hard, cutting off my words, then he took his hand away. He looked at me curiously, a smile playing on his bruised face. 'Maybe you put that cocaine in my room, maybe it was you, man. How do I know it wasn't you? How do they know?' He pointed towards the door. I felt a chill run through me. My heart was beating harder. Geno's eyes were as steely as the prison bars. I didn't doubt for a minute that he would carry out his threat.

As if he were reading my thoughts, Geno stopped eating. He raised a finger and said, 'Hey, man, no need to go that far, eh. You a clever guy, and we friends right? You look like you fucked … I tell you man, I more fucked.' He gathered up the last of the food and stuffed the small parcels in his pockets.

When I returned to Anak, I found him sitting on his mat, legs pulled into the lotus position, eyes closed.

As I rode back to the hotel, I was caught in Kuta's one-way traffic, inching along with a pack of motorbikes in the rush hour. I found myself bothered by what Geno had said: 'Tell Satchimoto to keep him there.' Wasn't that what he'd said? Then Satchimoto must be in touch with Paolo in Tokyo. What was the connection? And the cocaine in Geno's room … If Paolo was in Japan, then who could have put it there? Who else was involved? A disturbing picture began to form in my mind. How well did I really know Satchimoto? He'd always played his cards close to his chest. I'd always thought there was something he was hiding ...

A pack of motorbikes held me back when I reached Bemo corner, so I cut down a narrow lane, a short cut known only to locals, and rode quickly to the hotel. I found him in the coffee shop. After assuring Wayan and Ketut that Anak was doing okay, I went up to Satchimoto and asked if he would come for a walk with me. I saw his jovial face turn serious suddenly. He hoisted up his board shorts, buttoned his Hawaiian shirt and we set off along the beach.

'Satchimoto, I've seen Geno, and he's told me everything.' I said, calling his bluff. 'I know what's going on, but I would like to hear it from you.'

Satchimoto's face went through a spectrum of colour changes before turning pale. 'Has Geno confessed anything to the police?' he asked, avoiding eye contact.

'No, not yet, and if you tell me everything, I might be able to convince him not to.'

'How can I be sure of that?' he said, and in that instant I knew my suspicions were true. Satchimoto's selfish concern for no one but himself made my blood boil. He hadn't asked me how Geno or Anak were doing or what he could do to help them. Anak was innocent, and Geno, Satchimoto's business partner, sat in prison facing a death sentence, but Satchimoto was least bothered about them. Anger overwhelmed me. I grabbed him by the neck and dragged him into the water. I forced his head under and held it there to a count of ten. When I pulled him out again, he came up gagging and gasping for air. I allowed him one inhale then pushed his head underwater again. He managed to pull me down with him this time, but I forced my head to stay above water. Then he bit my wrist; he sunk his teeth into it and held on like a viper. I hauled him up and punched him in the mouth.

'Tell me what's going on, you sack of shit!' I yelled. A group of tourists had gathered around us. I pulled him out of the water, and we staggered along the beach, away from the onlookers, dripping wet. Satchimoto was coughing and wheezing. I took off my shirt, wrung out the water then wrapped it around my bleeding wrist.

'Talk!' I hollered. He made a few desperate noises and spat out some sea water. His voice was shot, so I walked him to a *warung* beneath some shade trees, ordered tea and waited until he calmed down.

'Okay, here it is,' I said calmly as we sat on a bench, sipping tea. 'I want to know everything that happened between you, Geno and Paolo. Take your time, but don't leave anything out. If I have all the information then I might be able to help. I'm the best chance you have of getting out of this mess right now.'

Through hooded eyes he cast me a suspicious look then followed it with an odd smile. He coughed, testing his voice, and began. He told me about the abuse of amphetamine in Japan and that many Japanese men took *shabu*, a type of the stimulant known as 'ice'. 'We considered smoking marijuana a bad thing, but smoking *shabu* was socially acceptable, amongst men anyway.' Satchimoto's tense tone and the fear in his eyes made me think he was avoiding my question.

'Hey, I don't want a lecture on drug use in Japan. I just want to know what happened here.'

'Of course, but in order for you to understand, I need to put it in context.'

'Okay, tell me,' I said, observing how bad his teeth were and making a mental note to put some papaya onto my bitten wrist.

'Some time ago, one of our divers asked Geno if he could get some *shabu*. Not understanding what he meant, Geno pulled out his freebase pipe and offered us smokable cocaine. The effect was similar to ice, only much better, with less side effects and no bad come-down like amphetamine. The freebase rocks even looked like ice … For us, it was like a bit of innocent fun, you know, something we were used to.' Satchimoto laughed nervously, and his upper lip bled. He wiped it with the back of his hand.

'Our clients couldn't get enough of it though. They hounded Geno until his supplies ran out. He went back to Brazil and brought two couriers into Bali, loaded with cocaine. Within a short time that was gone as well. Geno doubled the price but that didn't slow consumption. When we discovered some of the divers were buying it to take back to Japan, Geno came up with a plan. As cocaine powder is soluble in alcohol, Geno dissolved half kilos in whisky bottles. He had the labels, seals and screw caps replaced perfectly when he was done. Then he paid a duty-free delivery guy who worked inside the departure lounge at the airport to replace his normal whisky order with our bottles, which looked identical – only ours were filled with liquid cocaine.'

'So that's what all those girls from Brazil were doing here? They were the couriers, the drug mules?' I thought of Geno pushing the girl into the pool.

'Exactly,' he said, almost boasting.

'You know what's bothering me right now?' I said coldly. 'I saw all this … The girls, you guys hanging out, Geno and Paolo's trips back and forth, and I didn't suspect a thing. Am I that fucking naive?'

'No, you are not, Adam. This is just not your thing, that's all.' His patronising answer only aggravated me. I let him continue. 'The switch was made once our men had passed through Customs. They picked up what looked like the exact same bottles of whisky they had purchased on the other side. Our Japanese tourists returned to Narita Airport carrying their bottles freely, complete with a duty-free bag and receipt. It worked very well. Often, bags were randomly searched but Customs officers never gave the duty-free whisky a second look. Once in Tokyo, Geno took back the whisky bottles and gave the men new bottles he'd purchased in Tokyo. We gave them two for one, so our clients made on the deal.'

I had to steady my breath to control my anger. What Satchimoto was revealing to me was a detailed and clever drug-smuggling operation, but it seemed to mean nothing more to him than another business deal. He showed no remorse at all about using the Sandika as his base or about using our innocent clients as drug couriers, nor concern about the innocent Anak being locked up in prison.

'So, the men who travelled with the whisky bottles, didn't they know that they were full of cocaine?' I asked, keeping my voice even.

He paused and touched his swollen lip before he spoke. 'At first, yes, and we paid them in product. But as time went on, we couldn't tell them, or too many people would have known. You know, two bottles for the price of one kept them happy.'

Satchimoto's lip had stopped bleeding but had turned blue. He kept dabbing at it with a tissue. I felt revolted, betrayed by this man. He had made the Bali Blue Tours a front for a large-scale cocaine smuggling operation and kept it running right under our noses for such a long time. I wanted to drag him back into the sea and drown him this time.

A local beach-seller, mistaking us for tourists, approached us with a basket of woodcarvings on his head. But when he saw our faces, he backed away. We walked back to the hotel slowly. My wrist had begun to ache. I caught Satchimoto glancing at me. I noted his calculating look. I realised that I didn't know this man, but I did know that his main concern right now was how he was going to get out of this mess.

'We have to get Anak free, and you have to help. You owe us that much.'

'Of course, I will do everything I can,' he said, as we parted ways on the pathway leading to his room.

*　*　*

At Anak's compound, I told Dewi about all that had happened. The news had reached her already, but she didn't know the full story.

'I'm sorry to hear of your troubles, Adam,' Janna said as she opened her door.

'How are you feeling?' I hadn't seen her for a while.

'I am going to stay with Dewi because I feel it's too early to go home. I miss my boys but I know you're looking after them.'

'Your boys are good. Don't worry about them.'

'Adam, can I ask you a question?' She didn't wait for an answer. 'Why? Why did you do this? Why did you bring me here? Why do you care what happens to me?'

'I wanted to help,' I fumbled.

'That is not what I'm asking.' Her eyes were moist.

She laid her head against my chest, and I held her close in a silent embrace. Then she gazed into my eyes, searching for her answer. Her skin glowed, and her eyes were as blue as the sea. I wanted to kiss her but held back. Dewi was at the doorway with a parcel of food.

'Take these to Anak,' she said as she put a hand on Janna's shoulder, 'And she needs to stay here, so don't get any ideas about taking her away yet.' Janna's laugh was like the ringing of a temple bell. I left the compound feeling light and breathless.

13

'Satchimoto has left,' said Wayan as I pulled up at the coffee shop. 'He clean his room and go to airport. Don't know where he go. Ketut is hurt his friend didn't say goodbye.'

'Tell Ketut that Satchimoto is not our friend.'

Wayan told me that I missed two calls from my daughter. It bothered me that I hadn't spoken to her for some time. I didn't want to call her at Elisabeth's house. I didn't want to lay my troubles on Grace.

Ketut returned from the airport the next morning with an empty minivan. There were eight Japanese divers due to arrive, and he'd found no sign of them. 'There won't be any more diving business. That's over,' I said as he slumped into a coffee-shop chair beside me.

'And Satchimoto?'

'He's gone, Ketut. He won't be coming back.'

I wanted to tell him the whole story but decided against it. I assured Ketut and Wayan that we'd be okay; we still had some walk-in guests, enough to keep us going until I could figure out what to do.

Then I drove to the police barracks. The gate guard was happy to see me and quickly palmed the fifty dollars I gave him. I followed the rattle of his keys down a dark corridor to the cells. Anak sat in meditation, his face serene. I waited. After a long moment, he became aware of my presence. I told him everything I'd learned from Satchimoto.

'Pity you let him go. We could have used his money to buy my way out of here,' he said. Anak was finally showing an interest in getting out of his predicament.

'But Geno will confess to the cocaine being his …'

'That has nothing to do with it. That means nothing in Indonesia, as you should know by now. The only way out of here is by paying the prosecutor. And he'll want big money.'

'How much do you think?'

'We'd need about three hundred thousand dollars in cash.'

'That is huge. We'll have to mortgage the hotel.'

'I'm afraid the Sandika is mortgaged to the maximum the banks will allow. You see, I had a very bad run at the cockfights lately,' he said, holding my gaze.

'So that is why you wagered the hotel.'

'Of course, now you understand. I couldn't lose. The banks were going to take the hotel off me anyway. If Bas had won, he would have had to assume that debt, and if I'd won, well, who knows?'

'I thought the cockfight was a matter of honour, not a gamble to get out of debt!'

'It was both of those things,' he said, dismissing me with a wave of his hand.

* * *

Geno was in a shocking state. His face was a bloody mess of cuts and bruises. The wounds from his beatings made it almost impossible for him to speak. I wanted to give him a piece of my mind, tell him what I thought about his cocaine smuggling with Satchimoto, but his terrible condition made me hesitant. Besides Geno knew about my false identity and more. Now wasn't the time to risk antagonising him, so I merely reported what I knew.

'No problem,' said Geno, his speech slurred by his fat lips and broken teeth. 'You call Paolo. I give you the number. He gonna send money, and we get Anak free, and then we do my case. Anak's case is easy, man, easy, if we pay the money.'

He pulled me close and had me memorise a Tokyo phone number. After several tries, I broke it into small groups of digits and had it in my head.

'Go, call now,' said Geno. Further conversation became painful for him. He was struggling to eat the soft flesh of a banana. I left the cells, repeating the number in my mind.

I dialled the number all day to no reply. I returned to Geno. All he could say was, 'Keep trying, man. It's all we got.' I dialled many times, day and night, but still no answer.

I visited the police cells daily. Anak seemed unfazed by his imprisonment. He said he appreciated all the time he was getting to meditate. Geno's state was worsening. Every time I saw him, they'd beaten him more. 'Fuck them, man!' he hissed through broken teeth, 'Those pussies can't hurt me.'

* * *

Before my daily visit to the police barracks, I drove to Janna's compound and fed the orangutans. I had them down to ten milligrams of Valium mixed with half a bottle of arrack. I was astounded at the amount of fruit they now ate. They were lively and animated as I pushed the food in through the bars. I'd decided that on the next feed, I would further reduce their dose of arrack and Valium. I wanted the animals fully detoxed before Janna returned home.

I drove to Anak's place after to see Janna and pick up Anak's food parcel. Dewi was out. She had placed the food parcel on the bench before she had left. I tapped lightly on the door to Janna's room. Excited and agitated, Janna pulled me inside.

'Adam, thank god you're here. I nearly … I nearly lost it.' She pointed to a full bottle of arrack on the dresser.

'How did that get here?'

'I feel so foolish. Dewi went out this morning, so I walked to the kiosk outside the compound. It was like I couldn't stop myself. I had no control over what I was doing. I had no money so I gave the vendor my gold ring. I walked back here and was going to drink it, but then I stopped myself. I realised what I was doing and how stupid I was acting. Oh my god, I've been sitting here and staring at this full bottle and feeling very silly.'

I didn't know what to say. She hadn't drunk the arrack and that was good.

'Let's go out,' I suggested. 'Would you come with me? I want to show you where I work.'

At the *warung* I gave the man his bottle and asked for her ring back. He handed it over without a fuss.

Back at the Sandika, we sat at a sea-wall table. Janna was still very fragile, and she held her iced tea in both hands to stop them from trembling. Wayan watched us closely, her face questioning. There were no customers in the coffee shop nor guests in the hotel. The lady-grass roof had darkened as the new grass had aged, but it still looked magnificent. A tangle of colour lined the sandy pathway: the soft pastel of bougainvillea blossoms, the vibrant red of hibiscus and the delicate yellow of frangipani. The tide was in, and waves peeled over the reef with a distant hiss and roar.

'It is so beautiful, Adam. I love the roof. It looks like something from a Grimm's fairy tale.'

'How are you feeling?'

'Confused, excited, worried, angry, happy, all of those.' She caught sight of a surfer barrelling down the face of a wave, 'Look! Look at him!' The surfer disappeared into the pipeline then he reappeared, weaving and diving until the wave died. We watched him retrieve his board and paddle back out.

'You didn't answer my question last night,' she whispered.

'I couldn't. I didn't know what to say,' I said. Then I saw a cloud of confusion on her face. I had to say more. *Tell her the truth, that's enough*, came a small voice in the back of my mind. I took a deep breath.

'I've never felt so strongly about someone, and it's scaring the hell out of me.' I kept my eyes on her. She reached across the table and took my hand.

'I'm scared too. Terrified, actually,' she said softly.

* * *

A couple of days later, the Sandika had a visit. It was a representative from the bank where Anak had taken the mortgage. He made it clear that unless payments were made, he would have no option but to foreclose it. I talked it over with Wayan and Ketut. Using what little money I had, plus Ketut and Wayan's savings, we managed to put down the first instalment of the mortgage payments. It bought us a small amount of time.

Eddi showed up. He wanted to know Paolo's last name.

'It's Roberto,' I said. 'Paolo Roberto.'

'He's dead,' said Eddi flatly. 'Assassinated by Yakuza in Tokyo, a few days ago.'

My legs went weak, and I could feel the colour drain from my face.

'If there is something you need to tell me, something you're hiding from me, now is the time, Adam.'

'Do you know for sure it's Paolo?'

'Yep, an old police colleague attached to the Aussie Embassy in Tokyo called me because Paolo's passport was full of Indonesian entry and exit stamps. He faxed me a copy of it too, thought I might know something. The case has all the hallmarks of a contract hit, according to him. Someone had paid a Yakuza hitman to have Paolo killed. They cut his throat with a carpet knife – standard stuff in the Tokyo underworld, I'm told.'

I was feeling unsteady on my feet.

'The air's getting a little thick around here. You need to tell me what the fuck's going on.'

'I can't.'

Eddi threw up his hands in exasperation. 'Okay, but remember that I'm on your side, mate.'

* * *

Tired and weak, I walked out onto the sand. I stopped at the water's edge. I knew in my heart who had Paolo murdered. It was Satchimoto. He had killed Paolo, a gentle and decent scoundrel, a soft-hearted surfer, who would've followed his brother over the coal fires of Jimbaran if he had asked him.

Wayan and Ketut were inconsolable over Paolo's death. My most pressing concern was about telling Geno. I decided not to hesitate. I would go immediately to the police barracks and get it done. On my way there, I stopped at Eddi's office. I looked at the fax photo; as I held the black-and-white image, I had to force my hand to stop trembling. It was definitely Paolo. His eyes were peeled back, his lips stretched taut, and there was a gaping black gash where his throat had been cut.

In meditation, Anak didn't notice me pass. I reached Geno's cell and stood in front of him for a moment, unable to speak. He lay slumped against his cell wall. He'd been beaten again, and this time they'd broken his nose and for some unknown reason had shaved his head. He had bleeding razor cuts all over his scalp. I hesitated to show Geno the image of his dead brother, but felt that without the photographic evidence he'd never believe Paolo was really dead. No words passed between us as his hand reached out and took the rolled up paper from me. He looked at it, then at me. His face drained white. His palms turned out limply, and the image fell, landing face up on the floor between us. Paolo's face stared up at me like a ghost.

'Is this true?' I couldn't speak. 'Tell me, motherfucker!'

'Yes, Paolo has been killed.'

Geno held onto the bars of his cell and howled. The demented bellow from him brought the guards running, but they simply stood around laughing for a minute then left. I watched as Geno heaved with sobs, banging his head against the cell wall. Blood oozed from the cracked skin on his forehead, mixing with the tears and snot that streamed down his face. He smacked his head against the cell wall harder and harder until he collapsed onto the floor, where he lay curled up, moaning. Paolo's picture was balled tight in his fist.

'What the fuck have I done, what the fuck have I done …' he groaned.

I stayed until the guards led me away.

* * *

I spent a lot of time at the sea wall, looking out at the reef. I felt helpless. I couldn't talk to anyone. I visited the prison daily. I took food to Anak and Geno. Anak ate and meditated. He had little to say. Geno had become a changed man. The guards had come to realise they would get no information from him and had given up on the beatings. He didn't talk and rarely ate. I would find the food I'd left for him the day before still sitting in its bowl, covered in fruit flies. He spent most of the day slumped against his cell wall, head hanging low. A couple of times he made eye contact. The depth of his pain and grief made me shudder. Anak informed me that the police prosecutor had set the date for their first hearing. They would be formally charged with drug trafficking. The charge carried the death penalty.

Eddi came to see me. 'You've got to do something, Adam, and you have to move quickly. We're running out of time here.'

'I know. I think about it day and night. I hardly sleep. What can I do?'

'Find cash, and a lot of it. It's his only way out.'

I told Eddi that Anak already had the hotel mortgaged to the hilt, and we were only just keeping up with the mortgage payments.

'I went to the Polda yesterday,' said Eddi. 'An unrelated

matter, and I asked a contact if I could view Geno's passport. I looked at his date of birth, and then at the faxed copy of Paolo's, and it hit me. The two brothers were born on the same day. They were twins.' Eddi's information spoke volumes.

'What do you think will happen to Geno?'

'Well, he's going to do a lot of time. But that's not really the question. It's going to be the luck of the draw. If he gets a hard-nosed right-wing prosecutor, he's fucked. It'll be the firing squad. But if gets someone a little more lenient, he's got a chance of life imprisonment, and in Indonesia life really means life. He'd be a very old man by the time he gets out.' Eddi looked out at the reef as he spoke. Keening sea birds flocked around an incoming fishing boat, diving for scraps. The smell of freshly caught tuna hovered in the air. Wayan brought a couple of cold beers to our table. Eddi skulled his and left.

I walked down the pathway towards the Bali Haj Hotel. Hadn't Bas asked me to keep him informed? I would do that and more.

'I need three hundred thousand dollars, possibly four,' I said as we got seated in his office.

Mahmood didn't flinch, just tilted his head sideways a little. 'I think I can guess why,' he replied, and I told him everything that had happened until now, including the impending arraignment. I told him that the prosecutor would need to be paid in the very near future. I omitted telling him about the heavy mortgage taken on Sandika Hotel.

Mahmood paced as he thought. 'You will need to pay more than the prosecutor,' he said. 'We're probably looking at paying the police, from the arresting officer down. The judges will want money as well. I'd guess we'd have to pay the Governor of Bali something as well, and believe me, he won't be cheap,' he paused. 'What's in it for me, should I decide to find this amount?'

'Redemption.' The word was out of my mouth before I'd realised I said it.

'Come again?'

'Save Anak, and you save yourself as well.'

'Redemption is a big word, Adam.' Mahmood continued pacing. He ran his hand along the edge of the glass table. 'The moment for redemption passed a long time ago,' he said in a vague voice. 'I think the word you're looking for might be atonement. But you're clutching at straws here. When I ask you what's in it for me, I think you should speak the truth. "Nothing" is the correct answer.' Mahmood had seen through my desperate words. He was right. There would be nothing in it for him.

'But I'm still going to do it, on one condition,' he said.

I held my breath. I expected the condition would be a financial lean on the Sandika Hotel, so when he spelled it out, I felt the poignancy of his words.

'Anak must never know where the money came from. That is my condition …' He raised a finger. 'Because if he knew I was putting up the money to buy his freedom, he would rather face the firing squad.'

*　　*　　*

With Mahmood at the helm, we began the process of bribing the prosecutors and judges. I was astonished at the protocol we had to follow and the formalities we had to observe for corruption and bribery at such a high level. Mahmood, being well-connected with the upper echelons of the military power base in Jakarta, was able to secure the services of a high-powered lawyer by the name of Farbat Dingali.

'His name alone inspires fear in these lowly judges and prosecutors in Bali. Our job will not be difficult, but I must insist you accompany Dingali on all his excursions. That man may be the best lawyer in Indonesia, but I don't trust him. You will probably be invited to dinner at each of the respective houses of the judges, and at the prosecutor's too, and finally to the

Governor's mansion. You will visit them as guests and behave accordingly. Dingali will take care of the rest. The three of us will count the money together before you leave. It will be in American dollars and carried in offering baskets. I want you to keep your eyes firmly on Dingali as you travel, to make sure the money is not tampered with. Do you understand?'

* * *

Dingali arrived early the next day. Mahmoud had me meet him at the airport and booked him into the Bali Hyatt in Sanur. Mahmoud's black Mercedes with its tinted windows offered us perfect cover. The famous lawyer slipped through the airport without being noticed and into the car.

I picked up Mahmood later in the day for our first meeting at the Hyatt. We arrived undetected. Dingali had been on the phone all morning, setting prices. He insisted we pay more and have all the charges against Anak dropped before the arraignment. We were unlucky in one sense, he informed us. Both the prosecutor and the judges assigned to the case were hard-boiled nationalists, fiercely against drugs. But on the other hand, these guys were the most susceptible to bribes.

Mahmood opened his briefcase and produced the American dollars, piles of them. As I looked at them, I couldn't help thinking that my future could be sorted out with just one pile – one basket would cover Tula nicely.

I'd had Wayan weave the offering baskets to the sizes Mahmood had given me. With the money counted, Dingali and I left the Hyatt by taxi to our first rendezvous. We would begin with the prosecutor. With the arraignment date set in two days, we had little time to waste.

The prosecutor's house, set behind high walls, stood in the most affluent suburb of Denpasar, not far from the Governor's mansion. I carried a shoulder bag containing the preset amounts of money tucked into their respective baskets. The prosecutor's servants were expecting us and led us up the stairs to the house. The main lobby, where we were met by the prosecutor and his wife, was decorated in a traditional Indonesian style with carved wooden furniture and overhead fans. It smelled of furniture polish and other pleasant odours. They led us to a table laid with a traditional lunch. A servant stood behind each chair, politely offering dishes and drinks. Dingali and the prosecutor talked in Indonesian about a previous case they'd worked on. It appeared that bribery and corruption in Indonesia was conducted in a civil manner, all in the course of a day's business.

The prosecutor's wife spoke to me in perfect English with a British accent, 'Tell me about New Zealand. I've heard you have some of the most beautiful scenery in the world. I would love to visit there some day.' As I talked of the beaches and beauty of my home country, Dingali stood up, and I discreetly handed the prosecutor the basket. The two men left the room. I was so enthused by my conversation with his intelligent and charming wife that I almost forgot we were there to pay a large bribe to retrieve an innocent man from an Indonesian jail. I also realised that the prosecutor's wife knew exactly what was going on. Dingali and the prosecutor appeared in the doorway.

'Sorry to rush you, madam, but we must be on our way,' said Dingali. 'We have more meetings to attend, including one with the Governor.'

'Please give the Governor's wife my regards, and it's been a pleasure meeting you both.' The couple walked us to our taxi as if the purpose of our visit had been nothing more than a casual afternoon tea.

The next house we visited, also in the same suburb, wasn't as inviting. The issue in dispute, I gathered, seemed to be over the amount being offered. Both judges, who knew Anak, indicated clearly that they had little respect for him, and for the amount on offer they wanted to put him in the notorious Kerobokan Prison for at least a year. Dingali became red-faced at this turnaround but kept his cool. Negotiations continued on the balcony of the principal judge's house. Finally, Dingali threw up his hands in defeat. While he stayed with the judges, I took the taxi to the Bali Haj. Mahmood baulked, paced, raved and ranted, but finally opened his safe and added the necessary amount to the judge's basket. I returned to the house. The money was counted carefully. Dingali, impatient to get away from the judges, indicated we were late for a meeting with the Governor.

'How do we know they'll keep their word?' I asked the lawyer once we were out of the house.

'They will,' he said. 'Otherwise I'll have their faces splashed over the front page of *The Jakarta Post*.'

The Governor's mansion, built by the Dutch, was a stately white house of classical colonial architecture, set in rolling green lawns with a sweeping driveway leading to a pillared entrance. We were ushered around the back to the servants' quarters, where the Governor's secretary rushed out and almost snatched the basket out of my hand.

'Make the call,' Dingali said, and the secretary waved us away as if we carried a contagious disease.

'Disgusting behaviour. That man will one day get his,' said Dingali as we drove away in the taxi. Our next stop: the cells at the Polda police barracks. This time no bribe money was needed to be paid. The guards, clearly in awe of the famous lawyer in their presence, ushered us into the cell block. As usual, Anak sat meditating, but he opened his eyes when he heard the key being turned in his cell door. Dingali informed him that the police and prosecutors had dropped all the charges and that a taxi waited outside to take him home. Anak shook the lawyer's hand and looked at me suspiciously. He gathered his meditation mat and the few belongings I'd been able to bring to him and walked out.

I slipped down to Geno's cell to tell him that Anak was now free. The information had no effect on him. Slumped in a corner of his cell, he stared uncomprehendingly at me, his eyes blank and ravaged by pain. Untouched food sat rotting in its metal plate. Geno hadn't washed. Bruises and grime covered his body. A large scab on his forehead festered. His clothes were dirty and blood-stained. I worried for his mental health. His arraignment would be in forty-eight hours.

14

That evening we hosted a dinner at the Sandika to celebrate Anak's release. Wayan prepared his favourite dishes. The hotel was empty, and we had the coffee shop to ourselves.

Anak arrived in his Mercedes chariot, accompanied by Dewi and his extended family. After greeting everyone, he took offerings and incense to the four corner temples. He then returned and prayed at the temple under the banyan tree. After chanting a lengthy mantra, Anak ordered Gusti to dismantle the shrine. The cock-handler carefully removed the images of the several deities that sat up on a large flat stone. With Ketut's help they slid the stone aside. A cavity beneath the stone revealed an urn. I recognised it as a type of burial urn I'd seen in cremations. Anak picked up the urn and held it between his palms.

'This is my father,' he said. 'I felt it appropriate he should be with us tonight.' The urn containing his father's ashes sat centre table in the coffee shop. Anak, in fine form, laughed and drank and raised toasts of arrack. We ate and celebrated until the families tired and drifted off. Dewi and her family went home in the chariot with Gusti at the wheel. Wayan and Ketut went to their room, and Anak and I sat at a sea-wall table. As I gazed at the fishing boats' lights flickering on the horizon, I could feel Anak's eyes on me.

'Take me to him,' he muttered. I knew from the look he'd given me at the police cells that he knew who had given the money to buy his freedom.

Anak picked up his father's urn. We walked down our pathway and crossed the site of the temporary cockpit, the flattened earth with its rounded borders still visible. We passed the swimming pool, its underwater lights glowing turquoise in the dark, and walked across a stretch of grass to the entrance of the Bali Haj Hotel. It was late. Mahmood Bas sat in a lounge chair, sipping Cognac in the company of several guests. He turned as Anak and I entered the lobby then politely excused himself and led us to his office. Anak placed the urn on the glass-topped table.

'I have brought my father home,' he said. Mahmood was about to speak when Anak cut him off with an extended hand. 'Thank you,' he said. Mahmood crossed the room and shook Anak's hand. In place of the chilling hatred I'd seen at the cockfight in Singaraja, I saw willingness and relief on the faces of both men.

'I would like to build my father's shrine on the far side of the pool,' I heard Anak say. 'It was a favourite place of his, and where he taught me to meditate.'

'That we will do, Anak. We will build a temple in your father's honour. I'm sure Allah will approve.'

That night as I collapsed exhausted onto my bed, it didn't occur to me that I'd managed to bring Anak and Mahmood together and that as a consequence my prospects were back on track. No, my thoughts were with Geno. The brothers had bailed me out when I'd needed help. Regardless of the trouble Geno had caused us, I owed him.

*　*　*

The following morning, I bought a suit, shirt and tie at a Kuta menswear store. Geno's arraignment would be at two o'clock that afternoon. I arrived at the police barracks, and a guard led me to his cell and opened the door. With a bucket of fresh water and soap, I scrubbed him down as best I could. He didn't resist. Like a child being dressed, he let me help him put on the fresh clothes. He'd refused to speak with the court-appointed lawyer who'd come to his cell a few times, and even with me he remained sullen and silent. He pushed a comb away from my hand when I tried to put it through his matted and unruly beard. He hadn't shaved since the day he'd been arrested. This made me feel that the old Geno still lurked in there somewhere beyond his grief. The suit and tie made him look presentable, but with his shaved head and scruffy beard, he looked like a mad monk. He'd lost a lot of weight. I sat with him until the police van arrived to transport him to the Denpasar court house. I followed them on my bike.

The guards bundled the handcuffed Geno out of the vehicle and led him into the nondescript court complex in the centre of Denpasar. The old court rooms had no air conditioning, only a couple of rickety overhead fans that didn't offer any relief from the stifling heat. The courthouse had none of the trappings normally associated with such serious places, no stenographer or uniformed officials. Westerners on trial generally attracted attention from foreign newspapers or the media in Bali, but Dingali, through his contacts, had made sure our case would not be publicised.

The courthouse was a hall with back benches for the public, separated by a railing, beyond which stood a couple of chairs, one for the defendant on trial and the other for his lawyer. They faced a panel of three judges who sat behind a desk – the same judges that Dingali and I had bribed to secure Anak's release.

Geno's case came up first. His lawyer, a prim and proper young girl who looked like she was fresh out of law school, had earlier asked me why Geno refused to speak. I'd told her I didn't know. Geno looked up when he heard his name. He stood while the police guard undid his handcuffs and shuffled him forward. His lawyer took his arm and led him to the two seats beyond the railing. A long pause followed while the judges mumbled amongst themselves. They handed papers back and forth and asked the police guard, who'd been handcuffed to Geno, to come forward. A whispered conversation followed. The atmosphere seemed relaxed. Time didn't seem to be an issue. Mobile phones rang. *Warungs* delivered coffee and drinks, which could be ordered by calling out through an open window.

Then the courtroom silenced when the female judge spoke directly to Geno in English. 'Mr. Roberto, do you know where you are?'

Geno raised his head and looked around as if waking from a dream. 'Yes, I do.'

'And are you aware that the drug cocaine is illegal in Indonesia?' continued the judge.

'Yes.'

'So you must be aware of the consequences of importing such a large amount of the drug?'

'Yes.'

'Yet, you refuse legal representation. Do you intend to act on your own behalf?'

'No,' replied Geno. The short answers and Geno's unconcerned manner aggravated the judge. Her face reddened. Geno didn't wait for the next question. 'With respect, your Honour, I have nothing to say because I am guilty, and it is up to you to decide my sentence.'

'Mr. Roberto, please do not presume to tell me what I do or do not have to do!' she snapped.

On hearing this, my doubts about Geno's sanity vanished. The judge confirmed this with the outcome of her deliberation, 'Well, I can see you have all your wits about you, Mr. Roberto. We will remand you to Kerobokan Prison until a sentencing date can be determined.'

PART THREE

1

The Sandika's rat monkeys had either left the roof or returned to the banyan tree; their chatter was no longer bothersome. The leopard cat had done its job. I wanted to return it to the wild, and I thought that Joko would be the best person to ask.

At Putu's place, before I could get a word in, she wanted to know everything about Geno. I told her what I knew. Was Putu also involved in some way? Did she ask the questions to determine if she was at any risk?

Joko told me he knew about of a place in Banyuwangi National Park where animal hunters didn't go and the cat could run free without fear of being recaptured. So, carrying the leopard cat's cage, I met him at the Denpasar bus depot at the break of dawn. He was dressed in a black robe, his face hidden beneath a scarf. He carried his gunnysacks, knives and snake prongs fastened with twine. We loaded the cage onto the roof of a dusty relic of a bus and sat on wooden seats. The bus rattled its way up the western side of the island. When it stopped at townships, I climbed onto the roof to check on the cat. Its terrified demeanour worried me.

'Not long, friend, not long. You will soon be free,' I said softly.

Four hours later, we arrived at Gilimanuk and the ferry terminal. We passed under an archway covered with carvings of serpents with their tails entwined. We got onto the ferry. It was a short distance to Java. As we disembarked, taxi drivers and porters hustled around us for business. We found a taxi driver who agreed to take us where we wanted to go, some hundred kilometres along the coast. We drove through the town of Banyuwangi without stopping and meandered down the coast road, passing rice paddies and thatched huts. An hour later, we entered teak and mahogany forests as the taxi swung inland towards the National Park and the mountainous region of Pengarang. The road became a shaking juddering ordeal, which didn't bother the taxi driver or the snake man, but I could hear the cat hissing and snarling from the roof. We headed uphill to what seemed like the last outpost of civilisation: a coffee plantation on the edge of dense jungle. We untied the cage and asked our driver to wait.

In the dwindling daylight, Joko and I carried the leopard cat's cage between us. We followed a rocky uphill trail covered in dangling vines and tropical undergrowth. The trail led us out onto a grassy plateau. A group of monkeys scattered into the trees and a wild peacock watched us, its tail flared.

We placed the cage in the centre of the plateau then removed the cloth covering it. We fed the leopard cat a little meat. It paced and sniffed the air, eyes searching. Its nostrils twitched furiously, its ears flicked and its eyes darted. The animal's dulled instincts had come alive in the new surroundings. Joko limped to the cage. The cat froze. It hissed, eyes pinned on him. The ridge of fur down its back bristled. The snake man flicked the latch and swung the cage door open. The cat didn't move. It stared at the open door. Then it bolted to the forest's edge so fast that its yellow and black markings were no more than a blur against the green of the plateau. The peacock flew squawking to a high branch. Birds fluttered and rearranged themselves. The leopard cat stopped for a brief instant at the edge of the forest and looked back at us, as if unable to grasp its good fortune, then disappeared.

* * *

I continued to feed the orangutans. I'd managed to detox them over a very short period, and they had taken it well. They were off the arrack, and I had them down to two milligrams of Valium each. I gave them pure water in the arrack bottles with the tablets crushed and stirred in.

Both beasts would make an incredible racket when I arrived. They were humorous and intelligent, and I'd come to like them. Their black coats shone, and their eyes were expressive and clear. I could tell that they were clearly starving for affection by the way they held their paws out through the grill, indicating that I should approach them. I wasn't keen to do so. 'She'll be back soon,' I mumbled as I pushed the copious amounts of fruit they now ate into their cage.

*   *   *

Thoughts of Geno invaded my mind like some kind of virus there was no cure for. I kept seeing an image of him standing on the dock, asking to be shot. The depth of his grief for Paolo had touched me. I was acutely aware that I owed him – but more than that the truth of it was, and I hated to admit it, that I cared about him. A few weeks after his arraignment, the court-appointed lawyer called and asked to meet. I drove to her office in Denpasar.

She sat behind her desk, wearing a starched white blouse, her black hair pulled back into a bun. 'The prosecutor is asking for the death penalty,' she said as if reading from a script, 'and because Mr. Roberto shows no remorse for his crime, my guess is he'll probably get it. That means he will be shot by a firing squad once his mandatory appeals have run their course. A slow process that could take up to eight years, during which time Mr. Roberto will remain incarcerated. Is there any way we can find sufficient funds to pay off the prosecutor to reduce the sentence to life?' she asked without looking at me.

'I'll talk to him,' I said.

I drove directly to Kerobokan Prison. I'd driven past the building many times but never knew what it was until someone told me. The prison stood on the corner of Jalan Tangkuban

Perahu and the main road, between Legian and Semeniak. It was a stone's throw from Madame Putu's and from the main road it looked like a cheap pension. Nothing indicated it was a prison. A rice paddy surrounded most of the building and a *warung*, manned by inmates, was by the entrance way, catering to visitors. There were guard towers out of sight at the rear of the building. I was allowed inside for a bribe of two thousand rupiah. The guard led me into what I came to know as the 'blue room' and asked me if I would like to hire a mat for another thousand rupiah. As there were no chairs or tables in the large crowded room and the concrete floor was dirty, the only option I had was to hire the mat. I waited for the next bribe request, and it came immediately. The guard told me that Geno was a remand prisoner and was allowed visits only from family and I would have to pay a fee if I wanted to meet him. But the guard suggested I take a concession of ten visits, which I could have for only twenty thousand rupiah, and with that I could have a free mat as well.

A list of rules posted at the front door of the blue room stated that visits must last only fifteen minutes, but nobody seemed to take any notice. I could tell visitors had been there for hours. Indonesians and foreigners filled the room. I couldn't tell the prisoners apart from the visitors. A couple of guards stood around. A kiosk in a corner sold Fanta, *nasi goreng* and iced tea. Several couples had claimed the far wall, and my eyes widened in surprise as I saw a young Indo girl straddle her foreign boyfriend; fully clothed, she rocked back and forth on his lap slowly, her hand braced on his shoulders. Other couples fondled each other, their hands groping under clothes. A young girl I recognised from Madame Putu's was masturbating her client under a sarong. In another area, families sat in circles around plates of food, eating, taking no notice of what was happening against the far wall. A prisoner moved amidst the crowd, selling plastic-wrapped portions of sweet sticky rice. Another offered to sit next to me with a palm frond fan to keep me cool. 'Only five hundred rupiah,' he insisted.

I brushed him off as I found a spot on the bare concrete to spread my mat.

As Geno was hustled into the room by a guard, his eyes scanned the area and settled on me. A smile spread across his face, and he rushed towards me and pumped my hand. 'Man, what took you so long? I been waiting!' He grinned as he sat next to me on the mat.

'Sorry, Geno. You know, I've been kind of busy.'

'Hey, forget about it. You here now. That's the main thing.'

Geno's hair had grown. His clean clothes and close shave told me that the horrendous grief he'd gone through at the Polda had become manageable.

'I'm okay, man. I got a guard to get money in from Brazil. Fucker took twenty-five percent. You know I'm locked up all day but I can buy my way out for a couple of hours a day. I'm exercising, man, every day.'

'I talked to your lawyer. She wants money to reduce your sentence.'

'Fuck her, man! I don't need no reduction.' Geno pulled me in close and whispered, 'Listen up and listen good. Next time you come I'm gonna give you something. I want to make you a drawing.' I remained silent. The debt of twenty thousand dollars I owed Geno hung in the air between us. 'Hey chill out, man, nothing illegal okay. And go to Putu and tell her to get her cute little ass in here to see me. Okay? And find my guitar and bring it with you next time.'

We bought food and drinks and shared a meal. I told him about all the changes happening at the Sandika, including the cockfight that on account of Geno's bust had saved the hotel. At this, Geno roared with laughter and said, 'Hey, man, at least I did some good thing, eh?' I told him about the new friendship between Anak and Mahmood. He showed particular interest in whether we were continuing the diving tours and questioned me at length about what equipment Satchimoto had left behind.

'Do you think Satchimoto had anything to do with Paolo's death?'

'Think? What the fuck you talking, man? Satchimoto murder Paolo, no question about it.' The dark look on Geno's face made me quickly change the subject.

'Geno, I want to know this ... Why did you carry the cocaine yourself? It doesn't make any sense.'

'Ah, I knew you gonna ask me that, man,' he said. 'Those two *putana*. Listen, I tell you. I go to Rio. I pick up two couriers, beautiful Copacabana beach girls, just perfect. I buy tickets, fix them up with five kilo each and we fly Rio, Paris in transit, Singapore. Then between Singapore and Jakarta, one girl get sick. She look so bad, man. Sweating, vomiting, she go unconscious. All the flight staff, they hanging around us, and I got my five kilos strapped to her thighs. I start to shit myself, everything going wrong. I push her into the toilet and take the dope off her. Then the other girl she panic. She go into the toilet and take off her dope. I'm there with ten kilos of cocaine in a shoulder bag. Anyway, the girl, she get more and more sick. Scary stuff, man. I thought she gonna die. The doctor, he come to us when the plane stop in Jakarta. She must go to hospital now, he tell us. She has some kind of blood clot. Well, of course, the other girl go with her. I can't do nothing, man. I get back on the flight to Bali with ten kilos of coke in my bag. No choice, man. What I gonna do? So I know I gonna bin it. I go into the toilet, those fucking airplane toilets, they so fucking small. I start to unwrap the coke, 'cause I wrap it up good in Rio. It stink of acetone, then someone knocking on the door outside the toilet, then the fucking air-hostess saying, "Can you please vacate the toilet?" Fuck! So I stuff all the coke in my bag and take my seat. Man, what's with these Indonesians, they shit and piss every two minutes. There's a queue for the toilet, and I can't get back in. We now nearly at Bali. At last, I get into the toilet again, but I see I can't put ten kilos down that tiny little shitter. So I strap the dope to my gut and go myself. Fucking crazy, man. I know that now.' Geno stopped for a moment, a distant look in his eyes. 'Craziest thing I ever do in my life. Anyway, I knew Satchimoto gonna be there waiting and if there was any shit gonna happen with Customs, he pay the man. I get off the plane and I do passport okay. I walk up to the Customs guy. I'm sweating and shitting myself. I never carry dope before. You know the airport. You can see the outside from the Customs area. I see Satchimoto standing there, and he looking at me, and I start to feel safe. Then the Customs guy, he don't even look at my bag. Two cops come from behind and they grab me. They take me to a room and find everything. I'm fucked. I tell them to go get the little Japanese guy outside, that he pay whatever they want. They walk me out but Satchimoto was gone, man, gone. He could have saved my ass but he fucked off to save his own ass. You know that motherfucker is a clever prick. He murder Paolo because he think Paolo gonna talk.'

'You don't think he told the Customs here in Bali?' I asked.

'Nah, he didn't know I was carrying.'

'Maybe the two girls in Jakarta then? It seems strange that the two cops came up from behind.'

'Yeah, I'm thinking that too. Maybe one of them have a little coke on them … You know, they both coke-heads so they grass me up to get their ass off the hook. Those *putana*!'

'So what are we going to do about your case?'

'Nothing, man. Just come tomorrow and leave everything to me. Go now to Putu but tell her nothing about what you doing. Just tell her to come here, okay?'

I rolled up the mat and promised Geno I'd be back the next day. I passed the copulating couples and the eating families, and walked out of Kerobokan Prison, wishing that I'd never come. Here I was again, caught up in Geno's shit.

Outside the doorway of her brothel, Putu listened to my request suspiciously. She nodded and said she'd go. I asked her to give my regards to Joko.

Janna was ready to go home. Dewi was adamant that she stay longer, but Anak told me that the bloodstone cure was now complete. The alcohol had left her, and she was healed. I found her in her room, sitting on the bed. She turned away from me as I came near. Her hair covered her face. When I put my hand on her shoulder, she looked up at me, her face wet with tears.

'I don't know anymore. Don't know what is happening to me. Everything has changed, everything.' I sat with her and waited. I held Janna until she was calm.

'I feel silly,' she said. 'Everything was fine. I was waiting for you, excited about going home, and then ... I wasn't sure anymore, wasn't sure if I could do this.'

'Hey, I'm with you. I'm here.'

'Are you?'

'Yes.'

'Look at me. I'm a freak. I'm the drunk ape woman ... You are making a mistake. I'm not whom you think I am.'

Outside, a peacock strutted across the compound and it stopped beneath the banyan tree, crowing, spreading its tail feathers. The caged fighting birds set up a racket. I looked back at Janna. Her face was puffed a little, her eyes still wet but soft and searching. 'Adam?' she asked.

I had to find words but nothing came. 'Maybe *I'm* not who you think I am,' I said under my breath.

Anak and Dewi were waiting for us in the compound. Anak pulled Janna aside and said something that made her smile. The women embraced, with Dewi saying that she would visit Janna the following day.

We drove down the bush track to her compound. Inside, Janna ran straight to the cage. The apes were quiet. She took the key and unlocked the door. The orangutans smothered her. She mumbled a few endearments in Croatian, cuddled and petted them. They responded, gently petting and stroking her face, clucking. They took her hand and led her to their platform. She sat with them. One ape inspected her hair as if looking for nits, while the other laid its head on her lap and gazed up at her. I quietly entered the cage and placed a basket of fruit beside them.

'Come, Adam, sit with us,' she said absently. I wasn't ready. I left the cage. Janna followed, pulling herself away from the orangutans and locking the cage on the way out.

'How do you feel about that?' I asked, pointing to the lock and chain.

'It's okay, but I want to let them out into the compound at night. My boys need to have some space. We will be safe.' She stopped and looked back at her apes, 'I have treated them so badly. I am so ashamed … Thank you, Adam. I love them so much but I'm wondering if this is … Well, I'll think about that later. Can we go for a walk on the beach?' she asked. 'There is a small *warung* further down that makes really good food.'

The sea was calm on a low tide. We walked near the water's edge on a wide expanse of ruffled sand. Eddies of trapped seawater shone like silver. Small sea birds with stilt-like legs ran before us then took flight when we got close. Janna, absorbed in her surroundings, pointed out colours or stopped to admire the shape of a sea shell. The sun shadowed her, making her movements an elegant silhouette. Tinted amber clouds floated on the horizon and above them was a blaze of turquoise-blue. The evening sun was about to perform its magic. Janna walked up to me and ran her fingers over my face, then looked at me oddly.

'What's up?'

'Nothing, just making sure.' She handed me two little identical shells, crab shells that had been glazed by the sea to a delicate pink. 'Take one,' she said as she folded the other in her hand.

2.

I was back at the prison. The same guard at the gate held up two fingers to indicate I'd used my second visit and handed me a mat. I found a quiet spot and looked around. More couples canoodled in a secluded corner. Geno arrived covered in sweat, his muscles pumped, his face bright with a healthy glow.

'Hey, man, I been running. I do hundred press-ups and sit-ups every day.'

'You're looking good.'

'Yeah, and the thing you gonna get for me, you can only get in Denpasar.' Geno pulled out four little bamboo sticks of varying sizes from his pocket. 'Now, what you do is … You gonna find the exact centre of each stick and make a circle with it on a piece of paper, like a compass. These are the sizes, okay? Make sure you got it right. Don't fuck it up.'

I nodded. I knew I had no choice.

'Then you go to Denpasar to a truck supply store. You know, one of those places that sell all the parts for the cars and trucks.' I told him that I'd seen such places. 'Okay, now you buy me four pieces of rubber hose. You know, that really thick stuff used for water pipes in the motors. Like really thick, man, this thick,' Geno said, indicating the size with his fingers and thumb, 'and they must be straight, and about seven or eight centimetres each.'

'What's this for?'

'Don't ask, man. And where's that little Putu?'

'I went to her place and told her you wanted to meet her.'

'Okay, I know what she want.' Geno pulled me in close and whispered an amount in my ear.

'You sure?'

'Course I'm fucking sure. Go tell her, okay?'

I met Putu at the brothel again. She acknowledged the amount and told me she'd visit Geno that day. Then I drove straight to Denpasar, to the largest car-parts supplier I could find. The salesman gave me a compass to make measurements from the sticks. Then he offered me a selection of rubber engine-hoses with the diameter Geno wanted. The transaction lasted less than thirty minutes. Then, with the remainder of the money, I bought a cheap guitar at the local music shop. Back at the Sandika, I wondered what the hoses were for as I wrapped them in a sarong, keeping them ready for Geno.

* * *

That evening, Janna and I met at a jazz bar in Nusa Dua. I parked my motorbike and followed the sound of a piano to a large pagoda by the beach. The notes of a jazz ballad flowed with the sound of the surf. The pianist had his head lowered as his fingers danced on the keys. An audience of colourful sun-baked tourists drank cocktails at rattan tables. The open-sided bar led out onto the beach: it was the same beach where Geno and Paolo had taught me to surf an eternity ago.

Janna sat alone at a table, her expression serene and enraptured, lost in the music. She wore a black spaghetti-strapped dress, and her hair was teased up into a top knot and held together by a Japanese comb. I paused for a moment to admire her: the confident and proud way she held herself, the strong line of her neck, the soft curve of her throat, and the incredibly smooth texture of her skin.

The ballad ended to a smattering of applause. Janna filled her glass from a Perrier bottle, caught sight of me and waved me over. 'Did you hear that last piece? It was sublime.'

'Just the last verse,' I said. We sat looking at each other, hesitant and uncertain, each waiting for the other to speak. The waiter came and left. A group of tourists crowded the bar, calling for drinks. The pianist was signing CDs and the bar staff were clearing tables.

'Shall we walk for a bit?' asked Janna. 'We can come back for the next set.'

The Nusa Dua sands had been carefully raked, the beach chairs placed in perfect order and the palm trees trimmed. Behind us, the hotels were lit up like Christmas trees. This was an upmarket tourist area, so different from where the Sandika was. It made me feel a little uncomfortable. I much preferred the wild surf and sweeping sands of Kuta Beach.

'You look amazing,' I said as we stopped by the water's edge. Janna turned to face me. She smiled and took a deep breath.

'You know, I *feel* amazing. No, wait, that didn't sound right.' She shifted on her feet and dug her toes into the sand. 'What I mean is … Being alive feels amazing. I've missed out on so much. Like music, for example.' She waved her hand back towards the bar. 'I played the piano when I was a teenager and loved it. I think I'm going to take it up again.' She looked wistful for a moment but then her lightness returned. 'Adam, thank you for everything. For helping me get my life back. But I want you to know that I'm okay now.'

'What do you mean?'

She tilted her head and looked at me quizzically, then she said in a thoughtful voice, 'What I mean is … I don't want you to be here because you think you are saving me. Is that the right word? Well, anyway, I'm okay now, and I want you to be here because *you* want to be here, with me.' She raised her arms and fixed her comb. I understood what she meant. My heart pounded as I tried to find the right words. I'd never seen myself as her saviour, and I couldn't find a way to tell her how I really felt.

Here was my chance, my moment, but all I could say was, 'This is where I want to be.'

Anak and Mahmood Bas had plans for a joint venture, and I was often asked to sit in on their meetings. Mahmood paid the mortgage on Sandika Hotel in return for some Bali-Haj-style units that would be erected along one side of our property. Mahmood spared no expense when it came to the building of Anak's father's shrine: carved granite pillars led into a walk-in recess; the urn and the flat stone sat in the centre, surrounded by replicas of gods from Anak's temple of origin. The completed structure complemented the Bali Haj grounds.

But what really brought the two men together was their passion for cockfighting. Anak had the best eye for picking birds, while Mahmood had the right business acumen to make the betting work. They travelled together around Java looking for champion cockerels. Anak made the selections, and once back in Bali, with Mahmood's bush bankers in place, they couldn't lose. When they arrived at the cockfighting tournaments, very few people were aware they were cohorts. The punters assumed the old Hindu-Muslim rivalry remained in place.

The removal of the Sandika's tropical wilderness duly began. Workers hacked with machetes, so within a couple of days we could walk from our coffee shop straight into the Bali Haj. Although I missed the garden, the overall effect was pleasing. The temples were given an upgrade as well, but the mango tree and a few other ornamental shrubs were left in place.

* * *

One evening, Mahmood asked me to dine with him. I shaved and showered, ironed my best shirt, dug out a pair of new shoes and walked down the pathway to the back entrance of the Bali Haj. I was early, and a waiter escorted me to a plush leather couch with a view of the front entrance: a sweeping driveway lined with queen palms leading up to a set of marble steps with Romanesque pillars. The beautifully carved arched doorways looked like they belonged at a Raja's palace. Mahmood certainly had good taste, I had to admit.

'Adam, would you like to come with me and view the kitchen? Anak has told me of your previous restaurant,' he said as he joined me. I followed him to a large stainless-steel fitted kitchen, impeccably clean and modern.

'It cost me a fortune,' he said. 'I had a Swiss chef come in as consultant. He designed the thing. But the point of a kitchen is to produce good food, no? And in Bali, as you know, some of the best food can be eaten at a roadside stall or in one of those *warungs*.'

He then led me to our table. We continued our conversation over a glass of wine. 'Let me get to the point,' Mahmood said. 'I want you to take over my restaurant and make it into something. Our food is passable but it doesn't have a point of difference over the other hotels. My head chef tries hard but he needs direction.' I looked at the menu. He was right. It was all fairly standard fare.

'What do you have in mind? Given that we are in Bali and most tourists would expect to eat local flavours,' I asked him.

'Exactly, that *is* what I have in mind: New Asian with a European style presentation. Artistically presented traditional dishes with a modern flair ... Creative use of local spices and fruits, making in-house desserts. Do you get where I'm going with this?'

'Yes.'

'I have to confess that I sent a spy to your little coffee shop once to have him sample some of your dishes. I know why our Japanese prefer your restaurant to ours. I want that kind of food here, only better. You will have complete managerial control, and as many staff at your disposal as you need, both front-of-house and kitchen.'

I forced myself to look calm and only vaguely interested in

the offer although my heart was beating quickly. Here at last was something big. 'If I do decide to do this, I guess you're thinking of paying me a salary?' I asked.

'Yes, I have something in mind.'

'Mahmood, I can turn this place around. It's a huge undertaking, but I'm confident I can do it. However I need it to be worth my while. I don't want a salary.'

His hand came up and smoothed his moustache. A waiter approached us, and he waved him away. 'What do you want?'

'Twenty-five percent of the restaurant's profits.'

'That is preposterous!'

'Not if your profit is doubled.'

He looked at the sea. 'Strange how things turn out, isn't it? Adam, I swear, when you asked me to bail out Anak, I never imagined it would come to this.' He waved his hand at the view then spoke sharply, 'Twenty percent and a two-month trial period.'

'Done.'

'Start tomorrow?'

'I'll be here.'

'And before you start, see my clerk for an advance. You'll need suitable clothes, and I'll be deducting that off your twenty percent.'

*　*　*

Now, with a new job and good prospects, I felt comfortable about calling Grace. I was back on track and would be able to start paying my debts. But before I could make the call, Wayan called me from the office and handed me the receiver. I almost dropped it when I recognised the voice.

'Adam. Don't hang up. I know it's you. If you hang up, I'm calling the police.' Elisabeth's voice crackled through the telephone line.

'Adam, say something.'

'How did you know I was here?'

'I didn't. Grace told me and gave me the number. She's pregnant, Adam.'

'Whoa, come again.'

'You heard.'

'When? How?'

'And she's keeping the baby. She's left Steven, who was a complete egg. She's living with me. A couple of nights ago she had a sort of meltdown. She'd tried calling you but couldn't get through. I think that set it off. She told me everything.'

There was a muffled sound. I cursed myself for not calling earlier.

'Damn you, Adam. You don't know what I've been through because of you. David's left me, and those goons have only recently stopped coming around, and now our daughter's having a baby. And while all this is going on, you're lounging around on a beach in Bali. You have to come back.'

'I can't come back with nothing. That's why I'm staying here. I'm trying to get money together …'

'I'm going to cut this short,' she said. 'Here's what I've decided: either you give yourself up, or I'm going to turn you in. Is that clear?' The phone went dead. Typical Elisabeth, hanging up to avoid a reasonable discussion.

Grace was pregnant. I needed time to process that. I leaned back in the chair and closed my eyes. My little girl was going to be a mother. It just didn't feel right. I desperately wanted to talk to her. Would Elisabeth really give me up or was that just an empty threat? Either way, it hollowed my stomach. A group of guests were playing volleyball in the pool. I could hear their splashes and laughter, and smell their suntan lotion. A local woman arrived by the pool with a basket of fruit on her head. I watched them haggle over the price of a pineapple.

In an odd way, I was pleased that Grace was with her mother.

I'd always felt that I was the cause of their strained relationship. David was gone, and clearly Grace and Elisabeth were talking to each other. I picked up the phone and called Grace. She answered on the second ring.

'I was going nuts with worry. I thought something had happened to you,' she blurted.

'I hear I'm going to be a grandfather?' I said, trying to sound casual.

'Hah! Yes, you are, but to be a grandfather you need to be here.'

'I know.'

'Why didn't you call me, Dad?

'A lot of stuff happened here, things I can't talk about. I didn't want to worry you but it's all turned out alright, and I've just landed a big job running a kitchen. This is the turning point, sweetheart. I know it.' I regretted not confiding in my daughter, but then what could I tell her? That I was looking after a Brazilian drug dealer who'd lent me the money to pay Tula and that he's in prison now? Or that I've been busy bribing public officials and detoxing a couple of gay alcoholic orangutans?

'And you're going to be the youngest grandad ever,' she said. Clearly she didn't want to hear more excuses.

'How are you feeling about having the baby?'

'It's the best, Dad. I can't wait. We're going to be a family, even if it's just me and the baby.'

'You're going to make a great mum.'

'Thanks.'

'And what's up with your mum? Is she serious?'

'Yeah, sorry, you were right. I should have kept my mouth shut.'

'Think she'll go through with it?' The thought of being arrested and deported home broke was unbearable. Elizabeth knew exactly where I was. It would take the immigration police only minutes to track me down.

'Don't know. You never know with Mum, and you're not her most favourite person. But if she does drop you in it, I'll call and let you know, okay?

'How far along, are you?'

'About three. I can just feel a little bump on my belly.'

'You okay for money?'

'Yeah, I'm still at Pierre's and I'll have maternity leave when the time comes.'

'Take it easy, sweetheart. I'll call soon. And, hey, this is a bit of a shock, but I'm happy for you.'

'I knew you would be. Love you, Dad.'

* * *

I set out for Kerobokan with the four rubber engine hoses and guitar slung across my back. The gate guard showed no interest in the hoses at all but wanted a substantial amount of cash to allow the guitar in. When I told him that what he was asking for was more than what I'd paid for the guitar itself, he lowered the price. Geno came into the blue room, dripping sweat, fresh from training. He checked out the rubber hoses, a grin spreading across his face.

'Exactly, man, exactly.'

'Did Putu come?' I asked as Geno rewrapped the hoses.

'Yeah, she come, man.'

I was too tired with thoughts about home to press him for any information on what he intended to do with the hoses.

* * *

The heron's call woke me. I spent a few minutes on the balcony, watching the surf and thinking of Grace. Then I showered and dressed myself in a white linen shirt and trousers. In the coffee shop, Wayan had my breakfast ready, and we ran over the previous day's business. I was still the Sandika's manager although Wayan and Ketut took care of most of its running. We had become the overflow for the Bali Haj. When they were full, their guests came to us. I looked at the Sandika's gate, expecting to see the immigration police arrive at any moment. Wayan looked at me strangely; she sensed that something was up.

It was a good day in the Bali Haj kitchen. I made a lot of headway on the new menu. The staff were eager and responsive. I threw myself into work and enjoyed being back at the helm of a serious operation, even if it might all be over soon.

In the evening, I stood at the sea wall. Fruit bats swooped by me like old friends. I liked to imagine they were thanking me for getting the rat monkeys out of the banyan tree. On the soft sand below the wall, a few guests were playing a game of volleyball – foreign surfers on one side, Bali beach-hustlers on the other – the rubber ball smacking loudly against their fists, the players giving out loud hollers and secret signs. A couple of surfers were catching the last waves on the sea, visible only by the white trails they left behind in their wake. Wayan sidled up and handed me a Long Island iced tea. She stopped to watch the sunset.

'You okay, Adam?'

'Yeah.'

'You not leaving us?'

'Not if I don't have to.'

Wayan sighed; she wasn't satisfied with my answer.

'Beautiful sunset,' I said.

'Of course. The gods like to play with colours.'

* * *

Janna had prepared a candlelit dinner for us on her veranda. Her place smelled of jasmine and frangipani blossoms. Beyond her compound, a local gamelan orchestra was practising, its bell chimes weaving a counterpoint to the night noises. She'd been decorating her home. Her excitement overflowed as she showed me everything she'd bought: a hand painted lamp, a coffee table, a framed batik design. Her smile turned to concern as she picked up on my mood.

'Is everything alright?' she asked. 'Come and sit down.'

'Sort of, I think. You know I'm just feeling a lot of pressure. I've got this Geno thing and …'

'Why do you bother with that guy? He's given you nothing but a headache,' she said, moving around the table and arranging the food with a pair of chopsticks.

'And now my daughter tells me she's pregnant, and my ex-wife is threatening to tell the police about where I am.'

'Oh no, Adam.' Her eyes clouded a little. Silence wrapped itself around us. Then her breathing quickened, and she spoke in a rush of words. 'But wait, you could stay here. Nobody would find you here.' She pushed the food aside and moved onto my lap. I felt her hands against my neck, and the warmth of her breath as her lips met mine. There was a strangeness in our embrace, as if we had been apart for a long time and only just found each other. We kissed tentatively and she whispered lovingly in her own tongue. Then her coy hesitancy gave way to an overwhelming passion.

We fell onto the bed clutching and grasping, tearing at each other's clothes. She kissed my neck as she pulled down my trousers. Her sarong fell away. Her skin felt exquisitely soft as she moved onto me. I was inside her. We stayed like that until our small waves of movement became an ocean. After an infinite moment, she gave a prolonged shudder and collapsed beside me, panting hot breath against my ear, sweat beading on her brow. Too exhausted to move, we held each other in a deep, warm embrace, listening to the pounding surf and the rustling of palms.

I awoke to the chattering of apes. Shards of morning sun stabbed into the room. The air carried a brisk coolness. Sheets and pillows were thrown about the room, clothes lay strewn where they had fallen. We'd hardly slept; it was as if we had tried to squeeze a lifetime of lovemaking into one night. I looked at my watch. I was late for work. As I made to get up, I heard her behind me. Then her arms were around my neck.

'Work can do without you,' she said, running her fingers through my hair. Then she slid around and laid her head on my lap. There were delicate violet shadows around her eyes. Her hair cascaded in an unruly tangle to her breasts, and her eyes held a glint of mischief.

'This morning I am going to kidnap you,' she whispered.

I admired the length of her, the lift of her breasts, the cant of her thighs. Janna was a perfectly beautiful woman. It was written in the curve of her smile and in the way she moved and spoke her words that she was ready to embrace her future and that she wanted to take back everything life had denied her. And in that moment, I knew that our lives were woven together. I knew without any doubt that I loved her.

3

Geno walked into the waiting room full of enthusiasm. 'I feel like an athlete again. I pay more now and get to stay out three hours, running, stretching, doing push-ups and sit-ups. This what I do when I'm young and training for the Olympics, only then I do eight hours every day. Man, you can get anything in here: coke, weed, speed and smack. The guards bring it in, good prices too. I touch nothing, man, nothing. Look what shit that stuff do to my life! I finished with all that. Fuck that shit, man.'

'Has your lawyer been?'

'Yeah, she come, but I tell her to leave. She say I'm looking good, and I tell her I want to give the firing squad a good target, you know, a handsome motherfucker to shoot at.' Geno's laugh echoed through the blue room.

As I'd finished my concession of twenty visits, the guard had his hand out when I arrived the following day. Madame Putu passed me. She spoke harshly to the guard, and from then on I never had to pay another entry bribe. Putu asked about business at the Sandika and if there was any possibility of returning to our previous arrangement. I told her that most of our guests were not Japanese anymore and that she would have to approach Mahmood Bas regarding this. She frowned on hearing the Muslim's name and sashayed off.

'Putu, man, she all about money that one. Forget about it,' said Geno when I told him about our encounter. 'My little lawyer come today. Told me they set a date for sentencing. It is one month from now. For sure I get the firing squad. And the appeals could drag on for years, so I gonna be here a long time, my friend. I hope you don't get sick of visiting?'

I choked back words. What was he trying to say? That the debt between us didn't exist? I was beginning to get a glimpse of how Geno's mind worked.

'Okay, now listen up. Go to Putu's place. She gonna give you a box of money, American dollars. You take it and hide it in your room at the Sandika, and hide it good, man. It's a shit load, okay.'

Putu was expecting me. She led me to her room and opened a package containing one hundred thousand dollars, all in hundred-dollar notes.

'We're going to count this together so there can be no misunderstanding about the amount, okay?' Her lips moved as she counted. Putu could count money faster than a bank teller. She handed me the first bundle of ten thousand, and I began sorting piles of money. The money smelled slightly rancid. I rode back to the Sandika with the money in a shopping bag. I took a roll of cling wrap from the kitchen, rolled the bundle in plastic, climbed up the wall of my room and stuffed the package deep into the lady-grass roof.

* * *

I returned from a hectic lunch service. The weather was bad and our guests had chosen to stay in. Our boat tours had been cancelled on account of an onshore wind creating huge waves; raging walls of water pounded over the reef, so large that even the most accomplished board rider wouldn't attempt them. I stood at the sea wall and watched these monster waves break with uncanny regularity. The coffee shop was empty as the wind made it uncomfortable to sit there. Wayan and Ketut were at a ceremony, and the rest of the staff had the day off. It was early afternoon. I was leaving to see Janna when a motorbike pulled into the carpark. I recognised the dark flashing eyes of Putu through the visor of her full-facial helmet.

'Adam,' she said, looking around to see if anyone had seen her. 'I have a message from Geno.' I asked her to come inside, but she shook her head. 'You know the rice paddy behind the rear prison-wall, the one right under the guard tower?' she said.

'Yes.'

'Geno wants you to be there at exactly two o'clock.' She handed me a watch and told me to use it. 'Like I said, two o'clock. It has to be to the second, and take this.' She gave me a motorbike helmet with a pull-down tinted visor, similar to the one she wore. 'Clip it on your passenger seat and ...'

'Putu, what's going on?'

'I don't know. Really, I don't, but my guess is Geno wants you to pick up someone, and I think it has something to do with his release. You probably need to go pay someone, and Geno doesn't trust the person who's carrying the money. But that's just a guess.' Putu's cynical look suggested Geno didn't trust her either. It sounded plausible. I've been through this process before when we secured Anak's release. I was glad that Geno finally had a plan. He was going to buy back his life through the only way that worked in Bali, and hopefully this would be the last favour I would have to do for him. With Geno released, our debt would be cancelled. I guessed we would be going to the appeals prosecutor, and I would be transporting a prison guard who wouldn't want to be seen. Putu raised her chin to me then swung her motorbike out of the carpark. I attached the helmet to the passenger seat of my bike. The wind came in strong swirls and gusts, rustling the lady-grass roof.

At one forty-five, I drove to the prison as instructed and waited for a few minutes at a *warung*, watching the second hand on the watch I carried. At the rice paddy, I kept my motor running and unclipped the helmet to hand it to whoever would be arriving. I looked up at the guard tower: a uniformed guard sat inside, cradling an automatic rifle and watching television. I could hear the sounds of the actors' voices and the dramatic music that accompanied the local soap operas. A farmer rode towards me on a bicycle. He wore a straw hat and carried a load of freshly harvested grass on his carry tray and handlebars. He made eye contact, nodded and rode past me. Something huge almost knocked me off my bike suddenly. It shot past my face like a flying trapeze artist and landed in the rice paddy, causing such a thud and splash that the ground moved beneath my bike and I was showered with a fine spray of mud. Then a figure, covered in grey paddy mud, like some apparition from a horror movie, emerged from the shallow water beside me. A hand went up and wiped the mud from the face. I knew the grin. It was Geno. I shuddered. Panic gripped me. I looked up to see that the guard was still absorbed in his television. I looked all around. Nobody had seen us. There was no one else there except for the disappearing farmer who couldn't have seen Geno. Before I could open my mouth, he was on the passenger seat, pulling on his helmet. 'Go man! Drive!' he said. I hesitated, shocked into stillness. 'For fuck's sake, go!' hissed Geno. We drove away from the prison towards the main road.

'Back streets, man, take the alleys. You know the way. And don't go too fast.'

'Where are we going?'

'To the beach by your hotel, man. I need to pick up my money. And don't worry, I got a plan – that was best jump I ever make,' he said in an ecstatic voice. 'I tell you, man, if I'd made that jump in the Olympics I woulda got gold.'

'You pole vaulted out of the prison?'

'Exactly, man, exactly.'

'How many people saw you?' I asked in panic. I'd almost slowed the motorbike to a halt.

'Keep driving, man. Not one of those motherfuckers saw me. I jump from behind the cell block. The only thing I left there is a piece of bamboo. They won't know I'm gone until tomorrow, while taking head-count. Now, for fuck's sake, drive, man, drive.'

'I can't take you to the hotel.'

'Take me to Jimmy the Fish's hut, and go get my money and bring it to me.'

I drove around the airport road, figuring that would be the least likely route to run into anyone we knew. The fierce onshore wind caused people to keep their heads down. I pulled up at the end of a track leading to Jimmy's hut. The place was abandoned, as were several other fishermen's huts in the dunes, all of them vacant on account of the weather, their boats pulled high above the waterline. I pushed my bike in behind some scrub and walked with Geno.

'I'm fucking free, man. I did it. Every day I was training, man, to jump straight over the wall.' Geno made a motion with his hand like a bird taking flight. 'Like a fucking bird, man, like a fucking Olympic bird.' When we entered the hut, his euphoric mood turned serious.

'Okay, so far so good, but I have to get off this island quick. Now go get me the money and come back, like you taking a walk along the beach, okay? Then I tell you what we gonna do next.'

'Geno, I can't help anymore. I can't do this. You have to get that into your head. I have my job, my family, and I can't be involved in this shit. Please, man, let me out of this.'

'Okay, okay, I understand.' Geno flashed me a twisted smile as his green eyes zeroed in on mine. 'Listen up, man, this is it. This is payback time, so do this small little thing for me, and you done, Adam. Do this, and you don't owe me no more.' I could still smell the rice paddy mud on him.

'Now just get my money.'

I drove back to the still-empty Sandika. In my room, I dug out Geno's money, tossed it into a beach bag, changed into shorts and a T-shirt and walked along the wind-torn beach, sand whipping my eyes. I found him huddled in a corner of the hut. He'd washed himself off and looked clean. He set his green eyes on mine once again and said, 'Adam, man, now here comes the next thing you must do for me. If you help me, I live, man. If you don't help me, I die by firing squad. You know that, right? The only way off this island is by boat, your boat. I got it figured. You know the jerrycans we use when we go out, yeah? I gonna need sixteen of them, full of gas and inside the boat. I gonna need Paolo's and my surfboards, and I also need you.'

'What? I told you, I'm out.'

'You owe me, man. You gotta take me over the reef.'

I yelled above the roaring wind, pointing at the reef, 'Look! Look at the size of those fucking waves! Have you ever seen them that big?'

'Yeah, they big. I been looking at them, looking hard, and here's what I figure. We stack the jerrycans up front, to give us weight in the bow. We don't try to go over the wave, we go through it. We gonna come out the other side, trust me, man.'

'And another thing, everybody will see us,' I added, trying to think of anything I could to convince him of the madness he was suggesting.

'I thought of that too, you know. We can get those straw hats that the local fishermen wear, the ones they tie on with white cloth. We gonna be fishermen going out for the night. Also we leave just at sunset, when it is hard to see and the waves are smaller. With this wind, nobody gonna be on the beach anyway.'

'So you take the boat. What about me?'

'Ah, that one easy. Once we over, we go along the beach, past the reef. You take Paolo's surfboard and paddle in. It's gonna be dark, man, so no one see you. Dump the board and walk home.'

'Where will you be heading with the boat?'

'G-Land, in Java. If I take it easy I can make it. Gonna sink the boat offshore, paddle in on my board and mix in with the surfers.'

I knew about the isolated but popular surf spot of G-Land in Banyuwangi province. I have heard many of our resident surfers speak of it. The thing Geno's plan had in its favour was that all the local outrigger fishing craft looked the same. He had put a lot of thought into it, and so far nobody except Putu knew of my involvement in it. By moving quickly and using our spare Land Rover, I was sure I could get all the necessary stuff into our outrigger without being seen. The boat lay at the water line in front of the Sandika, so I could launch it easily on the incoming tide. I tried to think of less dangerous alternatives. There weren't any. Geno had thought it through. If we had to get the boat out, then crossing the reef was our only option. We had to find a way through those waves. We couldn't take the boat along the beach; it was way too heavy to transport, and if we tried by water the reef would form a horseshoe that came ashore further along the beach. What caused my throat to dry up every time I looked towards the reef was the size of the waves. Geno had picked the worst possible day to make his break. If the boat capsized, we would both be cut to shreds on coral and our chances of making it in alive would be slim.

'I know, man, I know what you thinking, and I really sorry. I sorry for every fucking thing … For you, for Paolo, for the whole fucking thing!' He wiped his eyes with the back of his hand. 'In prison, man, when you show me the photo of Paolo, I want to kill myself. I don't care to live, and I don't care about anything, but slowly I come back. A couple of things change my mind. You, man. Because you give a shit. And one more thing. I got something I gotta do, and after that I don't care anymore what happen to me.'

'Geno, you're on your own. I'll help you get the boat into the water, but I'm not going to do it. No amount of money is worth dying for. I'll pay you what I owe you, but you can't ask me to do this.' He looked as if this was he answer he had been expecting. I thought of Janna; we would soon be sitting in our favourite *warung* and spending the night together.

'Just listen, okay? I understand, but if you do this you are free. Free of me, and you won't owe me nothing.'

'No, Geno, you listen to me. I'm not doing it.'

'You know what this means?'

'What?'

'I gonna get caught, man. There's no other way off this island.'

'I know, I hear you, but this is your shit. I've done all I can for you. I didn't do the coke thing, Geno! I wasn't involved in that shit. You screwed up, not me, and to be honest with you, I still don't really understand why I've helped you until now. I'm over it. I'm not going to get involved any more than I already am. I'm going to launch that boat for you, and then I'm out of here.'

'Okay, okay, I hear you, man. You want to do it like that? But you should think about what gonna happen to *you* and Putu when I get caught? You think about that, eh? What they gonna do to you, man? We gonna be in that police cell together, man.'

I looked into his eyes, and for the first time I understood: I was caught in his trap. Yes, he would give me up. He'd do anything to save himself. He had me by the balls and he knew it. There was nothing in Geno: no friendship, no warmth, no empathy, just cold calculating self-preservation. Why hadn't I seen this before? Or had I, but refused to acknowledge it? Or was it because Paolo wasn't there to reign him in anymore? In Geno's eyes I saw the same look the leopard cat had flashed me before it'd made its final dash for freedom. Geno broke our gaze and turned away.

'Now you got it, eh? So let's move it.'

* * *

I returned to the Bali Haj and told my head chef that he would have to cope without me as I had an urgent matter to attend to. I wanted to send someone over to Janna's to tell her I wouldn't be coming tonight but didn't have time. I would get this thing done quickly, be shot of Geno forever and explain things to her later. Back at the Sandika, the grounds were deserted. I had to fight against the wind to strap the surfboards across the outrigger.

I took the Land Rover and made four different gas stops so as not to attract attention; these I carried two by two to the boat and secured them up front with ropes. I then bought fisherman's whites and two straw hats for myself and Geno at an out-of-the-way hardware shop. I also stocked the boat's hull with a supply of tender coconuts, dried fish and anything edible I could find in the coffee-shop kitchen, plus a hand-held compass and sea chart from the tour offices.

I went back to the hut an hour before sunset and sat with Geno. I listened to him prattle on about his plans: he was sure the money would get wet on the way into G-Land, but that would be okay, because he could dry the notes. He would mix in with the surfers; the place being so remote, the news of his prison break would not have reached them. Geno would make his way out of Indonesia through the group of islands between Singapore and Jakarta and buy himself a passport from a traveller somewhere.

'How did you pole vault out? I mean on what?'

'Four pieces of bamboo, man, connected together on the inside with four pieces of rubber engine hose. I sat there for weeks carving my bamboo and fitting the rubber. Nobody knew what I was doing, and nobody guessed they fitted together. Even me, I never knew it work, but I knew that pole wouldn't break. Man, I sailed over that wall an arm's length above the barbed wire. When I let go of pole, I push it backwards. The only thing those motherfucker guards going to find tomorrow is long piece of bamboo lying there. They ain't gonna figure that one, man.'

As dusk approached, we padded down the beach. I looked back towards the hotel as we boarded the outrigger. Nobody was around. A quick shove, and we were afloat. We paddled a short distance out of sight of the hotel before we fired up the motor. The wind had dropped slightly. I looked out at the reef. The waves seemed smaller, but were still some of the largest I'd seen in my time in Bali. Geno took the helm. From his years of surfing the reef, he knew every protruding coral head and every submerged cluster of rock in the lagoon. He steered the boat through the darkening water, heading towards the airport runway. Once near the reef, we intended to work our way back to the main break by manoeuvring through some dangerous shallows. This would allow us to reach the crossing point without having to deal with the rolling foam, the aftermath of these monster waves; this way we would be less noticeable to anyone who might see us from the shore. It was a risky plan, but if it worked we could sneak up on the crossing and move into our chosen wave side-on, then swing the helm into it at the last second before it broke. Dusk gave us cover, and the wind muffled the sound of the motor. Geno and I wore our straw hats tied on with white cloth. The surfboards were tied out of sight.

We soon lay close to the reef. The boat buffeted and swung in the eddies and foam. I took the helm. Geno braced himself in the bow. With a nylon rope, he'd tied two jerrycans full of gas together like saddle bags. He kept one eye on the waves to our port side while his hands worked frantically tying the knots. The rip beneath us pulled us closer to the crossing. We had to move soon. Massive waves pounded onto the reef as they broke, their noise deafening, their spray stinging our faces. We rose over them, bucking and weaving. I looked down and saw the jagged coral heads reaching out like black claws. I held the helm with one hand; the other gripped the throttle on the outboard, ready to jam it full on.

Seeing these waves from the shore had not given us the real picture of their size. As we sat below them on the outrigger, they rose like humongous walls of black water, the size of large buildings. They peeled away from the port side. The white water at their peak, illuminating their height, was whipped by the wind into a fine back spray. The water beneath us shifted wildly. I steadied the boat as best I could. We had to make our run now. I screamed at Geno. He raised his palm.

'Wait!' I saw his mouth move. I was deaf with fear. I felt

myself weakening and wavering. My nerves caused me to shake. It began in my hand and crept up; I feared my trembling arms wouldn't be able to control the helm. I felt myself being gripped by an icy paralysis.

'Now!' Geno yelled. The command brought me to my senses. I jammed the throttle full on, dug the helm in deep to make the outrigger turn. We motored sideways along the wave. We rose higher and higher, still breached. Then without waiting for Geno's second order, I swung the helm. It took every bit of my strength to bring the outrigger around. She turned head on into the black water. My fears were realised. Instead of going into the wave as we had intended, the bow rose up. Within seconds, the outrigger canoe became almost perpendicular. The bow where Geno clutched on hovered directly above me. The outboard motor revved uncontrollably, its propeller out of water. The tender coconuts I'd put in the hull poured out like deadly missiles. One smashed into my shoulder, and another hit the side of my head. I braced myself into a crossbeam with one arm and tried to push the outboard into water with the other. Then, just as we were about to lose control, our bow came down. Racing water submerged us. With the boat underwater, I held desperately to the crossbeam. Within seconds, we popped out the other side of the wave, as if a hand had reached in and pulled us out. I wiped my eyes and looked towards the bow. Geno was gone. The wave had swept him away.

I looked ahead; another wave lay in my path, as large as the last. The motor had died underwater. I had to start the motor. I pulled the start cord. Nothing. I pulled again and almost ripped the cord out of its socket. The spark plug was wet. I ripped off the rubber cover that housed the plug and blew hard on it as the boat rose on the fast-moving wave and began to breach. I couldn't deal with that now; I would have to get to the helm later. I had to focus on starting the motor now. My life depended on it. I jammed the spark plug cover back on. The motor spluttered and started on the second pull. I now had forward momentum; I swung the helm. We rose high, almost too high. Then the power of the motor pushed the boat over the peak of the breaking wave with only seconds to spare.

I'd made it. I motored over the next mound of water until I was out of danger. I looked back, trying to spot Geno. It was too dark. The boat rose over another forming wave as I motored forward. Then I heard a voice, 'Help, motherfucker, help!'

I looked forward and saw nothing. I brushed sea spray from my face and saw a nylon rope move. It was stretched across the curve of the bow. I scrambled forward and looked down. Hanging from the bow, Geno clung to the rope with his head out of water. Over his shoulders, on another rope, which was hopelessly twisted around his neck, hung two jerrycans. I understood why we'd made it through the first wave: Geno had jumped off the bow with two jerrycans hung over his shoulders and clung to the bow by the nylon rope, forcing it down through the wave. This had saved our lives. I was about to help him when it came to me … Here was my chance: I could cut the rope and be free of Geno. The rip would pull him into the waves, which would kill him. I knew that. I'd been there myself. Geno couldn't get back on the boat without my help. He saw my hesitation, and he understood. His challenging eyes stared up at me.

'You think you got the *conyos* for that, eh?'

A stray wave knocked us sideways, the sea spray blinding me for a moment, then I caught sight of him again.

'Do it, motherfucker. Now's your chance … You got me.' He laughed. It was a mad hyena cackle. 'I come this far, I suffer, I fight and I get to here, and now it's between you and me, man.' He laughed again. 'So make up your fucking mind!' A wave submerged him. When he came up, I had my arm extended towards him. He latched onto it and would have pulled me in with him if I hadn't had my legs braced inside the boat. I managed to get him aboard. He fell into the hull, spewing seawater and gasping.

I unstrapped Paolo's surfboard and launched it. Before Geno knew what was happening, I'd jumped into the swell. I would paddle around the reef and come in on Kuta Beach. There was some distance between us before I looked back. I saw Geno standing on the boat with his hands cupped to his mouth, hollering through the spray. 'Hey, you off the hook, motherfucker. You done it. You don't owe me no more. I was never gonna hurt you ... Never, man.' I paddled harder. Geno's voice became a faint echo coming through the roar of the waves. Soon I was beyond the reef. The beach lay in front of me. I was safe. Then I heard a motor behind me. I caught a glimpse of Geno motoring away through the windswept darkness. He was looking at me with one arm raised in a salute.

I belly-surfed onto the beach. The lights of the beachfront hotels lay a good distance away. I dragged myself out of the water. My feet wavered on solid sand for an instant. I tucked Paolo's surfboard under my arm and stumbled along the shoreline to the Sandika Hotel.

4

At dawn I awoke to commotion outside my door. They poured into the room, carrying machine guns. The police and prison guards searched the bathroom and balcony, all dressed in uniform and armed with holstered pistols, batons and guns. One guard held a revolver to my head. The commander who had shot the cockerels walked in.

'Where is he?' he said.

'Who?' I choked out the word.

He nodded to one of his men, who reversed his machine gun and struck at my chest using the butt with such force that I fell off the bed. Then they came at me like pack of dogs as I lay on the floor. They kicked, used their batons, stomped on my head. My ribs cracked. My nose broke, and the metallic taste of blood filled my mouth.

'Where is he?' asked the commander again.

'Who?'

Again his men began. The first beating was nothing compared to what happened next. I curled up on the floor, trying to cover my head. The blows and kicks rained down on me. A pain shot though my back like a searing hot knife.

'Where is the Brazilian?'

'I don't know.'

'Take him outside.'

They handcuffed me and pushed me down the stairs and out to the pathway where I was forced to kneel. Two guards stood by me, pointing their machine guns at my head, while the rest of them herded our guests out of their rooms and into the coffee shop. They walked past me, some with terrified expressions, others curious.

Back at the coffee shop, the Sandika staff watched the proceedings, keeping their distance. Wayan's hands covered her face; Ketut cried openly.

The guests were pushed into the coffee shop and held under machine-gun guard. I received another crack on my head with the butt of a gun, and a sharp command, 'Don't look.'

Over the next hour, the police tore the hotel apart. They went through each room methodically, throwing beds, dressers and guests bags out onto the pathway. The commander paced up and down. From my position, kneeling handcuffed, I watched guards rifle through guest's bags and steal valuables, watches, cash and jewellery.

Anak arrived and went to the commander. 'Leave my guests alone, set them free.'

'Be quiet and go away, or I will put you back in the Polda as well.'

Anak looked at the commander with disgust and left.

They shoved me into a police van, where a guard held me down on the floor. I knew my destination: the cells in the police barracks in Denpasar. I knew the police and prison guards would keep searching the area around the Sandika until they'd satisfied themselves that Geno wasn't hiding out here. They hadn't asked me about the missing outrigger canoe. I prayed that Jimmy would take care of that.

At the Polda they took me into a room. I recognised the farmer who had passed me behind the prison with his bicycle laden with grass, his kindly face wrinkled and brown from working in the rice paddies. The commander came in and asked the farmer, 'Is this him?'

'Yes, he is the man I saw on the road behind the prison.'

'Thank you, you are free to go.'

As the rice farmer walked past me, he bowed and whispered,

'I'm sorry, may the gods forgive me.'

Then they brought in the prison guard who'd sold me the twenty visit concessions. He was handcuffed; looking at me, he nodded. Then they took him away. I heard a cell door rattle shut. The guards pushed me into Geno's old cell at the end of the row. They removed the handcuffs and kicked me to the floor. Every part of me ached. I had a pounding pain in my head. My cracked ribs made breathing unbearable. My eyes and lips were swelling shut but were thankfully numb. I lay curled on the cold concrete floor, wheezing and gasping. I knew there was more to come. But I made a vow: I would never tell them. I would endure the pain, but I would not tell them where Geno was, or what I'd done. I knew that my life depended on it. I repeated this over and over to myself. I was innocent, I'd been conned into helping Geno. I didn't know what the punishment was for assisting someone with a prison break, but I knew it would be high. My only chance to get out of here was to keep my mouth shut.

I slept in fits and starts, and had vivid dreams. In one, I saw Elisabeth walk into the cell with two of Tula's men. She pointed at me and said 'get up'. I opened my eyes to see the guards standing over me. In another I was raped by Janna's apes, and in another I watched Grace give birth to a baby orangutan.

They came for me every day. Some beatings were worse than others, but all were extremely painful. The guards enjoyed coming up with new ways to inflict pain on me. During one beating, a guard, with the commander watching, bent my index finger all the way back and snapped it. The pain was so severe, I almost fainted. I began to understand from their interrogations that what angered them most was they couldn't figure out *how* Geno had escaped. But they were determined to find out. I was their only chance. After my beatings, I heard them beating the Kerobokan guard in his cell further along. They shouted at him questions like, 'How much did the foreigner pay you? How did you let the prisoner out?'

Clearly no man could climb up a bendy length of bamboo and jump his way out of prison; pole vaulting was something they'd probably never seen or heard of before. Fortunately, I was never asked about the missing outrigger canoe. Jimmy and the crew at the Sandika must have covered that up nicely.

*　*　*

Even though I could force myself to bear the breaking of my fingers and ribs, and the blows to my kidneys, and the stompings on my head, there was one kind of torture that almost made me blurt out Geno's whereabouts every time it was used on me: the cattle prod on my testicles. One particular guard delighted in using it. As soon as I saw the guard holding the instrument before me, my body would shake uncontrollably. He would stuff a piece of rag in my mouth first. When the electric prod hit my testicles, I would clamp down hard and bite back the truth. I couldn't speak. I had come this far. I resolved not to break down now. I poured sweat and convoluted. Snot would run from my nose, and my shorts would fill with shit. After that they would drag me back to my cell and toss me on the concrete floor like a slab of meat. All I could do was brace myself for the next round of beatings.

The pain from the electric shocks on my genitals became so unbearable I began to hallucinate wildly. Once, I dreamed that Janna and I were walking on Kuta Beach, and she was carrying a baby girl strapped to her belly in a sarong. Janna gently handed the baby to me, and when I looked down, I saw it was Grace I was holding. I woke up from the dream to the smell of vomit and shit-stained walls.

On one occasion, the guards arrived while I slept. They did not bring along my mouth cloth. When they applied the cattle prod on me, unable to bear the pain, I bit off a piece of my tongue.

*　*　*

In time, my body developed a kind of tolerance to the beatings; they still hurt, but not as much. The guards sometimes took pity on me and against the commander's orders threw me scraps of food and water.

The beatings and torture came to an end one day because of a particularly painful episode. Normally one guard would hold me from behind while another applied the cattle prod. That day, for some reason, he released his grip, and I fell. As I toppled backwards, my legs spread open. The guard holding the cattle prod decided not to use his instrument, but he kicked me in the testicles instead. A sickening pain tore through my body as the full force of his boot hit my balls. Vomit erupted from my mouth, and diarrhoea ran down my legs. I passed out.

When I came to, the guards had left. The unrelenting pain seared through me like a hot knife. I ran my hand over my balls and looked down. One testicle had swollen to the size of an orange. It looked hideous and strange, as if the blue skin could burst at any moment. In the course of the day, it had got bigger. It grew to the size of a grapefruit.

I slept intermittently and had more wild dreams. In one, Elisabeth walked in with two New Zealand cops and a doctor. The doctor took out a scalpel while Elisabeth pointed to my testicle and said, 'It needs lancing. Open it up'. I woke up to find the commander and two of his guards staring at me, looking worried. From that moment on, the beatings stopped. They'd realised they'd gone too far. At some point an Embassy representative would have to show up and this wouldn't make them look good. But then, I doubted they'd even notified the Embassy.

I lay in stupendous pain for a long time, but although it diminished slowly, the swelling of the testicle didn't. It did not hurt much anymore, but the thing remained the same size. Something was very wrong. I became terrified that I'd been made a eunuch, that I would live the rest of my life with an unfunctional mango-sized testicle. The commander came often and brought in random people to look at my deformity. They were curious and asked me if it hurt or if I felt any pain.

They never laid a hand on me again. Slowly my bruises and cuts healed. The ribs took the longest, and a raw nerve hanging from a knocked-out front tooth made eating painful. The gate guard brought food and water regularly. Soon I could walk around my cell. The interest in my mango-ball gradually waned, and I was left alone. I inspected it every day, hoping to see some sign of reduction, but it stayed as it was, rock hard and large.

Until now, all my energy had gone into surviving and recovering from the daily beatings. I'd begun every day by preparing myself mentally for what was coming and steeling my nerves and resolve. Every day that I'd managed not to talk had become my reward for the torture I'd endured. After the beatings I would lay in pain on the cold concrete floor, congratulating myself between tears on my daily victory.

Then the food began to arrive: delicious, healing food. I recognised the taste of Wayan's cooking. Two meals a day were brought in by the gate guard. A few days later, as I chewed on a spring roll, its hardness caused me to take a closer look at it. I found that it contained a rolled-up piece of paper. It was a note: 'Be strong my brother.' I chewed up the note and swallowed it. Then, a couple of days later, I found a note from Eddi: 'Hang in there, Adam. Working on it.'

The following day, Eddi walked in with the commander, who walked away after unlocking the cell and leaving the door open. I was too shattered and broken to fully understand what was going on. I knew that I might be released, but all I could do was stand there, mute and scared.

When Eddi saw me, his face turned white. 'Holy fuck,' he swore, taking a step back. Then he gained his composure and was all business. 'Adam, snap out of it. I'm taking you away from here but we have to move fast. Here, put these on.' He handed me a set of clean clothes. 'Your flight for Tokyo leaves in one hour.

I used an airline ticket that I found in the Sandika's safe. It was Geno's and still had the return portion. I managed to put it in your name. It's all we could manage. I have your Michael Brown passport with me, and my mate Bob will meet you at Narita.' Each sentence was like cool water being poured over my wounds. I now understood and moved quickly.

'How much did you have to pay for this?' I muttered as I peeled off my torn and ragged clothes.

'Very little. We couldn't crack the commander. He's got a thing about this case and he's taking it personally. In the end he thought he'd gone too far and wanted shot of you. Anak gave him a few grand and the deal is that you leave the country immediately. They still haven't found out how Geno escaped and that's what's causing the commander grief.'

I pulled on the fresh linen shirt, and it felt great. As I took off my shorts, Eddi got a look at the mango ball. His eyes flared. 'Jesus Christ! What the fuck is that?'

'I don't know, but there is no pain, and I have a lot to thank for it.'

'Mother fucking animals! Filthy pricks, they're not fit to call themselves part of the human race.'

'Eddi, it's okay.'

The trousers he'd bought were thankfully a size too large. As I slipped on the shoes, I saw he'd also brought along a small travel bag.

'Wayan's packed it. Now let's go.'

Eddi and I walked past the gate guard, who smiled and bowed us out of the Polda police barracks into a waiting taxi. The sunlight blinded me; I shielded my eyes. My swollen ball made walking difficult, and I had to drag one leg along.

'How long was I in there?' I asked.

'Five weeks. We couldn't do anything. The commander refused to negotiate. The Australian Embassy gave me your case, and believe me, that was the quickest we could work it. That commander was a really tough nut. As I said, he seemed to have taken the whole thing personally. Wayan and Ketut are waiting at the airport. I told the rest of them not to come. We want you out of here quick.'

I sat in the taxi, luxuriating in the new clothes, feeling the divine coolness of the air-conditioning against my skin, and admiring the tropical colours moving past my window. We turned onto the road leading to the airport when Eddi asked the question.

'How did Geno get out?'

My tongue stuck in my mouth. I couldn't answer. I'd spent so long and suffered so much to not reveal these words that they still refused to come out. I looked at Eddi, feeling my face contort into a frown.

'Hey, Adam, it's me, Eddi,' he said, placing a hand on my shoulder. 'Don't tell me if you don't want to.'

'He pole vaulted out.'

'Eh?' he raised an eyebrow.

'Yeah, I know.'

'Geno's got a lot to answer for the trouble he's caused us all. Oh, and before I forget, your daughter called. I said you were away on a tour ... I didn't want to alarm her. She's really anxious and wants you to call her urgently. Wouldn't tell me why, but I gather something's up over there.'

I limped through the airport to the departure gate. Wayan rushed to me and hugged me tightly. I felt her tears on my skin. She smelled so clean, the scent of coconut oil in her hair. Then Eddi hustled me towards the check-in gate, handing me the passport. 'Hey, your papers are ready. Your flight is waiting. Here's your boarding pass.' Eddi and Wayan led me to the departure gate.

Eddi handed me a wallet. I saw that it was full of money. 'This is from Mahmood, so you'll be okay in Tokyo. He sends his sympathy. And Bob will be waiting at Narita, and I'm going to call him to take you to a doctor and get ...' He looked at Wayan uncomfortably then back to me. 'Get that thing looked at.'

'Eddi,' I called. 'Can you ask Anak to meet Janna and tell her what's happened?'

'You talking about the ape woman?

'Yeah, her name's Janna.'

'Okay,' Eddi said, looking at me oddly.

The Japanese Airline flight taxied down the runway, and as it lifted off, I looked down at the Sandika Hotel. Construction was underway on the new units. I saw a small group of people gathered on the beach before the coffee shop, looking up.

5

After sleeping on a hard concrete floor for five weeks, the softness of the airline seat felt great and lulled me to a deep sleep. I dozed most of the way. I would be arriving in Tokyo as an Australian named Michael Brown, dressed in an oversize pair of pants and with a missing front tooth and yellow blotches on my face, plus a mango-sized ball.

I navigated my way through Narita Airport. In twelve hours, I'd come from a filthy dim shit-covered cell in Denpasar to one of the biggest and busiest airports in the world. Neon signage flashed, and bright lighting dazzled, and the chrome and glass walkways disorientated. I managed to keep following the passenger who'd been in the seat in front of me since Bali and soon found myself in a passport check-in queue. With an entry visa stamped in my passport, I passed through and travelled down an escalator to the ground floor. I got myself together and as I had no baggage to claim headed directly to the customs check-out. It took me a moment to convince the Customs officer that my baggage consisted of only my one carry-on bag. He shrugged and gave it a cursory inspection. I walked through glass doors and out into the arrival lounge.

'You must be Michael Brown?' came a voice from behind me. 'I'm Eddi's mate, Bob. I heard you've been through hell down there.' He was short, balding and ruffled with a slightly bemused expression. I found his Australian drawl welcoming.

'I have an Embassy car waiting, and you can bunk up at my place until we get you sorted. Eddi told me you need to see a doctor urgently. We have a Doctor Grey attached to the Embassies, and

I've got you booked in with him as soon as we get into the city.'

Thankfully Bob didn't talk much or ask too many questions. My broken finger had begun to ache, and the old pains in the ribs that I thought were long gone had resurfaced. I felt exhausted, and in the comfort of the Australian Embassy car, I once again fell asleep. We pulled into the driveway of an office block, and Bob helped me as I limped into the lift.

Doctor Grey, a middle-aged Canadian, inspected me for over an hour. His practice was like a small hospital. It contained units for performing ultrasound and X-ray tests, both of which he used on me. He also took blood samples from me and insisted that I be tested for tuberculosis and malaria.

'Bob's told me you were subjected to torture and that these wounds were inflicted by the Indonesian police. Is that correct?'

'Yes.'

'In that case, we could lodge a formal complaint with the Human Rights Commission in Geneva. To be honest, I've never treated injuries caused by torture in my career. I would like to see the people who did this held to account.'

'Doctor, my main concerns are my swollen testicle and my ribs. I don't want to lodge any complaints. I'm sorry, but I have my reasons, and another thing ... I really need to use a telephone to call my daughter.'

'I'm sure Bob can arrange that, but for the meantime, let's begin with the testicle. It's absolutely functional and the contusion, the swelling you have, will disappear over the next few weeks; you see, fluid accumulates around the testis when it's injured, and takes a very long time to come right. The condition is called hydrocele. In your case, you will first notice a softening and then the swelling will start to diminish.'

Doctor Grey's words were a huge relief.

'The bad news is your ribs; the X-ray tells me they were broken more than once and haven't knitted properly, and that's what's causing the pain. We'll have to fix them. And your index finger will have to be rebroken and reset.' He paused. 'All these procedures we can do here. Apart from these broken bones, you are remarkably intact.'

The doctor then looked over the top of his glasses and said, 'But if you change your mind about that complaint, I would like to help.'

'Thank you, doctor.'

Bob came in and informed the doctor he'd got the bill on the Embassy's account. 'After all, he is an Aussie, right?' He smiled sympathetically and winked. Eddi must have filled him in. When the doctor showed Bob the X-rays and told him there was quite a lot more to do, Bob was clearly shocked at the state of my ribs. 'I think I can swing it with the Embassy,' he said.

'Right now he needs a place to rest up, a telephone and some good food, and we'll attend to those ribs as soon as we can,' said the doctor as he handed me a bottle of Codeine tablets.

* * *

Bob took me to his apartment. It looked out over the south end of Roppongi, a suburb of tree-lined avenues where most of the foreign embassies in Tokyo were located. Bob was a good host, and although it was tiny, his sixth-floor apartment contained everything: a fully stocked refrigerator, a collection of books and a spare room with a comfortable bed.

'I'm afraid I'm going to have to leave you to it. Make yourself at home. I'm not here often so it's all yours.'

I took a shower and marvelled at the phenomenon of hot water and shampoo, and I enjoyed being able to brush my teeth in a clean bathroom once again. I paced the apartment, thinking about how I got here. I was free. I had survived the Polda and probably escaped a twenty-year jail sentence for assisting with a prison break. I had to consider myself lucky, but I didn't feel lucky, I was too shattered to feel anything. My immediate concern was Grace; I found the telephone and called her.

'Dad, you can't keep doing this, you know? You disappear all the time. Eddi called and said you were away on tour. Are you okay?'

'Yeah, I'm okay. I couldn't get to a phone, that's all.'

'You voice sounds different. Where are you?'

'I'm in Tokyo. I am living under a different name.'

'You sound all worn out. Is something wrong? What are you doing in Tokyo?'

Before I could answer, Grace cut in. 'Dad! Listen!' I heard the ruffling of fabric. 'Can you hear that?' she asked.

'I think so.'

'He just kicked like hell. I think he's trying to talk to you, asking you to come home.'

'I'm trying, sweetheart. I'm trying.'

'Just promise me you'll be here when the baby's born.'

'Okay, I promise.'

I stared out the window. It was evening, and below me, a heaving mass of people lit by stark street lights moved towards a subway entrance. Neon lights screamed from pachinko parlours, sushi restaurants and trinket shops. I heard the whoosh and screech of a train, and saw the people quicken their pace. I looked down through the blaze of light, and I thought of all the promises I'd made to Grace that I hadn't been able to keep.

*　*　*

The first week in Tokyo, I slept and ate, and felt my body heal. Grace and I talked almost every day. She rang early one morning. 'Can I ask you something personal?' she said.

'Fire away.'

'Do you ever think about your mother?'

'It's strange that you should ask that, because I just recently started thinking about her. Yeah, since you're expecting, and when

I was talking with Janna back in Bali, I was wondering about her … You know, what does she look like, where is she, does she have kids, that kind of thing.'

'She's my grandmother, Dad. When this one's old enough to travel, I'm going to go look for her.'

* * *

Bob took me to his dentist, who arranged a porcelain cap for my broken front tooth, and Doctor Grey reset my ribs and finger. I was told to rest up for another week. Slowly my swollen testicle softened and began to reduce in size. I wanted to call Bali and tell them I was safe, but I resisted doing so. Instead, I asked Bob to send a message to Eddi. I thought of Janna constantly; she had no telephone so I couldn't call her. I wandered around the shopping centres in Tokyo, walking listlessly through the malls and sidewalks. I saw Janna's face in reflections on shop windows, in advertisements on subway trains, in the faces of women I walked past.

All around me, life swirled, and people moved busily like the rise and fall of a tide. Whenever I stopped and closed my eyes, everything that had happened to me would flash before me. I saw the face of the guard who had used the cattle prod on me, and I would burn with anger. I would see Geno shouting through the dark surf: 'I would never hurt you.' I would remember the look he'd given me in the fishing hut. Why hadn't I noticed that self-obsessed look before? I had been prepared to do anything to stop my fragile world from falling apart, and he had known that and had taken advantage of it. In the prison cell, I had been seen humanity at its worst, but rather than breaking me, it had empowered me; behind the pain and exhaustion, I felt a new strength, positive and strong.

I walked back to Bob's and paced the apartment. I couldn't sleep. In the middle of the night I peered through the window and saw skyscrapers looming through the first rays of a foggy dawn like grey monoliths from some futuristic age.

* * *

The next day I went out to buy clothes with the money I had; Mahmood had packed my wallet with a good amount of American dollars. Bob had told me about a meeting place for foreigners looking for employment: Studio Alta, an area under a giant outdoor movie screen near Shinjuku Station. I found it and approached a young guy who worked there. He turned out to be an Aussie.

'No worries, mate. Just about every foreigner in Tokyo is teaching English.'

'I've never taught English before,' I said.

'Hey, neither had I until I got here. But as long as you can speak it, you can teach it. Just along this road, there's a bookshop ... Go to the top floor and get a copy of the *Tokyo Times*. Hundreds of jobs in there. Good luck, mate.' I wanted to talk more to him but he was swallowed up by the crowd.

Located in the shadows of skyscrapers, Shinjuku was a fast and furious place. The streets were lined with bustling restaurants, gaming parlours, computer shops and the ubiquitous noodle stands with their sour tang of fermenting soybeans. Neon signs rose up the sides of buildings, higher than the eye could see, and teeming throngs of people pushed and shoved their way along the pavements. As I tried to find the bookshop, I became caught in a group of schoolgirls moving in the opposite direction, chattering like a flock of sparrows, texting on their cellphones, totally unaware that they were pulling me along with them. I managed to free myself and found the shop. The Aussie was right. There were plenty of jobs available for English teachers.

I found a job within a week. The school was on the tenth floor of one of the smaller skyscrapers in West Shinjuku, a stark and sterile building of thirty-five floors. After a rigorous interview, I was asked to sit in on a class.

That night I brushed up on my English grammar, and the following day I took my first beginner lesson. It was basic stuff, and I enjoyed the enthusiasm of the young, mostly female group of students. After class they invited me to a coffee shop, where conversation revolved around a dozen English words and involved a lot of exaggerated politeness and school-girl giggles. They addressed me formally as *Sensei-san*, which translated to Mr. Professor. That night I called Grace to tell her I had a job.

It was time to leave Bob's apartment. He'd done so much for me, and I appreciated it, but I felt I'd overstayed my welcome and began looking for other accommodation. A friend of Bob's introduced me to an older suburb called Akebonobashi in Shinjuku; it was one of the few suburbs in Central Tokyo that had survived the blanket bombings of the Second World War. Ornate wooden buildings with tiled eaves lined its lanes and byways. You could find there trimmed bonsais and potted bamboo precisely placed on tiny balconies; a myriad small shops with shopkeepers wearing traditional clothes and hawking their wares in guttural tones; taverns and restaurants emitting mouth-watering aromas; people in kimonos, holding sponges and towels, shuffling on their way to the bathhouses.

I found a letting agency that specialised in cheap traditional rentals. They showed me a six-tatami mat room with an old handheld telephone and a little recess with a sink that doubled as a bathroom. The main room was also the bedroom. It had a duvet I could roll out at night. I didn't mind the size. I didn't intend to stay there too long. The day I moved in, I called Grace to give her the new number.

*   *   *

As I came to terms with my situation, I knew that Bali was over for me. I could never go back. I would never see Janna again.

The only option available to me was to save my money and fly home on my Australian passport and then hand myself in to the authorities and tell them what had happened. At least I would be keeping my promise to Grace. That night I wrote a letter to Janna. It was so long that it only just fit into an envelope.

A few weeks later, Bob called me at the school and asked to meet up. In a café outside, he told me that his colleague at the Brazilian Embassy wanted me to help identify Paolo's body. The Embassy couldn't find any relatives, so the body remained lying frozen in the police morgue since the murder because the Embassy could not go ahead with the cremation and other formalities until it had been formally identified. I hesitated at first then agreed. I could do that for Paolo.

We met a few days later outside an austere building in Yotsuya, which housed the police morgue. Bob introduced me to his Brazilian colleague, an older man in a suit and tie who spoke excellent English.

'I'm sorry to put you in this position. I know it must be difficult for you. I understand that you knew Mr. Roberto for some time.'

'Yes, I did. He lived in the hotel I managed.'

'Perfect, then you will be able to give us a positive identification,' he said as we entered the building.

Before we were allowed into the refrigerated area that held the bodies, we were required to sign an entry book. Bob signed but then the Brazilian stopped in mid-pen stroke.

'Somebody viewed Mr. Roberto's body two days ago. How extraordinary, after all this time. Look!' He held up the book for me to see, and there under the name of Paolo Roberto I recognised Geno's signature. I'd booked him into the Sandika Hotel so often that I knew it. A cold chill came over me. I said nothing as I put my signature on the page. I looked back at the entrance way, half expecting to see Geno. He was probably still in Tokyo if he'd visited his brother recently. I didn't know if the information of his escape had been relayed to the Embassy here yet. Perhaps not, because if they had been alerted of him then his signature would have caused alarm. But then his handwriting was almost illegible.

'Well, unless this person contacts us, there is nothing we can do. We still have our process to complete. The police want the body out of here and it's our responsibility, so we'll get on with it, shall we?' said the diplomat in a matter-of-fact manner.

The attendant led us to a chilled room with body bags on metal trolleys. Harsh fluorescent light reflected off metal tables and turned our skin pale. The place reeked of chemicals. The morgue attendant checked the number he'd been given and unzipped the bag. Before us on a stainless steel draw was Paolo's body, sheet-white but clearly recognisable. For an instant I wished it were Geno lying there instead.

I see Paolo laughing as I fall off my surfboard. I hear his lilting harmonies as he sings. Then he gulps down a shot of arrack, grins, and looks at me. I tried to push away the thoughts of Paolo from my mind but I couldn't. I turned to the diplomat, fighting to control my trembling speech.

'Yes, that's Paolo Roberto,' I stammered, and I tried not to vomit. The diplomat took a couple of photographs and asked me to fill out and sign a form in Portuguese, which he roughly translated for me. As I signed, I noticed Paolo's birth date. He would have turned thirty-five tomorrow. The diplomat and Bob paid this no concern. With the identification process done, we left the building.

Ever since I'd been in Tokyo, I'd thought long and hard about Geno. My hatred for him burned with such intensity that I sometimes had to walk the concrete boulevards of the city to try to get him out of my mind. Now that I knew he was here in Tokyo, something compelled me to find him. I wasn't quite sure what was driving me. I remembered his last mad words on the night of his escape: *I would never hurt you, man. You are free now. You don't owe me.*

6

The next morning I phoned my school to tell them I would be taking the day off. On the way to Shinjuku Station, I stopped at a trinket shop and bought a carpet knife and tucked it in my jacket pocket. Holding a colour-coded subway map, I navigated my way through half-a-dozen train stops until I surfaced at Yotsuya, near the police morgue. A café across the busy street gave me a frontal view of the entrance. I waited there for three hours. Then I walked up and down the pavement for an hour and sat at an outdoor noodle shop, eating a bowl of *udon* soup. It tasted hot and bitter, and I left it and returned to the café, where I waited for another hour.

It was Paolo's and Geno's birthday; I'd acted on the hunch that as they were twins, Geno would come to see his brother's body today. But I was beginning to think I was wasting my time. I paid for my coffee and decided to leave. As I opened the door and stepped onto the crowded street, I almost collided with Geno. He took one step back, mumbled what I assumed was a Portuguese prayer and held his crucifix before him. Then his face exploded into a smile. He grabbed me, lifted me off the ground and swung me around. When he let me down, he held my face in his palms and said, 'Man, this is fucking out of it. How the fuck did you get here?'

My heart thumped as I tried to get the measure of him. How incredible, I thought, that after all we'd been through, all the trouble and pain he'd caused me, he was able to push it all aside, disregard it all, and act as if none of it had happened. He seemed so genuinely happy to see me. My hand wrapped itself around the

277

carpet knife as we went back into the café.

When we took a seat, I caught a glimpse of him watching me out of the corner of his eye, a cold chameleon's stare, as hard as a nail. He was checking me out, trying to gauge me. Then as I sat to face him, his warm enthusiasm returned. I forced myself to pretend like I was happy to see him. Don't let him see the depth of your hatred, I told myself. As I began my charade, I was surprised at how easy it was. It was like slipping into an old and familiar habit. I told Geno everything that had happened since I last saw him. He listened and seemed to showed genuine concern, particularly about my time in the Polda.

'You'd make a crap detective. I been in to see Paolo already. Man, my own flesh and blood, we been together since we born, never apart. It's killing me, man. I go many times to that place to see him. I just wanna be near to him, you know.' Then he quickly changed tack. 'It's so good to see your face, man. I'm so fucking sorry. I never thought you would get into shit like that. Never thought they'd figure out you helped me. Those fucking Indo bastards at the Polda, man.' Geno then asked in a low voice, pointing his finger to his pants, 'And the *conyo*, it working, man?'

'The doctor tells me it's all good.'

'Thank fuck for that.'

'So how did you get here?' I asked, keeping my voice steady, hoping that my eyes weren't giving me away.

'It wasn't easy. Everywhere I go, I'm shitting myself. I been in Indonesia until now. The boat trip was perfect, man, perfect. I found G-Land in a couple of days, stashed the boat and made my way overland to Jakarta. I hid out there. Anyway, I see a backpacker place in Jakarta, but I can't go in 'cause I got no I.D., nothing, man, just this big bag of cash. I see a guy come out. He look a little like me, same height, same eyes, only brown hair. I follow him, and I hear him speaking Spanish to his friend. Perfect. I steal his bag. I didn't hurt him, okay? Anyway, I stop at a hair place, and they colour my hair brown, and then I take taxi to the airport. First flight out was to Hong Kong. When I arrive there, I take a flight to Tokyo straight. All the time, I'm thinking I gonna get picked up for the stolen passport. But I get through. And here I am. I got here four days ago.'

'Why Tokyo? You could've gone anywhere.'

'I have to get Paolo home, man, you know. My passport says I'm Antonio Solera from Spain. I can't just show up at the Brazilian Embassy.' Geno stopped in mid-sentence as if something had just occurred to him. He looked at me keenly. 'But you could, man, you could.'

'What?'

'Call that diplomat guy and tell him you've managed to find Paolo's family in Rio. Maybe you could say they visited the hotel in Bali once and you phoned and got their address from the hotel registrar.'

'Could work,' I said. I was keeping up the pretence, but at the same time warming up to the idea of having Paolo's body returned to his family.

'I'll give you a phone number they can call. My family, our Mama … Paolo was her favourite. I can't tell them. I tried, but I can't do it. It is better they hear it from the Embassy.'

'Okay, I'll do that. I'll call tomorrow … have you contacted Satchimoto?' I asked after a moment's pause.

'He moved from the place where he used to live. But I gonna find him, man, trust me.'

I left the conversation there; I didn't like the tone of Geno's voice. We left the coffee shop and took the subway to Shinjuku. We walked around Kabukicho and stopped at a sushi shop with a revolving bar to drink some warm *sake*. Back out in the cold night air, under a blaze of flashing neon and the rattle of pachinko parlours, I asked Geno where he was staying.

'I stay at love hotels. They don't ask for I.D., and they charge by the hour, and I can change hotels every night. Hey man, I gonna go. Can you make that call tomorrow?'

'Okay.'

'Is there a number I can call you at?'

I hesitated at first but then gave Geno the number of the school where I taught, and I reminded him that he'd have to ask for Michael Brown.

'Okay, Michael Brown. I gonna be in touch.'

I took the subway back to Akebonobashi. When I reached home, I changed into a kimono and went to the local bathhouse. The hot water stung my skin until my body adjusted to the temperature.

I didn't know what it was that I wanted from Geno. Perhaps it was simply the fact that I could finally see him for who he really was, and that gave me some kind of satisfaction. For some odd reason I thought of the Spanish guy whom Geno had robbed. Then Paolo came to mind; his loyalty to his brother had cost him his life. I pushed away the image of his body in the morgue when I made the call to the Brazilian Embassy the following day.

'Thank you for the information,' said the diplomat. 'I'm sure his family will be very grateful. We will take directions from them as to how they would like to proceed.'

*   *   *

I had found myself a peaceful place to unwind on the rooftop of my school building. Curved glass barriers sheltered the area from the wind, and bamboo grew from glazed pots. There was a slatted bench against the barrier where, between lessons, I would come and read or gaze out over the city. After a full day's teaching at the school, I would walk home to Akebonobashi, stopping at sake taverns along the way. These tiny wooden drinking-houses that specialised only in warm rice wine brought back the memories of a bygone era. Beneath the glitter and neon shine of modern-day Tokyo, most of the old Japanese traditions still remained: like the communal gathering at the local bathhouses, where corporate businessmen chatted freely with tattooed Yakuza, or the gold-and-gilded Shinto shrines, often found wedged between a fish shop and a fruit seller, where men and women dresses in kimonos would toss in a coin, pull the bell chord and pray. I was fascinated by the city. But even as I moved amidst the teeming mass of people, all jammed together in these confined spaces and narrow alleys, going about their business with extreme politeness, I knew I could never live here. I missed the warm tropical nights of Bali. I missed Wayan's cooking, the surf, the sunsets, the laughter and Janna. Every time I thought of her, my heart would beat harder.

*   *   *

Two weeks later, I got a phone call from the Brazilian Embassy, informing me that the family had chosen to have Paolo's body returned to Rio for a full Catholic burial. The casket with the body had left on a flight to Brazil yesterday.

Then Geno called. 'Hey, man, we have to meet. Tell me where you are.' I didn't want to give him my address, so I agreed to meet him that night at the revolving table sushi shop in Kabukicho.

I made my way past the gaudy strip joints, where doormen with punched permed hair and pointed white shoes tried to palm cards with pictures of hostesses into my hand. Groups of young Japanese boys stood lined up at peep-show parlours or checking out the mind-boggling sex toys arranged in shop windows.

As I took a seat in the sushi shop, Geno came in brimming with excitement. 'Let's walk, man. I don't like to talk here,' he said.

We walked out into the teeming crowds.

'I've found Satchimoto.'

'Where is he?'

'He's back in the travel business, runs an agency in Ginza.'

'How did you find him?'

'Don't ask, man, don't ask,' said Geno. 'Here, look at

this.' He handed me a key, a large brass key with a series of evenly indented lines running lengthways and an edge with a complicated cut, resembling a small saw. 'There are two of these,' said Geno. 'I keep this motherfucking key in my asshole, along with my crucifix, the whole time I was in the Polda, and also in Kerobokan. There is another key. Satchimoto has it, and together they open a safety box in the bank of Tokyo in Ginza. You need both keys to open that box. There's one million and two hundred thousand American dollars in that safety box.' He paused to gauge the expression on my face. We'd stopped at the doorway of a pachinko parlour. The rattle and hum from inside had almost drowned his words.

'That's twelve hundred thousand dollars,' he said louder. 'That's how we kept our money, you know. When it came to money, we didn't trust each other. We would both show up together, each with our own key, and open that thing.'

I didn't say anything. I knew there was more coming.

'I want you to call him. You tell him Geno is dead, shot by Indonesian Police when resisting arrest. That before he escape from Kerobokan, he give you this key and told you what's in the safety box. You're here in Tokyo, man, and you gonna negotiate price for the key.'

'Geno, I …' I couldn't speak. I was trying to act dumb, trying to do and say what Geno would expect from the old Adam. But it was becoming harder and harder. My anger and hatred threatened to burst through my façade. I'd got into the habit of keeping the carpet knife in my pocket. My hand was gripping its plastic handle now, nearly crushing it while Geno continued speaking. 'Just hear me out okay? You ask to meet Satchimoto, tell him to come alone and bring along the key so you can be sure he still have it. He will come. You can count on that, man.'

'Man, I …' Geno didn't let me speak.

'Negotiate a price, maybe twenty-five percent. Don't give him the key, but go to the safety box with him, open the thing and take your money.'

'And where are you going to be while I'm doing this?' I had my anger in check. All I had to do was humour him. Geno was so involved in making his plan that he hadn't noticed me nearly lose it. I eased my grip on the carpet knife.

'I gonna get the money. I gonna follow Satchimoto and take it from him. You can keep yours.' His absolute gall and certainty that I would be willing to participate again in one of his mad plans made me laugh. He looked at me curiously.

'So, is that a yes or a no?' he asked.

'It's a no, a big fucking no. You must know that, man?'

'Hey, what do I know? I know you need money, am I right?'

'Yeah. I do, but I'm not going to do this.'

Geno remained quiet for some time. We eased our way through the mass of people, pushing towards Shinjuku Station. 'Look, I gonna call you tomorrow,' he said. 'Maybe you change your mind. Think it over, man.' We parted under the Studio Alta screen.

* * *

Geno rang the following day.

'Yes, I'm prepared to negotiate with Satchimoto. Come to my school,' I said.

'Exactly, man, exactly. Now give me the address.'

I met him in the crowded lobby on the ground floor of my building. We walked to the bank of lifts. I pushed the button for the express lift to the thirty-fourth floor. Only Geno and I remained in the lift as it rose through the last twelve floors to the roof. It opened into a small lobby. We walked up a set of stairs and into the doorway that led out to the roof.

'Hey, this is beautiful, man, but what the fuck are we doing here?' Geno asked, looking down through the glass suicide-barriers.

'I'll call Satchimoto and ask him to come here. I'll tell him you're dead, like you suggested and that I have the second key and want to negotiate with him. I'll insist he brings his key. I'm going to bring him here to this roof. We will set a time, and you will be here too. You can hide down the stairwell, out of sight until you see us go through, and if there's anybody up here then the deal's off. Understood?'

'Of course, man, of course.'

'You take the key from Satchimoto and walk away.'

Geno looked at me suspiciously. 'That motherfucker kill my brother,' the words were spat out like bullets.

I felt my fists tighten at the mention of Paolo. I had to turn away in case my contempt showed. Yes, it was indeed Satchimoto who'd had Paolo killed, but it was Geno who had put him in that situation, who had ruined his own brother. I steadied my breathing and managed to regain control. I turned again to face Geno.

'I know,' I answered, trying to inject sympathy into my tone, but it sounded false even to my own ears and my voice cracked a little. Geno's eyes narrowed as he looked hard at me.

Panic set in. My heart thumped. I was afraid that he knew what I was up to and that I was bullshitting. I opened the carpet knife in my pocket and felt the sharp blade with my thumb and forced myself to continue. 'When he sees you and knows you're alive, he's going to have to spend the rest of his life in hiding, knowing that at any time you might appear and cut his throat. You take the keys and leave.' My voice steadied as I slipped back into character.

'You liked my brother Paolo, eh?' said Geno curiously.

'Yes, I did,' I said, uncertain about where this exchange was headed.

'And you wish it was me dead, not Paolo. Am I right?'

'I don't wish anybody dead … Not you or Paolo,' I said, pushing my free hand into my pocket to stop it from shaking.

Desperate moments passed between us. Geno turned away. He had his head down and was shuffling his feet. I felt my face burn, felt sweat break out on my brow. My throat tightened.

'And what do you want?' asked Geno finally. I exhaled slowly. He was normal again. I could see his suspicion had passed and he was struggling to grasp the reason for my proposal.

'Nothing,' I answered. 'You get the money, all of it, and Satchimoto gets to live in fear for the rest of his days.'

Geno sat silently on a slatted bench, then said, 'You're a strange man, Adam. You're a good man, you know. I love my brother too, eh. We got that in common. And Satchimoto walks away?'

'Yes.'

Geno put his head in his hands. 'Okay, we do it your way. I agree to that for you, man, not for that piece of shit. I let Satchimoto go for you.'

'Deal,' I said, and we shook hands. Geno handed me the key along with Satchimoto's number, and we descended the thirty-four floors in the express lift.

7

I called Satchimoto immediately. I wasn't sure that I could handle any more of this. My anxiety levels were going through the roof, threatening to break through my composure. I needed to act fast or I was likely to pull out. It had been a close call with Geno on the rooftop. I dialled the number. A receptionist put me straight through.

'Satchimoto, it's me, Adam from Bali. I'm in Tokyo.' I heard a grunt that told me he was listening. 'Geno is dead, shot while resisting arrest after his escape.'

This news brought forth an immediate response. 'When did that happen?' he asked.

'Recently.'

'Are you sure?'

'Yes, I was asked to identify the body.'

'What do you want from me?' Satchimoto's voice was flat.

'Before he escaped from prison, Geno gave me a key. He said you have the other one. Do you know what I'm talking about?'

'Maybe.'

'I'm here to negotiate. The Sandika needs money urgently; its survival depends on it. Anak's lost heavily in the cockfights and mortgaged the place. If I don't get the money, we'll be bankrupt,' I said, making it all up as I went along. I heard Satchimoto laugh, a staggered sarcastic goat-like laugh that indicated he believed my story.

'Where do you want to meet?' he asked.

I gave him the address of my building and arranged to meet him in the lobby the following day. 'Come at two thirty. And bring your key … I want to see it.'

'Of course, and you bring yours too. I want to make sure it's the correct key as well.'

I cautioned that he must come alone, adding that I would also be alone. He grunted in agreement. As Satchimoto hung up, I knew he'd bought my story. I was a person he trusted. After all, when Satchimoto had confessed about his drug-smuggling operation to me, I'd kept silent, which had allowed him to leave Bali. I knew he'd be there on time and that he'd come alone.

I hardly slept that night; panic and fear made it difficult to breathe. The hot baths failed to calm me, and the *sake* did nothing to soothe my nerves. I woke up early, got dressed in a linen suit and walked to work. The morning class was a group of beginners, about ten students in all. At twelve I received a phone call from Geno; I made it brief and said, 'Two thirty today.' Geno hung up without answering.

My afternoon class was a group of businessmen from a local I.T. firm. They were advanced English speakers and the weekly class revolved mostly around having conversations, learning the more obscure tenses, memorising irregular verbs and so on. I would often give them exercises to do and leave the room for short periods. As the time approached, I found myself sweating even though the air conditioning was on. I set my students an exercise of memorising twenty irregular verbs and writing sentences using the past participle and then excused myself, saying I needed to use the bathroom.

*   *   *

I had forgotten how short Satchimoto was until I met him in the lobby. He wore a suit that had obviously been tailored to fit his tiny frame, along with a blue shirt and white tie. But something was different about him. What was it? He smiled as he shook my hand, and I saw he had the most brilliant set of pearly-white false teeth. He appeared relaxed as we walked towards the bank of lifts.

'I know a private place where we can talk.' I led him into the express lift and hit the button for the top floor.

'And how is everyone at the Sandika?' he asked as the lift doors closed.

I didn't answer. I took out of my pocket the key Geno had given me and showed it to Satchimoto. He responded by showing me the key he had. They were definitely a pair; both were engraved with the same box number.

We were now speeding past the tenth floor, and I had to move fast. As floors twenty-two to thirty-four were mostly apartments, there was very little lift traffic, but I wanted to get my message across to Satchimoto before then. I positioned myself in front of the lift controls and steadied my voice. 'Geno is alive and well. He is waiting for you at the top floor. He will take your key and cut your throat with a carpet knife.'

I waited a second. Satchimoto smiled as if he thought I was joking. His false teeth flashed white for an instant, then he took in the seriousness of my face and turned pale, his eyes flaring with fear. 'Stop the lift!' he stammered, pushing at me, trying to get at the controls.

I shoved him away. We'd just passed floor twenty-two.

'Geno has a gun to my head. He forced me to make the call to you. I don't want to do this, but I have no choice. He'll kill me too if I don't.' The lift was fast approaching the top floor. 'There's a way out of this. We have one chance. I know that the money is more important to Geno than your life. Give me your key. If you don't have the key, he won't kill you. I'm sure of that.' The lift had reached the top floor. Satchimoto was scared witless and with a trembling hand, he gave me his key. I put it in my jacket pocket. 'And whatever happens, whatever he does, don't tell him I've got the keys. Or we're both dead. Do you understand?'

He nodded, his body shaking. The lift doors opened, but he remained glued to the back of the lift and I had to pull him away and shove him up the stairs and out onto the roof.

Geno moved swiftly. He was through the door instantly, charging at Satchimoto. He slapped his face, knocking him to the floor. 'Give me my key, motherfucker!'

'I haven't got it. It's back at the office,' pleaded Satchimoto as he got up. Geno looked at me for affirmation.

'That's what he said.' I shrugged.

'You didn't bring it, you piece of shit. You kill my brother, you kill my brother Paolo.'

Just as Satchimoto regained his footing, Geno slapped him so hard on the other side of his face that his false teeth shot out of his mouth and landed at my feet. Satchimoto staggered and fell again, close to the glass barrier. Geno was out of control, possessed by a rage so violent that all reason had left him. 'You think I care about money, you murdering motherfucker? You think I'm like you? You kill my brother, like you think you can do anything, and you come here with no key ...'

Satchimoto lay where he'd landed. Geno took him by both wrists and began to whirl him around in circles. He whirled him faster and faster until Satchimoto was horizontal; Geno was a powerfully built athlete, and Satchimoto a tiny Japanese man. Around and around they went.

There was nothing I could do. Geno was spinning Satchimoto around with such force, I would've been knocked down had I tried to stop them. After a couple of powerful circles, Geno let Satchimoto go. Like a discus thrower, arms extended in a final thrust, Geno heaved him upwards. Satchimoto's body went flying over the curved glass suicide barrier. His hand shot out to catch the edge of the glass, but he missed. Satchimoto started to fall. I caught a last glimpse of his toothless face, his eyes bulging out of their sockets. He slid faster and in an instant he was gone. The only evidence that he'd been there was a thin trail of snot that ran down the glass and a pair of false teeth on the roof. Then Geno came at me. His face was furious and wild, still possessed by the power of his rage. I could tell he didn't recognise me. A carpet knife appeared in his hand. His thumb pushed the razor-sharp blade out of its plastic socket.

'It's me, Geno! It's me, Adam!' I shouted. 'You've just thrown Satchimoto off the building.' I took him by the shoulders and shook him. He stared at me quizzically then the murderous look in his eyes changed to a confused green. He sheathed and pocketed the carpet knife.

'What the fuck!' he stammered. Then it dawned on him. The magnitude of what he'd just done and the danger we were in now. We rushed to the glass barrier. Far below, we saw Satchimoto. He'd landed on the road, his head split open, surrounded by a growing pool of dark liquid, his arms splayed and his legs bent at unnatural angles. Traffic had stopped. Stunned pedestrians stopped, hands covering faces, others staring motionless.

'Fuck,' said Geno. 'Quick, man, we gotta get outta here. Take the stairs.'

I followed Geno through the door to the stairwell. He moved fast, taking the stairs in jumps of three at a time. He didn't look back. Then I remembered Satchimoto's false teeth; I rushed back up the stairs and to the roof, and pocketed them. I went back out through the door. The express lift wasn't in use. I pressed the call button and waited. Seconds became minutes, and the minutes felt like hours, and then finally the doors slid open to an empty lift. I pressed the button for the tenth floor. I wiped the sweat off my face with a handkerchief on the way down and walked out into the reception area of my English school. I went to the bathroom, washed my face and hands. As I passed the receptionist on the way to my classroom, she didn't look up.

In the classroom, the group of men were chatting away in Japanese. As soon as they saw me, they chimed 'Sensei-san' in unison and reverted to English. The clock on the wall said two-fifty. I'd been gone twenty minutes.

'Please excuse me, I had to take a telephone call. We can make up the extra time in the coffee shop after class if anyone would like that. Now let's look at those irregular verbs.' I took my seat at the head of the table and placed my hands flat on the table top to stop them from shaking.

At three o'clock an announcement came through on the speaker system, first in Japanese then in English. 'Would all occupants of the building please use the north exit when leaving, on account of a traffic accident.' I looked around the room; nobody found this unusual.

After class I led my group of students into the groundfloor coffee shop, where we continued our conversation lessons. Police and uniformed guards were mixed with the crowded patrons of the lobby, questioning the people who left by the north exit. Luckily they didn't bother with a group of businessmen and their teacher, all of us well-dressed and carrying briefcases. We passed through unnoticed. I was so conscious of Satchimoto's false teeth in my pocket that they felt like they were burning holes in the fabric. I wanted rid of them as well as the pair of keys. I hadn't yet thought of a safe place to dump them. I walked a good distance with my students. At the west entrance to Shinjuku Station, we bowed to each other and went our separate ways.

On the way to Akebonobashi, past the Ni-chome district, was a Shinto temple. It was set in a park and as I walked through its entranceway, I came to a deep pond with water bamboo, flowering lilies and golden carp, whose fins rippled the tranquil surface of the water. I sat on a side bench beside the pond. A Shinto monk shuffled past in burgundy robes. I watched the movement of the carp for some time then reached into my pocket, looked around to make sure nobody saw me and tossed Satchimoto's teeth into the water. They floated on the surface for a short while. The carp inspected them, then determined they were not edible and glided away. Satchimoto's false teeth sank in short sweeping movements.

I chose the heaviest rock bordering the pond. Green carpet moss broke away as I moved it. I slipped the two safety-deposit keys under it, pressed the spongy green moss back into place and looked around. An old woman was praying at the shrine, head bowed, holding incense in her palms. Nobody had seen me. With the moss back in place, the rock looked as if it had never been moved.

That night I drank myself into a *sake* stupor. As I staggered home down a deserted alley I pulled the carpet knife from my pocket and snapped it in two. I tossed it to the ground and stamped on it again and again until all that remained of it was crushed plastic and tiny segments of blade. I slumped against a doorway, holding my head. From across the alley, an old lady in a kimono came out and without looking at me, she swept the mess into a tray with a straw broom. Then she disappeared behind a wooden door.

*   *   *

I went to work the following day. The receptionist told me that a man had died outside the building yesterday, but they were not sure how.

I tried to sound casual when I answered, 'I'm sorry to hear that.' Then I entered the class room to a chorus of 'Good morning, *Sensei-san*' and immediately in halting English a student gave me a full rundown of yesterday's death. It was the talk of the class.

'Maybe he jump?' wondered another student.

'Jumped,' I corrected him. 'It's the past participle, but the "ed" is pronounced as "t".' I made the class repeat after me as I said 'jump-t', exaggerating the 't'.

I forced myself through a full day of classes. I'd lost my appetite, and I had no desire to talk with anyone, and when I was alone, scenes from the incident on the rooftop invaded my mind as vivid as the day they had happened. I couldn't sleep, and at one point I considered giving myself up to the police. I didn't want to call Grace. I would hear the telephone ringing but could not answer it. It was all I could do to carry on teaching until enough time had passed so I could leave my job without arousing suspicion. I found myself looking over my shoulder constantly, worried that Geno would appear.

My solace was *sake*. I went to a local tavern every night. As soon as the barman saw me enter, he'd shout '*konnichiwa*'. And by the time I reached my seat a carafe of hot *sake* and a selection of pickles were placed before me on a bamboo tray. The ancient wooden tavern was packed tight with drinkers. I would listen to their guttural laughter and watch the dance of chopsticks while I worked my way through a number of carafes, as many as I could drink until the barman, who reminded me of someone I knew, held up his palm and said, '*Yamete kudasai*, Stop'. Then I'd drag myself home and collapse on the tatami floor.

A week later, at the end of a morning class, the receptionist came and asked for me to follow her. She led me to a classroom, where sat a Japanese detective and a young female translator. He had punch-permed hair and wore a black shirt under his dark suit. The translator introduced him as Detective Katsuki, the person in charge of the investigation of the man who had fallen off the building. Katsuki pushed his identification badge across the table and the translator began. I felt my face tighten and held onto both sides of the chair.

'We have been informed that you spend a lot of time on the roof garden of this building. Is this correct?'

'It is. I went there to read. It was relaxing.' I was surprised at how normal my voice sounded.

'Did you see any other people during the time you were there?'

'No. Occasionally someone would come up, but not recently.'

'When did you last go up to the roof?' My stomach sank. Had someone seen me there that day? I felt Detective Katsuki's eyes boring into me.

'A couple of weeks ago.'

'Can you give us an approximate time and day?' the translator asked, without looking up, writing continuously as she spoke. I pulled out my pocket diary, hoping my hands wouldn't shake, and thumbed through it. I looked at my weekly schedule.

'The fourteenth of this month, from twelve to two o'clock.' That *was* in fact the last time I'd been up to the roof to read. Detective Katsuki spoke in a guttural tone to his translator for some time.

'In your opinion, do you think it would be possible for someone to climb up the suicide barriers and jump? Or do you think there were other people involved?'

I breathed out, feeling numb. I could hear the words coming out of my mouth; they sounded distant, as if they came from another person, another voice.

'I really can't answer that. It's not something I have thought about.'

A long conversation followed between the detective and the translator. Although I did not understand Japanese, I kept hearing them repeat the name Satchimoto in connection with the word 'Yakuza'. My curiosity pulled me back.

'Can I ask a question?' I interrupted.

'Certainly,' replied the translator.

'Could you tell me about the man who died?'

'Certainly,' she said again and shuffled through a couple of papers. She came up with a file that had Satchimoto's photo on the right-hand corner.

'Iko Satchimoto was the name he most frequently used, although we know he had other aliases and a number of passports. Because of this, it's been hard to track his recent movements. We know he spent the last year offshore, perhaps in the Philippines, possibly in Indonesia. He was a well-known Yakuza boss. He was a money-man and organiser. His main operation was money laundering for different Yakuza factions through a group of travel agents he controlled with his wife.' The translator stopped. 'Would you like for me to continue?' she asked, looking up from her file.

'Please do,' I said.

'His wife left him for a rival Yakuza boss, and together they attempted to take over Satchimoto's operations. His life was at risk on account of this. We know the rival faction had a contract out on him. We believe Satchimoto got warning of this and fled Japan, taking a large amount of Yakuza money with him. He was gone for about a year but resurfaced recently. Our informants tell us he paid back all the money he owed with interest. We think the Yakuza would have no reason to assassinate him, and the way in which he died is not the way they carry out their assassinations.' The translator looked through a couple more pages then said, 'That is why we are asking you so many questions.'

'Thank you for explaining this.'

Detective Katsuki suddenly spoke in English. His voice growled, 'Satchimoto, no good man, you understand?' I nodded. 'Yakuza no good. In Japan, big problem, understand?' I nodded again. The detective stood and shook my hand. 'Thank you, *Sensei-san*. Maybe I take English lesson with you, okay?'

'Okay,' I answered, taken aback by the turn of events. I wasn't a suspect. They hadn't even asked to see my passport, and the information about Satchimoto explained volumes. In the lobby we bowed formally to each other, and Katsuki and I exchanged cards. I entered my classroom and looked at the expectant faces of my students.

'Good afternoon, class.'

'Good afternoon, *Sensei-san*,' they replied in unison.

That evening I wrote a letter of resignation to the school, explaining that I would be leaving Japan soon. I had two more weeks of teaching to be completed.

That night I sat again in the tavern, letting the hot liquor mix with relief. A huge load had been lifted from my shoulders.

I had to figure out what to do and where to go. As the barman refilled my glass, I knew who he reminded me of: Farbat Dingali, the Indonesian lawyer Mahmood Bas had used to get Anak out of jail. I settled for one carafe. I needed to remain clear. I fiddled with the chopsticks, pushing the pickles around on my plate. By the end of the night, I knew what I was going to do.

8

By the time I'd finished my morning class it was two o'clock. Indonesia was two hours behind Tokyo. From the phone in the lobby, I called the international directory and got Dingali's number. A secretary put me through, his voice condescending as he tried to remember who I was. 'Ah, of course, of course, how could I forget,' came his slippery tone as I told him what I wanted. 'I can try, but no promises though. I'll make some inquiries and call you back.'

I gave him the school's number and information about when I'd be available there. On a grey Monday morning, when the Tokyo smog smothered the view from my classroom window, I was asked to come to the telephone.

'Good news, my man. It can be done. Book a flight to Jakarta, call me with the flight number, and I'll meet you before immigration. I must warn you it's going to be expensive …' said Dingali.

*   *   *

At the Shinto temple, I walked around for some time before I took a seat by the pond. I was dressed as a tourist and carried a camera. I waited until I was alone then pushed the rock slowly with my foot. The two brass keys lay exactly where I'd left them. I reached down, picked them up and pocketed them while pretending to take a photograph of the pond, then replaced the rock.

I took a taxi to the Ginza and went straight to the Bank of Tokyo. A wall of safety-deposit boxes of varying sizes lined the interior of a large enclosed room to one side of the main entrance. Two uniformed and armed security guards stood outside, while a number of customers had their boxes open or were shuffling through documents on the tables provided.

I found the number I was looking for with ease and put the two keys into their slots and turned them simultaneously. The box slid open. Inside it, wrapped in brown paper and secured by tape, lay the money. I opened my shoulder bag and stuffed the paper parcel into it. I had to stop myself from looking over my shoulder, afraid Geno might come bounding in. I carefully closed the box then walked out past the security guards calmly, as if this was something I did every day.

I strolled the crowed avenues of the Ginza, mingling with the shoppers and lunchtime crowd. Reaching into my pocket, I took a tissue and wrapped the two brass keys in it.

On the way back to Akebonobashi, I stopped again at the temple. At the shrine I took a handful of Japanese yen and dropped it into the offering basket to made a wish. Golden carp circled the pond. It was spring in Tokyo, but I hadn't noticed. The cherry blossoms were in bloom and their petals floated on the ponds surface like pink snowflakes. I unwrapped the keys, bent down as if to feed the fish and let them slip from my hand. They sank instantly.

Back in my room, I locked the door, pulled down the blinds and in the dim light, opened the parcels and counted the money. It came to exactly one million and two hundred thousand American dollars. I repacked it into bundles and returned it to the shoulder bag.

*　　*　　*

One week later, I passed through Customs and Passport Control at Narita Airport and boarded a Garuda Airline flight direct to Jakarta. I'd found a suitcase and packed my clothes, but the case was still only half-empty, so I'd bought a collection of Japanese kimonos to fill it out; the bundles of cash were strewn randomly through my suitcase. There was no point in hiding them as I would be meeting Dingali before Customs, but I took the precaution of arranging the money in such a way that the lawyer wouldn't be able to see how much I had.

Ten hours later, as the plane began its decent to Jakarta Airport, from my window seat porthole I saw the myriad of small islands that lay just offshore. Then I caught sight of Jakarta, the sprawling capital city of the most densely populated island in the world. I exited the plane and at Passport Control, on viewing my passport, the controller made a phone call and asked me to wait to one side. Within minutes Dingali arrived with an official, who wore a tag that read 'Department of Immigrations'.

As we walked to his office, Dingali told me to pay the man ten thousand U.S. dollars. I dug into the case and produced the money. The immigration official put an entry stamp on Michael Brown's passport then led us through a side door to the arrival lounge.

'Okay, so here it is,' Dingali said as we seated ourselves. 'I've contacted the commander of the drug squad in Bali, the arresting officer in your case, and the bad news is that although there were no charges laid, the commander still has a personal problem with you. He'll allow you back into Bali for a price of course, but he insists you must tell him how the Brazilian escaped,' said the lawyer.

'I can't do that.'

'Then it's going to cost you, my friend.'

'How much?'

Dingali looked thoughtful, then shaking his head said, 'You couldn't afford it.'

'Try me.'

'Three hundred thousand dollars.'

'Done.'

He raised both eyebrows. 'And how do you intend to pay this amount?' he asked in disbelief.

'In cash, now.'

He didn't blink; he asked me to follow him to the toilet. As we reached the cubicles, I entered one. I quietly took the money from my suitcase and put it in my shirt front then flushed the toilet. Outside, apart from Dingali who stood there with an open briefcase, the toilets were empty. He didn't bother counting the money as I placed it in his case.

'I'm impressed,' he said as we walked towards a taxi rank.

I took a taxi to downtown Jakarta, where I bought a briefcase, arranged the remaining money in a tidy manner and walked into a branch of the Bank of Indonesia.

'I'd like to deposit nine hundred thousand dollars into this account,' I said, pushing across a piece of paper scribbled with an account number to a poker-faced teller. A manager appeared with a sly smile on his face and asked for me to follow him.

'I assume you know the owner of this account?' he asked as we sat in his office.

'Yes, he's a friend of mine.'

'So you would have no objection if we called him to verify?'

'Not at all.'

Over the speaker phone in the manager's office, I heard Mahmood affirming that he knew me and explaining that he was expecting the money. I recalled the conversation I'd had with him by phone from Tokyo:

'*Mahmood, I need to ask a favour.*'

'*Go on.*'

'*I need to deposit a large amount of cash into your bank account.*'

'*How much?*' I could picture him smoothing his moustache.

'*Close to a million dollars.*'

'*My goodness, Adam! You seem to be doing alright.*'

'*Not really, but I will explain later. I'll be in touch with further instructions about the money. Can you do this?'*

'Of course,' he said, and gave me his bank details.

I left the bank with fifty dollars in my pocket. It took me an hour to find a street beggar about my size. I took him aside and told him that I'd like to buy his clothes for fifty dollars and that he could have my suit as well. In a side alley, we made the exchange. His torn sweat-stained shirt and shorts stank, but they were a good fit. The only thing that didn't do him justice was that I insisted on having his tyre-sole sandals, leaving him barefoot as he couldn't squeeze into my shoes. On seeing my reflection in a shop window, I realised my face and hair were too clean, so I rubbed my fingers around the exhaust of a parked car and ran them over myself.

The last thing I did before entering the New Zealand Embassy was throw Michael Brown's passport into the sewer.

The receptionist looked at me with suspicion and made me wait. There was a stack of New Zealand newspapers on a rack, and in one of them, I found a recent article on the search for the missing sailor Adam Milano. It had a photo of me. It would make my explanation so much easier.

It was an hour before an Embassy official came to see me. I simply pointed to the paper in my hand and said to him, 'I believe I am this man. I am Adam Milano.'

Within minutes, the High Commissioner appeared. He had a missing person's file in one hand and a warm smile. He guided me into a conference room.

'We were almost ready to close this file … We were sure you had drowned. Where on earth have you been?' he asked.

'I don't know.'

'What do you mean you don't know?'

'I woke up this morning and remembered my name and that I have a daughter called Grace back in New Zealand. The last I remember is that the *Sea Rover* ran into a reef. But, unfortunately, I have no recollection of my life after that.'

9

The Air New Zealand flight banked to starboard. The familiar views of the Auckland skyscape and of the Pacific and Tasman Oceans thrilled me. I saw the rolling surf of the West Coast beaches and traced the Manukau Harbour back to the sand bar beyond the heads. Then the plane banked to port and the Waitemata Harbour shone like silver in the distance, and I could see North Head and Bastion Point rising up, blue and misty, like mythological fortresses guarding the entrance to the harbour. A lone sail bent against the wind and further out across the channel, Rangitoto Island sat humped like a huge prehistoric beast. But what was causing my heart to leap out of my chest was that I knew Grace was waiting for me on the ground below.

I cleared Customs, walked out of the arrivals gate and searched for her. I couldn't find her. I walked the length of the airport, looked outside then thought that I might have given her the wrong arrival time. I knew where Elisabeth lived. I would take a taxi there and wait outside. But then, suddenly, Grace sidled up beside me and put her hand on my arm.

'Hello, Dad,' she said quietly, and her hand slipped down to her belly. She took my hand and placed it on top of hers. Then she wrapped her arms around my waist and buried her head into my chest. Taxi horns sounded around us, and backpackers ambled by clutching guide books like bibles. The scrapes of trolley wheels and the hum of the airport were drowned out by the roar of a departing plane.

'You kept your promise,' said Grace as we walked towards a taxi.

I checked into the Y.M.C.A. and spent the morning on the phone, speaking with my former accountant, the liquidator and my creditors. A sum was agreed upon, so I called Mahmood to let him know I was ready to go ahead with the first stage of our plan.

The next morning, I wrote a check for Elisabeth's share of the restaurant and sent it to her address by courier post. An hour later, the phone rang.

'Is that you, Adam?' she said. I didn't answer, but as I hung up the receiver I felt light and free.

* * *

It was autumn in New Zealand, and a southerly wind with a cold bite blew down Ponsonby Road as I made my way to Tula's haunt, located on the second floor of a bar at Three Lamps. I carried a plastic bag with one hundred and eighty thousand dollars in cash, which I swung back and forth nonchalantly as if it contained nothing more than a loaf of bread. The Matua sat at a table attending to his affairs. As he saw me enter, he rose and crossed the floor to give me the traditional Polynesian greeting, the touching of noses.

'In the islands, we revere our ghosts and bestow titles upon them. In your case I think I'll take the money and hope that it is real.'

'I can assure you it is.'

'I miss your pastas. Your restaurant is still going, but the food is lousy.'

'So I hear.'

He looked at me evenly. 'That little girl of yours is a handful of trouble.'

I wasn't going to rise to the bait. I waited until Tula's men had counted the cash.

'You're a lucky man,' he said, as soon as he'd been told the amount was correct.

*　*　*

The duty nurse showed me to his room. Duncan sat wearing a dressing gown; his hair and beard had turned completely white, and although his skin was a blotched leathery brown, it wasn't the death-like grey I remembered. He'd pulled his chair up to the bed, which was covered in sea charts. A wooden architect's drawing-board held a chart of the North Australian coastline. Rulers, pencils and scraps of paper with nautical equations scribbled on them were strewn about the room.

'Hello, Duncan,' I said nervously.

He looked at me, and in his eyes, I saw no hint of madness. They were as grey as the ocean but held a touch of warm blue.

'What sea-route are you plotting?' I asked.

'My voyage, I'm trying to figure out how I managed it. If you follow the currents and tides of the region, I should have ended up here.' He stabbed his finger at a point on the chart.

'Duncan, I've brought you something.'

I placed the varnished wooden box on the bed before him. His eyes were drawn to it like a child to a toy. He opened it with care. Inside, on a deep blue satin lining, lay a sextant and compass. It was the Plath Navistar Classic compass and sextant, the very set that had been used on a famous polar expedition and been recently restored to original condition by the Plath Company themselves.

'They are magnificent.'

'They are yours.' He couldn't take his eyes off the instruments. He didn't notice as I left the room.

*　*　*

On a balmy humid night, Grace and I strolled along Mission Bay Beach. The clouds were heavy with rain. A group of teenagers hung around the fountain. We watched the water lights changing colour, and Grace told me how she didn't feel comfortable living with her mother. She had to figure out what she wanted to do, how she would support herself as a single mother.

We came to the fountain and saw Milano's restaurant on the other side of the boulevard. The terrace was crammed with dinners. The economic crisis had passed.

'Do you miss it?' asked Grace as she linked her arm in mine.

'A little. I often think about my father and Papa Milano.'

'I can understand that. So, old man, you have some explaining to do. I haven't asked you anything until now because I wanted you to settle in, but you have to tell me what the hell happened?'

It took walking several times across the beach until I'd finished my story. I left out the part about the swollen testicle. There was a sudden smattering of rain, and we sat under the shelter of a phoenix palm.

'That is incredible. It's out there, Dad! I had no idea. I can't believe that you never said anything. How are you really? You can't have gone through all that without feeling ... well, I don't know ... Do you think you need counselling?'

'No, sweetheart. I don't need to see a shrink. I'm okay.'

When the rain stopped, we continued our walk. The teenagers, already drenched, had now jumped into the fountain pond and were splashing each other, squealing with laughter.

We sat on a café terrace. I fiddled with my coffee while Grace used the bathroom. I had prepared myself and was ready to tell her of my plan. She took a seat, waved to a waiter and ordered drink.

'Grace, I'm leaving again.'

'I guess I knew this was coming. Bali?'

'Yeah.'

'When?'

'Well, Mahmood has given me my job back. My work visa should be processed by next week. The lawyer Dingali informed me that the commander of the drug squad will not trouble me anymore.' I took a sip of my coffee. 'Grace, would you like to come with me?'

'What do you mean?'

'Come and live in Bali. Would you consider that?' It took her only a second to decide.

'Hell, yes,' she said, rubbing her belly. 'Living in a luxury resort in Bali! Are you serious? Of course, we're coming. Are there good hospitals over there?'

'No, but we'll go private, and Wayan and Ketut are going to cherish this baby as if it were their own.'

*   *   *

We flew to Ngurah Rai Airport in mid-December. As we passed through Immigration and Baggage Control, we walked out into the warm embrace of Wayan and Ketut. Wrapped in frangipani garlands, we made our way to the Land Rover. Within minutes I was sitting at the Sandika's sea wall, drinking a Long Island iced tea and receiving guests like a returning soldier. Eddi, Mahmood, Gusti and then finally Anak arrived. He had little to say but I sensed his pleasure.

When we were alone, he leaned forward and whispered, 'Come and see me tonight.' Fire flies flickered in the headlights under a dusky half-moon as I rode to Anak's compound. He sat cross-legged on his dais under the giant banyan, framed by hanging aerial roots, which gave his rat monkeys access to the inner realms of the sacred tree. Several scampered upwards on my arrival. A candle flickered in a root cavity before an image of Arjuna. The compound was empty. In the glow of an oil lamp, Anak was meditating on something before him. I saw the bloodstone in a glass of water. He indicated where I should sit. We watched the stone begin to bleed; a red ink-like liquid oozed from points in the bloodstone and curled into the water's surface, as delicate as incense smoke. Slowly the water in the glass turned deep red. He then picked up the glass, removed the stone and satisfied with the colour handed it to me.

'Anak, I am home and safe and not in need of protection.'

'Of course, but drink it anyway. It will give you energy and clarity. You have much to tell me … I want to know everything.'

As Anak watched, I drank the tasteless red water. I knew he would want to know every single detail, from the time Geno pole vaulted out of the prison until the present moment.

Soon, I felt a surge of energy, followed by a deep peacefulness, and I was about to begin the telling of my story when I was suddenly filled with a compelling urge. I reached down, took Anak's kris from his sash, touched its razor sharpness with my thumb and slashed the curved dagger down on my outstretched arm. The blade hit my skin, but it didn't cut. I reached over and slashed at a piece of bamboo on the dais. The same kris sliced through it like it were a ripe mango. I slashed at my arm again in a quick succession. Apart from a few red marks, there were no cuts.

'Are you quite finished?' Anak asked impatiently.

'Yes, I believe I am.'

'Good. Now start from the beginning.'

Anak folded his arms and closed his eyes. I heard the chatter of monkeys, the cooing of cockerels, the chirping of insects and tree frogs. For a brief moment, the distant sound of a plane departing the airport drowned these night noises, then they returned, accompanied by the swaying and rustle of palm fronds. I took a deep breath and began.

* * *

It was the middle of the night when I returned to the Sandika. I peeked into Grace's room and saw she was sleeping soundly. Through the mosquito net, I watched the rise and fall of her chest, the curve of her belly. She'd been through enough on my account. From now on, I would be looking after my daughter and grandchild. Grace had taken to Bali instantly, and I knew she would be happy staying here.

I went back out and sat by the sea wall, revelling in the peacefulness and clarity of the bloodwater. A wave broke, its shimmering hiss blending with the night noises. I closed my eyes and a flood of images surfaced. I saw the plough-nose dinghy, with me floundering on the stern. I saw Jimmy the Fish at the helm, surfing an outrigger down a glassy wave-face. I saw Geno strapped to the bow of an outrigger, with a jerrycan on each shoulder. I saw myself lying on the floor of a prison cell. The next wave broke, and the sound reached me like an old friend, whispering secrets.

10

I smelled him: that sweaty musky smell he'd always had. He was behind me. His hand latched onto my hair and pulled at my head, and the blade of his knife was cold against my neck.

'Move, motherfucker, and I cut your throat.'

I froze. A wave crashed against the sea wall. Geno tightened his grip. The sharp point of his knife dug into the soft flesh of my neck, hard enough to penetrate and cut skin.

'How the fuck you thought you gonna get away with that one, man? You think you clever, motherfucker? Nice work, man, but Geno got you figured. You took Satchimoto's keys, and you got my money. You can't spend that much so soon, man, so I know you got it stashed. I gonna make this real simple. You take me to my money or you gonna be Mikey Brown for real. I gonna squeeze the fucking life outta you and dump your sorry-ass body at Blue Ocean. Just like that junkie scumbag.'

'I got your money, Geno, and I wanted to give you the keys back in Tokyo, but you were gone. I had no way to contact you. I was waiting for weeks, but you never came.' My voice trembled as I lied, and my body shook even though I knew he couldn't hurt me. I was safe. He knew nothing of the power of the bloodstone.

'Nice try, motherfucker. Just take me to my money.'

'It's stashed by Blue Ocean.' More lies rolled out of my mouth. I wanted to get Geno away from the Sandika, away from Grace.

Still holding the knife, he released his grip on my hair. I turned and couldn't recognise him. He'd grown a beard that covered his face. His long hair, as well as the beard, were dyed jet black and his green eyes were now dark brown.

'Coloured contacts lenses, man. I walk right past the same Customs asshole at the airport that busted me. I hand him my Spanish passport, and he didn't know nothing, man. After I finish with you, I gonna go get that commander motherfucker, who beat the shit outta me. I gonna do him nicely.' Twisting my arm up my back, he forced me towards my motorbike. We mounted it together. As we rode along the beach road, he leaned against my back, digging the knife into me. I hoped that a cop would stop us, but it was too late in the night. Kuta was deserted. The beachfront hotel lights were dimmed and wisps of steam evaporated from the tar seal of the empty road. When we reached Jalan Legian, a vehicle's headlights shone at us. I saw the pale faces of two tourists through the car's windscreen. I could crash, run right into the vehicle. I couldn't be hurt; memories of Ketut and the truck returned to me. Geno pushed the knife in harder. The car passed.

I swung the motorbike into Double Six Road and came out on the beach. The tide was out. We rode along hard sand, sea shells crunching beneath the tyres. When I saw the solitary lamp on the palm tree, I crossed dry sand. The back wheel revved and spun until we came to the track. I stopped outside the carved doors of the compound. I hammered on the door. I heard a sandpapery rustle from the palms above, and a dog barking. I hammered again. With each thump, I felt the knife in my back. We waited. Then came a scratching on the other side of the door, the sound of claws on wood, followed by throaty clucking. The door opened, just a crack at first. When she saw it was me, she opened it wide. Janna held an oil lamp in one hand and with the other she held back her apes.

'Adam!' she screamed. Geno pushed me into the compound. Janna saw the knife and froze.

The two apes took him from behind. One wrapped its arms around him like tentacles, enfolding him and throwing him to the ground. The knife fell from his hand as he was buried under the animal. The ape secured him easily, holding Geno's arms and legs splayed with its own four limbs. The second ape clucked, peeling its lips back and showing its sharp yellow teeth.

'Stop! No!' Geno screamed.

Janna was about to stop her apes. I held her back. While one ape held Geno, the other ripped his trousers away with its paw. His bare buttocks squirmed and writhed beneath the beast, trying to dislodge the ape as it mounted him.

'Please, Adam ... Oh, for fucks sake, man! Please.'

The ape on top of Geno threw back its head, pumped up its throat and let go a harrowing burst of clucking and gurgling. The sound reverberated off the compound's walls. I knew the sound: it was an orangutan mating call. Geno stopped struggling; his body stiffened, his butt cheeks clamping together, and his pleading face fixed on me in a look of abject horror. I moved cautiously towards the ape sitting on top of him, took him by both paws and pulled him off Geno. The ape stared at me and down at Geno, then a paw pulled away and swiped at me. Janna rushed to restrain the animal. The other ape wrinkled its nose and released its grip. I picked up the knife and knelt beside Geno, and while Janna held back the apes, I pointed it at Geno's eye.

'Apes can't swim,' I said.

He moaned and stammered something unintelligible.

'Apes can't swim,' I repeated, moving the knife in the direction of the beach. Janna could no longer hold back the animals. They were aroused and hell bent on getting at Geno. His face fell into a grimace as a paw swiped at him.

I pushed the animal away and said again, louder, 'Apes can't swim.'

Then he got it. In an instant, he was up on his feet and running, out through the door. Both the animals broke out of Janna's grip and charged after him, leaping and clucking. Janna moved to follow them but I held her back. I dug out my mobile and dialled Eddi's number.

'Geno's here. He's standing in the surf just beyond Janna's compound. The apes have him bailed up.'

'I'm on my way,' said Eddi.

I turned to Janna. She was watching me. Her face showed both shock and pleasure. Then she was walking towards me.

'I'm sorry about that,' I said. 'I thought the animals would be in their cage, I can explain … He had a knife at my throat. I thought you'd be asleep.'

'Shhh …' she said, raising her hand to cover my mouth. 'Enough. But if he hurts my boys, I'm going to hold you responsible.' Janna's eyes danced with delight. She was soft with sleep, her hair a radiant tangle. Then we heard Eddi's Land Rover pushing its way along the track. When I opened the door, he came in with a rifle held over his shoulder.

'So where is he?' Eddi demanded. He was all business.

'Standing in the sea is my guess. He won't be coming out unless you escort him out with that gun. He's unarmed.'

We walked towards the beach, and Eddi kept his rifle trained and ready just in case.

The gun wasn't necessary. Geno never made it to the sea. We found him lying on the sand halfway down the beach. It wasn't a pretty sight. Janna chained her apes and led them back to the compound. Geno didn't move when Eddi cable-tied his wrists and feet, or even when I stood guard over him when Eddi went to get the Land Rover. When we lifted him into the vehicle, he opened his eyes briefly. They were green and unfocused; he'd lost his coloured contacts.

'You look like you need to be away from here. Go, Adam. I'll handle this.'

I watched Eddi drive away with Geno.

Janna had caged her animals and changed her clothes. When I returned, she was sitting on the steps. Her eyes followed me as I entered. Oil lamps cast flickering shadows around us. The smell of dawn was in the air.

'So, are you here to stay this time?' she asked as I sat beside her.

'Yes, I believe I am.'

*   *   *

We drove up hill towards Mt. Agung until we came to the ridge road. The first rays of sunlight cast the island in a soft glow. The vegetation dripped with dew. To the south, through swirls of mist, past the sculptured rice paddies and the towers of village temples, we could see the teardrop peninsula of southern Bali. We could make out Kuta Reef, a thin white line on an azure pallet, and beyond, just visible through the haze, stood the temples of Uluwatu. A bird's song rang out like a chime, and moments later came the return call. Behind us, nestled within its dark cone, lay the crater-lake, where puffs of steam arose and dissipated, casting moving images like shadow plays on the lake's mirror surface. The majestic summit of Mt. Agung towered above us. I took a deep breath of the mountain air.

'Janna ...' I said, and I tried to think of something deep and meaningful to say, but no words came. So I handed her the diamond ring I'd had made in Auckland. She looked at it, her eyes alight with pleasure, and then she slipped it on her finger.

SIX MONTHS LATER

As Janna and I came out of the domestic terminal at Medan airport, we spotted Aafaaq holding up a handwritten sign for us. He wore a grey uniform with 'Indonesian Department of Conservation' written in English on its lapels. It was mid-morning, and the heat was stifling. A colourful group of backpackers were boarding a minivan with a sign that read 'Lake Toba'. Porters huddled around a freshly opened durian, stuffing the fruit's pungent white flesh into their mouths. Women wearing burqas haggled with taxis drivers over fares. Janna was anxious. Her orangutans had been sedated and were in two large packing cases in the cargo section of the plane. Aafaaq hardly had time to introduce himself when Janna insisted that we supervise the unloading ourselves. By the time we reached the tarmac in his van, the cargo staff were only too happy to let us take care of the two crates with their dubious cargo. The apes were calm and awake. The sedative had worn off, and they responded to Janna's soothing tones as the men loaded the crates into the van.

Two hours later we were weaving our way along a dense jungle track, the sunlight filtering through gaps in the rainforest canopy. Janna rode in the back, talking to her animals, slipping them food through the gaps in the crates, then casting worried glances at me. Earlier that month, we had spent several long telephone conversations with Aafaaq and considered ourselves fortunate that he had agreed to take our orangutans. For ever since we had made the decision to set free the orangutans, we had run into every obstacle possible. No rehabilitation centre in Indonesia was willing take Janna's apes due to their age and the length of time they had spent in captivity. Moreover, owing to the recent deforestation, most rehabilitation centres had more animals than they could cope with but not enough volunteers. I was referred to a centre in northern Sumatra that had closed its doors to new arrivals yet had immense tracts of uninhabited virgin rainforest. After we offered a substantial donation to the centre, Aafaaq took a personal interest in our case. It was agreed that we would bypass the centre's headquarters and travel upriver to an isolated part of the rain forest, where he was sure that food would be plentiful for the beasts. Janna and I would camp out with the apes until we were satisfied that they would be able to survive. Furthermore, Aafaaq would deliver fruit twice a week to the site and communicate with us by telephone with weekly updates.

Two of Aafaaq's men were waiting for us by the river with brightly painted long-tailed skiffs. These boats had outboards, with a unique propeller system that allowed the shaft to be levered out of the water to avoid rocks and rapids. Soon each vessel carried one crated animal and an abundance of fruit. Janna and I had brought along our camping gear and supplies. The journey up-river was spectacular. At times the rain forest almost covered the waterway as we manoeuvred through dangling vines and jungle flora. The sound of bird song was almost deafening.

'Adam, look,' said Janna, pointing to a spot high in the canopy. Above us, a large orangutan crashed through the forest, swinging from vine to tree. During our telephone conversations, Aafaaq had insisted that we ensure our orangutans would be able to climb trees. If not, they would not be able to forage for food. So, with the help of a few local boys in Bali, we had spent an interesting couple of weeks placing fruit high in the coconut trees and arranging a series of ropes to simulate vines. Janna's apes became competent climbers in a short time.

* * *

An hour later, we arrived at our destination. The crates were unloaded on a grassy riverbank, our camping gear dumped next to them, and the men were back in their boats before Janna could open the crates. Aafaaq called out to us, 'See you in three days,' as he revved up his outboard.

The orangutans stumbled out of their cages, dazed and confused. Janna huddled with them while I set up camp. As evening fell, the jungle noises intensified with all kinds of screeching, thumping and wailing. As I watched Janna and the apes, I was reminded of the night in the Blue Ocean surf, when I'd given them the vodka and then the three of them had held each other in a similarly bizarre communion.

The following morning the orangutans were alert and immensely interested in their new surroundings. They would venture out into the bush only to come scuttling back in fear of some noise they'd heard, but then their curiosity would prevail, and they would be off again exploring and rummaging. A triumphant moment came when one ape climbed into the canopy to grab a mangosteen fruit, and Janna turned to me with an expression of pride. On the second day we had a visit from an enormous male orangutan, fearless, with battle scars on his cheek flaps and face and with flame-orange eyes that watched us intently. He walked on all fours to our stash of fruit, selected a bunch of bananas, cast his intent glance at both humans and apes and meandered off. On the third day, our apes separated. At dusk, when the tropical noises had reached their peak, one returned. In his paw he clutched a bunch of wild berries, which he shared with his mate. That night, in our tent, Janna and I held each other close, listening to the night noises and the clucking of our apes.

'How are you feeling?' I asked, stroking her hair.

'Disturbed, worried,' she said, as she lay her head on my chest. 'They are going to be okay, I know that. They will make it.' Her words were a question.

'They will, darling, they will.'

* * *

In the morning Aafaaq arrived. Janna had made her way further down the river. She had decided to slip away without goodbye so as not to stress the apes. As I boarded the long-tail boat for our journey home, I looked back at the two animals that I had grown very fond of. We had been through a lot together. However, my nostalgia and sadness were quickly overcome when I realised that they would be free to roam the jungles soon, to live the remainder of their lives in the manner that they were born to live. We picked up Janna and rode back to the van in silence. On the return flight to Bali, Janna's mood picked up a little. I suggested we call Aafaaq as soon as we arrived home and check on our apes.

* * *

Wayan, Ketut and Grace were waiting for us at the airport. My grandson, Tai, was strapped to a sling on Grace's belly. Wayan had insisted that Grace follow the Balinese custom of not letting the baby touch the ground until he was six months old. I was surprised that Grace had agreed to it.

'How's the kitchen going?' Grace had been in charge in my absence.

'Honest answer?' she asked with a cheeky grin.

'Go on.'

'Better without you.'

I nodded. I had no answer. I suspected she was right; the kitchen staff loved her. She managed better than I could.

Janna prised Tai away from Grace as the two woman embraced. On the ride back to the Sandika Hotel, I looked out at the reef. There were a few hardened surfers catching the last waves as the evening light cast them in silhouette. Wayan and Janna were speaking to each other in Indonesian. I knew that they were discussing the plans for our wedding: a proper Balinese ceremony to be held at the Sandika. I was a little nervous about it, but Anak and Mahmood would settle for nothing less.

*　*　*

I entered the Bali Haj kitchen from the staff entrance. The evening service was in full swing. Grace stood at the stove, managing four flaming skillets at once, with Tai strapped to her back. She turned briefly to inspect some plates about to go out to our diners, nodded her approval to the waiter then returned to her stove. The skilful elegance with which she tossed a pan of flaming prawns reminded me of my father. The gravel tones of his voice came back to me. Hadn't I spent the first years of my life in a bassinet next to the stove? As if he could hear my thoughts, Tai opened his sleepy eyes and for an instant they settled on me. Then, with jerky movements, an arm came out of the sling and his face tightened into a blue ball, and he let out a howl that cut through the din of the kitchen. In the most natural manner, Grace manoeuvred the sling in front of her, put Tai on her breast, and continued cooking.

I left quietly and passed beneath the banyan tree to the beach. At the water's edge, I looked out beyond the reef to a turquoise sky streaked with magenta, the remnants of the sun an orange orb. Glassy waves peeled away effortlessly and broke like distant drumbeat as the sun's embers slipped beneath the shimmering horizon.

The sequel to *Shaman of Bali*

BLOOD MONEY

by John Greet

In the sequel to *Shaman of Bali*, Adam Milano, surrounded by family and friends, lives a prosperous and peaceful life in the sun-drenched Kuta strip. However, his conscience begins to torment him. His new life was made possible by the drug money he had hijacked from the Brazilian drug smuggler Geno Roberto, who is in Bali's Hotel K, waiting to be sentenced to death. Adam knows that his adversary is hell bent on revenge, and, through corrupt prison guards, Geno is able to set in motion a series of events that devastates Adam and his family. Adam exhausts every means to resolve the situation, but after a horrific incident, initiated by Geno, Adam realises that he has no alternative – he must find a way to kill the Brazilian.

If you enjoyed *Shaman of Bali* then this gripping sequel, inspired by true events, will keep you riveted as Adam digs deep to find a darkness within.